The Battle
of
Walnut Hollow

A Novel

ISBN   978-0-9787484-6-3

Published 2018

Walnut Creek Press
2970 Walnut Creek Road
Marshall NC, 28753

www.walnutcreekpress.com

Cover design by the author
Manufactured in the United States of America

Our policy is always to have good and friendly relations with everyone, but we never accept being oppressed, and we will never accept it.

Ahmad Shah Massoud

The Battle

of

Walnut Hollow

Dennis Ruane

1

The family home is a log building, a fact that elevates the value of the property, to my way of thinking. When the realtor senses this, she recounts more features regarding the Ramsey homestead, to which I listen politely and not without interest, but the sale has already been made. The property sold itself to me soon after I looked it over.

"The logs are black walnut, Mr. Stone, a native tree that thrives in this area, and walnut logs will survive for generations."

"Really, the house is built with walnut logs? Walnut is one of my favorite trees, Cathy. I'm finding the history of this property quite fascinating, so by all means, continue."

"I'm related to the Ramseys by marriage, so I happen to know a good bit of their story. In the early 1900s, Mathew Ramsey, the grandson of the original owners, encased the family home with chestnut planks, added the room in back, and covered the wood shingles with a metal roof.

Mathew and his wife, Anna, raised six children here. She outlived her husband by ten months and died in the house at the age of eighty-nine."

"How interesting, six children in this little house. Are any of their offspring still in the area."

"Yes, all of them, actually, but only two are still alive. The youngest, Edna, lives a quarter mile away, and Edna's brother, Ben, lives right across the road in that green house."

We talk for ten minutes longer, and while I appreciate the conversation, I feel I've taken up enough of the realtor's time. I thank Cathy and say that I would like to stroll across the tract one more time, but promise to be at her office in the morning to sign a contract.

Walnut Creek meanders through the property and provides a steady, comforting sound of rippling water, offsetting the traffic noise from Walnut Creek Road. This vehicular tributary marks the northern boundary of the acreage.

What caused me to settle on this property, isn't the history of the house or the charm of the creek, and certainly not the noise of the road. The decision was made after viewing the picturesque gray building, situated at the western end of the land. Measuring thirty feet by thirty-two feet and constructed of decorative cinder block, the structure was raised a century after the house, and for decades, was a general store for travelers on Walnut Creek Road.

While but one of many back roads that wind through Madison County and the mountains of Western North Carolina, this tree-lined avenue, which twists and turns along the course of Walnut Creek, is a major thoroughfare west to east. The store was built on the property when automotive travelers began to utilize the road.

Because I wish to enter into commerce myself, I'm confident that the building and it's location will serve me well. I speak of business tongue-in-cheek since I'm retired now. Let there be no mistake about that. At age sixty-four, I embark upon the trading of goods and services for amusement and pleasure, perhaps at some level for much needed therapy in my advancing years. I don't need the money; I need the occupation.

Whereas this particular tract was selected for the advantage of the store, I chose to establish my enterprise in Madison County because of another structure, one that exists now only in memory. That is my grandmother's house, a wood-framed, two story, Victorian house which once stood on this same road as part of a beautiful homestead. That was where I passed my boyhood summers, helping

Grandmother Wallin and Great Aunt Emma, and playing with my cousins who lived on the next farm.

Along the many complicated paths I have traveled in life, the peaceful, easy pace of those summer days have always hung gently on my mind. I've long sensed that I lost something when I stopped coming to Madison County, something that I've looked for ever since.

I'm a realist and have no illusions about recapturing those days from half a century ago. My hope is that by entertaining them in action and spirit, I can to some degree separate myself from the regretful memories I've accumulated in the years since.

For most of my life, I've been a forward looking individual, believing that when the truth is made known righteousness in humanity will follow. Over the course of my career that outlook was repeatedly compromised until my experience in Afghanistan dealt the final blow to optimism.

My fervent desire in returning to Madison County is to ensure that I do not depart from this life bent over and bitter, harboring, as I do in dark moments, the notion that civilization is, and perhaps always was, inherently flawed, a hopeless endeavor.

2

With so much activity, weeks pass like days. Two months have gone by since I closed on the Ramsey homestead, the bulk of which time I've devoted to working on the store building. Fortunately, this entails mostly cleaning and painting since I've never been much of a handyman.

The original store furnishings, including shelving and a long, wooden counter are still intact, so aside from some slight refurbishing to suit my particular business, I'm leaving most fixtures where Mathew and Anna Ramsey placed them.

The back of the building is where most of my renovation efforts have been focused. Partitioned off from the sales area, this space was originally designed for storage and as an office of sorts. Now it's become a workshop, with the most significant alteration being the installation of large windows, facing Walnut Creek.

Coffee mug in hand, steam rising into the cool morning air, I enter the back door of my work place, breathing in a musty aroma of old timber, saturated with wood smoke. The centerpiece of the shop is a cast iron potbelly stove, standing in the same location it has occupied for over a century. An Acme Giant Stove, no less, one of the premiere potbelly stoves of it's time, which my neighbor, Ben, tells me was purchased by his father through a Sears Roebuck catalog in 1905.

The bulbous firepot has a three inch skirt rail, and that's where I place my mug while lighting a fire. Firing up this grand old heater to offset the chill of these spring mornings is a ritual that I perform with solemnity, like a religious rite. Just as I reach for the handle of the stove door, I hear the sound of a vehicle pulling into the graveled parking area that fronts the building.

Retrieving my mug, I step outside to see the back end of a blue pickup truck, the bed loaded with firewood. The vehicle has obviously traveled some miles as evidenced by numerous scrapes and dents along with rusted areas above the wheel wells. A man steps around the corner of the building, comes toward me, and smiles as he glances at firewood that I recently stacked along the side of the building.

"Howdy neighbor. My name's Julian Runnion. You doing alright?"

"I'm doing well, thank you. I'm Ira Stone. How are you?"

"Good, better now that spring is finally here. I didn't think winter was ever going to let go this year."

Julian Runnion is about my height, six feet, with dark eyes punctuating a face, mostly hidden by a full beard and the low brim of a camouflage hunting cap. Auburn colored hair hangs nearly to the man's shoulders and, like his beard, is laced with gray. Faded blue jeans, well worn at the knees, seem quite natural on him as does a canvass jacket with work gloves, protruding from a side pocket.

"Say, I hear you're doing a little woodworking."

"Yes, that's my plan anyway. I'm just a beginner, mind you. Hand-hewn bowls, something I've wanted to do for years now. I lived near a man in Afghanistan, who made them and I was fascinated by what he did. He showed me the basic technique, and I decided it's what I wanted to do one day when I retired."

"Afghanistan, hell, you didn't have to go all the way over there to learn that. They make hewn bowls right around here. My granddad made them in fact, big bread bowls out of poplar."

"Ha, ha, well, I was in Afghanistan for other reasons. I'm a journalist, or I was, anyway. I was covering the war there."

"Damn, you sure were there for other reasons. Now that's

5

something I don't think I could handle."

"War, you mean?"

"No, being over there, in Afghanistan, for any reason. I think I could handle war if I had to, even though I was never in one. My older brother was in Vietnam, so I know about war.

Say, the reason I stopped is to see if you're going to be needing some wood. Family's got some acres up the road, and I sell a little wood here in the valley, firewood mostly, but whatever you need. I reckon you'll be wanting some logs to hew bowls from. Got lots of nice walnut."

"Well, I'll definitely take you up on some walnut. Firewood, I won't be needing right away. I suspect you think that's a measly pile I've got stacked there, but it's just what I've gathered on the property since I moved in. I'm adding to it every day"

"I wasn't wondering about the quantity. I'm just impressed with how small it's split and how neat it's stacked."

"Oh, yes, well I used to cut wood for my grandmother and that's the way she liked it."

"Old Mrs. Wallin, huh?"

"Y-yes, how did you know I was related to her?"

"Dad told me. We used to buy sausage from her."

"Oh, the sausage, yes, that was Grandma's specialty. She made it right up until the end of her life."

"I know. We had some of the last of it. Haven't found any I like as well since. You don't have the recipe, do you?"

"No I don't, but I'll have to see about that. Someone in the family probably does."

"There you go. Now if you sold sausage in your store, I can guarantee you'd have some business right off the bat."

"Hah, who knows, maybe."

"I'm just goin' on with you. What do I know? Anyway, I should get moving along here. I got a load of wood on the truck to deliver, and I suppose you're anxious to start to work. I'll bring you by some walnut logs in the next day or so. How big you want them?"

"Three to four feet long, at least eight inches in diameter and the greener, the better."

"Gotcha. Hey nice talking to you, Ira, and good luck with them bowls."

Julian walks back to his truck, inspecting the firewood pile again as he passes. I watch as he pulls away and then return to lighting the stove in even better spirits than I began the day.

Julian Runnion is an interesting character in both his speech and persona such that I wish the conversation would have gone on longer. I've met many people in my travels around the world, but this man from up the road impresses me as someone a bit different.

Opening the stove door, I lay short, dry twigs on the grate of the firepot to form a crisscross stack. Lighting a piece of cardboard, I turn it in my hand until it's burning vigorously, and then place it in the center of the kindling. The wood burns readily, so that by adding progressively larger sticks, I soon have a crackling blaze.

As I stare into the flames, life seems simple to me now. I realize this with a sense of guilt, considering all the trouble and complexity that I've witnessed in the world. *Did I act fittingly in the face of it? Did I do all I could to alleviate it?*

Despite this new course I've charted for my life, questions from the past trouble me. Shutting the stove door, I move to the hewing bench, determined to focus my thoughts on the present and not allow reservations about the past taint such a fine day.

3

The town of Walnut Creek is situated on a mile long tract between the French Broad River and a mountainside, natural boundaries that have prevented expansion beyond one street in width. The layout and architecture, including the century-old courthouse, remain much as I remember from when I was a boy.

Ben, who is twenty-five years my senior, tells me that Walnut Creek hasn't changed since he was young except that the town was more vibrant and busy back then. Ben talks of Saturday evenings, when he had to step out into the street to get by because the sidewalk was so full of people.

But with the coming of interstate highways, Route 25, Main Street, became US 25 *Business* and ironically, business withered, vibrancy faded, and the sidewalks emptied. The interstate is not entirely to blame since the era of small towns and main street shopping was coming to an end anyway. Rerouting automobile traffic around Walnut Creek was just the final blow.

Fortunately, for one who laments the loss of the old, there are a handful of stubborn businesses that remain: Robinson's Grocery, Penland Hardware, Riverside Café, and of course, the post office. I make use of these establishments whenever possible, and if they can't supply the goods and services that I need, then I try to do without.

Today, I have two destinations: the post office to send my latest dispatches out into the world, and the hardware store for a sack of concrete mix to anchor the post for a sign. My cousin, Amy, has worked at the post office for decades, a fact I was aware of, but I'm still taken by surprise when I'm face to face with her across the counter. In my mind's eye she's still my kid cousin, companion of summers in the valley.

Amy is the oldest of my Aunt Sadie's children, and we grew very close, during those long summer days of our youth, before life became so much more serious for both of us. Amy is a year younger than me and, back then, liked to boss me around to some extent. I liked to let her do it, since, after all, I was the city kid from Charlotte, and so unskilled in country ways.

As I pull into the parking lot, the mail carriers are preparing to embark on their routes, and I exchange waves with Barney Flynn, the mail carrier for the Walnut Creek Valley. A bell clangs above my head, as I push open the glass door of the post office, and Amy appears from the back.

"Well I was just beginning to wonder if you were still around."

"Hi Amy. I've been busy. That's the life of a shopkeeper you know, there's always something else to be done."

"I hear you. Are you open yet? My neighbor was just by there and said that it didn't look like anyone was around."

"I'm going to take care of that this afternoon. I'm putting up a sign at the edge of the parking lot that spells it out: *Wooden Bowl Shoppe*. That should alert the public that it's a going concern. I don't have many bowls finished for the occasion, but I don't expect a great rush of people first thing when I open the door."

"No I wouldn't think so, out there. You are working then, you're workshop's set up?"

"Yes, amidst everything else, I put together a workbench and spend some time at it every day. And now I seem to have a source of wood. A man who lives up the road is going to get me some walnut. His name is Julian. I can't remember his last name now. It begins with an R."

"Runnion?"

"Yes, that's it, Julian Runnion. He says his family has some land and there are many walnut trees on it."

"Walnut Hollow."

"Walnut Hollow, is that the name of their place? He never mentioned the name."

"I don't think that's what's on the map, but it's always been called that. That land has been in their family since way back, and part of it is planted full of walnut trees. One of the Runnions, back along the line, planted them. I've never really seen the trees, myself. In fact, not many people have. The Runnions have always been a private bunch."

"Well Julian seems like a straight forward fellow, so I hope he brings me some good wood."

"Oh he'll bring you the wood alright. Just be careful of what else he's selling."

"I don't quite get what you mean, Amy."

"Well, I don't really know what I mean either. I'm just going on. I haven't seen much of Julian in recent years. The man's secretive. Let's just say that the Runnions have always played by their own rules. But I suppose you'll find that out soon enough. Let's see here, back to business. Where on earth are you sending mail to this time? Hmm, Germany, Afghanistan, and Nepal."

Amy pronounces 'Nepal' with a long e, while accenting the first syllable, as if she had never heard the word. I wonder if I should say something, but when she smiles and winks, I know she's teasing, just like always. A woman comes in and lines up behind with several packages in hand, so I pay my postage fee and move away from the counter.

"I'll get out of your way here Amy; I'll stop back later. Oh, how's your mother doing? I meant to ask that first off."

"Better now. The bout with pneumonia was a scare, but she's out of the hospital and back at Laurel Courts. You need to stop up and see her. She doesn't know who's who most of the time, but she enjoys talking. Let me know; we can go together."

"I'll do that, Amy. Bye."

Bridge Street, named for the bridge that crosses the French Broad River to the west, runs perpendicular to Main Street and separates the hardware store from the Post Office. The bridge is intersected by a short span that leads to Island Park, a five acre tract in the middle of the river.

Once owned and inhabited by a wealthy lumber baron, the island and the family home were left to the town upon his passing. The island has since been developed into a delightful park and the house converted into a museum of local artifacts and memorabilia.

Crossing Bridge Street, I step through the open door of the Hardware Store and exchange greetings with Frank Penland, the proprietor, and a man who is leaning against the wall beside the counter. I don't recognize the other man, but the expression on his face as I pass, suggests that he knows me. Perusing the selection of wood screws at the end of the center aisle, I notice that the stranger has left the wall and is coming toward me.

The man is about my height, unshaven, clad in a well-worn canvass topcoat and a wide-brimmed hat. I might guess he's about my age as well, but a bent frame, and slow, measured gait suggests he's older. An arm's length away, the man leans against shelves, clears his throat, and speaks.

"How are you going to heat that place?"

The question catches me off guard. I assume he's referring to the building that is my workshop, but considering I've never met this person, it seems a number of introductory questions have been skipped over.

"The block building, you mean?"

"Yeah, the old Ramsey Store."

"Why, I plan to heat with wood. I've been gathering wood and I work with wood, so I . . ."

"You ever heat with wood before?"

"Yes, well never my own place, but I've lived in a number of places that have depended on wood heat."

"It isn't as easy as it sounds, you know."

"No, it takes some work, I know that."

The man looks at me in a peculiar way, as if his observation of me is of more interest than the answers to his questions.

"I know heating with wood involves some work, but you see, I work with wood, so there will be lots of scraps that have to be gotten rid of anyway. And I plan to buy some wood as well."

"Uh huh, that's good. Winter is always coming, you know. Good Luck."

He says this in a whimsical manner, then turns and walks away. I follow him to the front of the store, surprise giving way to irritation, and I address the man in a louder and somewhat indignant voice.

"Oh by the way, my name's Ira Stone."

The man turns in the doorway and smiles.

"I know who you are."

The stranger walks away, leaving me baffled and exasperated. I turn and look toward the counter, but Frank is leaning over some paperwork and seems not to have noticed the interaction. Drifting back into the center of the store, I pick up a box of wood screws and a few other items, all the while distracted and annoyed.

Frank Penland is familiar to me since I seem to need something from his inventory on every excursion into town. I came in today to get a sack of concrete mix, but as often is the case, I approach the counter with an armload of items.

"Finish nails, hinges, sandpaper, and a quart of white paint, will this be it for you then, Mr. Stone?"

"Yes, Frank, well, almost. I'm going to grab a sack of concrete mix off the dock."

"All right, then. Looks like you've got lots of projects going, as usual. Say, what were you and old Tom talking about?"

"Tom, is that his name? Not much really. He inquired about my heating plan for my business, and I don't think he was too impressed with the plan or with me for that matter."

"Hah, don't mind him none. He's a peculiar bird, but he's alright once he warms up to you. If he didn't think you were okay, he wouldn't have talked to you at all, believe me."

"Well that makes me feel somewhat better. Does he live here in town?"

"No, out your way, actually, further up the valley. Lives way back off the main road. Don't see him here in town too often, so I guess this was your lucky day. Say, how are things going out there? You about ready to open?"

"Yes, any day now. I'm not expecting a great rush of business though. Other than people going to and from work, things are pretty quiet out my way."

"Well it may not be like that for long. Have you heard about the gas people that are in the county?"

"No, I haven't. Natural gas, you mean?"

"Uh huh, natural gas, the kind they get from shale, these days. They lifted the moratorium on hydraulic fracturing in the state last year and have started issuing drilling permits."

"Hydraulic fracturing in Western North Carolina? I read that the moratorium was lifted, but I thought that the only significant shale basins are in the middle of the state, down near Raleigh and Durham."

"Well, I guess they found gas here too. They've been in this part of the state since last year, buying land and getting people to sign contracts, mostly in Yancey County, but now they're here in Madison."

"Well that's no good."

"Hey, tell that to the ones who are signing some of those fat contracts for lease of their land. From what I hear, people are struggling to hang on to their farm one day and the next they're off in a Cadillac to a condominium in Florida."

"Hmm, I see. Have you talked to any of these gas people?"

"No, but I see one of them around: white haired guy, seems to be about in his fifties. He drives a Porsche and dresses kind of citified."

"I think I know who you're talking about; I've seen that guy around town. Sticks out like a sore thumb. I thought he was someone with a second home in the area."

"He's been around for a while, and he does have a place here, which means he plans on being around for a while longer. He's out near you, too, as a matter of fact. You've seen that big house that went up right around the bend on Fisher Lane, haven't you?"

"Sure, how could I not notice it? I wondered why someone was building such a big place there. I mean it's an okay spot, but with the money that's gone into it, he could have picked a more secluded location."

"My guess is it'll be sort of an office too, because he wants to be in the center of things once the action starts. The valleys around here are where they'll be doing the drilling."

"Damn it!"

"You against gas drilling?"

"I don't know if I'm against it or not. Up until now, I haven't really paid enough attention to have an opinion one way or the other, but I'd rather not have a rig in my backyard."

"I hear you there, but it does mean jobs for the area, and hey, I might put up with a rig in my backyard for one of those big money contracts. From what I hear, you can make millions off the royalties."

"Well, can't argue with that, or, at least not now. An electrician is coming at noon to do some wiring in my workshop, so I better get back there."

"Who you got doing the work?"

"Dave Barnwell, my neighbor recommended him."

"Good man, Dave, he'll fix you right up. He knows his stuff, and he tells some good stories, too."

4

According to the deed, I'm the owner of two acres of land, roughly divided in half by Walnut Creek. The property is laid out in a long, narrow strip, such that I have the luxury of a quarter mile of the stream as part of my estate. Across the creek the land rises abruptly, making it unsuitable for any sort of development or farming, and so it remains a tree-covered backdrop, framing in my homestead.

Walnut Creek does not flow like a high mountain stream, with churning waters, tumbling in a rapid descent over rocks and boulders, but instead snakes through the valley with little fanfare, dragging sand and silt, making just enough noise to please the imagination. What it lacks in grandeur and drama, it makes up for with it's varied wildlife: fish, frogs snakes, turtles, ducks, herons, and many smaller creatures that one has to get down close to the water to see.

Like the French Broad River, of which it is a tributary, Walnut Creek is an ancient waterway, predating the mountains, wearing away tectonic uplift to maintain its prehistoric course. Old-timers tell me that the creek used to run much higher when they were young, that it hasn't been the same for many years. But I suspect that all creeks run higher when we're young, just like all snows are deeper and life seems so much simpler. Walnut Creek runs high enough for me at this stage of my life.

In the time since I've settled on the creek, daily walks along its bank have worn a discernible path. I particularly like to stroll this trail with a cup of coffee in hand, the water sound providing a suitable background tone to focus my thoughts. While awaiting the electrician, I employ this exercise to assimilate the information I received during my excursion into town.

What did Amy mean when she said that the Runnions play by their own rules? Who is this character, *Old Tom*, who already knows me, apparently well enough to impose his opinion about my heating plans? And last, but not least, there is now the possibility of natural gas drilling in Walnut Creek.

It's just that, however, a possibility, which may or may not come to be. I mustn't allow my plans to be disrupted by thoughts of what *might* happen. And this Tom character, I may never cross paths with the man again, but if I do, I won't be caught off guard next time.

A huge poplar tree, four feet in diameter, stands at the northern tip of the property and marks the boundary as far as anyone can say, since there's no survey of this line on record. The poplar has most likely been spared these many years because it straddles the line, and as a result, has grown in girth to such a size that I cannot reach my arms half the way around it.

Placing my hand on the furrowed bark, I look upward, along the trunk, a straight shaft extending seventy feet into the air, like the mast of a great sailing ship. The topmost branches sway in the wind while the trunk, anchored firmly in the ground, remains unmoved.

As I turn and walk back toward the business end of my estate, I see that a white pickup truck has pulled into the parking area of the shop. A man, who I presume is Dave Barnwell, stands beside it and raises a hand in my direction. Returning the gesture, I walk at a faster pace, retracing my steps along the creek.

Rounding the house, I come upon the man looking up at power lines projecting from the roof of the shop. Smiling, he extends his hand as I approach.

"Dave Barnwell; you must be Mr. Stone."

"Yes, Ira Stone. Call me Ira, please."

"Okay, Ira it is. Well, Ira, power lines don't look too bad from this end. Must have been redone at some point."

"Well I don't think that's the case on the inside."

"I would guess not. Wouldn't be surprised if most of it's the original wiring in this old building. You'll be wanting to bring it up to a two hundred amp service I suppose."

"Not really. Whatever it is now is probably fine."

"What about running tools? You said you had a woodshop. That can draw a lot of power."

"I don't have many tools and none that use electricity. Come in I'll show you."

We enter the building through the back door and Dave smiles at the sight of the potbelly stove. I built a fire earlier to offset the morning chill and the room is a comfortable temperature now. The electrician turns, steps through the doorway into the showroom and rubs his hand across the countertop.

Dave Barnwell is a big man, several inches taller than me, stout and strong looking with large, calloused hands. His hair is short and mostly gray, his features affable and disarming. Dave takes a deep breath and exhales as he turns toward me.

"Man this brings back some memories. I can remember coming in here as a kid with my parents. I can still see Mr. Ramsey standing right here, behind this counter, talking and grinning. He was always joking, just like Ben does. You know how Ben is."

"Yeah, I've gotten to know Ben pretty well."

"Well, he's a chip off the old block. I remember Mr. Ramsey standing here with an apron on, and a visor. He was always wearing a green plastic visor and had a pencil behind his ear. And back here in this room, old guys would be sitting around the stove, talking, smoking pipes and cigars."

"When was that, Dave, can you remember what year?"

"Let's see, sixties, it must have been. Store wasn't open much longer after that. I'll check with my mother, but it seems to me it closed down for good by sixty two, or a . . . No wait, it closed down in nineteen sixty-four. I remember now because it was still open when President Kennedy was killed. I remember being here while my father and Mr. Ramsey talked about it."

"How interesting. How old were you then, Dave?"

"In sixty three, I was six, so I wasn't really sure what was going on, but I do remember how upset everybody was. People in this valley are mostly democrats, at least back then they were, and they took it hard when Kennedy got shot.

Haven't been too excited about a president since, and I don't expect that'll change with this guy we got in now. People around here have been hurting for a long time, and they're fed up with the government. I'm just thankful I got my own trade and it's in demand."

"Business is good, then?"

"With all the new people moving into the area and building homes, it couldn't be better. But, I'll tell you, at the same time I'm grateful for the business, I worry about all these new places going up. Everybody wants to be up on a ridge with a view or else at the end of the road in some secluded hollow. If it keeps up, pretty soon there won't be any more secluded hollows or clean ridges to look up at.

Used to be, people built little places in the valleys, along a creek bottom, places that fit in, like this one. Now these folks want big houses, places that don't fit in or make any sense to me. I think a lot of the time it's not for the sake of a place to live; it's mostly for show."

"You mean like that place around the bend on Fisher Lane?"

"Exactly what I'm talking about. You ever meet that guy?"

"I've seen him around; heard a little about him this morning at the hardware store. I know he works for a gas company."

"His name is Don Oldsmar. He's a classic, believe me. I did a little work for him early on, but I keep my distance now. Pushy and full of himself, thinks he's God's gift to Madison County and the rest of us are here to serve him. Talks like he's got lots of money, but at the same time he's rushing me with my work and questioning my hours.

Then he kept me there for half an hour after I was set to go, telling me about his house in detail, down to the special lighting above the toilet. I could hardly get a word in edgewise. That's what these places are, not a home to live in so much as they're some kind of statement or an investment."

"Well, I'm not trying to make a statement here, or if I am it's the opposite of Don Oldsmar."

"Right, this is different, what you're doing. You took something that was here already, something that was run down, and you're fixing it up and making something nice out of it. He took something that was already nice and tore it all up for his own purposes.

As far as I'm concerned, the only statement he made was in ruining part of the skyline forever, and now we're stuck with looking at that big house for the rest of our lives. But don't get me started on that. I best stick to what I do best. Let's see where you want lines run."

I lead the electrician to the back of the building, where a partially finished walnut bowl sits on the hewing bench. Next to it, lies a bowl adze and a leather glove that I wear on my left hand while I work. A denim apron hanging on a hook, and walnut chips scattered in all directions, complete the picture of my workspace.

"By God you weren't kidding about not having many tools. This is it, this little thing? What's it called? I've seen them before, but I can't remember what it's called now."

"A bowl adze, it's my main tool, but I do have a few more tools besides this."

"But no power tools, huh? I hate to ask this, but what do you need me for?"

"Ha, ha, lights; I need better lighting. That one fluorescent light just doesn't cut it on a cloudy day. And some more outlets: a couple back here and a few more out in the showroom."

"Now we're talking. You had me worried there for a while. Well that won't take long. Point me in the right direction here and

I'll have you fixed up before you know it."

While Dave occupies the building, I take the opportunity to set the post for my business sign. I took the time to carve the sign myself, utilizing a limited collection of carving tools and even less carving ability. Incised letters on both sides, painted a forest green against a white background, spell out my new trade: *Wooden Bowl Shoppe.*

To my knowledge, mine is the first business to occupy the building since the store was shut down. The Ramsey family maintained the building, but never revived it as a general store or leased it for any other purpose.

The parking area in front of the store is still well defined even though it hasn't been subject to much traffic for decades. With some effort I dig at the west end of the lot, working down through layers of gravel deposited here through the years.

The parking area separates the building from the Walnut Creek Road by about fifteen feet, so that my efforts are clearly on display to passers-by. One vehicle slows so that the driver can get a better look, and when a horn toots, I glance up to see a young man wave in seeming approval of my efforts.

Working with a digging bar and post hole digger, I excavate a hole eighteen inches deep and ten inches in diameter, four inches wider than the signpost. Dave emerges from the building as I shovel wet, sticky, concrete from a wheelbarrow into the space around the upright post.

After I check with a level to see that the post is in line, the electrician holds it in place while I tamp in a layer of stones on all sides and fill in with the last of the concrete. Dave and I stand back to view the sign, just as Ben pulls to the end of his driveway in a red Chevrolet pickup, that he keeps spotlessly clean.

Before he retired, Ben was employed as the school bus repairman for Madison County and has known Dave since the electrician was a boy, riding those same buses to grade school. In fact, Ben recommended Dave when I mentioned that I needed electrical work done. He smiles as he sees us, standing together in the parking lot of what was once his family's store, and then he shouts at the electrician in a put-on, scolding voice.

"You better treat him right, David, you hear me."

"I'm after his money, Ben, you know me. I'm after his money."

"You better treat him right, you hear me," Ben shouts again, grinning. He toots his horn, waves, and pulls out.

5

"Hey Ira, you doin' alright today? Got you a load of wood out here. Didn't mean to scare you. I heard the tapping and figured you were back here working."

"Oh, Julian, I didn't expect you back so soon. I was working but daydreaming at the same time, so I didn't hear you drive up. With this window open, the sound from the creek drowns other noise out."

"She's runnin' high ain't she. That's the way I like it, the way the creek runs in the spring, cold and clear, too. Hey, I like how you got this fixed up in here. And you're working on a bowl right now, huh? Ain't that something. I swear, if I didn't know, I'd think this was always a bowl-making shop."

"Well that's good to hear. Sometimes I wish that I had been here all along. That would have made for a pleasant career. So you have some wood for me?"

"Yep, big old walnut tree that came down this winter. Tree was healthy. Branches just got weighed down with snow and it came out by the roots."

I lay the bowl adze aside, brush the wood chips from my apron, and follow Julian outside. As we approach his truck, he lights a cigarette, takes a long deep drag and blows smoke in the direction of the road. Julian stands square-shouldered, with a lean, angular frame. He's a handsome man, in a rough, natural sort of way, although I doubt such thoughts concern him much.

"I cut you six logs for now, so you can see if this is what you want. If it *is* what you want, I can bring you more anytime you need it. Tree ain't going anywhere and walnut will last a while outside. What do you think?"

"Wow, this looks great, Julian, just what I had in mind. Look how nice the sapwood stands out. That will be interesting to play with on a bowl. This ought to keep me busy for a while and make for some nice bowls. We can just roll them off right here and I'll start cutting them up today. How much do I owe you."

"I figure a hundred bucks will do it. How does that sound for you?"

"Sounds real good, we have a deal, and in fact, I'll take another load from this tree right away. Do you sell much wood like this?"

"Not like this, mostly firewood on the road here, but lumber's the main business. Cousins and I run a little mill. I do farming on the side, run some cattle. I get by. Don't need much, that's the key. As long as I got a little cash coming in, I get by all right."

"You have a family?"

"Yeah, a son, grown now. Wife and I divorced a while back. She moved to Virginia where she's from. My boy, Dakota, lives with me. Well, he does most of the time, anyway. He's been working construction over in Weaverville. Got a girlfriend over there, too, so I haven't see much of him lately. How about you?"

"No girlfriends."

"Hah, I hear you there."

"I don't have a family; never married."

"Where you from?"

"Charlotte is where I grew up, but my family's scattered around the country, and I've been overseas so much of the time that I've pretty much lost touch with them, except for the occasional email or phone call. Seems we only get together for weddings and funerals, if then."

"Well, my family's mostly here in the valley or somewhere

hereabouts, so we never lose touch with each other. There's advantages and disadvantages to that. I don't want to be sticking my nose in your business, but why did you decide to move back here?"

"I always liked it here, that's one of the reasons I stayed with my grandmother in the summers. My brothers and sisters gravitated the other way, Raleigh, Phoenix, Philadelphia and one brother still in Charlotte. I've moved around a lot, but I've always stayed in small towns. They were just scattered all over the world.

I don't regret the way my life has gone, really, but lately I find myself wishing I had stayed with my Grandmother, and lived my life here. But you can't change the past. I'm back here now and as Grandma used to say, 'there's a reason for everything'."

"My grandma used to say about the same thing, so it must be true. Well Ira, I got to get moving here. Plan to cut trees along a fence row this afternoon, mostly firewood stock."

Julian drops the tail gate and climbs into the bed. He's able to slide the walnut logs out without my help, so I go inside the building and get a hundred dollar bill from the money box. When I hand it to him, Julian folds it in half and slides it into his shirt pocket.

"You need a receipt."

"No, we're good."

"Well thank you Ira. Been a pleasure doing business with you."

As he turns to go, a car pulls into the lot and stops in front of his truck. Julian tilts his cap back with the palm of his hand, and draws on his cigarette. A woman emerges from a Subaru Outback and walks toward us, focusing her gaze on Julian.

"Hello Julian."

"Hi Pat. You caught me. Can't get away with anything these days, can I?"

"No, you can't. How is he today?"

"About the same. A little crankier than usual. Still says he wants to get out on the tractor."

"You didn't let him did you?"

"No I didn't let him, but I can't be there all the time."

Julian turns and introduces the woman to me as his sister, Patricia. Patricia half smiles and nods. She's shorter than Julian by several inches and I guess that she's close to his age. She's a pretty woman, but with a serious demeanor accentuated by distinct lines on her forehead. Her hair is flaxen colored, and tied back in a ponytail. An oversized, denim shirt hangs midway down her thighs, over bluejeans.

"I'm heading up there now. What are you doing?"

"Just sold Ira here some wood. He's going to be making walnut bowls. We're done; I'll be right behind you."

Patricia nods, gets in her car and drives away. Julian takes one last puff on his cigarette and crushes the butt out on the bed of his truck.

"Whew boy, wait till she sees what a mess the house is. Dad had a stroke a while back and never really came back from it. Mom's been dead for five years now. He never really got over that either.

Well, I better head up the road, Ira, and let you get back to work. Wish I could stay here and make bowls with you."

"You think your sister's going to be mad?"

"She's always mad about something. Nah, I'm just saying that. Pat just worries too much about all of us. Since Mom died, she's taken over that job. I'm glad she keeps after the old man though, cause he'll listen to her. He sure as hell won't listen to me. You take it easy Ira."

"You, too, Julian, and thanks for the wood."

6

During the time I lived in Afghanistan, I came to appreciate a simple diet, one based mostly on rice. Rice is the most important part of any meal in that country, and Afghans take much time and effort in creating their rice dishes. The fact that rice is so readily available in any part of the world, is heartening to me.

I would prefer to have rice scooped into a bag as it is in the open marketplaces in Afghanistan, rather than wrapped in plastic packaging made from petroleum, and sold in a grocery store, but one must adapt to the circumstances at hand. I now live in Walnut Creek, North Carolina and the marketplace is Robinson's Grocery.

Now bread is even more of a compromise in this geographic locale. I certainly can't expect to dine on naan, the bread I grew so accustomed to in Afghanistan, a thin, oval-shaped flatbread, topped with sesame seeds. One day, when my list of projects clears somewhat, I plan to try my hand at baking naan.

Of course I could drive to Asheville and procure bread and other staples in a form more pleasing to my imagination, but since I have no other business in Asheville today, such an excursion would amount to driving a two ton machine forty miles and burning two gallons of gasoline. Thus, even while adhering to such a simple diet, I find myself in a moral quandary.

In the end I choose the least extravagant use of petroleum, proceeding to the checkout with two bags of rice in my cart, alongside a loaf of sourdough bread, curry powder, and onions.

Upon reaching the jeep, I notice a sleek, black car with tinted windows cruising in my direction. The insignia on the hood identifies the automobile as a Porsche and as I try to remember what significance that fact has relative to something I just learned, the driver pulls in a few spaces away from where I'm parked.

The license plate catches my eye because of an unusual, personalized script: ITSAGAS. 'It's a gas', I suppose is the message, which also has a familiar ring, and might have been sufficient enough a clue to prod my memory except the driver emerges and resolves the mystery.

He's the man I've noticed around town who stands out for his appearance and mannerisms. Frank at the hardware store, mentioned him because of his involvement with the natural gas industry, and Dave Barnwell identified him as Don Oldsmar.

Oldsmar looks to be in his fifties, is short in stature, and seems fit and spry for his age. His clothes are casual and stylish, but more typical of what a man of his age and deportment might wear in a cosmopolitan setting.

I turn toward my vehicle, and unlock the door, having no desire to attract his attention, but the stranger walks in my direction. He has handsome, boyish features, white hair, and sports an atypical tan for this time of year. Oldsmar smiles broadly as he comes up to me, exhibiting teeth that are too bright for his age.

"How do you do, sir, I'm you're neighbor from right around the bend. You're fixing up the little store on Walnut Creek Road, right? I saw the sign you just put up."

I transfers my grocery bag to my left hand so that my right is free to shake the outstretched hand offered to me.

"Yes, that's me, at the old Ramsey store. Ira Stone's the name."

"Don Oldsmar, pleased to meet you. I hear you're a writer."

"Really? Where did you hear that? I've been trying to establish myself in the area as a bowl maker."

"Uh, I guess from someone in town, I heard it. You know how it is in a small community like this, everybody knows everything about everybody."

"I sure do know that. In fact just the other day, someone told me that you work in the gas industry."

"Y-yes, that's true. I'm a consultant, you might say, the go between. I represent the gas company and deal with the local people, or, what I mean is, I work out contracts for the lease of their land.

It's a real satisfying job, I can tell you that. I've made some people a lot of money, people who were struggling to get by. Places like Madison County get an economic boost when they work with me. Have you by any chance, heard of Blue Ridge Power Corporation and what we do?"

"No, not your company per se, but I do know about hydraulic fracturing for natural gas. That's what you do, right?"

"Yes, for the most part, that's what we do, but there's much more to the picture than that. At Blue Ridge Energy we're committed to a clean energy future, and hydraulic fracturing is a key step in that direction. Natural gas burns cleaner than coal, so it's a bridge to the time when we can convert to renewable fuels.

I have some literature here in the car if you're interested in more details. But hey, another time. I didn't really want to talk about that. I just wanted to touch base with you and say hi. After all we're going to be neighbors, you and me."

"Yes, I noticed the house you built there on Fisher Lane."

"Yes, hey, how about that, sweet spot, huh? I was lucky to pick up that little piece of real estate. Wait until you see the view from up there. That's been my dream for a while to have a cabin in these mountains. They're some of the oldest in the world, you know, and there's almost something . . . I don't want to get too heavy here, but, almost something spiritual about them. I sit out on my deck in the morning, drinking coffee and I can feel it. I feel like I was meant to be here. You know what I'm saying?"

"Yes, I think I know what you're saying."

"Yeah, you know what I'm saying. That's what pulled you here too. That's probably why we picked the same area, you and me. But hey, I'll let you go. I'll be around though, talk some more. After all we're going to be neighbors and, well, most of the people in this area have lived here forever, for generations, so, you and me, we're, uh, we're . . ."

"Both outsiders?"

"Outsiders, yes, we're outsiders, so in some ways it's you and me in our neck of the woods. I'm originally from Chicago. How about you?

"I grew up in Charlotte."

"See, that's what I'm saying. We're both from cities. So I'll be over, check out your work. I want to trim my place with as much local art as possible, so I definitely want to check your bowls out. Take it easy, Ira. I got to bop into Robinson's here. Some guys are coming over this afternoon for a business meeting, and I need to pick up some steaks for the grill."

The window is down as I wend my way along Walnut Creek Road, but in spite of the cool morning air, I feel warm and uncomfortable. Everything about this interaction is bothering me. I know that this meeting with Don Oldsmar wasn't nearly as simple as it would seem to be on the surface. This wasn't just an effort to be neighborly. Was Oldsmar trying to form an impression of me or to make an impression on me?

I don't like the man or trust him, a reaction born of my many years of observing people, trying to discern the nuances in their demeanor that often foreshadowed the true character I would be dealing with. I'm quite good at such analysis after all these years, a skill that furthered my career on occasion, and in some instances, saved my life.

Oldsmar has a tense smile that plays on his lips far too often to fit the conversation, suggesting to me that it's a forced gesture. And while he looked me in the eye for the most part, he glanced about himself as if he was impatient, like he had more important matters to attend to.

The fact that we are both outsiders seems to be a weak basis for establishing a relationship, considering how vast the *outside* is.

In truth, I am far more comfortable with the people who reside in Walnut Creek, *insiders* like Julian or Ben, then I ever could be with someone like Oldsmar.

Aside from his demeanor, the fact that in his opening sentence, Oldsmar mentioned that I was a writer, raises a flag of caution. It would seem that he got a little ahead of himself, and perhaps blurted out the basis for the interaction. After I deflected the comment, Oldsmar never addressed the point again, suggesting that he adjusted quickly to his misstep and decided not to press the issue further, for now anyway.

I have a distinct feeling that the subject of my profession, or rather, my former profession, will be brought up in a future encounter.

How much does Oldsmar really know about me? If his source of information is indeed the local hearsay, then I can assume, very little, because I've been careful not to make known the details of my career, especially the turn it took in Afghanistan. However, if Oldsmar has acquired knowledge of my résumé through his own research, or if that knowledge was furnished to him by those who finance his presence in Madison County, then he knows far too much for my liking.

Intuition tells me that the latter is the case. That same insight cautions me to tread carefully around this character, and if further discussion is unavoidable, to keep the focus on my current profession, hewing wooden bowls.

7

The bench creaks and groans as I maneuver a piece of walnut into place, and I guess that if my hearing were more acute, I would hear my old bones doing likewise. Yesterday's prolonged session with the gardens was well worth the stiffness I'm experiencing today.

The warmer weather seems to be finally taking hold after an unusually cool April such that even at this early hour, a long-sleeved shirt is sufficient to offset the morning chill and a kindling fire provides ample heat to warm the workshop.

The sound of Walnut Creek, running high from recent rains, provides soothing background noise to offset the commotion of traffic on the road, my neighbors, rushing to their various occupations. I chose this location for my business because it's a well traveled route, yet I never imagined just how much traffic would go by each day on this country road.

Hundreds of people, leaving their homes and traveling to a job so that they can finance the home they abandon each day and pay for the vehicle that transports them back and forth.

I try to imagine what this setting would have been like before civilization became so reliant on these machines for transportation. Instead of the grinding of tires on asphalt and discordant engine noises, I might hear the sound of horse hooves as they clapped along an earthen Walnut Creek Road, or the rattle of a wooden wagon, being pulled behind.

Rather than fleeting images of faces speeding past, I would greet people passing by on horseback or on foot, making their way to or from town. That was not so long ago. The oldest people in the neighborhood remember when the road wasn't paved and some of them traveled it by just such means.

I'm only somewhat less dependent on a vehicle because I work at home, but I could hardly live without one. I assuage my guilty conscience over this dependence because of my occupation, wherein the tools I use are powered by my own effort. Except for the use of lights when daylight is insufficient, I use no electricity.

Is such an approach the answer to humanity's great dilemma, our addiction to fossil fuels? If the human race were to voluntarily revert to a simpler form of technology, could civilization be sustainable?

I smile at the thought, remembering when I once posited this very question to a colleague years ago near the end of a hot and dusty car trip from Gardez to Kandahar. Eric, a longtime environmentalist, was in a prickly mood on that uncomfortable, sweltering day in Afghanistan.

"Civilization is unsustainable at any level", he answered, staring out the window at irrigated farmland surrounding Kandahar, a region that is one of the oldest known human settlements. Eric sighed and turned toward me as he continued.

"To reach a sustainable level of technology we would have to go back to the stone age. We're going to get there, Ira, sooner or later, whether we like it or not. It's just a question of how much of the human race will be alive by then."

I understood Eric's point at the time and I appreciate the truth of his statement even more clearly today, but I don't want to entertain such melancholy thoughts this beautiful spring morning. I want to make bowls.

I secure the wood with my left hand and test the sharpness of a buck saw I recently purchased at a flea market in town. I rake the saw's teeth across the contour of the walnut log, but stop when I hear the sound of footsteps on gravel. My neighbor, Ben, appears in the doorway. He's a little man, skinny and stiff, but alert and active as he approaches his ninetieth year. He places a hand on each side of the doorway and pulls himself up the step and into the shop.

"Hello, hello, I just came over to make sure you're working hard. Spring is here and the tourists will be flocking to the mountains. Do you have enough bowls ready for them?"

"Not yet, but soon. Some of these on the shelves are about dry enough to finish up, and I'm hewing out more every day. I'll be ready, although I don't think there will be a great rush through the front door."

"You never know. I can remember when this store was a hot spot. It was the first one of it's kind on the road here; the first place you could get gasoline, too."

"I didn't know your parents sold gasoline here."

"Yes sir, only one pump, one of those tall ones with a clock face on the front. It used to be out there by the corner of the building, opposite my place."

"Well I'll be. I never would have guessed that."

"Wasn't there long though. My mother didn't like the smell, and for what money my parents made, it was more trouble than it was worth."

"More trouble than it was worth, now that I might have guessed."

"Say did Dave Barnwell get you fixed up the other day?"

"Sure did, Ben. New lights, outlets galore, I'm all set."

"David's a good man. I've known him since he was a little boy. I think I mentioned that I was the school bus repairman in the county for thirty-eight years, and buses broke down a lot back then.

The kids used to hate to see me coming, because they knew Ben would get the bus running and they'd still have to go to school. No one complained louder than David. He was a rascal. Ha, ha, yes sir, I got to know all the kids and their parents, too.

"I'll bet you did. That reminds me. I've recently met a man that lives in the valley. His name is Julian Runnion. Do you know him?"

"Julian Runnion, yes, sure, I know who he is. I used to know him better when he was young, but I haven't really seen much of him in recent years. Ever since his wife left, he pretty much keeps to himself. I know he still lives on the family property up the road. You say you recently met Julian?"

"Yes, earlier this week. That's who I bought this walnut from."

"No kidding. So that's who was in the blue truck. I didn't recognize him. Beard's longer and grayer than it used to be. The Runnions have always been a private family, long as I've known them, but their good neighbors in their own way. The old man, Adam, quit coming around years ago; he rarely leaves the farm. His father was like that, too. They've lived up in that hollow for as long as I know.

Runnions were one of the first families to settle these parts and just about everyone is related to them. My grandmother was a Runnion, a distant cousin to Adam, in fact."

"How interesting. Apparently Adam isn't doing real well, health wise."

"I knew he had a stroke a while back, but I haven't really heard how he was doing lately. I'm surprised Julian told you so much though."

"His sister, Patricia, stopped by while we were talking. She was on the way to see her father and pulled in here when she saw Julian's truck. That's how it came up about Mr. Runnion's health."

"Patricia, I almost forget she's part of that family sometime, she's so different from them. Their mother was a Boyd and she takes after that side of the family: more outgoing, speaks her mind, too. Her husband was killed some years back, tractor accident. I met him once, and he seemed like a nice fellow.

They had a farm north of here, up over the mountains, into Tennessee. Her children must be grown by now, but I guess she's stayed up in Tennessee all these years."

"I don't know. She really didn't say very much."

"Hah, maybe the Runnion in her is showing through now.

Anyway, that's not the reason I stopped, to gossip. We can do that anytime. My sister is concerned you aren't eating enough. She wants to have you up the road for dinner, like on Sunday next. What do you say?"

"Sunday, sure, that would be nice. What time?"

"We eat earlier on Sundays, about four o'clock. I can pick you up if you like, say at ten till. No sense both of us driving."

"Okay, Ben, sounds like a fun afternoon. Can I bring anything?"

"No, no, just yourself and your appetite. Anyway, I'll let Edna know. And now that I delivered my message, I'll let you get back to work. I got to get back across the street. Man's coming to do trimming around my place. I can't keep up with it anymore. Yesterday I went to use the weedeater on the bank above the house, and I just plain gave out. So I figure it's time to hire some help."

"That's understandable, Ben. I hope I still have you're stamina at ninety."

"I'm not ninety yet. Now don't go rushing things. And I don't know if it's stamina or stubbornness that keeps me going, but I keep going. Anyway, I better get over there and let you make bowls. If I don't see you before, I'll see you Sunday."

I move to the doorway to watch my aged neighbor walk back across Walnut Creek Road, to the house he and his wife, Daisy, purchased in 1945. Daisy died twelve years ago, and Ben has lived alone ever since. I wish I could have met his wife who he speaks of often, but I'm glad that I got here in time to at least make Ben's acquaintance.

I turn back to the workbench, raking the saw's teeth in a steady motion back and forth across the contour of the log. I'm buoyed up with thoughts of the dinner engagement at Edna's house. This is the first such invitation I've received since moving here and I welcome the opportunity to get to know more about the valley and, in particular, about the family that preceded me at this locale.

Dining at another's table is a pastime that I came to enjoy very much while in Afghanistan, and doing so endeared me to the country and it's people. I have fond memories of Afghans as very good cooks along with warm recollections of their hospitality. They love to have guests, and as opposed to Western culture, where unexpected arrival of a guest is seen as rude or inappropriate, guests are welcome in Afghan homes at any time.

Before the Soviet invasion and the ensuing decades of war, the people were even more open and generous. Today, many view Afghanistan as a place of endless warfare, but in 1974, when I first traveled there and had nowhere to eat or stay, I could knock on a stranger's door and would likely receive something to eat and possibly gain shelter for the night. The owner of the house would welcome me without knowing who I was or where I was from.

Afghans became more reserved in the years that followed, and with good reason, but I still found their generosity intact even up until the time I left.

I stop sawing and gaze out the window, distracted by one particular memory. Wally and I were near Gardez, on the way back to Kabul, when our truck coughed to a halt on a dusty, hot roadway. In my estimation, our journey to Khost had been a waste of time, so I was in an agitated state even before the vehicle broke down.

I was traveling with Walter Simpson of BBC News and we'd made the journey to meet with a Taliban commander who was well known in those parts. Not only was the commander a no-show, but upon our arrival, there seemed to be no knowledge of the supposed meeting.

Wally was upbeat as usual, claiming as he often did that even gaining no information, still told something. He just about had me convinced of that when the truck broke down in the middle of Gardez Road. After numerous attempts to revive the aged Toyota, we pushed it off the graveled surface and walked to a nearby house.

When Mahmud Safi appeared at the door, I read concern in his eyes, but saw kindness as well. Mahmud invited us in and sent his son, Habib, to fetch a man who could help with our automotive trouble. Wally and I were soon seated cross-legged on pillows sampling the cooking of Mahmud's wife, Lakhta.

I was familiar with Afghan dining etiquette by this time, but

I still watched to follow the lead of our host, unlike Wally whose easy and casual manner was not to his advantage in this situation. He leaned back carelessly and placed one foot forward, such that it was pointing toward Mahmud. Sitting with legs outstretched or with the feet facing people is considered rude in Afghan culture.

This was not the reason Mahmud did not warm to my colleague, but the indiscretion was symptomatic of an attitude that resulted in Wally not being invited back. And it was more than the fact that I kept my feet tucked in that allowed a relationship with Mahmud to go forward.

Despite a world of differences, we were two of a kind in intrinsic ways. In the years that followed, we shared many meals together in affirmation of these commonalities. Alas, those days are gone now. The spark of curiosity in Mahmud's eyes that I so treasured was replaced with a blaze of anger, and one day, the light was extinguished forever.

I'm not making much progress with this walnut log. I'm not keeping my mind on the task at hand. I retuned to Walnut Creek to let go of the past and begin to live for the moment. The past cannot be changed. I reposition myself over the log and focus, raking the saw blade in long, even strokes, concentrating on what's in front of me.

8

With each end cut off, I split the log down the middle with a froe, a tool that I purchased from an antique mall in Asheville. The froe is well designed as a splitting tool, with a long iron blade and a short, round piece of wood attached at a right angle for a handle. Grasping the handle, I place the cutting edge on the end grain of the log and strike the back of the iron with a heavy wooden mallet, driving the blade into the center of the log.

Because the tree came down recently, the wood is pliable and yields to my assault, slowly separating from end to end with sounds of ripping and splintering fibers. The split runs true, attesting to the fact that this walnut tree grew straight and fast, shedding its early limbs and shooting upward in competition with surrounding trees for sunlight.

With one of the halves, I repeat the splitting process on a line parallel to the first cut, removing about two inches of the outer surface. The result is a rough walnut plank about twelve inches long, ten inches wide and six inches thick.

With a hatchet, I bevel the ends and corners to mimic the curvature of the log, resulting in a crude rectangular bowl shape. Upon the inner surface, I draw an oval outline, spacing my sketch half an inch from the edges to allow suitable width for the bowl and leaving myself room for error.

Before wielding my adze and starting the hewing process, I determine that a cup of hot coffee sitting close at hand would complete the picture of a proper workplace. When I step outside and start toward the house, a vehicle pulls into the parking lot, prompting me to retrace my steps.

So few people frequent my place of business that I'm caught off guard when I have to assume the role of shopkeeper. Smoothing stray hair behind my ears, I step into the showroom just as a woman enters the door. I smile, and when the gesture is returned, I recognize her as Julian's sister, Patricia.

"Oh, hello, Patricia, right?"

"Patricia, is it? I like that. My mother always used Patricia. The guys call me Pat. But you may call me Patricia, if you like."

"I like Patricia, and I've always preferred calling people by their full name, provided it's not too long. You see, I've never had a problem with my name being abbreviated. What would you shorten 'Ira' to?"

"True, it seems it's already shortened from something."

"Funny you should say that. A colleague of mine likes to tease that 'Ira' is short for 'irascible'. Ira is actually an ancient name, and depending on which origin one adheres to, it can mean anything from one who is watchful to a warrior."

"Which meaning do you prefer? Julian told me you're a writer, so I would guess the first one suits you better."

"Yes, considering I've been a journalist most of my life, I like to think of myself as one who is watchful. However, in the course of my career, I've watched and associated with many warriors, and although I tried to remain neutral in my observations, the warrior tendency did show through at times."

"That's when you become irascible."

"Y-yes, I think that's what my colleague was getting at."

"Well, I prefer Ira, if that's okay."

"Yes, I prefer Ira, too. I'm a long way from the fight now."

"Well, Ira, I'm on my way back home to Tennessee, and I thought I'd see what you have here. A friend has a birthday coming up and she loves wood. I thought maybe a wooden bowl from the old neighborhood would be a nice gift."

"Good, I'm glad you stopped in. I was just preparing to work with some of the walnut Julian brought me, but once a bowl is roughed out, it needs to dry before it can be finished. So unless you're friend's birthday is in a month or so, I don't think I can have a bowl ready from that tree."

"No, her birthday is Thursday, so I can't put this off for even another day. One of these bowls you have finished will be fine. Clara's never been to our farm, so she's not sentimental about it, like I am. I'll get a walnut bowl for myself later. Did I interrupt something? I saw you here walking toward the house."

"Oh, no, I was just heading over to get another cup of coffee before I get too engrossed in my work."

"Go ahead then, and I'll look over what you have. It takes me a while to choose."

"Okay, I'll be right back. Would you like a cup?"

"Yes, actually that would be nice. I didn't expect this kind of service though. I didn't see 'coffee' on your sign."

"I hadn't really thought of it, but that's an idea. If you come by here some day and I'm advertising coffee, you'll know that the bowl business hasn't gone so well. I'll be right back."

I pour the remaining coffee down the drain, rather than reheat it in the microwave, which is my usual practice. Refilling the percolator with water and the filter basket with coffee grounds, I place the old, appliance on the burner. The coffee pot has been part of my estate since I was in graduate school and has accumulated many miles along with it's tarnished appearance, percolating in far-flung regions of the world, sometimes over open fires.

While the pot is gurgling and bumping on the stove, I take the opportunity to check my appearance in the mirror, something I often forget to do in these days of solitary living.

Such an unexpected surprise, for Patricia to stop in like this. She seemed quite indifferent about me or my business when she passed by two days ago.

I was intrigued by Julian's sister at our first meeting, and became even more interested after the information Ben passed on to me this morning. I make a quick perusal of my features in the mirror, smoothing my beard and wishing I had trimmed it this morning.

In the kitchen, I pour coffee into two new earthenware mugs I purchased last fall but have not had occasion to use.

As I enter the shop, Patricia is standing at the counter looking down at two bowls she has selected from the display. She looks up and smiles as I hand her the coffee.

"I've narrowed it down to these two. What do you think?"

"I like them both, but I'm partial to walnut, so this one gets the nod. I especially like the sapwood on this end and the color variation. This other bowl is birch and comes from a tree that was cut down across the street on my neighbor's property. I assume that you know Ben?"

"Yes, everybody knows Ben."

"Ha ha, I'm finding that out. The walnut bowl came from the tree right behind this building, near the creek, a large limb that broke off over the winter."

"Well that settles it for me. What could be more homegrown than that, a walnut bowl, made from a walnut tree, growing on the bank of Walnut Creek? Clara will love it."

"Wonderful, and I thank you for the purchase, the first sale at the Wooden Bowl Shoppe."

"How nice. I'm sure many more will follow."

"I, uh, don't have the gift wrapping department set up yet. Is paper and a brown bag okay?"

"That will be fine."

"How is your father? Julian told me he was having some health problems."

"Oh, Dad's doing pretty well, just frustrated that he can't get outside and work like he wants to. He suffered a pretty bad stroke, and he's been a long time coming back from it. He told me more than once if he had it to all over again, he'd take a heart attack over

41

a stroke. He says, that at least with a heart attack, you get the damn thing over with, one way or the other."

"That's an interesting opinion and I can see his point. Well, Julian was glad to see you arrive. He said that your father will listen to you."

"Oh, Dad listens to Julian, too. He just doesn't do what he says or he'll do the opposite just to show him. He and Dad are two of a kind in many ways. I wish Julian would listen to me, too, about his health, especially. He doesn't take care of himself like he should. He's diabetic, you know."

"No, he didn't mention that."

"He wouldn't. Nearly killed him once and it will in the end if he doesn't start taking better care of himself."

"It's that bad?"

"Yes, it's been very bad at times. Smoking and drinking doesn't help, but you can't tell Julian anything. That's where he's a chip off the old block. Anyway, I don't want to get started on that. I better get my bowl and let you get back to work."

"Oh, no rush. I'm not on any time schedule here and I'm fortunate in that I'm not dependent on the business to survive. I take it seriously, but I take time to enjoy it, too."

"That's nice; that's real nice. You like it here, then?"

"I love it here. I really feel at home like I haven't felt anywhere in years. In many ways, I wish I had gotten here sooner, especially before things started to change."

"Yes, Madison County was overlooked for a long time, but people are definitely zeroing in on it now. My grandmother used to refer to all outsiders as 'people from the north' no matter which direction they came from."

"That's interesting."

"Yes isn't that funny? I don't think she was referring to a geographic location so much as an attitude."

"I know what she's talking about; I know that attitude. In fact I experienced it up close just the other day at Robinson's with a man who recently built a house on Fisher Lane."

"Let me guess, the big house up on the hill right at the last turn. I come in on Fisher Lane and I noticed it right away. That house sticks out like a sore thumb."

"So does he, believe me, and his attitude may be the least of the problem. He's a consultant for an energy company that's planning to drill for natural gas in this area. He's here laying the ground work, getting people to sign contracts for drilling rights on their land

"Oh no, gas drilling, here, you mean fracking?" That's been going on for a while north of where I live and believe me, if you've never seen one of those operations, it's not a pretty sight."

"I can't say I know much about it. I know that the gas rigs are a bit larger than they were in the old days."

"That's putting it mildly, and it's not just the well itself. The whole area turns into an industrial site: day and night trucking, pipelines, bright lights, not to mention outside workers, taking over the area. My God, I hope that's not what's coming here. Do you think Julian knows about this?"

"We never discussed it. I actually just learned about it myself."

"Darn it, my father doesn't need something like this now. I know that change is inevitable and new people are going to move in, but I never expected something like gas drilling."

"Well, if it's going to happen, I hope they stay out of Walnut Creek Valley at least."

"I do, too, Ira, I'd rather things stayed like they are, farmers and plain folks going about they're lives, and a bowl maker, too."

"At your service. And I plan to do my best to keep things the same. That's why I came back here, because of my fond memories of the valley."

"Well that's good to know. Anyway, I do need to get home. I have to work tomorrow and chores are piling up around the house."

"Thank you for your business, Patricia, and the conversation. Please come again."

"Thank *you*, Ira, and I will be coming again soon, Memorial Day weekend. My father loves holidays, especially the patriotic ones, so we always get together for this one. I'll stop in then and see what you've made out of our walnut."

"I'll be looking forward to it."

9

*M*y God, what's happened? An explosion, the house is on *fire. Another explosion, the house seems to have exploded. Mahmud runs toward his home and I follow. Helicopters, I hear helicopters; I see a Blackhawk circling. Something is protruding from my leg, a piece of wood. I feel nauseous, faint, limping toward the house, I stumble into the doorway and onto my knees.*

Through the haze, I see Mahmud pulling at rubble, his shrieks of anguish punctuate a crescendo of human misery. The wedding party has disappeared. I hear wailing and crying, see people crawling on their hands and knees. Blood, smoke, the acrid odor of explosives. How can this be happening?

I open my eyes to darkness and hear only the sound of Walnut Creek through open windows. I chose this room as my bedroom for that very reason, so that I can hear the peaceful, reassuring murmur of Walnut Creek as I lie in bed. I'm in desperate need of that reassurance now after another dream about the event that changed my life forever, the moment when a delightful, enchanting occasion was transformed into a hellish nightmare.

This valley is the source of my most pleasant memories, and I came here hoping that I might build a new life, relegating recollections of war to the past. But Afghanistan is still close behind and tonight my hopes are undermined by a poignant flashback. I glance at the clock to see that it's just after four and knowing well that I won't get back to sleep, I roll out to start another day.

While coffee is perking I sit at the computer, scanning the news, reading between the lines, seeking distraction for my thoughts. Instead, I find myself irritated with how shallow and predictable most of the journalism is.

I could probably write most of the mainstream news myself, in advance, especially with regards to the Mideast. Domestically, it's safe to report that budget negotiations have stalled, that republicans demand greater domestic spending cuts and the democrats won't yield—except a little more each time. Serve all this up with the latest celebrity scandal and there you have it.

Mornings are usually reserved for writing or correspondence, but after such a troubling dream, I know I can be neither sociable nor objective with words. Assured that the world is still intact, I turn from the computer, pour a cup of coffee and step onto the porch to see what news is in the morning breeze. I'll *experience* what's happening in the world rather than be told about it second hand.

The scene is bathed in moonlight such that I'm able to discern the contour of Walnut Creek and the gnarled boughs of trees that grow on its bank. I'm drawn toward the scene, cross the lawn, and place a hand on the furrowed trunk of a large tree behind my workshop, a mighty walnut that likely sprouted about the time Mathew and Anna built their store. The creek and town are named for the ancestors of this tree.

The moon is low in the southern sky and its brilliance is reflected countless times in the rippling water of Walnut Creek. I'm mesmerized by this light show and comforted by the accompanying water sounds. Following my footpath, I stroll east along the creek bank, in the direction of Walnut Mountain, the hulking bulwark of the valley and the origin of the stream.

At the end of my acreage, I lean against the giant poplar tree, standing straight and resolute as it has for a hundred years, marking the boundary between the Ramsey and Flynn properties. Gazing back in the direction of the house, I marvel at how well the structure fits into the landscape, almost like a natural outcrop of the land. Such is the case for most of the older homes in the valley, simple dwellings that were built for function and use, and are aesthetically pleasing for that reason.

These same characteristics are what I appreciated in the house in which Mahmud and his family lived. Their's was a conventional Afghan home, a mud-brick structure with one entrance and a greeting room just inside the door, the same room where Mahmud welcomed two stranded journalists into his home. The house was located with other homes within a walled compound where Mahmud lived with his wife, children, parents, and his sister, Parisa.

The wedding of Mahmud's son, Habib,was a time of great celebration. For a western journalist to attend such an event was not customary, but by then Mahmud and I were good friends and he treated me as one of the family. I felt quite honored by the invitation and was captivated by the ceremony.

Unlike a wedding in the United States, traditional Afghan weddings span several days and are characterized by unique customs and rituals.

On the first day, the bride's family traveled to Mahmud's house to get to know their future in-laws. The following day Habib led a procession on horseback to the house of his betrothed, Shandana, accompanied by musicians and dancers. Ceremonial rifles were fired at intervals along the route.

On the evening of the third day, the wedding feast began at Mahmud's house with music, dancing, and singing. Shandana arrived on horseback, and as she and Habib entered the room, the musicians played a beautiful piece, *Ahesta Boro*, which means, walk slowly, a song that is the Afghan counterpart to the American *Wedding March*. A Quran was held over their heads, and we stood up to pay our respect.

When it was announced that dinner was ready, all the guests formed a line and walked alongside a beautifully decorated buffet. Four different rice dishes were offered, many kinds of kabobs, and three types of Afghan bread. A variety of pastries completed the dinner table.

After the meal, Habib and Shandana walked to the wedding cake and the musicians returned to play another traditional song as the cake was cut and served. Then was to follow, hours of merriment with people dancing as the musicians played songs of a faster beat. Wedding festivities, I was told, will often go on until dawn.

But there was to be no more ceremony, not another minute of celebration. As the cake was being served, terror was unleashed from above, and the nightmare that will surely haunt me to my grave, unfolded before my eyes.

Mahmud and I had stepped outside to talk and were nearly knocked down when the first missile struck. We turned back toward the house and witnessed the second rocket strike. I was hit in the leg and fell to the ground, but struggled to my feet and followed Mahmud as he ran toward the ravaged building.

Inside was wailing, agony, and death, where moments before there was joy and life, a scene of merriment and celebration turned into a war zone. When I reached Mahmud, he was bent over his sister, Parisa, who was still alive, but so terribly wounded, I knew she would not live for long. When I knelt beside her, Mahmud stood and turned his attention to the wreckage, pulling at the rubble, calling Habib's name.

I repositioned Parisa, hoping to make her more comfortable, but she hardly seemed to notice, her eyes were fixed, staring straight ahead. The smoke began to clear and I saw Mahmud's father, Abdullah, lying against the wall a few feet behind his daughter, one arm torn from his body, his clothing covered in blood. Mahmud appeared out of the gloom and knelt between his family members, sobbing.

I felt faint, grasped my leg and closed my eyes. I had seen the face of war before but never this close and personal. Parisa's breathing quickened, and I opened my eyes to witness her tremble, stiffen, and relax into death.

A screech owl sounds from the dark woods across the creek, a sonorous, mournful call that resonates with my thoughts. I turn and peer into the shadows as another owl answers from higher on the ridge. I concentrate on the somber calls as they go back and forth in the darkness, focusing my thoughts on the present.

Life goes on, and I must go on as well. Dwelling in the past solves no problems. My remaining time in this life, will be devoted to fighting against war by striking at the root of the problem, the greed that motivates the war makers.

10

Encompassing an area of two square miles and with only one runway, the Asheville Regional Airport is charming in comparison to its sprawling, metropolitan counterparts. I had no trouble finding a parking space just outside the terminal, and with time to spare, I'm sitting in the waiting area of Gate 7, anticipating the arrival of Justine Chantal, my friend, former colleague, and at one time, lover. We have not seen each other in four years, now, sustaining our relationship through handwritten letters, as we have since we were young.

The fact that I've retired from our profession does not seem to surprise her nearly as much as I might have expected, although I'm sure she will not fully accept it as fact until she hears the details. I'm somewhat nervous about this reunion. Justine has a knack for asking complicated questions, the answers to which I'm still working out in my own mind.

Justine says that she has made a major decision regarding her own career as well, but wants to wait to discuss it over a glass of wine. Knowing her as I do, I can guess the direction she's going. I've seen it coming for some time.

When Justine and I were young and just starting out, we seemed to be in agreement about everything. Our politics were progressive and for us that called for the utmost integrity in our profession. We were committed to observing news as it happened and relating it in all its wholesomeness or meanness to the world, truly believing that when the truth is known, righteousness will surely follow.

The scene grows indistinct, the crowd noise waxes nostalgic, as the memory of another small airport on the other side of the world is conjured up. Justine and I waited to depart for Cambodia soon after the overthrow of the Pol Pot regime by Vietnamese forces.

We were in love and with all the naïve freedom that youth proffers, I imagined us continuing as a team beyond that assignment, partners throughout an illustrious and rewarding life. I remember that little airport in Vietnam so well because that was the last time I harbored such naive optimism for the future.

Nothing I had learned to that point in my life prepared me for what I experienced in Cambodia. Not only were the horrors of the Pol Pot regime revealed to me, but I was made aware of how the covert bombing of that country by Richard Nixon and Henry Kissinger cleared the way for the rise of the Khmer Rouge.

Had I simply described Pol Pot for what he was and relayed only the overt details of the Cambodian catastrophe, my career would have proceeded along a smoother, more conventional path, but I could not separate my observations from the knowledge of my own government's collusion. Cambodia became my first lesson in how empires operate.

Justine was better able to remain detached from the larger picture and reported just what was before her eyes. We eventually parted ways in our careers and our lives, but never in the spirit of those early days together. Her career flourished in association with many major publications, while mine moved forward in fits and starts, dogged by controversy and censorship.

The major news outlets and the moneyed interests that own them, couldn't get rid of me by conventional means, but not for lack of trying. I went rogue, came back at them through independent news channels and with books, always a thorn in their side. In the end, I walked away from journalism of my own accord, having finally observed too much.

A voice, announcing that Justine's flight is unloading rouses me from my reminiscences and I take a position among the crowd gathered near Gate 7. I readily spot my friend among the disembarking passengers, and she acknowledges me with a beaming smile. Justine is an inch shorter than I am, lean and athletic looking for her sixty-two years. Her salt and pepper hair is shorter than when I last saw her, just brushing the shoulders of her khaki safari shirt.

We hug, kiss lightly on the lips and clasp each other again, more tightly.

"Ira, you've grown so distinguished looking. I love the beard. If I didn't know you, I'd guess you were a seasoned college professor, classical literature, perhaps, or maybe philosophy."

"No, nothing so intellectual, just a humble bowl maker. Now with you there's no uncertainty. Had I never met you before, my first guess would be that you're an international correspondent on a brief layover here in Asheville before you're off on assignment to some exotic region of the globe."

"Ha ha, you know my life isn't nearly as exciting these days. I can't wait to see your place. Is it far from here?"

"Not at all, less than an hour away. We head north, take a left and then a right, and we're in the Walnut Creek Valley, Madison County, Jewel of the Blue Ridge, as they say."

"Jewel of the Blue Ridge, now I read that, and I think it's a charming saying. I must confess, when my plans to visit you were finalized, I spent some time researching your new home and I learned a number of interesting things, some that you may not know about, but let's save that for later, over a glass of wine."

Justine and I chat nonstop on the way back and then continue filling each other in through lunch. I surprise myself with how much I have to tell about my new locale and Justine seems to delight in the information, almost as she would if I were describing my experiences in another country. After a lunch of portobello mushroom sandwiches and a rice dish, prepared especially for the occasion, we move to the back porch, and I pour more wine.

"The sandwiches were superb; you've outdone yourself. And the rice dish was delicious, Ira. What did you say it's called?"

"Bor Pilau, a classic Afghan recipe. It was served with the first meal I ate at Mahmud's house and remains one of my favorites. Mahmud's wife, Lakhta, was a wonderful cook and she seemed to love to feed me. Nothing is more important at the Afghan table than the rice. Most important is not to overcook it. Each grain should be distinct from the next. Sticky rice just will not do in a respectable Afghan kitchen.

For special occasions, there is always a variety of rice dishes. For her son's wedding, Lakhta truly outdid herself. Her spread was a work of art in more ways than one. I wish I would have taken a picture of . . . Well, I wish a lot of things. That seems like a long time ago, now."

"Well you're rice was perfect, Ira. Lakhta would be pleased. Are you still in touch with them, Mahmud's family, I mean?"

"No, not really. What remains of the family is scattered now; most have left the country. Lakhta remarried, one of Mahmud's brothers who was a widower. The youngest daughter and I exchanged letters a while back, when she was in Pakistan, but I haven't heard from her in a while. I can hardly blame the family for not wanting to keep in touch with me."

"Ira, I can't understand why you blame yourself for what happened. You more than anyone else did your part to . . ."

"I'm sorry, Justine, forgive me. I've worked hard to keep myself from wandering down that path again, but I had a terrible dream just the other night and the whole hellish incident has been fresh in my mind again.

So allow me to change the subject. As I recall, you have an agenda, select topics that are to be talked about over a glass of wine, something concerning a career change, and information about Madison County even. We have our wine in hand, so let's talk."

"Oh, okay, good idea. Well let me start with the more intriguing part of my agenda. Have you ever heard of an organization called

Backbone Mountain Militia?"

"Hmm, no, I can't say I have. In fact, I've never even heard of Backbone Mountain. Is it around here?"

"Apparently, somewhere in Madison County, one would think, since that's where the militia is supposed to be located, but I couldn't find any mountain with that name on the county map. The reason I know about it at all is because I did a search on Madison County in anticipation of my visit, and while reading through the titles that came up, I saw a familiar name: John Perkins. Do you remember him?"

"Y-yes, I think. He worked for Reuters, right?"

"Yes, and he still does, in fact. After the Oklahoma City Bombing in 1995, John followed the growth of the militia movement in the United States and published a number of articles about it. The reason his name turned up in my search was because, in one article, he mentions a group known as Backbone Mountain Militia, presumably located in Madison County, North Carolina."

"How interesting, and I'm quite surprised that I haven't heard of the group by now, especially since I, too, have been intrigued by the growth of the militia movement in this country. It's the sort of information I would have attended to."

"Actually, it's not so surprising since other than the name and the general location of Madison County, the article disclosed very little about the group. In fact the secretive nature of Backbone Mountain Militia is a feature that distinguished it from other militia groups around the country and was the reason John included it in his article.

Well, you know me, I needed to learn all I could, especially if I was going to bring it up with you, so I contacted John to see what additional information he might have, and the story only became more interesting. He said that he wouldn't know about the militia at all except that during an interview with a member of the East Tennessee Militia the name came up.

The man that was being interviewed brought it up because John was asking him questions about the origin of his own militia and to what extent they trained. In the course of his answer, he said that there was a militia in Madison County, North Carolina, which was the oldest that he knew of. He said it was formed right after the Civil War, and it was highly trained, run like a modern army. And get this, he said that he didn't know the names of any of the members, but he did know that the chief officer was known as the Field Commander."

"Justine, have you concocted this story just to stir me up? You know I'm retired now."

"Ha ha, no, I wouldn't do that to you, and I don't want to tempt you out of retirement. I never expected to uncover this information. I was looking for mundane facts such as who Madison County is named after, or what's the highest mountain in the county. And rest assured, after what I've told you, there's not much else to get stirred up about. John said that once he started asking more questions about Backbone Mountain Militia, the source from Tennessee clammed up, like he had already said more than he should have."

"John told me that all inquiries he made in this area went cold and even the North Carolina Citizens Militia, which is the main militia organization in the state, was unable or perhaps, as he guessed, unwilling to give any information about the group. He hoped that when he mentioned Backbone Mountain Militia in the article, it might prompt someone to come forth with more information, but, no such luck."

"Well doesn't this just beat all. All we know is that somewhere in Madison County, a mysterious character, known as the Field Commander, leads a secret, well trained army named Backbone Mountain Militia. I like it though. This reminds me of information I might have stumbled upon in Afghanistan about a local Taliban company led by some enigmatic tribal leader."

"Well it could all be conjecture. The information is incomplete to say the least. I wouldn't have even given it more thought if it hadn't pertained to this area, and I knew that you would find something like this interesting."

"I do, very much so. I'm retired from journalism, but my

curiosity is as active as ever. I'll certainly keep my eyes and ears open with regards to Backbone Mountain Militia. There's a man I buy wood from, Julian is his name, an intriguing fellow. His family has lived in this valley for generations and if anyone would know about this, I bet Julian would. But, enough of this for now. What about you Justine, what are your plans going forward?"

"Well, okay, here we go. I've decided to stay with National Public Radio for the foreseeable future; I've been offered a senior analyst position. Now don't wince. I know your feelings about NPR."

"I haven't said a word, Justine."

"You don't have to speak; I know what you're thinking. I agree with you to some extent, but I don't think you're being entirely fair. I know that NPR depends on some of the same funding sources that control commercial news, but you can't put it in the same category as the other major media outlets.

NPR does its best to extend the parameters of debate within the limits of political pragmatism. If NPR wants to receive sufficient funding than they have to be somewhat selective about what is reported."

"That they are."

"Oh, you have to admit that those who get their news and information from public broadcasting are better informed than those whose information comes from mainstream media. Right?"

"More wine, my dear?"

"Oh, Ira, you're impossible."

"And by that, which connotation of the phrase are you implying, that I am *not* possible or that I am unbearable?"

"Ahem, yes, I'll have another glass of wine, my dear. I'm sorry, but I can't move to the country and make bowls for a living at this stage of my life."

"How do you know that until you try? Tomorrow morning we'll go over to the shop and I'll give you your first lesson. I may save your soul, yet."

"Hah, I doubt that. But tell me, speaking of saving souls,

how is your study of Buddhism coming along?"

"Oh, fairly well. I'm sticking with it, and from what I've learned, that's the hardest step for most people. I consider myself a secular Buddhist as far as the philosophy itself. For me it's a way of life rather than a religion.

Meditation is not coming easily for me, but I'm starting to see a little improvement there. It's going to take some work to focus this old mind that has been allowed to run rampant all these years."

"Well I'm glad you're still enthused about it, Ira. I have to say, you seem more relaxed and happy than I remember you."

"Really? That's good to hear, especially from you, Justine. Did I tell you what steered me toward Buddhism?"

"Yes you did mention that in a letter, the giant Buddha statues in Afghanistan, the Buddhas of the Bamiyan Valley."

"Yes, or what was left when I got there. The Taliban dynamited and destroyed the statues in 2001, but I was inspired by the site, anyway."

"You first went to the site when you were young, back in the seventies, right?"

"Yes, a side excursion while I was working with my father, and I revisited Bamiyan a number of times after that. I almost didn't want to go there again, knowing that the statues had been destroyed, but something drew me back.

The fact that the Taliban would view such peaceful symbols as a threat to their religious beliefs rekindled an interest in Buddhism for me. So at least in my case, their act had an effect opposite to what they intended. I think Afghanistan, and the world for that matter, would be far better off if more people practiced Buddhism."

"Why?"

"War, that's why, or lack thereof. Have you ever heard of a Buddhist nation going to war? Since the time Buddhism was conceived, twenty-five hundred years ago, there has never been a conflict involving Buddhists that led to war, while during that same period, humans have fought hundreds of wars. This is because tolerance and compassion are an integral part of the teaching."

"Okay, I'm convinced. So tell me, *oh enlightened one*, are you here in the Walnut Creek Valley to spread the word?"

"Uh, well, perhaps, in time. I'm not ready just yet to go up against Reverend Lacey at the Walnut Creek Baptist Church."

"Ha, ha, best of luck to you, if you do. But you have a bit of the warrior in you, Ira; you're not a Buddhist by nature. You followed wars most of your life, and sometimes you did everything but take up a gun for the cause you believed in."

"Yes, and that's something I struggle with still. Buddhism in a time of conflict requires great patience and a sincere belief in compassion for all human beings. I was never ready before, but perhaps I am now. I need to accumulate a great deal of wholesome karma to offset the negative karma of the past, so that the next time I'll act accordingly."

"I hope there will never be a next time, Ira. You were true to your profession and worked hard at it. You deserve a peaceful retirement, whatever karma you've accumulated."

"I'll drink to that. More wine, my dear?"

"Yes, thank you."

11

"The first step is to split the log, using this handy tool."

"What is it? I've never seen a tool like this before."

"It's called a froe, and not many people have seen one, but not so many years ago, it was a common tool on every homestead. With the advent of power tools the froe was one of the first hand tool to be hung up."

Justine watches as I work through the preliminary steps, procedures that would be difficult and even dangerous to a novice, but my concern that she might find this roughing-out procedure boring was unwarranted. Instead she seems fascinated with the process. Recognizing this, I slow down and place the tool with more deliberation, happy to have an audience for whom to demonstrate the skills I've developed.

The eighteen inch length of walnut is straight grained and splits easily under the edge of the froe, driven by the weight of the wooden mallet. I cut two inch slabs from opposite sides and then split the log down the middle to form two six inch planks. With a draw knife, I level the outside of one plank, place this surface down on the hewing bench, and draw an oval pattern on the inner surface.

Until this point, Justine watched with a befuddled expression, but with the addition of this illustration, she smiles, recognizing in my crude procedure an image that hints at a bowl.

"Now I see, what's going on. You're going to cut everything out from the center of that drawing and you have a bowl."

"Basically, yes, but it's not so easy, as you will see, since *you* are going to cut everything out. I'll introduce you to the bowl adze, demonstrate the process, and then you can take over."

With the adze I make a series of cuts within the outline, working more slowly than usual for the sake of demonstration. When I've dug down about half an inch, I turn the bench and tool over to Justine who after several awkward hits, gains a feel for the process and removes wood with increasing confidence.

She becomes engrossed in her work and is doing so well that I see no need to interrupt her with further instruction. Instead, I retrieve my coffee mug from the skirt rail of the wood stove, step out the back door, and stroll to the creek.

The water is running at a vigorous clip with a churning and babbling noise that intermingles with the steady tapping, emanating from the workshop. I've never heard the sound of my trade from such a perspective and find it to be pleasant acoustic accompaniment to the creek music.

An inharmonious sound disrupts the composition, engine noise. A pickup truck backs in beside the building, Julian delivering the second load of walnut. As I reach the truck, the tailgate is down and he walks toward me, putting on gloves.

"Howdy Ira. I thought you would have these first logs used up by now."

"Hah, not quite. Business is a little slow still, so I haven't geared up to full production yet. I do have an apprentice inside working, so there's no down time here."

"I wondered how there could be tapping coming from the shop when you're over by the creek."

"Yes, Justine Chantal, a friend of mine is visiting for a few days, so I put her to work. I'll introduce you after we unload these."

"Say, Ira, before we get started, I want to talk to you about something. A fellow stopped up at the farm yesterday, Oldsmar's his name, said he knew you."

"Don Oldsmar, you mean? We met a few days ago is all, so I wouldn't go so far as to say he knows me."

"He talked like he did, even said something about you being a writer. In fact he talked like he was friends with you and everyone else around here, and looking at me all the while with a big smile on his face, like we were friends, too."

"I can't speak for everyone else, but Oldsmar and I are *not* friends. All I knew of him before he introduced himself was what I learned at the hardware store from Frank. Oldsmar introduced himself to me in the parking lot at Robinson's, and I'll tell you this much, my first impression of him wasn't good. Had you heard about him before?"

"Oh yeah, everybody has. He's the one who built that big house on Fisher Lane."

"What did he want? Somehow I guess he didn't stop just to make more friends."

"No, he stopped to talk business. Wants dad to sign a lease on the farm so this company he's with can drill for gas."

"Damn it, that's what I was afraid of. What did your father say?"

"I never let Oldsmar get to him, figured Dad didn't need the aggravation. I know what he would have said though. He'd say hell no, and if Oldsmar didn't get the message, he most likely would've escorted him off the farm with a shotgun. I didn't go that far, but I had half a notion to. I don't like the guy. I just straight out told him no."

"Did he get the message?"

"He got the message, but he didn't like it. His pearly whites disappeared real quick. He told me all my neighbors would be signing leases and says that the Mooneys, family that lives out beyond us, already signed a lease on their land.]

Oldsmar said that the company would get the gas underneath us anyway by drilling down on their property and then sideways until they got under our land. Says they can get the gas anyway, so we might as well sign and make some money out of the deal. I says to him, if you can do that, then why even ask us for a lease."

"Good point."

"Yeah, and he didn't have a good answer. Said something about wanting to be fair with everyone and spread the profit around, but I didn't buy it. Then he said, 'if you ask me, you're passing up a good business opportunity here', and I looked at him and I said, well mister, I *didn't* ask you."

"Let me guess, Oldsmar didn't like that either."

"No sir, he sure didn't. For a few seconds, he had a look on his face like he wanted to hit me. But that's when it got kind of creepy. Smile came back and he got all polite again. Thanked me for my time and turned to go. Before he got to his car, he looked around and said, 'sure is pretty up here. It's no wonder you like it. You have a nice day now'. He left on that, but he's going to be back, sure as I'm standing here.

But hey, I didn't want to take up your time with this, Ira. It's just that the guy acted like you knew each other and I thought I might find out what his story is."

"Can't help you there, Julian. Like I said, I just met the guy. I know the type though, so I bet I could make a good guess at his story. Glorified salesman, public relations man, all smiles and handshakes on the surface. He comes in first and paves the way for the company he works for."

"But why would he build a house like he's set to live here?"

"Building that house and moving here is all part of the sales pitch, making like he's part of the community. My guess is, he'll sell that place as soon as his end of the job is done, so it's an investment, too. By the time the drilling is in full swing, Oldsmar will probably be long gone. I can guarantee that he never gets his hands dirty on a drilling rig."

"Well, I'm not buying what he's selling, but others around here have, so he isn't going away. I need to find out more about this guy and about the gas drilling."

"What about talking to the family that already signed a

contract?"

"The Mooneys? Nah, haven't talked to them in years. No surprise they'd be the first to sign on though. They're always looking to make an easy buck."

"I'll tell you what I can do, Julian. Oldsmar happened to mention to me that he's from Chicago, and I have a friend there who can get the inside story on just about anybody."

"Oh yeah, is this friend of yours a detective or something?"

"No, even better, a journalist, and one with over fifty years experience, a tough nut from the old school of journalism. Saul Griffin is his name, better known as Buzz Griffin. He's mostly retired now; just writes an occasional article for a magazine or an editorial for the Chicago Tribune. He's getting up there in years, but when I last talked to him, Buzz was as sharp as a razor and he has contacts that would make the FBI jealous. He'll get the story on this Oldsmar, if anyone can."

"I'd appreciate that, Ira. I don't think I'm going to learn much more about him around here."

"What's this, a labor strike? Am I the only one who works around here?"

Julian and I turn to see Justine standing in the doorway, smiling, wood adze in hand and wood chips clinging to her sweater.

"Justine, I was wondering how you were getting along in there. Julian and I are just discussing business. We're the chamber of commerce of sorts, in the valley here.

Julian, this is my friend and new apprentice, Justine Chantal. Justine is between jobs and is visiting for a few days. Justine, Julian Runnion, local woodsman and the source of the walnut you're working with."

"Howdy ma'am. Pleased to meet you."

"Nice to meet you, Julian. The wood you brought is really beautiful. It cuts well, too, even for a novice like me."

"I heard you in there. Didn't take Ira long to put you to work, did it? Don't let him work you too hard. That must be why he got this second load, because he knew you were coming.

Speaking of work, I best be heading back up the road. Got hay to cut and if I don't get to it, I'm afraid Dad'll be out on the tractor. Step back a few paces, Ira, and I'll slide these off."

Julian unloads the logs, dropping them into a pile alongside the previous load.

"Well, Justine, you get these turned into bowls and I'll bring you another load. We got plenty of walnut on the farm."

"You're on, Julian. Nice to meet you."

"See you Julian. I'll be in touch."

"Okay Ira. Stop if you're up that way. We're out Runnion Lane. Don't mind the dogs, they're all bark and no bite."

Julian pulls away and Justine turns to me with a smile.

"I didn't mean to break up your meeting."

"Julian and I were finished, at least for now. Why are you smiling at me like that?"

"Oh, it's just that wherever you go, you seem to befriend the locals."

"And what's wrong with that. As far as I'm concerned, that's how you really get to know a place, by experiencing it through the eyes of people who live there."

"I agree with you, and I envy you. It was never as easy for me to do. It's something that always seemed to come naturally for you."

"Well I like to think that even though I don't really have roots in any one place, I have small town roots, be that as it may. I don't make friends in a city nearly as easily."

"No, you certainly don't."

"What's that supposed to mean?"

"Just what I said, but let's not go there. What were you and Julian talking about so intently, if you don't mind me asking? I didn't mean to eavesdrop, but I couldn't help but hear you mention Buzz Griffin. That's a clue that you weren't just discussing walnut logs."

"You're right, we weren't. There's a potential problem, seeping into the neighborhood—gas drilling. The vanguard is already here

64

in the form of a smooth-talking, city-type, named Don Oldsmar. He's embedded himself in the area and has been advocating the idea. He's already gotten at least one property owner in the valley to sign a contract and recently he approached Julian about leasing his family's farm."

"Do you know this Oldsmar character?"

"He introduced himself to me in the parking lot of the grocery store. I still can't figure out just what his angle was in doing so, but I'm certain it wasn't just to be neighborly. In the course of our chat however, he did mention that he's from Chicago."

"Ah, Buzz's home turf. You want the inside story on this guy, and from Buzz you'll get it plus a whole lot more."

"Yes, and it's the whole lot more that I'm eager to hear. The first step is to see who's behind this Oldsmar, just what kind of money we're up against. Besides that, I haven't spoken to Buzz since I left the business, so I'm anxious to hear his opinion about my departure. And of course, I want to hear his opinion on the state of journalism in the United States."

"Ha ha, well I'm sure you'll get an earful. Buzz was pretty down on the profession years ago, and I doubt that age has mellowed him out any. Well, I hope Buzz can help you with this. I'd hate to see some problem developing here and you get drawn into it. I think retirement becomes you, Ira."

"Thanks Justine. I don't think there's a problem, yet. But intuition tells me the more informed we are at the outset the better we'll be able to prevent one from developing. At any rate worrying about what might happen is not going to do us any good at the moment. We must focus on the present and attend to the task at hand. Right now I want to see the bowl you're hewing."

12

"**I** did hear you left the business, Ira. Word is you've given it all up, moved back to the states and settled in the south somewhere."

"Yes, that's right Buzz. I've seen enough of war, especially the war in Afghanistan. Let's just say that as a journalist, I was losing my objectivity. I was taking sides."

"Hah, well who doesn't, but I know you were on the right side. Too bad for journalism though, because you're one of best we have. American journalism is in a fundamental crisis, Ira. The so-called mainstream media is nothing more than a cartel run by a handful of powerful corporations. They use their control of news to shape the public's understanding of issues, and it's all in the name of their corporate agenda.

I'll give you one glaring example, something I've recently covered in an editorial. The United States accounts for half the military spending in the world. Think about that, Ira, *half of the total military spending of the entire world*. We have bases in over a hundred countries, taxpayers are supporting them, and yet it's not an issue that's debated or even widely known about.

The military-industrial complex sees that the public is never well informed about such details, and the news establishment is completely complicit. Old Eisenhower hit the nail right on the head when he warned us about the military-industrial complex, although today, I would expand his description to military-industrial-media complex.

But you know this stuff, Ira. Don't let me get started. So what's up with you? What the hell you been doing with yourself?"

I smile, amused to hear one of Buzz Griffin's classic rants, and delighted that he still has his gritty edge. While he speaks, I picture him, as I saw him last, at his desk, cigar clenched in his teeth, smoke swirling about the room, black suspenders against a white shirt with sleeves rolled up.

I fill in my mentor as to where I'm located in life, and how I'm occupying my time. This discussion inevitably leads us to the point of the phone call.

"Oldsmar, Oldsmar, that name doesn't ring a bell, but from what you tell me so far, I'm sure there's one waiting to be rung. I don't blame you one bit for being leery of this guy, Ira. He has all the earmarks of a corporate shill. And he's got big money behind him, you can bet on that.

This new energy boom and the money to be made from hydraulic fracturing has spawned a gold rush mentality. The big energy companies are running roughshod over the country with promises of energy independence for the nation and jobs for the people, when gold is all that really matters to them.

They're even going to start drilling here in Illinois now. I just read that the DNR has started accepting applications."

"Well this phone conversation serves as a wake up call for me, Buzz. I was aware of the new push for oil and gas extraction in the country, but haven't been paying as much attention as I should. It's something I didn't think about in Afghanistan. Oil and gas extraction isn't the overriding concern there, it's war and survival. And besides, extreme extraction methods, like hydraulic fracturing aren't necessary yet. There are reserves that can be tapped the old fashioned way."

"Bullshit, Ira, oil and gas *are* the overriding concerns in Afghanistan, just not with the people you associated with on the front lines. Let's face it, war is the most extreme extraction method of all. And don't think there isn't a connection between the people

67

behind hydraulic fracturing in this country and the corporations profiting from the wars in Iraq and Afghanistan.

What's been taking place in the Middle East for decades is happening here now, just not in such a violent way. But don't kid yourself, if it comes down to it and, *we the people*, show any real resistance, the full weight of the military-industrial-media complex will come down on us just like it does to resistance over there."

"I certainly hope that's not what's in store for Walnut Creek. I was looking forward to a quiet retirement, hewing wooden bowls."

"I don't think there's such a thing as quiet retirement anymore, especially for a thinking person. Corporate control is closing in on us all, Ira, the monster that capitalism created. In this country, we've undergone a corporate coup d'état, and the game is over now, they've won.

The corporations control the courts, elected officials, the press, and the systems of financial regulation. The only way we can assert our right to life, liberty and the pursuit of happiness is to resist the machine in what ever way we can, however daunting the prospect. There may be only a slim chance now, but if we don't try, there's no chance.

But there, you got me going again, Ira. Let's start with this Oldsmar character. I'll find out what I can and get back to you on it. My suggestion is to pay attention to everything he says or does, keeping in mind that no matter how benevolent he may seem, it's all designed to enrich his employer. At the same time, never show him your hand.

I'll bet that finding you there has probably thrown them a little off balance and they're not sure how to deal with it."

"What do you mean Buzz?"

"These outfits are used to rolling into areas unchallenged, completely controlling the message, and they didn't expect to run into a journalist of your status and your politics in an obscure setting like Madison County, North Carolina."

"Hmm, so you think they know who I am?"

"I'd be real surprised if they didn't. Assume it, Ira, and play the bastards accordingly."

"Okay Buzz, thanks for your help. I appreciate it."

"It's my job, Ira. And it's your job, too, young man. Enjoy your retirement, make some wooden bowls, but don't let up on your writing."

"So what's new with Mr. Griffin?"

"Oh same old Buzz, I'm happy to report. He's going to get me the story on Don Oldsmar. What I told him so far piqued his curiosity, to say the least, and in turn he's got me all stirred up about politics and resistance. Imagine that."

"Hah, you should have expected it, but it doesn't take much to get you motivated in that direction. You know Ira, I have to wonder why you settled back in the states after the run-ins you've had with the government over the years."

"I thought about relocating, Justine, Switzerland maybe, the Netherlands, and for a while I even considered disappearing in a country like Nicaragua. But in the end, I felt I would just be running from a problem that in a sense I'm responsible for, too. If I don't like the direction the country is going, *which I don't*, then leaving isn't going to help anything. So I decided to come here to Walnut Creek and do what I could to change the direction. But not in a confrontational way; I'm done with that now.

I say I'm retired, and in a sense I am, but I'm still working to change the world, this time as much with my hands as with words. If there's any hope to alter the destructive path we're on, we must curb our dependence on fossil fuels, because that's what keeps the corporate machine running, our energy addiction. If we don't buy what their selling than they have no power over us."

"My, my Ira, Buzz certainly has got you stirred up. But is it possible after all these years, doing what you did, that you can confine yourself to such a simple and passive approach?"

"No, it isn't, but first I want to prove to myself that I can do this, live a simple life in the country, a life that is both fulfilling, productive, and as much as possible, off the power grid. The

69

notion has always fascinated me. I've lived at times with people who did just that, whose lives were never affected by the industrial revolution, and they seemed no less happy than you or I.

Some year down the road, depending how my experiment plays out, I'll write about it, preach what I'm practicing, and encourage others to transition away from energy dependence.

What I'm attempting is nothing new, but each era brings different challenges, so I don't think there can ever be enough voices promoting such ideas. I hope to add mine to the list.

Why are you smiling?"

"Because I know you, and I knew that there was more to this undertaking then a desire to live out your days as a simple country bowl maker. It's good to hear the passion in your voice again, and I like the direction of your resistance now. You worried me at times, talking as if there was no longer any option to affect change except with armed resistance.

When I didn't hear from you after the wedding, I half expected to learn that you'd taken up with some militia in the Hindu Kush Mountains."

"No, I was too old and worn out at that point or I might have. The truth is, I was rudderless there for a while, both spiritually and politically. I visited Bamiyan on a whim, because it was such an inspiring experience for me when I was young. I was hoping that the winds of the old days might stir me again. That didn't quite happen, but the experience prompted me to take up an offer made by Aamir Sadi, to visit him in Nepal."

"He's the photographer you worked with in Afghanistan, right?"

"Yes and Aamir and I have stayed in touch since then. I spent a month in Nepal, talking with Aamir about our war experiences, visiting Buddhist sites, rethinking my career. That's what led me to come back to Walnut Creek, to start over again with a different philosophy and a different approach to life's problems."

"And from what I can tell, so far so good."

"Yes, I still have my moments. I'm dragging a lot of baggage from the past with me, and I'm getting old. But for the most part, I focus on the day to day, what's in front of me, my homestead, and my simple little business. Regretting the past or fretting about the future serves no purpose. Here and now is what counts."

"Are these the sort of things Julian and you talk about?"

"No, not really, not yet anyway. But Julian is a perceptive man, and I believe he'd understand such a point of view. In fact I wouldn't be surprised if he adheres to a similar philosophy, himself, but from a different perspective.

In an effort to minimize distractions in my life, I'm striving to become independent of the social and monetary system that society imposes on us, whereas, from what I can tell, Julian never quite bought into either."

"My, it does sound like you've found someone to talk to."

"I enjoy talking to Julian. Even though his worldly experience may be somewhat limited, he has a nonchalant and pragmatic attitude about life that I envy."

"What your saying reminds me of the way you used to talk about Mahmud."

"Uh, well yes there are similarities between the two of them, now that you mention it."

"I'm glad you like it here, Ira; I think it's a wonderful place. And I've enjoyed my visit very much, even though I didn't quite finish my bowl."

"Next time. I'll keep it on a shelf with your name on it. So, you're off tomorrow to a new career."

"Yes, I am. This will be a different experience, not as exciting, but I think I'll enjoy staying in one place for a change."

I cross the porch and join Justine on the swing. We clasp hands and she lays her head on my shoulder. The cool spring air is pleasant and we are warm enough sitting close to each other.

In the dim light of a flickering candle, with eyes half-closed, I can imagine this to be another evening ten years ago or even thirty years ago when Justine and I might be doing the same thing, reaffirming our feelings for each other before another good bye.

71

"I wish you the best on your new path, Justine, I mean that."

"Thank you, Ira. And I hope you find everything you're looking for here in Walnut Creek. I sleep better at night, knowing that you're in a place like this and finally out of harm's way."

13

"How many years were you in Afghanistan, Mr. Stone?" "I was there on and off for seventeen years, starting in 1998, but I spent time in the country before that. My father was a photojournalist who was on assignment in Afghanistan back in the seventies, and I accompanied him a number of times. That's when I really fell in love with the country and is one of the reason, I took the opportunity to go back."

"Wow, I can't imagine, being in a place like that. Were you scared? I mean from all I've heard and seen on television, it seems like a dangerous place to be."

"It is at times, there's no denying that, but I was a war correspondent, and covering events as they happened was part of my job, so I had to be out on the street. I was always aware of the danger, and I'm not a great risk taker, but early on, I came to accept it."

I'm dining at the home of Edna Rice, sister of my neighbor, Ben. Edna's daughter, Susan, and Susan's husband, Michael, are also at the dinner table. Edna and Susan have prepared a meal of traditional southern cuisine: pan-fried chicken, field peas, collard greens, mashed potatoes, sweet tea, and blackberry cobbler for desert.

Susan is especially intrigued by the notion of a person willingly going to a place such as Afghanistan, and while she asks most of the questions, all present seem intrigued with what I have to say.

"Weren't you ever worried that you might be kidnapped by the Taliban?"

"Yes, that was always a concern. In fact, in high risk areas, I was often escorted by a driver who had an automatic weapon at his side. But on one occasion some U.N. staffers were kidnapped in broad daylight, right on the streets of Kabul, so there's a limit to what a person can do to protect themselves. Traveling with armed guards or in bulletproof vehicles doesn't help establish trust, so sometimes I just had to take chances.

I had some reassurance in a remark made by an Afghan colleague and it was intended to be funny: 'The Taliban will not want you,' he said, 'and if they do take you, within twenty-four hours, they will be begging us to take you back'."

"Oh my, a friend of yours said that, someone from Afghanistan?"

"Yes, a good friend, Mahmud Safi."

"Are you still friends? I mean, are you still in touch with him now that you left Afghanistan?"

"N-no, unfortunately I'm not. Mahmud is dead now."

"I'm sorry. Did he die in the war?"

"Yes, uh, yes, he died in the war."

Susan starts to ask another question and stops mid sentence. An awkward silence ensues. I sense that my audience would like to know more, but are too polite to ask. I would like to tell them more, especially about Mahmud before the wedding tragedy, let my audience know what a buoyant and happy man he was, but I opt to finish my desert in silence.

The quiet deepens and I struggle for something to say in hopes of changing the subject. I don't want to spiral into one of my dark moods, not in the presence of such wonderful company. Fortunately Ben bails me out with a suggestion for an after dinner recreation.

"My, my, I think I'd like to stretch my legs after such a hearty meal", he proclaims. "Edna, Susan, you've outdone yourselves again, and I think I need some exercise now to work off all I ate. What say we stroll up the hill to the cemetery and introduce Ira to some of our family?"

The unhurried walk to the Ramsey Cemetery proves to be the tonic I need. We follow a grass covered lane that winds behind the house and up a hill through a pasture that's burgeoning with spring flora. I walk beside Edna, chatting about simple things: spring and gardens and family.

"The Ramsey Cemetery was on this land long before Andy and I built our house. I didn't like the idea of living so close to a cemetery when I was young, but now with Andy buried here and so many other members of our family, I find it comforting in a way."

"I think I can understand that, Edna. How long has the cemetery been here, do you know?"

"It's been a cemetery longer than anyone can remember. My grandparents fenced it in after they bought this land and their parents were the first of our family to be buried here, but it was a cemetery before that. I remember coming up here with my grandfather when I was just a little girl and I would play while he worked. He would haul dirt up here in his truck to mound up the graves."

"Mound up the graves?"

"Yes, people were just buried in pine coffins back then, and over time they would break up and the graves would sink. Granddad would use the dirt to mound them back up again."

"I've heard that expression before, but never thought about it in actual practice. It makes perfect sense, though."

At the crest of the hill, our party comes to a fenced-in tract of about a quarter acre, divided by intermittent rows of tombstones. I've been intrigued with cemeteries since I was a boy, particularly small family plots, and although I have long wanted cremation to be the way in which my mortal remains are dealt with, the thought of a peaceful interment among family members in a cemetery such as this, is pleasing to my imagination.

"Ira, do you think this is strange, all of us traipsing up here to the cemetery after a Sunday meal?"

"Not at all Edna. I find it a fitting and meaningful activity. My parents are buried in a cemetery so large that it would take an hour just to walk around it. An interstate highway borders it to the north, and a hospital complex marks the south end. This is what I like to think of as a family cemetery, an ancestor park of sorts. A stroll to such a peaceful and meaningful setting seems to be the perfect activity on a Sunday afternoon."

"Ira, where is your family? Ben told me you were from North Carolina, down near Charlotte. Is that right?"

"Yes, that's right, Edna, that's where we're from, but my family is scattered wide now, and I have only occasional contact with my brothers and sisters."

"Well that's too bad, I guess, but I can see advantages to that, having lived in Walnut Creek my entire life, with family all around me. Everybody knows what you're doing all the time. But then, it can be a nice thing when times get hard, and you need someone."

"Here lies Mom and Pop, Ira," Ben proclaims, waving his hand toward a headstone centered in the second row of graves. "Mom died within the year that he did. We figure she couldn't allow Pop go too far into eternity without her."

I stand before the headstone of Mathew and Anna Ramsey, the ancestors of the wonderful family whose company I keep today and occupants who preceded me at my homestead. Their graves are flanked on each side by those of their siblings, their deceased children and some of their grandchildren, even. Ben introduces me to his departed family members in a reverential tone with the occasional humorous anecdote about one or another relative.

I gaze from headstone to headstone as the narrative changes, moved by my neighbor's words and captivated by the setting. I stare at the headstone of Lucas Ramsey, Ben's uncle who fought in the Second Worlds War. Lucas was part of the 101st Airborne Division that parachuted onto Utah Beach to retake France from Nazi Germany. Ben relates that he jumped into enemy-controlled territory the night before D-Day, and he survived the ordeal to return to the Walnut Creek and live out his seventy-six years.

While Susan and her mother stoop to pull crabgrass from around the headstones, and Mike wanders off to smoke a cigarette, Ben and I move further into the cemetery. The graves of preceding generations are marked with thin, weathered tombstones, some with dates that are scarcely legible.

Here the oral history is not as complete since the occupants were buried decades before Ben was even born. Among these are the graves of two ancestors who fought for the confederacy in the civil war, one of whom died in battle. History is interwoven in this small family cemetery and war has left a mark on every generation.

Ben and I reach the other end of the cemetery where a cluster of large maple trees shade ground, matted with fallen leaves and twigs. Stones are obvious in the shadows among the organic detritus, a large stone offset by a small one, placed about four feet apart in an apparent row made up of four such parings. In any location, such a configuration would suggest the boundaries of a grave, while in this particular setting, the symbolism is particularly poignant.

"These are the oldest graves in here, Ira, and nobody knows who's buried here. I remember playing around them with my brothers and sisters when we were kids. Nobody knew even back then who they belonged to. But I guess that's the way all our graves will be, given enough time."

"Yes, that's true, Ben. For me, these graves are symbolic. They stand for all humans that have lived and died before us."

"Like the Tomb of the Unknown Soldier."

"Yes, something like that, I suppose. Let's hope they died a more peaceful . . ."

"Mr. Ramsey, the cattle pushed in another section of fence on the west side. They can't get in yet, but they will if any more posts get bent."

"What, not again. I told Haney we needed an electric fence up here. I best go have a look, so I can call him first thing in the morning."

Ben and I are interrupted by Michael who has discovered the

most recent breach by the cattle that belong to a neighbor who rents Edna's pasture. Ben excuses himself and follows Michael, leaving me alone with my thoughts.

The vague familiarity that I'm experiencing upon viewing these graves of the unknown becomes clear now that I'm alone. In the cemeteries of Afghanistan it's common to see graves marked only with stones because just the wealthy can afford inscribed headstones.

Mahmud and I sometimes walked in the cemetery and he would tell the stories of his ancestors with pride in his voice. That was a cemetery outside of Gardez, and while much different in topography from where I stand today, the emotion and symbolism of such places are universal. As I walked with Mahmud among the graves of his family, I had the same sentiment as I do here in the midst of the Ramsey family.

Just weeks before his death, Mahmud and I walked the cemetery for the last time. The wedding tragedy was two months in the past, but my friend was weighed down by a great despondency, his face sallow, his voice cheerless.

When we parted that evening Mahmud clasped my hand and bid me farewell, since I was leaving for Bamiyan Province the following day. I held his hand a moment longer, sensing perhaps that when I let go, it might be forever.

"Good bye to you, my friend", Mahmud said, "I hope that we'll meet again someday, when this is all over."

14

When weather permits, I drink my coffee on the back porch, immersing myself in the melodious sounds of the creek as I assess the progress of this grand experiment in living. Steam rises from my mug and blends with mists that fill the valley this cool morning.

My reverie is interrupted only by the passing of vehicles on the road, the sound of my neighbors, rushing to work. I certainly don't begrudge them for the interruption, since after all, it was my choice to live on Walnut Creek Road, a business decision of sorts. I wish instead that they, like me, could stay here in the valley and still make a living, the way it used to be.

As I rise to refill my cup, I hear a vehicle slow and pull into the parking area of the shop. Because of the evergreens between the house and the building, I'm unable to see who it is, so I wait, mug in hand, to learn if someone is here for business, or as is more often the case, they're just using the parking area to turn around.

Then Julian appears, walking alongside the building and stopping at the back door. He cups his eyes, peers through the glass, and when he sees no activity within, he turns toward the house and spies the idle proprietor on the porch. I raise my mug and Julian turns up the path towards me.

"Good morning, Julian. I was just going into the house for a refill. Would you like a cup of coffee?"

"I'd like to Ira, believe me, but I can't. You see, I got sugar, so decaf is all I can drink—doctor's orders."

"Oh I'm sorry, that's right. Patricia mentioned that to me. I'm glad you're sticking to your doctor's advice."

"Yeah, on that one. He wants me to quit smoking and drinking, too, which I ain't done, so I figure I had to meet him part way. Say, reason I stopped by is I got a broken off cherry tree, pretty good size, snapped off about ten feet up. Wondered if you'd be interested in it."

"Hmm, I've never worked cherry, but I know it's a nice wood for bowls. How did it break off?"

"Probably in the last big wind we had. Cherry doesn't do well in the woods, grows all crooked and leans out to try and get the sun. Can't get any good lumber logs out of it, and no one's fond of cherry firewood, so I thought I'd see if you could use it."

"Sure, I'll give it a try."

"I'm headed up there now if you want to take a look at it."

"I can come now. It's early; the morning rush won't start for a while yet. Let me grab a coffee to go and I'll be right behind you."

The road is less familiar to me, heading east, since I don't have a reason to come this way with any regularity. I follow Julian through dappled shadows, created by sunlight filtering through the canopy. From side to side, I view small homesteads such as my own, sturdy structures of stone and wood, nestled along the banks of Walnut Creek. One ancient log house that appears to be long uninhabited, huddles up against a steep bank, nearly hidden by undergrowth, and looks as if it may soon be reclaimed by the landscape.

My perusal of these upstream homesteads is interrupted when Julian turns left onto a dirt road, crossing Walnut Creek by way of a narrow bridge. A weathered, plank sign with painted letters identifies the route as Runnion Lane. Pastures stretch along rolling hills on both sides, and to the east, cattle graze on a long verdant incline, bordered by a distant forest.

At the top of the slope a cluster of trees seems out of place, an incongruous island of forest in a sea of grass. As the road draws near, I discern a fence, fronting dark boles, and tombstones are visible among them, identifying the enclosure as a cemetery.

On the backside of the hill, the road is lined by rough walls of stacked field stone, and to the left, a log tobacco barn comes into view, ancient and forlorn, a relic of a bygone era. Two deer, grazing beside the structure look up, but show no alarm. As we descend into a shadowed valley, the road is hemmed in by forest and runs alongside a narrow stream, a tributary of Walnut Creek.

A stone house comes into view, and four dogs of assorted sizes and colors herald our arrival with much barking and commotion. The door of the house opens and an elderly man moves onto the porch with a hesitant, unsteady gait.

Julian's brake lights flash, he pulls off to the side, and I park behind him. The man on the porch who I presume is Julian's father stares with a blank expression. Julian comes up beside me with a wry smile and speaks in a hushed tone.

"This is your lucky day, Ira. Dad seems to be in the mood for socializing. He doesn't hear too well and he won't wear his hearing aids, so when you talk to him, speak loud and clear and let him see your face. I think a lot of what he gets is from reading lips, but don't tell him I said that."

The dogs surround me, vying for attention and seem quite pleased at discovering a new person in their territory. I approach the porch with slight trepidation, a somewhat familiar feeling, reminiscent of times in Afghanistan when meeting a family elder.

My guess is that Julian's father is well into his eighties, but seems to be a strong and sturdy man. His craggy, weathered face is framed by a wild shock of white hair that obviously hasn't been brushed this morning. His eyes are dark, accented by large, bushy eyebrows, and his stare is steady and intense, but not threatening. Faded bib overalls partially cover a tan shirt and hang down over boots that aren't tied.

Supporting himself by holding onto a porch post, he extends his right hand as I approach.

"Adam Runnion", he says in a deep, resonant voice.

"Ira Stone. Pleased to meet you."

"Do you like living here, Ira Stone?"

"Y-yes, I do. I feel at home here, but I lived here once before. You see when I was young, I . . ."

"Yeah, I know, with your grandmother. I remember you. And your grandmother made the best sausage in these parts. She was a good woman. Kept the family going after her husband died. You come from good stock, Ira."

Julian chuckles at his father's words and lights a cigarette, prompting Adam to turn in his direction.

"Where are you going?"

"Other side of the hollow. Cherry tree come down and I thought Ira might be able to make bowls out of it."

"Humph. Mind the roads. It's still pretty wet in there."

"I will, I always mind the roads, Dad."

Adam turns back to me. "Will you make me a bowl, a small bowl out of one of our trees, something to eat walnuts out of?"

"Sure, Mr. Runnion, I certainly will."

"Good, I thank you. And good luck to you, Ira. I have to go sit down. I give out easy these days. I need to rest now. I may need to cut hay later, if it's ever to get done."

Julian blows smoke into the air, almost as if he's letting off steam, and he wags his head in a gesture of frustration. Before Adam turns I notice a twinkle in the man's eye and a smile playing on his lips, indicating that the remark had elicited the intended reaction from his son.

Julian suggests we ride in his truck rather than driving two vehicles over dirt roads, softened by winter thaw and spring rain. Before we get in, he calls toward the dogs, and a large, reddish-colored hound who answers to the name Wagon, separates from the pack and lopes toward us. Julian lowers the tail gate of the truck and Wagon bounds onto the bed, alongside a chain saw, gasoline can, and an assortment of tools.

We rumble over loose stones on a sandy roadbed, as Julian

guides the vehicle along a track as familiar to him as it is novel to me. A quarter mile from Adam's house, the road runs in a straight path alongside the creek for about a hundred yards.

Midway along this stretch, a meadow opens on the left, revealing a two-story log house, set back forty feet from the road. Dark and weathered, the structure has an air of abandonment, with patches of rust on a metal roof and brushwood encroaching from all sides. When Julian notices that the log building has drawn my attention, he brings the truck to a stop.

"That's the oldest house still standing. It's built on the site of the original home place that burnt down. I'll show it to you up close sometime. I think you'd appreciate it, doing what you do. It's built of eight inch walnut planks, hewn from whole logs. Some of them are two feet wide and thirty feet long."

"Wow! All cut right here I suppose."

"Yep, and most are the original logs, cut by my great-great-great grandpa, Julian Runnion. I'm named after him as you might guess. He had a thing for black walnut. You'll see what I mean right up the road here."

We continue driving, the road curves to the left away from the creek before it straightens out again, bringing into view a broad, orderly tract of trees. Gray-black bark, deeply furrowed, characterizes trunks that extend from the edge of the road to the creek bank and into the distance as far as I can see, Twisted limbs merge into a continuous canopy, a distinct web against the morning sky. The identity of the trees is familiar to me even without the leaves, but the sheer number takes me by surprise.

"Goodness, are these all walnut trees?"

"Yep, ain't it something? Been seeing it my whole life, but it still amazes me every day. They run for a mile along the creek, about twenty acres in all, and my best guess is around three thousand trees. Grandpa Julian who built the house we just saw, started planting them in the years after the War Between the States. There was no chance he'd ever cut any timber or harvest the nuts, and he knew it, but he planted them for his kids and grand kids and for all of us who've come along since. It was his way of making sure our family could always be independent."

"I'm impressed, Julian. I've never seen anything like it, such healthy looking trees and everything so neat and organized."

"Well he worked hard at it and we've worked at it ever since, those of us that stay around here, anyway. Probably me as much as anyone now, since I live right here. I was named after him, so I feel a calling to mind the trees."

"Do you cut them for lumber?"

"Yeah, we harvest some every year, plant new ones to take their place. Got cousins over in the next hollow that work here, too. They got a mill over there, so we cut lumber to pay the taxes on the land and give us some money to spare. Don't make a lot of money at it, but we can always make money, and that's what's important. We harvest the nuts, too. Make even less at that, but then if we didn't harvest them, we'd make nothing at it.

You've eaten black walnuts haven't you?"

"Yes, but not in a long time. Back when I stayed with my grandmother, I was introduced to the whole process: picking, hulling, cracking, and eating. Since then it's been store bought walnuts or whatever is served in restaurants, English Walnuts, I guess."

"In my opinion, the flavor of black walnuts is five times stronger than grocery store walnuts. My mother used to say that one teaspoonful will flavor an entire cake. And why pay for walnuts grown somewhere else when we have our own here for the taking? It's like that with a hundred other things, too. Grocery store closes for a day and people are in a panic, wondering how they'll survive."

Julian looks straight ahead as he speaks, steering his truck slowly along the majestic, ancestral woodlot. I'm lost in reverie with the scene before me and captivated by the narrative that goes with it, until the smell of wood smoke gets my attention. I turn to see another cabin, overlooking the walnut grove on a slope that rises from the valley floor. The structure is partially of logs with a plank addition protruding from one side, and is obviously of more recent vintage than the first house we passed. A wispy plume of smoke curls from a stone chimney and dissipates among overhanging hemlock boughs.

"Is that your place, Julian?"

"Yep, home sweet home. My grandpap built that years ago, or at least the log part of it. My wife and I added on to it and modernized it some. My boy Dakota lives with me, on and off, depending on his love life. And then there's Wagon, he followed Cody up the road one day and moved right in."

"What a great spot. I envy you."

"I like it, but I don't think it would work for you, for a business I mean. You're going to have a hard enough time getting people to pull off Walnut Creek Road, let alone drive back someplace like this."

"I agree. And if one were to get people to drive back in here to do business, then before long, it wouldn't be such a great spot."

"Right, you can't have it both ways. That's why so many people drive out of the valley every morning to work somewhere else, trying to have it both ways."

"Well, if you don't mind me saying, Julian, you seem to have it both ways. You live in this wonderful location and make a living here, too."

"That's true, but it ain't easy. I make enough money to live on, but that's because I live so that what I make is enough. That takes time, too, cutting wood, growing food, tending to the walnut trees, but it's the kind of work I like. It makes a whole lot more sense to me than selling my time to someone else, doing something I don't want to do, just so I can buy a bunch of things I don't really need anyway."

At the end of the walnut orchard, the road turns to the left along a steep incline. At this point, Julian steers the truck into a meadow where spring grasses protrude from the brown stubble of last year growth. He angles up a slope for fifty yards, turns to the right and after another fifty yards, steers back in the direction from which we came, now close to the stream. Julian explains that if he had cut straight across the bottom, it would have taken a tractor to pull us out.

As the truck nears the tree row that lines the creek bank, I see a cherry tree, lying in the field. A rich red color is evident on jagged, exposed heartwood at the point where it broke off. Julian pulls alongside the fallen tree, turns, and then backs up to within a few feet of it. As we exit the truck, Wagon leaps from the bed, and sniffs the fallen bough, as if he knows that it's out of place.

"Well, here she be, Ira. What do you think?"

"Looks good Julian, healthy and solid, classic cherry color. I'm sure I can get a lot of nice bowls out of this."

"Well let's do it then, since I got the saw with me. It'll only take us an hour or so."

"Okay, I'm all for it? What can I do to help?"

"If you would, stack the small branches over there in the tree row. Crisscross them some, so they pile up high. Makes a good shelter for small game animals."

Julian is soon slicing off the upper limbs of the tree, the whine of the chain saw reverberating throughout the valley. I take my job seriously and strive to create a brush pile that a rabbit or grouse would be proud to inhabit. Wagon hovers about me at first, but soon the novelty of a newcomer wears off and he wanders to dig for moles in the meadow. The tree is cut up in less than an hour, including the standing trunk, which Julian cut off at ground level.

Silence envelops us when the saw is turned off, and we load the wood onto the truck to the accompaniment of water noise from the stream, which Julian informs me is named Runnion Branch. When I hear gunfire, I look in the direction that the sound came from. Julian doesn't stop working, but speaks when he sees me turn.

"Someone shooting up on Backbone Mountain. We have a hunting camp up there."

"Backbone Mountain?"

"Yeah, it's a ridge off Walnut Mountain. We've always called it that even though it's not on the map. That's what the old-timers called it, my grandpa and great grandpa. I always supposed it was called that because it runs down the middle of The Land, like a backbone."

As another gunshot sounds, I remain silent, recalling what it was I heard about Backbone Mountain. Backbone Mountain Militia, is the mysterious organization Justine learned of, purportedly based in Madison County.

I hesitate for a moment, uncertain as to whether I should ask Julian about the militia, a caution born from experience, but I yield to curiosity, trusting the camaraderie that has developed between us.

He shoves a log to the front of the truck bed then turns to look at the me with a puzzled expression and says nothing at first, causing me to wonder if I crossed some line that I shouldn't have. There's no doubt the question has affected Julian and his reaction tells more than is said aloud.

"Yeah, Ira, I know something about it. Where did your friend, Justine, hear about the militia?"

"From another journalist who wrote a piece about militias some years back. John Perkins is his name, and he told her that a man he interviewed in Tennessee gave him the information. Justine did some research on this area in preparation for her visit and she saw an article John wrote about the militia movement in the United States. He mentioned Backbone Mountain Militia, and Justine was intrigued, so she contacted him to learn more."

"Did he say who this guy from Tennessee was?"

"No, and he wouldn't, not even to a fellow journalist."

"What else did he say?"

"Not much, John's contact didn't really know too much. He was just going on hearsay. But besides being located in Madison County, he did say that the militia was the oldest that he knew of and well trained. Oh, and he said their leader is known as the Field Commander."

"I'll be damned. Well, Ira, like I said, I know something

about them. For now let's just leave it at that. We'll talk about it again some time, okay?"

"Sure Julian, I understand."

On the way out Wagon runs alongside until we reach the jeep and then jumps into the passenger seat of the truck when I exit. Julian grins and tells me that the dog was just being polite before, and that I had been sitting in his seat.

We pull into the parking lot of the shop just before opening time, and Julian and I slide the logs off the back. He takes off his gloves, closes the tail gate, and lights a cigarette.

"Well, Ira, have fun with this. I'll be anxious to see what you make."

"Wait, Julian, let me get you some money."

"Nah, we're okay. You did half the work and I was going to clean it up anyway. Tell you what, you make Dad that bowl he wants and we'll be square."

"That's no problem. Are you sure that's enough?"

"Yep, that's enough. Take it easy, Ira. And hey, uh, do me a favor, don't bring up the Backbone Mountain Militia to anybody until we talk, okay."

15

I placed a bell above the front door such that I'm alerted when someone opens it. The bell rings so seldom that I'm startled when it does. I brush wood chips from my apron, and clear my throat before entering the showroom. Two women are inspecting bowls I have on display. One of them appears to be about my age and the other quite elderly. The younger women looks up and smiles.

"Are you the artist?"

"I make the bowls, yes. I'm still relatively new at it, so I don't think I can go so far as claiming to be an artist. A bowl maker is how I describe myself."

"They're quite lovely and very artistic to me. I'm Wendy Richardson and this is my mother, Ida Ponder."

"Wendy is from Florida, and she's visiting me for the holiday weekend. I live up above you a few miles, on Sprinkle Branch Road. I've lived here in the valley my entire life."

"I'm pleased to meet you. I'm Ira Stone. Thank you for stopping. I don't get many people coming in."

"I wouldn't think you would, being back here on this road. Coming up from Jacksonville, it always surprises me how remote this area still is."

"That's one of the reasons I chose to live here. I've lived in cities before, and wanted to spend my retirement years off the beaten track."

"You might think differently when you reach my age, Ira. I'm in my late retirement years and I've decided to move to some place more populated and warmer—Florida."

"Mother is moving down near me to Jacksonville."

"Goodness, that will be a change. I've never been back on Sprinkle Branch Road, but I was recently nearby on Runnion Lane, so I know it's isolated back in that direction."

"Runnion Lane, the Runnion property, you mean? Their property borders ours at one point, but I can't say I've been up in there more than one or two times in all my eighty-five years, and that was when I was a little girl. My grandfather built a barn for Ethan Runnion and took me along with him. Wendy, you've never been up in there, have you?"

"No, Mother, and I don't know many people who have been. You see, Ira, the Runnions are, well, lets just say, they've always been private people."

"Let's just say oddballs."

"Mother!"

"All right, I know I shouldn't say that, but it's just an opinion. But tell me, Ira, I'm curious, how did you happen to visit the Runnion property?"

"Julian Runnion stopped by here one day to see if I needed wood for bowls, and I bought some walnut from him. That's how we became acquainted."

"Julian, he's Adam's boy. I haven't seen him in years. He was married there for a while, a woman from Virginia, but his wife left him. You say he actually came here and asked you about wood? I declare, that's not like a Runnion."

"Yes, he did indeed. Two loads of walnut were delivered here, and then a week later, Julian took me back to Walnut Hollow to look at a cherry tree that was down. I was working on some bowls from that very tree when you came in."

"You've seen Walnut Hollow, then? What do you think of that, Wendy? I told you I saw it."

"Walnut Hollow does actually exists? I thought that was just

90

folklore. What's it like?"

"Magnificent, a stand of walnut trees that stretches along Runnion Branch for over a mile, and the entire orchard neatly groomed and healthy. It's an inspiring site. As common as walnut trees are, here in the valley, there's nothing I've seen like the ones there."

"I'd often tease mother that she just made that up, that Walnut Hollow doesn't really exists. You would think that the Runnions would be proud to show folks something like that. Why be so secretive?"

"They keep to themselves, keep things within the family and a close circle of friends. People around here were more like that in the old days. But times change; people talk more now. The Runnions have never changed. Actually, for the same reasons, they've been good neighbors over the years, so I can't complain.

But that won't matter to me one way or the other soon. The farm is sold and I'm heading south."

"Oh, you've already sold? Is it to someone in the area?"

"No, unfortunately it's not; I would have preferred that. I'm not a greedy person, but I'm not wealthy either, and the farm is all I have. I want to be comfortable in my old age and I want to help my children and grandchildren.

The property sold before it was even put on the market. I just talked to a realtor and a man bought it the next day. Paid full price, too. Nice man, said he worked for a company out west. His name is Don something. Let me see, Oldman or is it . . ."

"Oldsmar, is it Don Oldsmar?"

"Yes, that's it, Don Oldsmar. Do you know him?"

"No, not really. Well, yes, in a way. He's a consultant for an energy company based in Texas."

"Yes, that's right and he said that his company would most likely do some drilling for gas on the farm. I really didn't like the sound of that, but he said that it wouldn't change things much. Says that once the wells are in place, they'll be like big fire hydrants sitting out in the fields. Nobody will even notice them.

Quite honestly, I never thought I'd get the price the realtor put on the farm and was shocked when a buyer came along so soon. As I said, I'm not a greedy person, but I'm alone now, and my family is scattered all over the country. I have to look ahead."

"I certainly understand, Mrs. Ponder, anyone would probably have done the same thing."

I continue to speak, determined not to mar an otherwise pleasant interaction by revealing the dismay that has come over me. When I notice Wendy examining a bowl, I take the opportunity to change the subject.

"That bowl is made from a birch tree that was cut down by the power company on Ben Ramsey's property right across the street."

"I know Mr. Ramsey. I rode the school bus when he was the bus repairman. Mother used to work with him."

Sure, sure, years ago, I worked at the high school, during the time Ben was repairman, so I knew him well back then. I haven't talked to him much lately, but then I don't get out much. You know, he's related to the Runnions."

"Yes, he did mention that."

"On his mother's side. Her father was a Reese and he married a Runnion. If you go back far enough, probably everyone around here is related to the Runnions, even you, Ira."

Ida Ponder laughs upon saying this and her daughter smiles and nods. Wendy Purchases the bowl that caught her attention, and she and her mother depart on as amiable a note as they arrived.

This is just the sort of friendly transaction I had imagined for my little business, but I can hardly muster any pleasure because of the information I've gained along with it. Sitting at the work bench, grasping the bowl adze, the weight of what I've learned concerning the sale of the Ponder farm, presses down upon me.

I've only just begun to investigate the mechanics and logistics of hydraulic fracturing, but from what I've ascertained thus far, it seems to be an invasive and destructive process. Oldsmar told Julian that his neighbors would be signing leases and that they could get the gas under his property anyway, which was disconcerting enough, but the sale of the Ponder farm is a much worse prospect. Blue Ridge Power Corporation will actually be the Runnion's neighbor.

I reposition myself at the hewing bench, tool in hand, but set the adze down, unable to focus on hewing bowls any longer this morning. I decide to break for a cup of coffee and a stroll along Walnut Creek to think this through. Why did Oldsmar buy the Ponder farm, property, bordering the Runnions? Intuition tells me that it's no coincidence and probably has much to do with Julian's rejection of his business proposition.

While coffee is perking, I feel a sudden need to speak with Julian about what I've learned. I'm not surprised when I don't find his name among the Runnions listed in the phone book and decide to chance a drive to his cabin in hopes of catching him there.

As I approach Adam Runnion's house, the dogs come out to greet me and I slow as they come alongside, but keep moving when Adam doesn't appear. While uneasy about not stopping, I'm relieved as well. I don't want to trouble this ailing patriarch with the purpose of my visit.

When I reach Julian's cabin, his truck isn't there but I turn up the drive anyway so that I can at least leave a note. Stepping onto the porch, I perceive the low, cautious woofing of a dog, and guess that Wagon is inside. The animal grows silent at the sound of my knock and in the interlude, I hear gunfire, faint but unmistakable. Stepping to the edge of the porch, I discern that many guns are firing, and the noise seems to come from the same direction as it did two days ago when Julian and I were loading the cherry logs.

Descending the stairs, I pause at the jeep, and listen again, but the gunfire has stopped. Then, as I'm searching for writing materials, I hear the sound of a vehicle approaching, and look up to see Julian's truck coming toward me. He pulls up with a look of concern but not of surprise, as if he knew I was here.

"Hey Ira, what's up?"

"Julian, I didn't mean to drive in unannounced like this, but I just learned something I think you'll want to know and the sooner the better."

"Sure Ira, I want to hear it then. Let's sit on the porch and talk. I've been on my feet all morning."

Julian climbs the stairs, opens the cabin door, and Wagon greets him with great enthusiasm before the dog turns his attention to me. I sit on a bench up against the cabin wall and rub Wagon's knobby head. Julian eases himself to the porch floor, trailing his right leg down the steps and placing his back against a post.

He's dressed in camouflage clothing from head to boots, and I wonder if perhaps he's been hunting. I don't ask, however, sensing that Julian is being polite about my unexpected arrival, but he wants to know first and foremost the reason for it.

So I tell him of the conversation with Ida Ponder and concern appears on Julian's face as soon as he senses the direction the narrative is going. He reaches into his shirt pocket for his cigarettes and nervously taps one from the pack. Lighting it, he takes a deep drag and exhales before speaking.

"You say it's already sold?"

"That's what she said, Julian. It sounds to me like the whole deal was orchestrated behind the scenes, with Oldsmar driving it along."

"Damn, I knew there was a chance Mrs. Ponder would be moving, but I didn't think it would be so sudden like. Her kids have all moved away, but I figured they would still be in line to get the farm."

"Mrs. Ponder didn't mention the price, but she implied that she received far more than expected and couldn't turn it down."

Julian shakes his head, takes another drag from his cigarette and nods to his right.

"Top of that ridge, on the other side of the creek, that's where they'll be. We border the Ponder farm up there."

"I'm sorry to bring you this information, but I thought you would want to know."

"Yeah, thanks Ira, it *is* something I need to know. I'll talk to my family about this and see what they think. I sure hate to tell Dad, cause this'll stir him up to no end. Maybe I'll just wait until Pat comes in and let her tell it."

"Last time I spoke to your sister we talked about gas drilling as a matter of fact. She knows about hydraulic fracturing, which is the type of drilling that's likely to happen here in the valley. She's seen it up close where she lives in Tennessee, and what she told me doesn't sound good."

"Damn it. I remember Pat mentioning that before, but I didn't pay it much mind because I never thought it would happen around here. I guess next time I will. Did you find out anything from your friend in Chicago about Oldsmar?"

"No, not yet. I'll call Buzz today. In fact, I'm going do that right now. Seems like I caught you in the middle of something, anyway."

"Nah, I was just up at the hunting camp, doing some cleaning up. Needed to break for lunch anyway, let Wagon out."

"I'll get out of here then and let you eat. Stop by the next time your down the road and I should be able to tell you more about Oldsmar."

"Yeah, I'll do that. I need to know what the deal is with this guy. I got a feeling that he and I are on course for a serious disagreement."

16

"He's a snake in the grass, Ira."

"Hmm, I might have guessed that. So is Oldsmar's behind what's going down here?"

"Oh no, hell no. He's a big fish, and he's probably calling the shots at your end, but he's working for a bigger fish, a shark in fact. You ever heard of Lawrence Kahn?"

"No, I can't say I have, Buzz. No wait, I seem to remember that name. Didn't he run for president once?"

"Yes, Khan was the Libertarian Party's presidential candidate some years back. He advocated for the abolition of Social Security, the FBI, the CIA, and public schools. Quite an agenda, huh? Khan put two million of his own money into the race, but that's chicken feed to him. He's a billionaire many times over, inherited a multinational energy company from his father and has steered it with a steady and callous hand ever since.

"Khan parted ways with the Libertarians shortly after his failed presidential bid, and since then, he's been pretty careful about keeping a low profile. His PR people have worked hard to overshadow Kahn Industries with Kahn Philanthropies. But with the recent energy push, brought on by new extraction techniques, his name is getting out into the light again."

"Let me guess, he wants to control it all."

"He already controls it all, Ira. Kahn Industries is the largest privately held company in the world. Petroleum, natural gas, fertilizers, ranching, commodities trading, you name it, Kahn Industries has a stake in it. But the biggest piece of the pie is still in energy production and in your part of the country, that means shale gas."

"Well damn it, Buzz, I was hoping you'd give me a more innocuous report on this Oldsmar character. I hoped that he might be the face of a small upstart company that was trying to get a footing in the gas industry."

"No, this is as big as they get, lot's of money and political clout. Oldsmar is one of Kahn's golden boys, the son Lawrence wishes he had, and he gives his boy lots of room to maneuver, to the point that they're almost operating autonomously. Oldsmar oversees the entire shale gas development in the southeastern United States. He's just chosen to base himself in your neck of the woods for some reason of his own, and I'm sure it's temporary.

Oldsmar earned his credential out west where this shale gas development started. He has an excellent track record for obtaining drilling rights, by hook or by crook. Lawrence Khan trusts Oldsmar's judgment and appreciates his ruthlessness."

"Well this is troubling to hear, Buzz, but at least now I know what we're up against."

"You're up against it all right, friend, capitalism at it's worst. Who do you mean when you say we?"

"Oh a local man who's had contact with Oldsmar. Julian Runnion is his name. He was approached about leasing his family's land, which he refused to do. That's what prompted my inquiry about Oldsmar. Since you and I last talked, Oldsmar purchased a tract of land that borders the Runnion property."

"Uh oh, that doesn't sound good. But the people who live there are who you want to be allied with in a fight like this, people with roots in the ground. You can trust their motives because they're fighting for their homes and families. If they're on your side, you know you're on the right side.

I'll find out what else I can and let you know. While I'm at it, maybe I'll just attack the beast a little from the rear. The information I've dug up on Khan Industries has got me intrigued. With hydraulic fracturing, coming to Illinois, I think a column about what's coming to town is in order, and I'll see that Khan gets star billing.

'Fracking' is the more commonly used term these days, although the industry doesn't like it. I prefer 'fracking' for the same reason they probably don't: it sounds like some sort of profanity.

"Ha ha, be careful, Buzz."

"You be careful yourself, young man. I don't have to worry too much. They don't know what to do with an old timer like me. They can't wreck my career at this point. No, Ira, at my age, I haven't time to take light jabs, I only go for the knockout punch."

I walk along Walnut Creek, crushing undergrowth and brushwood beneath my boots. Evening traffic has slowed to a trickle so that water sounds provide melodious accompaniment to my plodding cadence. At the trail's terminus, the giant poplar stands firm, as it has for hundreds of years, silently witnessing and unyielding in the face of change.

Anger and apprehension stir within me, and yet I sensed trouble was nigh before conversation with Buzz affirmed it. My sixth sense, developed over decades of observing trouble, was aroused when Don Oldsmar and his business affiliation were first brought to my attention. After he introduced himself at Robinson's, I had no doubt he was a problem, but hoped that his plans for this area would not affect mine. But it never works out that way with these types. Intuition tells me that confrontation with Oldsmar is inevitable.

Being the seasoned professional that he is, Oldsmar has no doubt come to a similar conclusion about me. My guess is that he's done his research, knows my background, and for that reason made contact with me as a first step. He wouldn't have had to go too deep into my résumé to guess that I would stand in opposition to his campaign. I doubt, however, that he realizes just how much I'm opposed to his plans.

Yet, I didn't come here to fight; I'm through with that now. I came here to live a simple life, to make wooden bowls, to change the world by example. The part of me that's grown old and cautious wants to make every effort to steer clear of Oldsmar and stay focused on my plan.

But I've never been one to duck a fight and perhaps it is as Buzz said, that for a thinking person, there's no such thing as a quiet retirement anymore. I'm a journalist first. At the least, I can find out what's going on here and put it in print, so that people know the real story and can make decisions accordingly.

I pat the neatly furrowed bark of the poplar tree and gaze upward along its vertical shaft through a web of limbs into the twilit sky. From somewhere far off in the distance, I hear gunfire, scarcely audible over the rippling water of the creek. The sound seems to reverberate from the direction of Walnut Hollow. I listen to the distant echo for a moment longer, a stirring sound in a strange way, and I'm compelled to walk back to the house at a brisk pace, suddenly inspired to work.

At the computer, cup of tea in hand, I open a folder titled *Hydraulic Fracturing,* a collection of articles I've read over the past few days and peruse again with a new sense of purpose. One in particular, an article on the National Geographic website, lays the groundwork for a fundamental understanding of the process, and beyond a description of the mechanics of hydraulic fracturing, the author presents pros and cons of its utilization.

Proponents point to the economic benefit to be gained from the vast amounts of formerly inaccessible hydrocarbons the process renders available. This translates into a boost for local economies, job creation and potential enrichment for some landowners. Oldsmar used these very same points as an argument for fracking in Madison County.

Environmentally, the case goes that natural gas is cleaner burning than coal and serves as the ideal transition fuel, to supply our energy needs during a conversion from fossil fuel to alternative energy sources. That point is hard to argue with.

Energy independence is another advantage the country stands to gain from hydraulic fracturing, and with it comes the promise of freedom from reliance on unstable regions of the world for our energy needs. Some go so far as to portray the support of fracking as an act of patriotism. To exemplify this, a number gas companies emblazon the sides of their gas trucks with the American flag.

Opponents of hydraulic fracturing point to environmental consequences of the process: contamination of ground water, air pollution, noise pollution, and the negative health effects on humans and other animals from chemicals employed in the process.

While these risks seem reason enough to question the desirability of such an industry, the social costs of fracking are also not easily dismissed. Heavy trucks crowd rural roads and out-of-state workers flood small towns, overwhelming local housing, police and health capacities. And whatever monetary benefits there are to be gained by local economies, or individuals, they are temporary and minuscule compared to the huge profits reaped by the energy companies.

I want to be objective, but to my mind, the facts speak for themselves. Hydraulic fracturing is another version of same old formula, whether it happens here or anywhere else in the world. The corporations and the wealthy individuals who own them are the ones who profit, while the people in a community or even a whole country suffer intrusion in their lives, destruction of their land, and ill effects on their health.

I won't let my opinion set the tone for what I write, but at the least, I intend to counter the claims made by Oldsmar and let the community decide. It seems to me that I need but present the facts and it will be obvious that despite his claims, the ultimate price of his plans will be the destruction of the environment and an unraveling of the social fabric of Walnut Creek.

Light is fading outside my window and cool air wafts into the room. I stand to lower the sash, but before I do, I listen for the murmur of Walnut Creek, perhaps to assure myself that at least for now, the valley is at peace, life goes on unchanged. I still don't want to concede that a storm is on the horizon.

Is this how people in other countries feel, in the face of foreign invasion? No, there's no comparing the situation we face here to the hopelessness or fear in a populace whose country faces incursion by military force. After all we're American citizens confronting an American institution, and we don't have guns pointed at us.

I move back from the window, but pause upon hearing a percussive sound, somewhere up the valley. I lean forward, and recognize it as gunfire. Somewhere up the valley, even as darkness falls, somebody is shooting.

17

"When we know how to be at peace, we find that art is a wonderful way to express our peacefulness." Words of a Buddhist monk, that I've aspired to live by since my retirement. This morning, however, I worry that, the anxiety I'm wrestling with will be expressed in the bowl I'm hewing. I returned to Walnut Creek to make bowls, to garden, to change myself. I have to focus my thoughts on the task at hand, and stop worrying about what *might* happen.

But why do they want it all, these billionaires, the Lawrence Khan's of the world? They have more money than they'll ever need and more power than anyone should have, but it's never enough. Khan will exploit these good people and destroy this valley, destroy the whole earth, even, for the sake of profit.

He will be stopped. All of them will be stopped. Sooner or later, people become angry enough, a tipping point is reached, and a human tide of resistance wells up around them, no matter how much money they have and regardless of how mighty their armies are. Do they think the French Revolution was an aberration? But here I go again, envisaging a confrontational resolution to the problem. I can't allow myself to revert back to that type of thinking.

I wonder though, can people like Lawrence Kahn be stopped through nonviolence, by peaceful resistance and example, rather than counter violence? Counter violence *does* work; I've seen it work. Peace and harmony may not engulf the earth through such means, but at some point, I think there's no choice but to make a stand and strike back.

The door chime rings, someone has entered the showroom, and I have no choice, but to shift from thoughts of violence and revolution to bowl making and peaceful interaction. I stand, brush the wood chips from my apron, transform the scowl on my face to a positive expression and enter the showroom. A women is inspecting my wares and looks up as I enter.

"Hello, Ira, sorry to interrupt. I know you're probably busy, getting ready for the holiday weekend."

"Patricia, what a surprise. That's right, Memorial Day is upon us. You said that you would be back this way. So, tell me, how did your friend like her bowl?"

"She loved it. She went on about it so much that she made me jealous, and I want one for myself. I can see you've been busy; there are number of new ones here. Are any of these made from the wood from Walnut Hollow?"

"No, not yet, but they're coming along. I've roughed quite a few out and they should be dry enough to finish before too long."

"Oh, I'll wait then. I've become sentimental lately, and I'd really like a bowl made from one of our trees."

"I'll hold them for you. I presume you're in for the weekend?"

"Yes, and in fact, I'll probably be staying a little longer. Dad hasn't been doing well and I'm trying to convince him to allow someone to come in and look after him."

"Oh, I'm sorry to hear that. I just met your father last week as a matter of fact."

"So I hear, and you made quite an impression, too."

"Really? He didn't say too much."

"Believe me, that's a good sign. You must have made an impression on him. And you must have made an impression on Julian to have been there in the first place."

"Really?"

"Oh yes. Julian doesn't make friends easily."

"I'm surprised to hear that. He seems to be a friendly enough person, and I haven't heard anybody speak ill of him."

"Oh, he doesn't make enemies easily either. He usually just keeps to himself and stays on the farm, a chip off the old block."

"Now *that* I was beginning to realize, and it reminds me of something I recently heard, that, the Runnions play by their own rules."

"Ha ha, I like that. How true, especially of the men. Speaking of the men, I should be heading up the road. I want to fix Dad a hearty lunch. Um, tell me Ira, do you have plans for Memorial Day?"

"No, not really. Same old routine, I guess: wander down here and make bowls, some gardening in the afternoon. I do sometimes observe Memorial Day in my own way. Perhaps in the evening, I'll sit by the creek with a glass of wine and remember the friends and colleagues I've lost to war."

"I like that idea, but the Runnions commemorate in a little more traditional fashion. Dad is a former marine and we celebrate with patriotic music on his old phonograph, and with steak from the grill, served with potato salad, and coleslaw. It's been the same music and same menu as long as I can remember."

"Hmm, that sounds like Memorial Day out of a Norman Rockwell painting, and I mean that in a good way. It does have a real nostalgic appeal."

"Good, would you like to come and join us, then?"

"Sure, I-I'd love to. That would be a pleasant break from my routine. Can I bring anything, a bottle of wine maybe?"

"Oh, no, we have everything. We even have homemade wine. Julian supplies the meat from our herd. The eggs and potatoes are from the farm, too."

"This sounds like fun. Are you sure it will be okay with everyone?"

"Yes, I'm sure. Besides, if the guys are being so sociable these days, so can I. You'll get to meet some more of the family: Julian's son, Cody, a cousin or two. I don't know who all will be there yet."

"It will be just you and Julian then from your family? He mentioned an older brother."

"Y-yes, we *had* an older brother, Samuel, but he was killed in Vietnam. He was a marine, like Dad, so our Memorial Day celebration is for him, too."

"I'm sorry. Julian didn't mention that."

"He wouldn't. In some ways, he's still not over it. He and Samuel were very close. Julian wanted to be like him and would have enlisted, but my mother wouldn't allow it. Dad agreed with her and convinced Julian that he was needed on the farm. I think to this day, Julian feels guilty that he never did his part, maybe even guilty about Samuel dying.

Dad has a little bit of the same feelings but for different reasons. He was a marine during the Korean War and he saw action, but never talks about it. Whatever his experience in Korea, he wasn't in favor of the Viet Nam War, and I think he regrets that he couldn't stop Samuel from going. So if the two of them seem moody and quiet tomorrow, I mean more so than usual, that's probably why."

"How sad. War affects a lot of people on and off the battlefield."

"Yes, it certainly took it's toll on our family and lots of families in this area. Early on in the war, Samuel and some of his friends decided to enlist. They just thought it was the right thing to do. Two of them ended up in the same company, Samuel and Thomas Gosnell, and they saw heavy fighting. Thomas is a cousin and was Samuel's best friend since they were little boys. His family has land back behind ours."

"Thomas made it back, then?"

"Yes, he made it back, but he was never the same after that. He kept to himself and rarely went anywhere for a long time, and he's still like that, in a way. I haven't seen him in years.

He and Samuel seemed like they had everything going for them when they were young. When I was little, I thought the two of them were the handsomest and smartest boys anywhere. But I don't want to reminisce on that now, that's what Monday is for. If you'd like to join us, after dinner, we take a walk up to the cemetery. Samuel is buried there, right next to my grandparents and my mother, and many other family members."

"Yes, I'd like that, I'd like that very much."

"Good. Anyway, I better get up the road to make Dad lunch and let you get back to work. If something comes up, and you can't make it, just let Julian know or give us a call."

"Well thank you for the invitation and I can't see what would come up. I'm going to mark the date in my planner right now."

From under the counter I pull out a day planner, a gift I received from my bank but have yet to open. I do so now and page through to Memorial Day.

"Oh, good it looks like I'm free that day."

Patricia looks at the empty pages and smiles.

"It looks like your free all right, Ira. I wish my day planner looked like that. See you on Monday."

18

To say that I've experienced an attitude adjustment from my mood of this morning would be an understatement. After hewing two walnut bowls out of the wood from Walnut Hollow, I'm in such good spirits that I've decided to employ myself for the rest of the workday at my garden project.

I last gardened decades ago, and it was a favorite activity when I stayed with Grandma Wallin. Great Aunt Emma was in charge of the gardens and was only too happy to delegate work in the vegetable plot to me so that she could devote more of her time to the fruit trees and berry patch.

I was an avid learner and absorbed all that my aunt taught me, such that in spite of the fact that I have not so much as picked up a hoe in the years since, I feel quite comfortable with one in my hands again.

Times have changed, however and ideas about growing vegetables have evolved such that in spite of my past experience, I strive to develop a system with an eye to the future, one that meshes with my overall plan for the homestead.

While educating myself on such topics as raised bed gardening, and composting, I find that much of what I'm learning is a more refined and analytical version of the skills that Aunt Emma taught me. Thus it seems, gardening has come full circle, and fortunately, I've circumvented the era of industrial gardening in my personal experience.

While thus employed at this agricultural enterprise, it's possible for me to realize some hope for the future of our species, in spite of these precarious times. Each foot of land I turn over is a gain; each layer added to the compost pile helps to secure the future. In the face of the coming collapse of civilization, I'm helping to lay the groundwork for a soft landing.

Few people realize as they speed by on Walnut Creek Road that this elderly gentleman, quietly turning the soil is actually striving to save the human race. All, very much fanciful thinking on my part, but for the moment, I allow myself to indulge in such daydreams.

Now I must confess that this newfound buoyancy can't be entirely attributed to the joy one experiences from gardening. My optimism has returned on the wings of a pretty smile and attention of a fair lady. How can I still be so silly at my age? I thought I had retired from such notions.

Beyond her obvious charms, there's much about Patricia that intrigues me. I labor on cheerfully, anticipating dinner on Monday and further conversation with Patricia and her family.

Stepping back from my work, I survey the small patch of land that I've cultivated. The sod is quite dense on this ground which has been sown with grass for so many decades, but beneath that is a deep layer of dark soil, deposited over centuries by the ebbing and flowing of Walnut Creek.

Labor with my hands, trouble-free endeavors, these are the simple gifts in life. How I wish I could remain in my present state, with my feet firmly planted on the ground and my mind focused on what's in front of me, this most primary of tasks, the procurement of food. I must adhere to my plan and not be distracted by events, swirling about me.

Eh, what's this? Hello there. A dog is swirling about me, wagging his tale and looking at me as if we are old friends.

"Wagon, hey Wagon, stop," comes a voice from behind.

I turn to see a tall, lanky young man, trotting towards me from the direction of the workshop.

"Sorry Mr. Stone, I didn't know he'd run up to you like that."

"That's okay, Wagon and I have already met. And I'm guessing that you're Cody."

"Yes, Dakota Runnion, but Cody's what they call me. I'm staying with Dad now and he told me I should stop and see what you do, you're woodworking, I mean."

"Hah, and here I am, a gardener."

"Nothing wrong with that. I garden too, sometimes, when I'm home. But what're you building here? Are these cedar boards?"

"Yes, it's cedar. I, uh, I'm trying something a little different, raised bed gardening. Like a big flower box that makes it easier to keep the garden under control, which is especially important for an old timer like me."

"I've seen raised beds before. My girlfriend's Mom does that, with flowers though. And that's your compost bin under the willow tree?"

"Yes it is. I plan to build a couple more, and ramp up production a bit. You see, I've done some research on gardening and my goal here is to have the most productive garden I can, in the smallest space possible. On top of that, I want it to be easy to maintain, and, last but not least, good to look at, year round."

"Makes sense to me, but I don't think it would work for us. Dad puts in about an acre garden, so that would take a pretty big box. And we always have plenty of manure to spread on it. Say if you want some manure for your compost, I'll bring you down a load. I'm going to be around for a while, maybe through the summer."

"I'll keep that in mind; I just might take you up on that. So you say you'll be here through the summer. You're father told me you were living in Weaverville?"

"Yeah, I was. My girlfriend and I split up and her uncle owned the company I was working for, so we kind of split up, too. Dad always needs help on the farm. It doesn't pay well, but at least I have something while I look around."

"Any prospects in the area?"

"No good ones. Aunt Pat thinks I should go to AB Tech, but

I don't know about that. She went to college you know."

"No, I didn't know that."

"Yeah, a college up in Tennessee, and did real well too, and she always has a job. Grandpa thinks I should just stay on the farm, but he thinks everyone should stay on the farm."

"Well, Cody, it's a tough decision, but one argument I can raise in favor of school is that at the least, it will give you some time to consider what you want to do. I majored in English when I went to college. I wanted to be a writer, but I was thinking in terms of a fiction writer. I wanted to write novels. But while I was in college, the people that I met and the events that were occurring in the world at the time, steered me towards journalism."

"And now you make wooden bowls."

"Yes, now I make wooden bowls. Speaking of which, let me give you and Wagon a tour of the workshop."

Cody is not much like his father, in appearance or demeanor. He's the same size as Julian, but has more sculptured, distinguished features, with no hint of a beard, which is the defining feature of the elder Runnion's face. He speaks more casually, without the reserve that sometimes comes across in conversation with his father.

Wagon runs circles around us, stopping abruptly, muzzle to the ground, and then trotting to keep up with us. Such a happy creature, tongue wagging, boundless energy, and ever attentive to Cody's voice.

As we walk toward the shop, Cody stops and stares at a rock garden, located in the center of the lawn.

"Did you put that there?"

"The garden, you mean?"

"No, the statue."

"Oh, yes, the Buddha, I just placed that in the garden last week as a matter of fact. I went by a yard sale outside of Weaverville and saw it. Solid concrete, five bucks, I couldn't pass it up."

"Is that your religion?"

"No, not my religion, really. I'm trying to live my life by Buddhist principles these days, and the statue is a reminder to keep trying."

"Well, I think it looks pretty cool there."

"Oh, thank you. Yes, whether it works out for me or not, I think it looks cool there, too."

Upon entering the shop, Cody turns a circle, inspecting tools, partially finished bowls, and walnut slabs, leaning against the wall.

"This is the workshop, where the logs from outside are split into the planks you see against the wall. Bowls are hewn from them and then set aside to dry on these shelves. After they're dry, I finish them with a mixture of oil and beeswax.

The finished products are moved to the business end of the establishment, the showroom out here, where hopefully they will sell, and then I can pay the bills."

Cody walks into the display area with me and looks slowly from side to side, examining the bowls with obvious surprise.

"Wow, you made these from those logs outside? I'd love to be able to do something like this."

"Well, Cody, it's not as hard as it seems, it's just mysterious like a lot of handcrafts are, and only because not many people do this sort of thing anymore. I can give you lessons, if you want to give it a try."

"Aw, man, I'd really like that."

"We'll do it then, once you know what your schedule is for the summer."

"Cool, Yeah, I'd like to give it a try."

Cody wanders about the gallery a bit longer, then we exit the building at Wagon's beckoning, following him to the bank of Walnut Creek. The dog rushes down to the water's edge and a frog jumps into the water, just out of his reach.

Conversation with Cody comes easily. He's open minded and curious about what I'm doing here. It's times like this I imagine the pleasure of having a son or daughter, someone to whom I could share what wisdom I've accumulated over the years. Our conversation reminds me of similar exchanges I had with Mahmud's son, Habib. He was about the same age as Cody is now, and he possessed the same curiosity about me and what I did for a living.

I explain to Cody in general terms, what my plans are for a self-sufficient homestead.

"That's really a good idea, Mr. Stone. You know it's really like a smaller version of what my family has done for years."

"Hmm, I never thought of it that way, but now that you mention it, you're right. And here I thought I was on to something new."

"No, I guess not. It's pretty hard to do something new in the world, even here. People have been around too long. Well, I better be going. I'm helping my cousin, Jerry Dale, this afternoon, at the sawmill."

"Oh, yes, you're father mentioned the sawmill. Are you cutting walnut today?"

"Uh, no, not today. I guess we're cutting some hemlock for the Messers, two by fours for a barn—pretty boring. I'd rather make bowls."

"Well, we'll work on that."

"I hear you're coming for the cookout on Memorial Day."

"Yes, I am. I have it written in my planner, as a matter of fact."

"Okay, so I'll see you then. I best be getting back up the road. Come on, Wagon, in the truck, boy."

19

I've entertained such pleasant company of late that it is with dismay that I respond to the showroom bell to see Donald Oldsmar bending over my wares. He turns and smiles, displaying those unnaturally white teeth, which for me, typify the man as a fraud. With a walnut bowl in his left hand and his right extended, he approaches the counter. I hesitate momentarily, but give in to tradition and shake the man's hand.

"Ira, good to see you again."

"Donald, right? We met at the supermarket."

"That's right, I'm your neighbor from around the bend, and please call me Don. I need a wedding present for a niece. She and her fiancé live in Vermont, and their tastes are traditional in many ways. I think one of your bowls will be perfect for them."

"I guess I can take that as a compliment."

"It is because there's nothing wrong with being traditional. I'm traditional myself in many ways. That's one of the reasons . . . You look skeptical Ira, why."

"That's my nature, the journalist in me. I'm skeptical until I'm convinced to be otherwise."

"Hmm, that's an interesting way to explain it. But I'm glad you brought up the fact that you're a journalist, because besides shopping for a wedding present, I want to talk to you about journalism. I mentioned to you before that I represent Blue Ridge Energy Corporation, and not surprisingly, we are in the business of energy production. While this is not so traditional, I mean, as say handhewn bowls, we are also in the business of job creation. Now *that's* an American tradition, and it's a big part of why I'm in this business, to, uh, carry on that tradition.

I come into sleepy little communities like this, monetarily depressed, without much business prospect, and give them a boost, specifically, with an influx of money. And this doesn't just apply to those we employ or lease from. The benefits extend to hotels, restaurants, and . . . Um, why are you going skeptical on me again?"

"Hydraulic fracturing for natural gas, right? That's what your company has planned for this area. If I hadn't already known, I could have guessed, because you're restating the standard talking points put forth in every article that promotes the industry."

"Aha! So you've done some research. In that case you must have also learned that our industry gives farmers, such as those who inhabit this valley, a source of income that can make the difference between keeping their farm or having to sell. Leases are often worth hundreds of thousands of dollars, money that's unheard of under normal circumstances.

In addition to the local benefits, there are many companies that make hydraulic fracturing equipment, and this has created thousands of jobs around the country. I could go on and on."

"I bet you could. But tell me, what does all this have to do with journalism?"

"Oh yes, of course, excuse me. Sometimes, I get carried away with my message, but then, that just shows how enthused I am about the possibilities here. Your talent as a journalist has come to my attention and I know this would be a valuable asset in promoting our new economic development plan for this area.

Now, I'm also aware of your time in the Middle East, particularly in Afghanistan, and I've read some of what you've written from that period. It's obvious that what you've witnessed has left you with a negative opinion of our country's involvement over there. And hey, let's face it, the war on terror or whatever you want to call it, is bogus. The real reason the United States is in the Middle East is oil."

"I'm surprised to hear you say that."

"I don't like to admit it, I'm not proud of it, but I'm not going to mince words with you. That's because I'm with you. We should not be at war there, and that's one of the major reasons I'm so upbeat about the current energy boom here at home. With the new technology we've developed to extract natural gas, we won't need to depend on unstable parts of the world for our energy needs."

I can hardly believe Oldsmar is trying to persuade me with these well-worn lines. I study the man closely, trying to find some indication in his deportment of the real motivation behind his words. How much does he know about me? Is his knowledge firsthand or has he been briefed by corporate handlers?

I question as well if he truly wants me to be part of his enterprise or he's trying to draw me out in the open, to find where I stand, so that he can deal with me accordingly.

Although many words come to mind in response to his banter, especially his reference to Afghanistan, I take Buzz's advice and respond so as not to show my hand. For now all he needs to know is that I'm retired from journalism and I plan to devote my time to bowl making and gardening.

"Because of your experience in the Middle East, I would think you'd be especially hopeful that we could become energy independent here in the United States, and to that end you might lend your journalistic skills."

"I appreciate what you're saying, but I'm really not interested. *Because* of my experience in Afghanistan, I decided to retire from journalism to pursue other projects. Making bowls is one of them, gardening another. I just want to work with my hands now."

"I, I see, but you will consider it, perhaps? The workload won't be excessive, and believe me, the pay will be very good."

Oldsmar stares at me intently, wearing that bizarre smile that I noticed at our first meeting. Why is he backing off so easily? Is it to truly give me time to consider his proposal or has he found out all he needs to know? I hear the sound of a vehicle pulling into the parking lot and welcome the interruption, especially when I glance out the window to see Julian, exiting his truck. Oldsmar turns and stares out the window as well.

"You have a customer. I should get out of your way here. Ah, I know this man. Is he a friend of yours?"

"Yes, a neighbor from up the road. I buy wood from him."

"How charming. I hope you're happy with his services because he doesn't strike me as much of a businessman."

I start to respond to this remark, but stop when I hear Julian rap on the frame of the open back door. He stops at the showroom doorway when he sees who I'm talking to, and gives Oldsmar a less than friendly look.

"Well, well, Julian, we meet again. I know you two have business to conduct so I best be getting out of your way. Never let it be said that I'm one to slow down the wheels of commerce. Think of my proposal, Ira. As I said the work wouldn't be demanding and . . ."

"I don't need to think about it: I've thought all of this out before I came to Walnut Creek."

"I see, well that is unfortunate. We'll just have to be good neighbors then, won't we? And about this bowl, I think I'll pass on it. On second thought, it may be a little too traditional, even for my niece. Hey, you two gentleman have a nice holiday."

Oldsmar returns the bowl to the shelf and ambles out the door. From the tension I detected in his voice, I'm more inclined to think he's just feeling me out to learn my position on his plans for Walnut Creek. If he hadn't concluded already that I'm not in his camp, the fact that Julian and I are acquaintances, back door acquaintances in fact, told him what he wanted to know.

"I didn't mean to interrupt."

"You interrupted at just the right time, Julian. I had more than enough of his company. We need to talk, too. I spoke with my friend, Buzz Griffin, and from what I learned, I'm afraid there's a real problem brewing here. Oldsmar is just the front man to get the ball rolling, a pretty face to charm landowners into signing contracts for drilling rights. The root of the problem is in Texas, Kahn Industries, a huge corporation, run by Lawrence Kahn."

"Never heard of him."

"I heard his name years ago when he made a run for president, but forgot about him until Buzz gave me the lowdown. Oldsmar works for Khan, and Khan Industries is the biggest privately owned company in the world. In fact, the economy of this company is bigger than many countries. Blue Ridge Energy Corporation is just one part of a huge operation."

"I ain't afraid of anyone, Ira. I don't care how much money they got. We're talking about my home, and I won't be bullied on my own land. And I ain't the only one around here who feels this way. If this Khan or Oldsmar is looking for a fight, they're going to find it, believe me."

"I don't doubt that's true, but my guess is they're not looking for a fight or expect one. That would only slow them down. I'm sure they're assuming that they can apply the usual formula, which is to completely overwhelm an area like this with their money and political influence before any opposition is mounted. By the time people realize what's happening it's too late.

If any laws happen to be broken, the repercussions and fines will be petty, relative to the profit. They're lawyers will clean things up behind them and it will barely slow them down."

"Damn, it's like an invasion in a way, like an army is taking over the county."

"It's not like an invasion, Julian, it *is* an invasion. Other words are used to make it more acceptable, like free enterprise, job-creation, or energy independence, but have no doubt, profit is what Khan Industries is after and for that they're invading Madison County."

"What's Oldsmar want with you?"

"He says he wants me to work for them, to do some writing in support of their project. But I think he's just feeling me out, making me an offer that he knew I would turn down."

"I don't get what you're saying. How would he know you'd turn him down?"

"Most of my years as a war correspondent, I've been a critic of American foreign policy, which I consider to be mostly driven by an imperialist agenda. Towards the end of my time in Afghanistan, I became an outspoken opponent of the war. The mainstream media wouldn't touch any of my articles; right wing pundits even started referring to me as a traitor. It wouldn't take much research to uncover my history and learn my politics."

"But what's the war in Afghanistan have to do with drilling for gas in Madison County?"

"Because the same motivation that keeps us in the Middle East is behind Oldsmar and the people he works for: huge profits that can be made from fossil fuels."

"Now hold on there, friend. I don't see that connection. We got into Afghanistan after nine-eleven. We went there after we were attacked here. There's some from Madison County that signed up and went over. We're in the Mideast to fight against terrorism."

"Fighting terrorism may well be part of it, Julian, just like part of the reason Oldsmar is here, buying up land and trying to get you to sign a contract, may be to make the United States more energy independent and lessen the threat of terrorism, but profit is the driving force, both here and there. If the Mideast were rich in bananas instead of oil, we would never even hear about it, let alone be fighting wars there."

"I can't say I agree with you on this one, but I can't stay here now to argue it out either. I was on my way to Southern States and they'll be closing on me if I don't take off right now. I almost forgot why I stopped in the first place. You ain't a vegetarian are you?"

"No not really. I don't each much meat, but I'm not a vegetarian. Why?"

"Pat wanted me to ask. She's planning dinner for Monday and said she should have asked you. More people are vegetarian these days, and she got the notion you might be. You *are* coming on Monday, right? Pat said you were."

"Yes, I'm planning on it, as long as you promise not to argue politics."

"I ain't promising anything, but I'll be good, for the old man's sake. You better watch it, too, Ira. I wouldn't be spouting off your communist point of view around Dad, if I were you."

"Julian, it's not a communist point . . ."

"I know, I'm just going on with you. Hey, I got to run."

Julian steps out the door and looks back toward me, smiling.

"I'll see you Monday, Ira."

20

"This is my cousin, Jerry Dale Runnion, and his wife, Sandy. Jerry Dale works on The Land here with me. Sandy works at the high school."

I stand and shake hands across the table with Julian's cousin, who is at least a decade younger than Julian and an inch taller, with a muscular, athletic build. Jerry Dale has thick dark hair and brown eyes that study me closely, seemingly with an air of uncertainty.

Sandy is the opposite of her husband, petite, blonde, and unassuming. She seems curious about me too, but in a simple, curious way.

"So have you had much business at your shop, Mister Stone?"

"No, I haven't had much business, but I have had a few sales. I'm not in a hurry about this, soI'm content to let it develop by word of mouth. I can say that while I haven't had a large number of customers, the quality of the patronage has been exceptional."

I say this as Patricia brings a covered dish to the table. She looks at me and smiles, but doesn't comment.

"Can I help with something, Pat?"

"Thanks, Sandy, yes, I can use your help. Everything is pretty much ready and just needs to be moved out here. But Dad's starting to stir, so if you can relieve me a little, I can tend to him."

"How's he doing today?"

"Not real good, Julian. He was a little out of his head early this morning, and the whites of his eyes have a yellowish color again Did you notice that?"

"No, I ain't seen him yet today. What do you think is causing that?"

"Could be a lot of things, but my guess is that it's his kidneys, like before. He should see the doctor."

"I agree, but you know how that goes. If anyone can convince him you can, so have at it."

"I will, but not today. I just want him to enjoy himself. Sandy, are you ready to get this show on the road?"

"I'm right behind you. "

The women leave and an awkward silence descends around the picnic table. Julian has an uncertain, worried expression, as he stares toward the house. While I'm struggling to think of a topic of conversation that might engage the three of us, Jerry Dale addresses me.

"Do you hunt, Mr. Stone?"

"Uh, no, not really. Well, I did a handful of times when I was young. My uncle took me deer hunting with him when I was just a boy, but the truth is I never even took a shot. All I did was sit and watch, so I don't know if you can really call that hunting."

"Sure it is, sometimes that's the best part. Where was it you hunted?"

"Here in Madison County over on the other side of town. My uncle, Harold Caldwell, and my Aunt Nan had a farm over there, about fifty acres."

"I know where you mean. I knew old Harry Caldwell, too. You ever consider hunting again? The deer are starting to come back around here. You might get a shot this time around."

"N-no, I don't think so. I haven't shot a gun in years."

"Hey Julian, I think you need to bring Mr. Stone up to the hunting camp sometime. What do you think? Julian, you listening?"

Julian turns in response to his cousin's question then looks above us in the direction of Walnut Creek Road. I follow his gaze and see a vehicle on Runnion Lane, just rounding the hill.

"Good, here comes Fred. Wasn't sure if he was going to make it today. What did you ask me, Jerry Dale?"

"I was saying that you need to bring Mr. Stone up to the hunting camp sometime."

"Sure, yeah, I should do that. I was thinking the same thing, myself. Say, I hear Dad inside talking, and Fred's here, so it looks like we're about to get started. What say we go around back and see how Cody's doing at the grill. Better make sure he's not overcooking the meat."

We follow Julian around the house to where Cody is standing over a rustic grill, built into a stone fireplace that stands on the bank of Runnion Branch. Cody has his back to us, and doesn't notice our approach. Wagon turns in our direction but remains sitting at attention, close to the grill.

Steaks are sizzling and sputtering over hot coals, filling the air with an aroma that is nostalgic for me, conjuring up memories of picnics and cookouts of the past. Julian steps close to his son and inspects the steaks.

"I'm not overcooking them, Dad, if that's what you're thinking."

"I'm not thinking anything. These guys were concerned that you might be, so I thought I'd come over and check. Meat looks good to me and like it's about ready to go. Pat's ready, Fred's coming down the road, so the timing is right. You've done it again, Dakota."

"Thanks, I guess. Say Dad, did you hear that Mrs. Ponder moved out."

"No, I knew she sold, but I didn't know she was gone already."

"She sure is. I was just talking to Joel this morning and he told me. He and his brother helped her move on Thursday, and she left for Florida the next day. Joel said that the new people were already hanging around the property, even before Mrs. Ponder was gone."

"Damn, I didn't think it would be so soon."

Julian pats at his shirt pocket and pulls out a pack of cigarettes.

He lights one and takes a deep drag, tilting his head back, blowing the smoke into the sky. He looks at me shaking his head, and them turns toward his cousin.

"Damn it, Jerry Dale, I wish we could have bought that property."

"Didn't have a chance. It was sold before anyone knew it was on the market. But yeah, I sure hate having somebody we don't know up there, especially those people. They got the high ground on us."

"What say we don't talk about it over dinner, spare Dad the aggravation for today. There'll be plenty of time for aggravation tomorrow."

"I grew up during the thirties, one of eight children. As a matter of fact I was the eighth. My mother didn't give up easily, but I guess when she got a look at me, she'd decided she better quit."

Dinner is a delightful affair with pleasant conversation, delicious food, and entertaining stories. Fred Davis, a boyhood friend of Adam, joined us for dinner and as he and Adam recollect their past, I find myself wishing I had a voice recorder with me.

"I had three sisters and there were five of us boys. We were poor, but we didn't know it, cause we were happy. I guess there's truth in the old saying about ignorance being bliss, because we just simply didn't know there were other people that had it any better than us. Isn't that right, Adam?"

"Yeah, that's right, Fred. When school was out, kids worked all summer long, right on the farm. We didn't go to the big town of Walnut Creek too often, even though it was just three miles away. We didn't have money to go to the show. We didn't have much money at all, but we always had what we needed here on the farm. Hell, we wouldn't have even known if there was a depression going on if someone hadn't told us."

Adam does not look well. Since the time I saw him last, he seems more gaunt and unsteady, and there is a definite yellow hue about his eyes. Yet he's in a good mood, gracious and cheerful, such that I'm disappointed when he decides not to make the traditional excursion to the family cemetery after dinner. I see concern on Patricia's face, that lingers despite her father assurance that he's fine.

Adam and Fred retire to the house and the rest of us begin the trek to the cemetery. Julian stops at his truck, reaches through the open window and takes something from the dashboard. When he turns I can see it's a cluster of small American flags, rolled up round the sticks they're attached to.

The Runnion Cemetery is situated on a hill in the middle of a large pasture, and like the Ramsey Cemetery, no road leads to it, only a passageway through a grass field. Hardwood trees, green with spring foliage, are interspersed throughout the cemetery, while along the perimeter, the brush is cut close, such that the gravestones and the fence that borders them are obvious, even at a distance.

Patricia, and I lead the way, while Jerry Dale, Sandy and Julian follow several yards behind. Cody ambles along to the side of us, stopping occasionally to throw a stick for Wagon, who runs circles around our unhurried expedition.

"This is the second family cemetery I've visited within a week and I'm wondering, why do they tend to be placed on top of hills?"

"I don't really know, Ira, I've never really given it much thought. That's just the way it's always been for me. I can't think of any graveyard around here that isn't on a hill."

Patricia turns to the trio behind us and puts the question to them. Julian just shrugs, but Jerry Dale speaks up.

"Keep them away from floodwater, maybe. All kinds of debris could get washed into them, or if it's bad enough, graves could get washed out. I heard that if the water's deep enough, caskets can come popping right up out of the ground."

"What, who told you that?"

"Gus told me, Julian."

"Gus? Well that's all I need to know."

"Ha ha, I know what you mean, but it might be possible. Think about it, gasses build up in there over time, then everything under water. If the ground gets soft enough, up they come like a ball bobbing to the surface.

"Uh huh, I hear you, Jerry Dale. Say Cody, What do you think, why are graveyards up on hills?"

"Probably out of respect for the people that are buried there, to make them higher in the sky and closer to heaven. And maybe it's so we can see it better. When I look up at our graveyard, I remember people that have died. It reminds me that I'm going to be there someday too, so I better get on with living."

Cody drifts away from us, making a mighty heave of the stick, and Wagon races after it. We walk the remaining distance to the cemetery in silence, and I think the others in the party are just as moved as I am with the young man's insight.

An iron picket fence, rusted in spots and intertwined with vines, surrounds the Runnion Cemetery and separates it from pasture. Without the enclosure is a uniform meadow of cropped grass maintained by generations of cattle. Within is a fragment of the forest that once covered this field, preserved by generations of a family that's buried here.

Patricia opens the gate against resistance from tufts of grass, and we file inside. Cody is last and he closes the gate before Wagon can follow. The dog arrives at the entrance, stick in mouth, tail wagging, with what could be interpreted as a look of incredulity that he's been excluded.

"You stay, boy. I don't want you in here, digging around."

"He's okay Cody. Go ahead and let him in. He won't tolerate staying out there anyway with us in here."

"Nah, last time I had him in here, Dad, he dug right on top of grandma's grave."

"So what. He ain't gonna dig down six feet, and I'm sure your grandma wouldn't mind anyway. You might as well let him in because he won't give up until you do."

No sooner had Julian spoken when Wagon charges the fence,

clearing it in a mighty leap. He runs up to Cody, wagging his tail, as if jumping the fence was what he was supposed to do. Cody smiles and rubs the dog's head.

The graves are arranged in neat rows, with headstones facing toward us as we move in among them. Patricia beckons me to follow as she walks toward the center of the cemetery along a narrow lane, carpeted with wet leaves. The rest of the party follows Julian, moving along the perimeter, to an area where the tombstones are more contemporary.

I come up beside Patricia when she stops in front of two tall, thin tombstones, so dark and weathered that it is difficult to read the information inscribed upon them.

"These are the graves of Buford and Abigail Runnion, the first to settle this property. They bought five hundred acres just after the Revolutionary War and we've been here ever since. Abigail was a Rector and as the story goes, they met at church, and got married within a month, even though her family didn't quite approve of the match. I think the Rectors still hold a grudge against us for that."

"You're kidding."

"Yes, I'm kidding. The Runnion and Rector families are so intermarried now that it's hard to tell us apart. I married a Cartwright from Tennessee and believe me, at first that caused a stir too. But my family got to like Mike.

He had different ideas about farming, but he *was* a farmer and a hard worker and that counts for a lot. He loved me and the kids, and he went to church on Sundays. In the end, my family couldn't have asked for a better in-law."

"How did you meet your husband, Patricia, I'm guessing that you didn't meet him at church."

"I met Mike in college at East Tennessee State University when we were both freshman. He didn't quite make it through to graduation, never could see the relevance of what he was being taught to farming. And farming is what he did, raised cattle and grew tomatoes and he did it well, right up until his death. He was cutting along a slope, a place where he had worked his whole life, and the tractor turned over on him."

"That's so sad. I'm sorry to hear that."

"It *is* sad, but then, he died while he was healthy and happy, doing what he loved to do. Not many people are lucky in that way."

Patricia looks behind her to where the other members of our party are congregated. The flags that Julian brought are now unfurled and fluttering beside a number of the graves.

"We should join the others. I just wanted to show you how this all got started."

Julian and Jerry Dale are leaning against the fence, deep in discussion and stop talking as we come up to them. The inscriptions on the tombstones in this area of the cemetery identify graves of more recent generations. Most prominent is a large stone, spanning two gravesites, that of Florence Runnion, dated 1928 to 2013, and the other of Adam Runnion, with the birth date only, 1926.

Julian has placed one of the flags on the grave to the right of his parent's marker. The engraving on the stone reads: Samuel Runnion, Born 1948, Died 1968, aged 20 years. Samuel died the year of the Tet Offensive, the event that brought the United States to realize that it wasn't winning the war in Vietnam.

Poor Samuel, a young man from this peaceful valley, killed on the other side of the world in the jungles of Vietnam, in a war that should never have been fought. Had he been born a few years later, he would likely have spent his life as a farmer in Walnut Creek, and be standing here with us today.

Cody comes up beside me and stares at the grave of his uncle, a person he knows about from stories, and whose image he's seen only in old photographs.

"This is Samuel's grave, Ira. A new flag is placed on it every Memorial day as per Dad's instructions. He usually does it himself, but isn't up to it today."

"Aunt Pat, was Uncle Samuel like Grandpa? I mean did he act like him and have the same opinions as him."

"No Cody, he was more like your Grandmother, but really different from all of us in some ways. From what I can remember, he liked to joke and laugh and he liked to be with family. Now if you ask me, your father is the one who's like Grandpa."

We turn and look toward Julian and he looks back at his sister with a straight face and a twinkle in his eye, but says nothing to dispute her supposition.

Suddenly, there is the sound of an explosion, perhaps a gun firing, coming from somewhere up the hollow beyond Adam's house. We all start and turn as another bang reverberates toward us, and another closely follows that. The last sounds more hollow than a gunshot, more like the noise of fireworks. When a series of small explosions sound in rapid succession, it seems certain that someone is setting off fireworks.

"What the hell is that, Jerry Dale. Is that on The Land?"

"Sounds like some fireworks to me, up on the ridge, the Ponder farm, maybe."

"Well who the hell would be setting off fireworks today, on Memorial Day?"

"I don't know, Julian. Can't be Mrs. Ponder, that's for sure. Maybe it's the new neighbors, introducing themselves."

"Some introduction. Maybe I should go up, there and introduce myself with some fireworks of my own. Come on, we better head down to the house and make sure Fred and Dad are alright."

We leave the cemetery and walk down across the pasture at a faster gait than we ascended it. The explosions continue, some of them quite loud, such that they suggest bombs rather than fireworks or guns. I wonder what the point of this disturbance could be. Is this some sort of intimidation tactic? This is no noise of celebration, but quite the contrary. To my ear, it's the sound of discord, an overture to conflict.

21

"Your dad's a tough old bird, Pat. He'll be all right once he sits a while."

"I know Fred, and if something like this had to happen, I'm glad you were here."

"Hey, your dad and I go way back; we're like brothers. As long as I can still get around, I'll be here for him. You take care now Pat. It's good to meet you, Ira. I'm going to stop into your shop one of these days."

"Nice to meet you, Fred, and I'll be looking forward to your visit."

Patricia and I stand in the roadway and watch in silence as Fred Davis drives off in his pickup truck, grinding and crunching up the gravel slope away from the home of his lifelong friend. When the truck dips below the crest of the hill, Patricia turns to me with a strained smile.

"Thanks for coming, Ira. In spite of the trouble, I hope you had a good time."

"I had a wonderful time, Patricia, and the disruption didn't take away from that. I do feel bad that it upset your father so."

"Yes, I'm not surprised though. This has always been a special day for him, not just for the remembrance, but a celebration of the new season: we made it through the winter, the family is here and we're still safe and secure on the farm. The truth is, he didn't make it through the winter so well, and he knows it better than anyone.

As far as the family, this was the least family I've ever known to attend Memorial Day dinner. Dad's brothers are dead, and his sister rarely travels. The younger people have their own events to attend. I'm sure this was all weighing on him, and then the noise pushed him over the edge."

"I just hope it was something relatively innocent, like kids, goofing around, and there's not more to it."

"Whatever it is, Julian and Jerry Dale will find out, believe me. Whoever is behind it, Dad didn't need this. When he didn't go to the cemetery with us, I knew he must be feeling bad, so it's no wonder the noise unnerved him so much. He looked scared to me, and that's what hurts me the most, because I've never seen him like that. Not too many years ago, he would have gone up through the woods, himself, on foot, and found out what was going on."

Patricia and I lean against the jeep, silent for a moment, each lost in our own thoughts about this afternoon's turn of events. When the noise on the ridge finally stopped, we did manage to distract ourselves from the interruption with conversation. I talked to some extent about my experience in Afghanistan, which I am always open to do when in company that is truly interested.

Julian and the women were just that, asking pertinent and engaging questions, but no one was more interested than Fred who seemed fascinated with what I had to tell. Only Jerry Dale said nothing. Not that he was uninterested, in fact he seemed to pay close attention to every word.

Adam didn't participate in our conversation because he never reappeared from the house, and I knew that Patricia was distracted for that reason. I really wanted to stay, but decide that it's time for me to take my leave, so that she can attend to her father. She walked with me to the jeep and I sense that she welcomes the opportunity for us to talk alone.

"How much longer are you in for, Patricia?"

"Oh, I don't know, I'm going to take it from day to day. I took the whole week off because I know something has to be done for Dad now. He can't take care of himself anymore and he's not going to leave the farm unless he's carried off it."

"Well if I can help, let me know. I enjoy talking to your father. I could do that and give you a break. My schedule is flexible."

"I know, I saw your planner. I might just take you up on that. I heard you're making a bowl for Dad. He told me that, himself. Have you finished it yet?"

"What a coincidence you should ask, I just did, or at least the hewing part. A few coats of beeswax and it will be ready to go in a day or two."

"How about bringing it on Wednesday? There's a woman coming Wednesday morning from the clinic who does home health care and I want some time to talk to her alone. If I think she's up to it, she'll stay here part of the day, starting that afternoon. Could you bring the bowl Wednesday morning around ten?"

"Sure, that's no problem. And, if it does work out with the health care worker, would you like to go to lunch?"

"Yes, I don't see why not. I'd like that. I haven't really done anything like that in a while."

Patricia turns and faces me, standing only a few inches away. I can see that she's nervous and worried. She glances at the house, then turns to her left and stares up the hollow for a moment before she speaks.

"Ira, do you ever feel overwhelmed with all that's happening around you? My father is unable to take care of himself anymore, but ready to fight if you mention it, and at the same time I'm dealing with the usual day to day issues with family and friends and work. And to add to the worry, there are big problems looming, things we have no control over, like the possibility of another war, or something like this gas drilling now. And I'm getting older, too, wondering what I want to do with the rest of my life.

When I was young, I believed that if I was an honest person, worked hard, went to church, paid my bills, and raised my kids right, that some day I would be rewarded for it. In spite of the work, there was security in the promise of the future. I felt that by now, I would be sitting back and enjoying my life, playing with grandchildren, and

131

having big family dinners on holidays. Instead, the road ahead seems more uncertain than when I was young. I lost my husband, my children moved away, and I live alone now in a town with my in-laws.

I was looking forward to this weekend, hoping for a little taste of the past, I think, maybe to find a reason to believe again. But between Dad taking a turn for the worse and the noise from the Ponder property, I feel more scattered and uncertain than ever.

The old days are definitely over, and I even wonder sometimes if those memories are just something that exist in my head. Maybe there's no such thing as the good old days, just new, uncertain days always in front of us. Am I making any sense?"

"Yes, what you're saying makes perfect sense to me."

I know what I want to say to her, but I'm not exactly sure how to word it. I hesitate, and then on impulse, I reach out and touch Patricia's elbow. She doesn't looks up, but steps closer, leans against me, and I encircle her with my arms. I'm silent for a moment, but now that we've established this level of trust, I feel more confident to speak.

"Patricia in my line of work, I saw many terrible things. I saw the worst of humanity, which, in my opinion, is the definition of war, and seeing it up close like I did, affected my view of the human race in a very negative way. In fact, by the time I walked away from it all, I had come to the conclusion that civilization is a lost cause. So why worry about it, why try?

I considered disappearing, moving to some obscure part of the world, and living out the rest of my days away from the problems of society. Instead, I went to Nepal at the invitation of a colleague, and spent some time thinking about my life and reflecting on the events I had witnessed.

I came to realize that I thought too highly of myself, that I thought I was somehow separate from these events. I'm a human, too, so if there's a problem with humanity, then I'm part of the problem, and therefore, I should strive to be part of a solution.

I didn't mean to ramble on, Patricia, *which I can do*, and I don't know if I'm answering your question. I guess what I'm saying is that yes I do get overwhelmed at times, but that's just part of being human and as long as we're alive, we have to accept the bad with the good. We can't avoid trouble and doubt along the road, all we can do is alter our route and press on."

"I like that thought, alter our route and press on. I think that's what I need to do."

"A friend of mine said it to me. Mahmud Safi. I mentioned him earlier this evening."

"Oh yes, your friend in Afghanistan. And so did he alter his route and press on?"

"Yes he did, he certainly did."

22

My raised bed frames are six feet by four feet, twenty inches high and constructed of red cedar. Cedar is a durable wood for outdoor use, with color and figuring that makes for attractive planters. I want my garden to be as aesthetically pleasing as it is nutritive. The addition of bench tops allow me to sit while I work, an accommodating arrangement for an old back such as my own. I didn't plan to work on this project now, but I can't seem to confine myself indoors on such a beautiful spring day.

While I work, my head is filled with thoughts of conversation with Patricia. She passed by this morning as I was crossing the lawn and stopped to have coffee on the back porch. She revealed that she has been considering moving back to Walnut Creek, an announcement that was not so surprising considering how fondly she talks about her family farm. But I was taken aback when she revealed a long held desire to restore the old log house, the family home place, built by her great-great-great grandparents.

I would find it a captivating idea under any circumstances, but considering that Patricia would move here and immerse herself in such a project, right up the road from me, makes it an especially exciting prospect. With such thoughts in mind, I work with greater enthusiasm on my own venture, and for today that entails raised bed gardens.

Stepping back to view my operation from a distance, I hear

a strange noise. It's the sound of vehicles coming up the road, which is hardly unusual, but there's a difference in the tone and magnitude this time. Something big is coming from the direction of town, moving slowly and deliberately this way.

Along with the sound, I sense vibration under foot, which arouses my curiosity to the point that I walk to the road for a better view. Around the bend comes flashing lights on a white pickup truck, that bears a yellow banner with the words, 'Oversize Load'. The driver raises his hand to me as he coasts by and then turns his gaze to the rear view mirror.

A tractor trailer rounds the bend, loaded with pipe, another follows, and another. Truck after truck rumbles by, loaded with pipe, huge, black pipes and smaller, orange pipes that stand out in glaring contrast to the green of the valley. Next comes a truck loaded with a bizarre apparatus that I guess is part of a drilling rig.

'Oversize Load' is an understatement for this truck, which takes up three fourths of Walnut Creek Road as it creeps toward me. Another vehicle with similar cargo is close behind and after that, one after another tractor trailer follows, carrying an array of cargo, including bulldozers, and front end loaders.

A pickup truck approaches from the east, and slows as it nears the convoy. The driver pulls to the right, riding the shoulder, and works his vehicle past the oncoming fleet, pausing at Ben's driveway, and skirting between trucks to cross the bridge.

Ben comes to the edge of his yard and shrugs when he sees me as if to ask what's happening. I can only respond in kind, although I know too well what this intrusion is about. For the moment, the din from the traffic renders vocal explanation impossible.

The hardware for gas drilling is being transported up the road, perhaps headed to the Ponder farm. I'm shocked at the immensity of the equipment as well as the quantity. I've never seen anything like this anywhere, let alone on a back road this narrow. Even on an interstate highway such a cumbersome procession would stand out. The stench of diesel fumes wafts about my homestead, dusting the garden and violating Walnut Creek. By the time the trailing vehicle comes into view, another white pickup truck with flashing lights and an oversize load sign, I guess that forty tractor trailers went by.

Following close behind, another convoy comes into view, a mixture of smaller trucks and cars, the vehicles of daily commuters, backed up behind the slow-moving caravan. As these pass by me, I note expressions of aggravation and confusion on the faces of the operators. Some look at me and nod or wave, and some gesture such as Ben did, wondering what's going on.

One truck leaves the line and pulls into the parking area of the store. I assume that it's someone who decided to wait rather than creep along in traffic. I'm not familiar with the vehicle, but when two men exit, I recognize the passenger as Julian.

"Hello there, Ira. You watching the parade?"

"I am, but I can't say I'm enjoying it much."

"You know what it is don't you? It's the damn drilling equipment. They been up on the ridge all week, making noise, so I figured they'd be starting soon. Doesn't this suck? I'd like to take that little weasel, Oldsmar, and wring his damn neck for bringing this in here.

But say Ira, before I get going on that, this is Lamont Greely, cousin of mine. I was telling him about what you do and when we got hung up in traffic I told him to pull off, so he could see for himself. Besides that, Lamont here cuts trees for a living, so I thought he might be able to help you out with some wood."

"Good to meet you, Lamont. Do you cut trees for lumber?"

"Nah, people's yards. Trim them, cut them down, whatever they want. But I see a lot of wood, all kinds. Just yesterday, I cut some dogwood trees over in Barnard. You should have seen the wood, boy it's beautiful. You ever use dogwood?"

"I haven't yet, but I'm definitely interested. Well come on in and I'll show you what I do use."

I lead the two men through the back door and after a brief introduction to the techniques and tools, I show Lamont the bowls I have on display. His appreciation for the work is obvious and his comments very flattering. He picks each bowl up and examines it with a woodsman's eye.

Lamont is younger than Julian and markedly different in appearance such that I would never guess them to be related. He's heavier than his cousin although not overweight, clean-shaven, with dark, wavy hair that cascades off his head in all directions. A gap-toothed grin, which he displays often, animates his boyish features and puts me at ease in his presence.

Julian remains beside me at the counter and is silent until there's a break in the discourse between Lamont and me. Then he speaks in a hushed voice, not intending to exclude his companion, but meant to denote gravity.

"That was Oldsmar on the ridge on Memorial Day, lighting off firecrackers, shooting guns, drinking, he and some other guys like him."

"How did you find out?"

"One of the boys got up there and watched them. He said they had a grill going, but it seemed that making noise was their main purpose because there wasn't any family with them. Considering they set up right near the line, I have no doubt it was for us. From the looks of all this equipment going up the road, I guess there'll be a lot more noise,"

"I'm afraid that's true, Julian. From what I've learned, this convoy is just the beginning of a long process, and we're probably just looking at the equipment for one drilling site. Unfortunately, more will follow."

"I know that already. Mike Jennings, on the other side of Walnut Mountain just leased out his land, the son of a bitch. Could have guessed that he would be next to jump in bed with the gas people. Money's always been his main goal in life, right Greely?"

"That's for sure. I think that man would sell his mother to make a buck."

"You find anything else out, Ira? How bad might it get?"

"Well I hate to say this, but from what I've read, if it's like

137

other places in the country, Blue Ridge Energy Corporation is going to take over this valley. This convoy that just went by, is just the first wave of traffic. When they're ready to do the drilling, many more trucks will come in, hauling water and sand. Just one well requires between two and four million gallons of water, and then the waste water will be hauled out."

"And that's all hauled by truck?"

"Yes, all by truck. Trucks are one of the most immediate impacts of fracking, thousands of trips to and from the wells. Can you imagine that many eighteen wheelers on this road?"

"Jesus, they'll wreck the road; they'll wreck the whole valley."

"That's right, and the traffic will be bad enough, but with the drilling sites, the pipelines and compressor stations, the valley will be turned into an industrial zone."

"There's got to be something we can do. This is our land; these are our homes. Most of the license plates I saw are from Texas. How can these people roll right in here and do this?"

"Money, that's how. They've got lot's of money behind them, and the man that's putting up the money has an intense desire to make more. If everyone in the valley would stand against fracking it might be stopped, but there again, money comes into play. The opportunity to make it rich will cause some people to get on board with the gas company, like this Jennings fellow. It'll pit neighbor against neighbor. Some are going to get rich, but most are going to lose in more ways than one."

"Hey Julian, the traffic's cleared. I got to get going up the road here."

"Yeah Greely, that's right, you got to go. We'll take off."

"Nice to meet you, Ira. I like your stuff, man. If you need some wood, get in touch with me. I go through quite a bit of it. Walnut's your favorite, huh."

"Yes, it is, but I'm up to try any hardwood."

"Ever try birch?"

"No I haven't."

"This lady I'm going to see right now wants some trees taken

138

down in her yard and one is a yellow birch. The heartwood of yellow birch is a reddish color, looks kind of like cherry. If I do this job for her, I'll drop a couple logs off here. I got to haul it off anyway

"I'd appreciate that, Lamont. I'll make you a bowl out of it."

"It's a deal."

I follow the men to Lamont's truck and Julian turns toward me just as he's getting in.

"Dad took a turn for the worse, so he's in bed most of the time now."

"I'm sorry to hear that, but I'm glad Patricia can be here with him."

"Yah, me too. He sure didn't need this crap happening on the Ponder farm."

"He knows about the drilling then?"

"We had to tell him. He knew after what happened on Memorial Day that something was up."

"What did he say about it?"

"He pointed his finger at me and said, 'Julian, no matter what happens, don't let them cross the line, don't let them come into Walnut Hollow'. And damn it, Ira, I won't. I gave Dad my word on it."

23

"My father asked you if you've ever been in the service?"

"Yes, one of the first questions he asked me, and the answer was no, of course. I told him that I had been in a number of wars because of my profession, but as an observer, not as a participant. Then he asked me if I *would* fight in a war. I have to say, the question caught me off guard. I don't recall anyone really asking me that before."

"Leave it to Dad. If you don't mind me asking, what did you say, Ira?"

"I said that I would, depending on the circumstances. Years ago, I would have readily said no, but that's not the case anymore. After my experience in Afghanistan, my opinion is that even people with high morals and with great respect for life, can be pushed to the point where they feel they have no other choice."

"So you would fight in the Afghanistan War?"

"As an American, no; if I were an Afghan, I might."

"You would fight against Americans, then?"

"Yes, and not because I'm anti-American—the Afghan people aren't anti-American. They're opposed to an outside army, occupying and controlling their country. They're opposed to the violence that ruins their lives. In fact, if I had remained in the country any longer, I might have opposed the American occupation with more than just words. Perhaps that's a reason I got out.

"Did you tell Dad that?"

"No, he seemed satisfied that I *would* fight if I felt there was no other choice, so I didn't go into specifics. And I didn't want to bother your father with my complicated brand of politics."

"Hmm, I think you might have been surprised. Dad's politics are complicated, too. I think he would appreciate your point of view. Now if Afghanistan was occupying our country, you would fight against them, right?"

"Uh, y-yes of course. You caught me off guard there. It's hard to imagine such a thing, occupation by another country. If it came down to it, I would fight against anybody that was threatening to take away my basic freedoms, fight even against my own country in my own country, if it came to that.

Patricia and I are interrupted by a waitress who welcomes us to the Riverside Café, a charming little restaurant on Main Street. Through many owners and a number of renovations, this brick building that overlooks the French Broad River, has been an eating establishment as long as I can remember.

Patricia and I have been perusing the menu while we converse, but haven't made a decision on what to order. I decide to try a black bean chipotle wrap and a glass of French Broad Ale, and she chooses the grilled pimento cheese sandwich along with a glass of Chardonnay.

"I never would have expected this sort of menu at the Riverside Café. That's the influence of Asheville and all the people that are moving into the area."

"Is that good or bad?"

"Good and bad. I'm happy to see the town revive under any circumstances, but I still have fond memories of the old days when Walnut Creek thrived and stood on it's own. I guess I'm old fashioned."

"Nothing wrong with that. In fact it's one of my goals, to become more old fashioned. I use to find change exciting, but now it worries me. These days, the marketplace drives change, not human needs or desires, and that's evident even in small towns like

Walnut Creek."

"Why does that worry you?"

"Because there's no end to it once that mentality has set in. Profit becomes synonymous with progress, money is considered to be the same as wealth, and as a result, people who have accumulated money are considered winners and those who haven't are losers.

The drive to make money corrupts individuals, degenerates families and brings down societies. In my opinion, greed is the flaw in humanity that might doom civilization."

"Goodness, I didn't expect such an answer, but I do agree with you about how money corrupts. The love of money is the root of all evil, as the bible says. I've seen it happen with people I know."

"Yes, and it's happening all over the world at an accelerating rate. Everybody wants to be a millionaire, then a billionaire. There are over a thousand billionaires in the world now, did you know that? And they're applauded, almost as if their financial status is an indication of great virtue. That's ludicrous.

If some are incredibly rich many others are incredibly poor, there's no getting around that. The divide between the rich and poor has grown into a chasm. How can it be justified in any civilized society that some of its members live in mansions while others are living on the street?"

"It can't be justified, but what's an average person to do? I don't really have the means to help other people out in any big way, and besides it's not our fault that people are homeless."

"Not directly, but at some level, we're all guilty. To whatever extent we participate in a system that puts people on the street, we have a hand in it. The same applies to war. Wars are fought because we are fueling the need for them with our lifestyle, and . . ."

"French Broad Ale?"

"Ah yes, that's mine."

The waitress smiles as she places our beverages on the table and informs us that the entrées will be out soon. The interruption is welcome, because I can hear myself going off on one of my tirades and I don't want that to happen. Patricia sips her wine and stares at me, a mischievous smile playing on her lips.

"So what's the answer, Ira? What's an average person to do to save the world?"

"I believe the answer is to stop cooperating with the current system in every way possible, and the first step is for us to wean ourselves off the marketplace. The people who are selling us their products aren't doing it because they're concerned about quality of life, or the health of society. Profit is what motivates them; if it sells, they'll keep making it.

It's not a change that comes easily because we're up against decades of conditioning. Billions and billions of dollars are spent in advertising, convincing us of how we should live and what we should buy.

Even people who realize there's a problem with the way society is going, still expect well-paying jobs with good pensions, cheap air travel, a car for every driver, state of the art medical care, and the thermostat set at seventy two degrees, year-round. People raised in industrialized societies have come to consider all this as a right."

"But why can't we expect that and try to make it true for everyone?"

"Because it's not possible for every one to live like that. There are seven and a half billion people on the planet today and it's impossible for all of them to have the same standard of living that even I do. There aren't enough natural resources.

The only reason you and I and the rest of the population of developed countries can live the lifestyle we do is because of cheap energy, fossil fuels. Nearly everyone in this country has lived their entire life with this cheap energy and knows no other way."

"So you think the answer is to stop using fossil fuels?"

"Yes, not all at once, but over time, yes. To stop using them all at once would result in chaos, the collapse of civilization. There must be a gradual transition, but a complete makeover is needed, a revolution. But it won't happen. There's too much money to be

143

made by the standard formula, and the illusion that profit equals progress is too fixed in the human psyche.

Instead of making the transition to a more sustainable way of life, wars are being fought in the Middle East for oil, the environment is being ravaged worldwide, and now an energy company is here in Walnut Creek to drill for natural gas."

Just then the door opens. I turn to see Don Oldsmar walk in with an older, well-groomed man who is carrying a brief case and sporting a black leather jacket. They seat themselves at a table on the opposite side of the room, and I lean toward Patricia.

"Speak of the devil."

"You don't have to tell me. That's the guy with the gas company."

"Uh huh, that's him. Let me see if I can hide in the menu here."

"Too late, Ira, he's coming this way."

"Ira, good to see you again. And I see your in much prettier company than when I saw you last."

"Hello, Don. Allow me to introduce Patricia Cartwright, Julian Runnion's sister."

"Oops, excuse me while I take my foot out of my mouth. Your brother doesn't strike me as the type that would want to be called pretty, anyway, Ms. Cartwright. Don Oldsmar, pleased to meet you."

Patricia offers a weak smile, but does not speak. Perhaps, sensing the coolness in her demeanor, Oldsmar turns his attention to me.

"So Ira, have you given any more thought to the writing proposal we spoke of last week? Things are starting to roll now, and we certainty would welcome you on board."

"No, I've made up my mind and I . . ."

"Say, let me interrupt here. Do you have a second? I'd like you to meet someone, Jim Hamlin, vice president of operations at Blue Ridge Energy. He's in town to oversee some legal matters. I'm sure he'd like to meet you and perhaps he can make a more convincing argument to prod you out of retirement."

"I-I really would rather not, right now. I see our food is coming and we need to be mindful of the time. Patricia's father isn't well and she's down here from Tennessee, looking after him."

"Oh, I understand, and I'm sorry to hear about your father, Ms. Cartwright. Perhaps Jim and I will catch you later, Ira. Jim's from Texas and he's just gaga over the mountains, especially all the trees, so I know he'd like seeing what you make out of them."

"S-sure, I'll be there."

The waitress arrives at our table, Oldsmar returns to his own, and I'm left to wonder what his ploy is this time.

"So that's the gas man, the guy who wants to lease our land and who was making the noise on Memorial Day."

"That's him, all right."

"What does he want with you?"

"On the surface he seems to want me to do some writing for his company, and that would be to extol the virtues of natural gas and the many benefits such an industry would bring to this area. But the more I've learned about this guy, the more convinced I am that he's playing a game of cat-and-mouse with me, trying to draw me out into the open."

"You think he's trying to find out where you stand."

"Oh I'm sure he knows where I stand by now, and that I would never write the public relations drivel that his company wants. I think what he's trying to learn is if I'll take a stand or remain on the sidelines. He doesn't necessarily want me with them, but he doesn't want me working against them either."

"Does that bother you?"

"No, it's somewhat encouraging because in a backhanded sort of way, it's a compliment, and an admission that their vulnerable. They're worried about what I might write."

"How did you learn about this Don Oldsmar guy? Didn't you just meet him?"

"I got the details on Oldsmar from a colleague of mine who lives in Chicago, Buzz Griffin. He was a mentor to me when I was starting out and one of the reasons I went the direction I did as a journalist. Buzz is up in age now, in his eighties, but he's still at it, telling it like he sees it, calling out the government, corporations, or individuals without fear of reprisal. If ever in the course of my career, I got to feeling conservative and yearned to flow with the current, I'd read Buzz's latest editorial and it shook me right out of it."

"Is this friend of yours aware of what's going on here?"

"Oh yes, quite aware and even more so because hydraulic fracturing is moving into Illinois now. I just read his latest piece and it's a blistering attack on the whole industry and particularly the heads of the big energy companies. And get this, Blue Ridge Energy Corporation, the company that Oldsmar represents and Midwestern Energy, the principle player in Illinois, are both subsidiaries of the same conglomerate, Khan Industries."

"Really, small world, isn't it?"

"Yes, even smaller with the far reaching tentacles of corporations like this. Lawrence Kahn is a multi-billionaire who owns the company and from what Buzz tells me, he's as ruthless a businessmen as they get."

"How can people like us go up against someone like that. It's scary in a way. Doesn't it worry your friend to be going up against him?"

"Not Buzz, I don't think he's afraid of anybody."

"But will it do any good? Will his writing be enough to change things?"

"Ah, actually, probably not. That's the sad part of it, and he knows that better than anyone. But, as Buzz put it, if we don't make the effort to push back against people like Khan, than there's no chance at stopping them."

"Well, I just wish this wasn't happening here and especially now with my father doing so poorly. Speaking of Dad, we should be getting back to the farm soon. I like the woman that's with him, but I don't want to push it just yet."

Patricia and I finish our meal amid discussion of lighter topics. We make observations about Walnut Creek and the changes that are occurring on Main Street, and she talks about her son and daughter.

Oldsmar and his colleague get up before we do and stand outside the restaurant conversing for a few minutes. Oldsmar is talking in a jovial manner, with animated gestures, such that if I didn't already know him, I would guess that he's a likable and friendly fellow. Yet intuition tells me that I will be dealing with an odious side of the man soon enough.

24

"You and Pat seem to be getting along pretty well, from what I can tell."

"Well, I enjoy being with your sister. She's a nice person, honest, intelligent, and witty."

"It's funny you know, since her husband got killed, she never seemed too interested in getting involved again. So, I'm glad to see you two hit it off."

"I really didn't expect it because in recent years, I haven't been too interested in a relationship either."

"You see, that's probably why it happened, neither of you were trying, and so you had that in common from the get-go."

"Hmm, I never thought of it that way, but you might be right."

I'm surprised that Julian mentioned the relationship between Patricia and me, but glad he did, since he seems to approve. We're in his truck, driving up a steep, rocky slope winding our way to the mysterious hunting camp that I've been hearing about. I met Julian at his cabin and we drove to the end of Walnut Hollow before turning north on this dirt road.

"What about you, Julian you seeing anyone?"

"Nah, no one can put up with me anymore. They couldn't before, and now I'm even more set in my ways. I've seen a couple women since Denise and I divorced, but it didn't last long."

"You mentioned that your wife was from Virginia. How did

you two meet, if you don't mind me asking."

"Years back, I used to sell at the farmer's market over in Mars Hill. She came to Mars Hill to teach at the college. I was smitten from the start, and she kept coming to my booth every week. Denise was from Richmond, and kind of a hippie-type, back then.

She fell in love with the whole area, the mountains, the lore, and I think she figured she found the real McCoy with me. We done all right for a while, had Cody along the way. But I think the things she liked about me in the beginning are the same things she hated about me in the end."

"Ha ha, I know what you're saying there. That friend of mine that you met, Justine, I think that was true of us. Not hate in the end, but just an acceptance that I'll never change and the knowledge that she couldn't put up with me the way I am."

"You seem to get along well enough."

"Oh yeah, we do, but we had some rocky times before we finally came to terms. We love each other, we would do just about anything for each other, but both of us know we can't ever live together. Justine would never move here anyway, under any circumstances."

"She didn't like it here?"

"Oh yes, she thought it was wonderful here. Justine enjoyed her visit very much, but DC is much more her style. To her, coming here was like visiting a foreign country, and she came open minded and ready to make the most of it, but I'm sure she's happy to be settled back in Washington."

"That's hard for me to imagine, living in a place like that."

"It's hard for me to imagine too. I've lived in cities for short periods of time, and I never felt comfortable. One thing I know for certain, we aren't in a city now. Where are the hell are we? I'm completely turned around here."

"We crossed the property line a quarter mile back. We're on land that belongs to Jerry Dale's family now, this ridge we're starting up now is Backbone Mountain, and the hunting camp is right on top. There's a group of us, mostly family, that between us, we have several thousand acres, all told. When we're speaking of the whole thing, we call it The Land. Backbone Mountain is sort of the dividing line right down the middle. Not many people besides us have been back in here for a long time."

"Goodness, I feel honored then."

"I wouldn't go that far yet. Wait until you get there and then decide. But everyone did agree on you coming up here, so that says something."

I do feel honored, however, in a manner similar to how I felt when I was accepted by Mahmud's family and then by his tribe. The reference to Backbone Mountain was the first mention of that name since my question about the militia. While my curiosity has remained unabated since Julian's reaction to my initial query, I haven't broached the subject since then.

As I mull over it now, I hear a gunshot somewhere up ahead of us, and then another. When Julian doesn't react, I assume it's related to the hunting camp.

"Is that somebody hunting?"

"Nah, at least they shouldn't be. Nothing's in season now. From the sound of it, I guess it's someone sighting in their rifle."

We grind around turn after turn, always uphill, and then the road begins to level off. Daylight is evident on the horizon beyond the tree trunks, a sign that we're at the summit. To the left, a cabin comes into view, nestled into a stand of hemlock trees twenty yards off the main road, and Julian turns into the drive. The structure would hardly be noticeable if it weren't for the vehicles parked outside.

The cabin is a one-room, plank structure with additions jutting out from each side. A thin plume of smoke curling from the chimney reminds me that we're up high, and it can be cool at this altitude, even in June.

As we exit the truck, I'm surprised to see several, saddled horses tethered to a hitching post to the right of the building. I'm about to comment on them when two men, carrying rifles and dressed in camouflage clothing, appear from behind the building. One of the men, I recognize as Lamont Greely, and he introduces his companion as Pete Rice, a second cousin whose family has property that borders to the west. Pete appears to be about half my age, tall and lanky with an easy going attitude and a firm handshake. The men inform us that they had been target practicing just before we pulled up.

Within the cabin, a rich aroma of food hangs in the air, a spicy, meaty fragrance that reminds me that I skipped lunch. That was at Julian's suggestion because he said that Jerry Dale's father, Amos, was preparing a pot of venison stew for the occasion.

I presume that it's Amos Runnion, standing over a wood cook stove as we enter, stirring the contents of a large pot. He's dressed in camouflage as well, and wears a green apron that looks like it could be an army issued garment. He raises a wooden spoon in greeting and informs us that the stew is about ready.

Two other men are seated at a table in the middle of the room, each with a glass of beer in hand and between them is a mason jar, three quarters filled with a clear liquid. One of the men seems to be about my age and the other much younger, thirties maybe. Both are dressed as the others, in hunting apparel. The older man looks up and grins at Julian.

"Hey Jules, got some Mountain Dew for you here."

"Thanks Gus, but I got to pass, I uh, . . . ah, okay, maybe just a taste. I got to be careful. Stomachs been acting up again. You get it over in Wolf Laurel?"

"Uh huh, only the best for you guys."

"Tommy ain't here?"

"No, he got tied up; he'll be by later."

"All right, good. Say, Ira, this is Augustus Ramsey and his nephew Tim, cousins of mine on my mother's side. They live over in the next hollow.

Ira's the one who bought the place down on the bend, Your family's old place. Gus is Ben's cousin, Ira. Ira fixed up the store into a wooden bowl shop, Gus. You ought to see it."

"Nice to meet you, Ira. I've been watching your progress there, as I drive by. I can't see how you can make a living there, selling wooden bowls. Are you sure that's not just a front, and you have a still out back?"

"No not me, just wooden bowls. I can't say I've ever tasted moonshine."

"Well, then you've come to the right place. Before you sit down, Greely, grab some glasses there. Fill one a quarter full with water, if you would."

I situate myself in a chair that Gus pulls out next to him, and Lamont places several glasses on the table and takes a seat across from me. The glass with water is placed in front of me and Gus fills another glass with an equal measure of the contents from the mason jar.

"Now, Ira, the best thing to do for your first time is to drink the shine down in one swallow then follow it right away with an equal amount of water."

"Hey, Gus, don't pull that. Don't believe a word he says, Ira. It's an old trick. The second glass won't be water but more of the same, like throwing gasoline on a fire."

"Come on, Jules I'd a stopped him."

"Ha ha, like hell you would have, Gus. We got beer in the fridge. I'll get you one, Ira. Take my advice, just a sip of shine and chase it with a swig of beer."

The other men join us at the table and are chuckling at what is apparently a common prank. Adhering to Julian's advice, I have my first sip of moonshine, followed by a swallow of Budweiser. The moonshine reminds me of vodka but with faint taste of whiskey. It burns slightly as it goes down and the swallow of cold beer is soothing relief.

With the second sip, I detect a slight corn taste and my throat is less irritated, I hold off on the beer so that I can more fully appreciate the taste of this local beverage. The alcohol, coursing through my bloodstream, along with the heat of the cook stove, causes me to glow with warmth.

Amos Runnion announces that the stew is ready, we fill our bowls in turn, and reassemble at the table. The stew is delicious, with generous chunks of venison, and, according to the cook, also contains chopped onions, carrots, celery, and crushed juniper berries, all seasoned with rosemary and basil. He says the recipe has been in his family for generations and has always been made with deer meat from these woods.

The mason jar gets passed around again and I chase my shine this time with a mouthful of stew. The conversation grows merry, mostly with tales of hunting: the big buck that got away, the legendary tom turkey that Greely shot with a bow and arrow, the huge, wild boar that ravaged the fields for years and was finally brought down two years ago.

I'm entertained by the personalities who tell the stories as much as I am by the subject matter, content to listen and observe, not having any hunting stories of my own. Eventually the conversation becomes more general, even to include hand hewn bowls. Lamont brings it up, I think to draw me into the conversation, and now that I'm talking, I can see that there are many questions these men have about me.

Inevitably the discussion turns to Afghanistan, and once the subject is raised, I notice that I have everybody's attention. As I have on other occasions, I try to paint a genuine picture of the people of Afghanistan, relating details of their lives, and naturally, I mention Mahmud and some of the happy times I passed with him and his family.

I try not to focus on the effect war has had on the country, and I especially don't want to get into a position where I must express my opinion of that particular war. But war is just what Tim Ramsey wants to hear about and after patiently listening for some minutes, he poses a question that steers me in that direction.

"Were you ever actually in the war? Did you see fighting up close?"

Tim looks at me with that same expression of excitement I see on the faces of many young men who ask such questions of me, almost as if the query is about a sporting event. The room is silent in anticipation of my answer, but I'm hardly put on the spot. Over the years I've developed skillful answers to such questions, telling what I've seen of war in all its inglorious detail. Fueled by the moonshine, I decide to give these men my honest opinion of that war.

"Yes, Tim, I was in the war; everyone in Afghanistan is in the war to some extent. I've heard the sound of bullets whizzing past and bombs detonating. I've seen people die, men, women and children, and I've seen body parts strewn about the street after an explosion.

I attended a wedding that was turned into a war zone by a hellfire missile. The bride, groom and six other people were killed and dozens more were wounded. The groom's father was my good friend, Mahmud, and he wasn't killed, but was so shattered by what happened that his death soon followed."

I pause and there's no sound in the room except crackling and hissing noises coming from the cook stove. I have everyone's undivided attention, so I take the opportunity to voice a conclusion that I've come to from my many years of observing armed conflict.

"All war is hell, men. Nobody wins. In the end, one side loses more than the other, and the only thing that's for certain about the outcome is that everybody loses."

Silence ensues, and I wonder if I have said too much. I doubt it was the sort of report they were expecting. I start to say more and then stop myself, preferring to let my statement stand. Swirling the last of the moonshine in my glass, I drink it down without a chaser. After an awkward pause, Julian breaks the silence and purposefully changes the line of conversation.

"My God, Ira, I might have just let Gus leave that second glass of shine on the table, if I'd known you was to take to it so well."

I chuckle, then everybody laughs, and our discussion of war comes to an end. The conversation turns back to less complicated topics such as moonshine and deer hunting. Julian makes his way over to me and taps me on the shoulder.

"Hey, Ira, come on with me now. I want to show you something."

25

"This is spectacular, Julian. What a view."

"Isn't it. What we're seeing is about two miles away, as the crow flies. That white building in the clearing, that's the Community Center."

"No kidding. I would have never guessed that, in fact I would never have guessed that we were even pointed in that direction."

"Yah, that's it all right, with the road right in front, and Walnut Creek's, running behind, just like at your place. With binoculars you can see who's truck's going by even."

Julian and I walked a hundred yards past the cabin on the same road by which we arrived and turned left on a wide footpath to come to this overlook. I suspected that he was trying to get me out of the building before I caused a stir with my opinions of war and Afghanistan, and that may be partly the case, but it's obvious that Julian wanted to show me something special as well. I have to wonder, however, what he thinks about my comments.

"I've been coming up here since I was a kid, but I never get tired of it. The Community Center wasn't even built then."

"Thanks for showing me this, I think I needed some fresh air, too. Say Julian, do you think I said too much in there about war and all? I didn't mean to get carried away. It's just that . . ."

"Nah, you got ask a question and you spoke your mind. You weren't bullshitting anybody, so that not getting carried away. What you said made them think; it made me think, too. Now let me ask you a question, Ira, and tell me if I'm stepping across the line here. What happened to your friend, Mahmud? You've mentioned him to me before. How did he die? Was it fighting in the war, was he killed by Americans?"

"Well, Julian, no, not exactly. You see, Mahmud was, uh, how can I put this?"

"Ah, hell, Ira you don't have to say. It's none of my business. You seem like you really liked the guy and had respect for him. I was just curious is all."

"No, it's okay, I should just tell you. I'll tell it like it was, and let you decide. Mahmud drove a truck wired with explosives to the outer gate of a NATO supply compound in Kabul and detonated it. He was killed along with three American marines and two Canadian security guards."

"Jesus, are you kidding me? Your friend blew himself up? Now see, that's something I don't get. That's where they have a whole different mentality over there than we do. Fighting for what you believe in is one thing, but what kind of way is that to fight?"

"Mahmud wanted to strike back at those who destroyed his family, and from the start, it was never a fair fight. How do you strike back at an overwhelming force like NATO, an army with unlimited resources and the most modern weaponry in the world at their disposal.

Believe me, Julian, Mahmud was an honorable man. I think you would have liked him if you would have known him. But he had his back up against a wall and for the sake of his honor, he had to avenge the loss of his family. Wouldn't you want to?

Imagine it's Cody's wedding, you're having it here and a helicopter launches a missile right into the middle of the celebration. Cody, his bride, Patricia and your father are all killed along with other relatives and friends, and you're powerless to respond in kind."

"By damn, I would respond though."

"How, Julian, how would you respond against the most powerful army in the world? Can you launch a Hellfire Missile back at them? Even if you could and did, they'd strike again with greater force. Suicide bombing is cheap, effective, and it makes the point to the enemy that you'll stop at nothing to get them."

"Would you do it, blow yourself up to get back at someone like that?"

"I can't say what I would and wouldn't do anymore, Julian. I always tried to believe that compromise and negotiation are the best ways to settle conflict, but in an instance where one side is totally dominant and uses that dominance in their own best interest, with no regard for the welfare of the other side, than I don't know. Where do you begin the negotiation when so much has already been taken from you?"

"And that's the way you see the United States."

"No, if I did, I wouldn't be here now. Most citizens of this country are decent, compassionate people. It's just that they don't realize what's really being done in their name because the media portrays it all as the fight against terrorism.

When they talk about defending America's best interest, what they really mean is corporate America's best interest. If it wasn't for the oil in the Mideast, we would never be there, and Mahmud and his family would be alive.

And what's been happening in other countries for decades is happening here now. A corporation wants the gas under your land and they intend to get it one way or another. What can you do to stop them?"

"Say no and not let them on my land."

"What if the government backs them up? What if they throw up the same sort of power and money and weaponry against you, like they do in other countries.

"They can't do that here. They wouldn't go that far."

"I used to think that, too, but I'm not so sure anymore. What if they did?"

"I wouldn't blow myself up, I'll tell you that much. But, by God, I'd fight back."

"Against an army?"

"We have an army, too Ira; we're trained and ready."

Julian exhales and looks away, shaking his head.

"Damn it, I didn't mean to say that. You got me stirred up, and the damn shine loosened my tongue. Let's head back to the cabin. I was hoping Tommy would have been there when we came. I think I heard someone pull up, so I think he's there now.

You ask me once about Backbone Mountain Militia, and I told you we'd talk about it some time. I want Tommy to talk to you first. He knows about you and wants to talk to you anyway."

We follow the path to the road without speaking such that I wonder once again if I've made known too much of my politics. And then, as if he read my thoughts, Julian begins to talk, relieving my unease. He tells me about the first time he walked up here as a boy, with his brother Samuel, and he points out the stunted growth of the trees and brush, claiming it's a result of the high altitude.

"We're up over four thousand feet here, Ira, so the weather is the same as hundreds of miles to the north. I've seen a frost up here in late June. Many a man's got caught up here at hunting camp without enough gear and froze his butt off up in a deer stand."

As the cabin comes into view, Julian seems relieved at the sight of a Chevy Blazer that I'm guessing belongs to the person named Tommy. Before we reach the porch, Jerry Dale steps out and comes toward us.

"He's over at the range, Julian. He wants us to bring Mr. Stone over to talk."

"Oh, okay, say why don't you just do that, Jerry Dale. I need to go in and sit down a bit."

In the sunlit clearing, I notice that Julian doesn't look good. He appears tired, and his face has a pale and ashen hue to it. He pats me on the shoulder and smiles before turning toward the cabin.

I follow Jerry Dale around the building and then along a grassy lane that leads through forest in a straight line to the south. As we approach an open space, I start at the sound of several shots, fired in succession. Jerry Dale stops as we enter the clearing and nods across a meadow to where a man is standing, inspecting a target on a wooden backstop.

"He knows your coming. He wants to talk to you alone, so I'll head back to the cabin, I guess."

"His name is Tommy?"

"Y-yes it is, but I'd call him Field Commander. At least at first I would."

I'm surprised at how serious Jerry Dale is as he offers this advice, adding to the mystique surrounding this person I'm about to meet, the Field Commander himself. What will the enigmatic Field Commander be like? What does he want to talk to me about? Crossing the meadow I experience a familiar feeling, a mixture of apprehension and excitement like I felt when I was meeting face to face with a tribal warlord or a Taliban leader.

The man at the target becomes aware of my approach, shoulders his pistol and walks toward me. He isn't smiling but he wears a relaxed, friendly expression and something about his features are familiar to me. I'd swear that I've seen him before, but how is that possible?

The man is dressed in army fatigues, combat boots and wears a cap, tilted forward on his cropped head. He could be any one of a number of American field officers whom I became acquainted with in Afghanistan, but why would one of them be here in Walnut Creek, North Carolina? No, this man reminds me of someone I've seen recently. He smiles as we shake hands and I sense that he's aware of my confusion.

"Mr. Stone, good to see you again."

"Call me Ira, please. You look familiar to me, but to be honest with you, I can't recall where we met, Field Commander."

"Ha ha, okay Ira it is, if you'll call me Tommy. We spoke with each other in town this spring, a short discussion about heating with wood."

I wrestle with my memory a moment longer and then I remember that I spoke with this man in the hardware store. This is who Frank, the proprietor, referred to as Old Tom. He certainly doesn't fit that name as he stands before me now, clean shaven, erect and tall, with a sharp and knowing gaze.

"Yes, yes, I do remember now. Heating with wood is still the plan and it's going well. But I have a feeling that isn't what you want to talk about today. In fact, I now suspect that isn't what you were really interested in when we first talked."

"Not the only thing, but I was interested. I burn wood for heat, so it's a subject I take seriously. But I wanted to meet you, too. I had heard about you and I've read your writing for years, but I wanted to get my own impression."

"And?"

"That's why we're talking now. Well, not the only reason. Julian speaks highly of you, and I trust his judgment. He's careful about choosing friends. He's a good man; I've known him since the day he was born. I grew up with his brother, Samuel, and we were best of friends right up until he died. I was there with him in Viet Nam in the end."

"What? You're his cousin, Thomas Gosnell, is that right?"

"Y-yes, but how did you know that?"

"Julian's sister, Patricia, mentioned it. We were talking about Samuel, and you came up in the conversation."

"Oh, I see. Well, that was a long time ago, that day in Khe Sanh, the worst day of my life. My best friend died right alongside me, and even though I made it through, something inside me died, too, something I've never quite gotten back."

"Khe Sanh was a terrible battle. I covered it and did my best to tell what happened."

"I know, I read what you wrote, and I appreciated it. It's one reason I've followed your writing ever since. And I'm a believer in fate, so I have to think that you ended up coming here for a reason."

"I'm flattered, and I believe in fate, myself, but I've retired from covering war, so I would hope I'm here for other reasons. My inquiry about the Militia stemmed from curiosity, it wasn't for professional reasons."

"I understand that and I trust your motives either way. We're not a secret organization, we just keep to ourselves, and if all goes well, we'll stay that way."

"Are you the founder of the militia?"

"Oh no, that was my great Grandfather, Ethan Runnion. He and his brothers were raised on stories of the civil war and weren't so sure where their allegiance would have been. The story goes that they decided that it was best to remain independent of all sides and not be drawn into fights designed by politicians from the cities."

"And the militia has remained intact since then?"

"Yes, in essence, but not in spirit. Over time it became more of a men's hunting club than a militia. The lessons of the civil war were forgotten, and young men drifted off to fight in new wars, I among them, Samuel, too.

After Viet Nam, I had a changed opinion of this country, especially of the people running it. That's when I reformed Backbone Mountain Militia, and used my experience to bring it up to modern times. This was no hasty decision on my part, and there are reasons that go beyond my experiences in Vietnam. But as the years have gone by, I'm more convinced then ever that we're doing the right thing.

We're not looking for trouble, but we will not have trouble pushed on us without a fight. And if there ever is a fight, I won't get caught on the wrong side this time. We'll do whatever it takes to protect our land and our freedom, that's basically what it comes down to."

"Well, I must say, this is a lot for me to take in. On the way here, I only had some slight information that there was a group named Backbone Mountain Militia somewhere hereabouts, and now I not only know that the militia exists, and is located right up the road from me, but I've met the leader.

I've had similar experiences in the past, but I didn't expect it here. Judging by what you've told me so far, let's just say, I understand the stance you're taking."

"I believed that you would, but it's good to hear it from you in person. As I said, I've read your writing over the years, and I agree with your opinion on most matters. That's really what I wanted to do today, let you know we're here and basically what we stand for.

As much as I would like to continue this discussion, we should get inside and be more sociable. Most of the men here this evening are officers, and I'd like you to get to know them in an unofficial capacity. But I'd like to talk in more detail sometime. I'll stop in at your shop if that's all right, check out your bowls *and* your wood stove while I'm at it."

"Sure, that would be fine. I'm there just about every day of the week."

"What day is best, when do you have a some slow time?"

"Just about every day of the week."

26

Walnut Creek is high and cloudy after a morning of heavy rainfall. Strolling along the creek is meditation for me, but I'm finding it difficult to focus this afternoon. My introduction to Backbone Mountain Militia and the Field Commander, has left me with a mixture of feelings.

To a large degree, I admire these men for the stand they're taking. Perhaps the warrior in me wishes I were one of them. Theirs is a selfless mission, not an effort undertaken for gain, but rather to preserve and protect something they have, their land and their freedom. I worry for them, too, a concern born of my experiences with comparable groups with a similar cause.

My unease is exacerbated by the incursion of Blue Ridge Energy Corporation into the valley, an entity that has come to exploit their land and challenge their freedom. Having met the leader of each camp, conflict seems inevitable. The Field Commander never mentioned it, but surely that possibility was on his mind as we spoke.

The irony is that I feel no menace from a secret militia, that trains in the forest, just up the road from me, but feel threatened by those who come openly into the valley with smiles on their faces, bearing promises of prosperity.

Upon reaching the terminus of the trail, I shake my head and try to clear my mind once again. I'm getting way ahead of myself, fretting about things that might happen, instead of focusing on what's in front of me right now. I'm not attending to the water, flowing past me on its resistless course to the French Broad River, or pausing to appreciate this tremendous poplar tree, standing unperturbed at the edge of my field, defiant against the ages. Though its leaves get tossed about, and it's boughs sway in the wind, the trunk remains firmly planted in the earth, immovable.

With that thought, I turn back toward the house with a desire to write. I've read that meditation enhances ones writing, so perhaps that works in reverse, and writing will help me to focus on the present. The treatise on homesteading is what I'll work on today, a positive theme to help me shake off this resignation to conflict.

Nearing the house, I hear the telephone ringing, and decide to not risk more distraction by answering it. I change my mind and hurry inside when I hear Justine's voice, as she leaves a message.

"Hello, hello, Justine, I'm here. I just got in from a walk. What's up? You sound upset."

"Ira, hi, I'm so glad I got you. Are you okay?"

"Y-yes, I'm fine, well, as fine as I can be at sixty-four years of age. What's wrong?"

"Have you read the news this evening?"

"No, not since about noon. Actually I decided to avoid the news for the rest of the day. Why, what's happened?"

"Ira, Buzz Griffin was found dead this morning in his office."

"What? I just talked to Buzz last week. Everything was fine then. What happened?"

"It's being reported as an apparent heart attack; he was found at his desk."

"A heart attack? Humph, I, I guess it's possible. Who did you hear it from?"

"The AP wire. Ira, hello, Ira, are you still there?"

"Yes, I'm still here, just a little shaken up."

"Ira, I-I've heard other things, too. I don't want to talk about it now. Please be careful. Promise me?"

"I promise. Do you want me to call you?"

"No. I'll be in touch, soon. Love you. Bye."

I'm stunned by the news of Buzz's death and alarmed by the apprehension in Justine's voice. In his latest editorial Buzz singled out Khan Industries, divulging the corporation's plans for Illinois and went so far as to refer to Lawrence Khan as a 'capitalist thug'. Then today, he's found dead at his desk of an *apparent* heart attack. I don't want to believe that he was murdered, but I'm skeptical that this is coincidental.

In the kitchen I pour myself a glass of wine. I don't know if my hands are shaking more with fear or with anger, but when the alcohol courses through my bloodstream and focuses my thinking, anger wins out. Another glass of wine and I'm at the keyboard, in a fighting mood, ready to pick up where my mentor left off.

You were one of a kind, Buzz. If only we all could be so true to our cause.

Where am I? Awake in the dark, late at night or early in the morning, I don't know which. My mouth is dry, and I reach for the stein on the night stand. When my grandmother's estate was settled, it was one thing I requested. Grandmother Wallin drank her tea in it, sweetened with honey. I filled it with the same mixture before I came to bed, having had my fill of wine.

A Buddhist precept advises abstinence from substances that lead to intoxication and heedlessness, and in my grief and anger, I disregarded that wise principle. Fortunately, inebriation wears off and heedless writing can be edited. I can deal with grief; I've done it many times before. Anger is the emotion I've struggled to control my entire life. Buddhism cites anger as one of the three poisons that are the root causes of suffering in life. Greed, and ignorance are the other two.

Greed has never been a character trait of mine. I never wanted much in the way of material possessions, and I'm generous when I can afford to be. I believe that greed may be the fatal flaw in humanity that will lead to the collapse of civilization. Greed is ultimately the motivation behind the trouble that we face in

Walnut Creek.

I've worked most of my life to transform ignorance into wisdom, and while I still have much to accomplish along that line, particularly in light of the wisdom I seek now, I believe I maintain the right course in this regard.

Anger is the poison I can't seem to manage. I have long been aware of how much more effective compassion is in affecting positive change than anger or aggression. Aggression is quick and effective, but does not solve the underlying problem and ultimately leads to more aggression.

Compassion takes time to be effective such that it's often dismissed as ineffective. But while the results aren't immediate and dramatic, in the long run it's humanity's best hope. As Grandma used to say, "you can get more with sugar than you can with salt".

I take a drink from her stein and lay back on the pillows, listening to the sound of Walnut Creek. She was such a strong woman and never wavered in the face of adversity. After her husband died, she raised four children on her own. One of them was my mother who left this valley soon after high school and never returned except in proxy, arranging for me come back each summer while she traveled the world with my father.

I returned to Walnut Creek to live out my days in reflection, letting the anger and aggression of the past drift back in time. Yet here I am, getting entangled in a growing web of intrigue that is fomenting the bellicose side of my nature.

Did I choose to come back to Walnut Creek because of the fond memories of my youth, or was I pulled here by fate, as the Field Commander suggests? Is this karma catching up with me?

The sky is lighting; it's morning after all, a new dawn. Maybe I have no right to relinquish the past. Perhaps I'm turning my back on unfinished business. I talked myself into believing that it was still possible to change the world in a peaceful way, but I don't know anymore. Maybe it's too late for that approach; the power of greed is growing too fast. If there is any hope for a better world to arise, the old order must be brought down first.

I rise and make my way to the kitchen in the dim light, brewing more coffee than usual in anticipation of a prolonged session at the computer. As the percolator thumps and gurgles, I look out the window and my gaze fixes on the raised bed frames of my garden project, distinct and impressive in the brightening scene.

A voice in my head tells me that I should be passing my day in the garden and workshop, growing food and hewing bowls, and not veering from the peaceful path I've chosen.

What revolution, whether from the right or the left, ever led to real change, a positive elevation of humankind? Would I forsake the vow I made at Bamiyan so easily and revert back to baser instincts. No, I've walked that route and the experience broke me. I'll leave the computer off today, plug into my higher instincts instead, and give peace a chance.

27

A simple and methodical process, the hewing of bowls from a piece of wood. The sound is soothing, a slow, metrical thud, fitting percussion to accompany the melody of the creek. This is why I came here. I want to remain in this moment always, employed at a simple task, thinking peaceful thoughts.

A vehicle appears in the parking lot and quickly backs in beside the building. I assume it's Julian because that has become his unofficial parking space. I sense alarm because of the uncharacteristic speed with which he maneuvers the truck, grinding the gears as he shifts into reverse. I get up, Julian meets me at the door, looking haggard and angry.

"Ira, hey, I need to talk to you. You got a minute."

"Sure, Julian, what's wrong?"

"Everything, just everything. I think Dad's dying. He hasn't got out of bed today. And it's because the goddamned gas company is planning to put a pipeline down through Walnut Hollow. They sent the letter right to Dad, says they've claimed a right-of way by eminent domain. Can they do that?"

"I, I wouldn't have thought so, not in this situation. The government *can* seize private property for public or civic use, such as for a highway or a railroad. An oil or gas company can do the same, but only when it's clearly in the public interest. I can't imagine it being used in this case."

"Hell no, it ain't in the public interest. There are other

ways they could run the pipe with a lot less trouble. And why our property? They're talking about a fifty foot wide gash right through Walnut Hollow. It's for spite. It's that son of a bitch, Oldsmar who's behind this. He's getting back at me for turning down his offer. If they bulldoze down through those walnut trees, they might as well bulldoze Dad under, too, because it'll kill him for sure. What can I do, Ira? I can't fight this in court."

"I don't know, Julian. This seems like a definite abuse of eminent domain to me, but I'm sure they have a team of lawyers to argue that it isn't. I'll see what I can find out though."

"Thanks, Ira. Do you think that friend of yours in Chicago would know anything about this?"

"I'm sure he would have, but Buzz died two days ago. He was found dead at his desk."

"Oh God, I'm sorry to hear that, Ira. What did he die from?"

"Heart attack is what they're saying. Buzz was in his eighties, and he drank and he smoked cigars, so it's not that unlikely. But what bothers me is that in the weeks leading up to his death he was writing articles against fracking in Illinois. And not only that, he was zeroing in on none other than Khan Industries, the parent corporation of the company that's setting up operations there."

"The same company that's here in the valley? You think they could have had something to do with killing your friend?"

"I can't say yes, but I can't definitely say no either, and that worries me?"

"Jesus, how big is this outfit?"

"Bigger than you can imagine. From what Buzz told me, Kahn Industries is the largest privately held company in the world."

"Well good for them. The bigger they are, the harder they'll fall. I'll be damned if this Khan, or his lapdog, Oldsmar, or anybody else is going to mess with Walnut Hollow without a fight. I'm serious about this, Ira."

"I know you are Julian, and so am I. Buzz didn't give up; he fought right to the end. I'm not going to give up either. In fact I'm going to pick up where he left off and go after these bastards."

169

"I'm glad to hear that, Ira, I really am. And hey, any wood you need, from now on, is on me. I can bring you vegetables from the garden or cuts of beef, whatever you need. I just can't help you writing. It's never been a strong point with me."

"You've helped me a great deal with my writing, Julian. You've made it real, given me names and faces to connect to a story. That's what Mahmud did in Afghanistan, he let me be part of the story, so that I could tell it right, not just talk about it from the sidelines."

"Well be careful, Ira. I don't want you to end up like your friend in Chicago. Do you have a gun?"

"N-no, I don't. I haven't carried a gun in years."

"Do you want one?"

"I don't think so, Julian. Writing is my weapon. I want to beat them that way."

"Well I hope you can, I really do, but I don't think I'll let go of my rifle just yet."

"No, I don't blame you. Tell me something. How long have you been a member of Backbone Mountain Militia?"

"Since a few years after Tommy came back from Nam. He lived way back, in a cabin on his family's property and kept to himself. I wandered back one day, during deer season, and he was dressed for combat, shooting and training like he was at a boot camp or something. He told me right then that he would never forgive the government for what they did to him and Samuel. Tommy said it was the mistake of his life going over there and that the next time he storms a hill, it'll be Capitol Hill."

"Whew, how old were you then?"

"About twenty, and I can tell you, I was pretty shocked to hear that kind of talk. But the more I hung out with Tommy, the more it started to make sense to me. He's a smart guy, reads a lot, cabin's full of books. He told me way back then that sooner or later the government would try to take our land from us, and that we had to be ready. And he was right, now it's happening."

"Are you ready?"

"Hell yes, we're ready."

28

I want to be objective about this, but from what I've learned so far, I'm of the opinion that the whole concept of hydraulic fracturing is flawed, from the process itself to the way it's being imposed upon people. When I read the same catchwords repeated over and over by both industry and government: jobs, energy independence, patriotism, I suspect that something is wrong. I've experienced this sort of party line approach too many times in the past—that's the same way wars are sold.

And as far as the guarantee of riches that lures landowners such as the Mooneys or Mike Jennings into the fracking camp, it seems many of these promises never materialize or unravel soon after a contract is signed. Some even report that because of reclassification of their land as an industrial zone, leasing to a gas company has wound up costing them money.

I hold my opinion in check for now, adhering to the facts, hoping that the evidence will speak for itself. My message is that despite the promises of riches, and the appeal to patriotism, Blue Ridge Energy Corporation is in Madison County primarily to make a profit and that the local culture, the environment, and property rights will all be at risk if they are given a free hand. I emphasize the last of these by detailing the seizure of land through eminent domain, using the Runnion property as an example.

I learned that this is indeed legal under the auspices of the Natural Gas Act of 1938. At the time, nobody could have foreseen the huge number of pipelines necessary to accommodate hydraulic fracturing. By design, eminent domain is to be used as sparingly as possible, but in most recent cases, government regulators are ruling in favor of the gas companies.

Blue Ridge Energy Corporation can swoop in with heavy machinery, carve up Walnut Hollow, pay what they decide is fair compensation, and the federal government will back them up. Another example of the unholy union of industry and government, which is not just a threat to Walnut Creek, but to the United States, and the whole world.

I'll keep that judgment out of the discussion, for now. I believe that the possibility of having their land appropriated by eminent domain will be alarming enough to the county landowners.

Happy with what I've written and before I yield to the temptation to say too much, I email the file to the *Herald*, Walnut Creek's weekly newspaper. I hope the editor remains as enthusiastic about my article as she was when I discussed it with her on the phone.

I glance at the clock to see that it's just past eight, time to make my way to the bowl shop for the morning shift. I'm a little late, but I was determined to get this article on it's way this morning. I pour another cup of coffee and walk the path to the building, trying to refocus my thinking, which has been in a whirl since Julian stopped in. I'm a bowl maker again, and hopefully can pick up where I left off yesterday.

As I reach the door, I hear a discordant sound against the usual background noises, a siren. The wail of an emergency vehicle is unusual on this road, so it always catches me off guard. It sounds faintly from a distance, fades to nothing, and then sounds again, the result of the circuitous path the vehicle is following along the creek. It will be another minute before it comes by here, so I place one foot on a walnut log and wait, coffee in hand.

Most likely it's a medical vehicle from the Mission Hospital outpost on the other side of Walnut Creek, racing back here for someone who needs transport to the hospital in Asheville. The siren sounds louder, probably rounding the bend at Lee Ramsey Road, and only seconds away now. Here it comes around the curve and across the bridge.

Such a bizarre spectacle on Walnut Creek Road, this large van, racing by, siren blaring, lights flashing, sights and sounds that are commonplace in a city, but very out of place here in the valley. The wail becomes deafening, and then quickly fades as the vehicle passes and accelerates up the road.

I anticipate the noise, waxing and waning again as the van winds its way up Walnut Mountain, but just as I step toward the shop, I realize that the sound of the siren is reverberating through the valley differently than usual.

I walk to the road and look toward the mountain. The vehicle isn't visible, but I can tell that it's turned north. While I'm estimating the distance and speculating as to where it might have turned, the siren stops, and an uneasy feeling comes over me. From the auditory cues and considering the time lapse, a good guess would be the Runnion property.

Even if my deduction is right, there's nothing I can do, so I return to the shop and situate myself at the hewing bench. Focusing on the walnut bowl I started yesterday, I make a few light cuts with the adze, but I'm distracted again, wondering why I'm not hearing the siren, sounding the medical van's return trip.

I lay my tool down and step outside. As I gaze up the valley in the direction of Walnut Hollow, I notice Ben crossing the road at a hurried gait. He seems to have guessed my thoughts because he gets right to the point.

"It was Adam Runnion. Edna just called me. She heard from his cousin, Cora. Said there was nothing they could do; he was dead when they got there."

"Ah, I'm sorry to hear that, Ben, but I was afraid this was about him."

"Probably a heart attack, but who knows. He was doing poorly. Patricia found him slumped over in his chair. Cora says he's been all worked up over this pipeline they plan to put through

Walnut Hollow."

"Damn them. They're doing that for spite, Ben. It's something that's not even necessary and look what's happened."

"I know what you're saying, I had the same thoughts myself, but what can you do? Nobody has the money to fight . . . Oh look, here comes the hearse."

I turn to see a black Cadillac Escalade with tinted windows cruising toward us. Ben raises his hand as the vehicle passes and we watch in silence as the hearse continues up Walnut Creek Road.

"Lordy, lordy, the ranks of we old timers are thinning."

I smile and turn to look at Ben and as I do, another dark vehicle approaches, a black Porsche. The car slows to a stop and the window comes down to reveal Don Oldsmar, staring in a condescending manner. He says nothing and after a few seconds, he looks forward and drives on.

"Now what do you suppose that was all about? What did I ever do to him? That's the fella that works for the gas company, right?"

"Yeah, Don Oldsmar, and I think his stare was for me."

"Why, what did you do?"

"I think it's more about what I won't do. He wanted me to do some writing for Blue Ridge Energy Corporation and I turned down the offer."

"Well that's your choice, but it don't call for him giving you a look like that. Do you suppose he knows Adam passed away?"

"Wouldn't surprise me if does, and I doubt that he feels any remorse or empathy. Probably feels he's gaining the upper hand with one of the Runnions out of the way. Oldsmar's a snake in the grass, Ben."

"Well, he wouldn't gain an upper hand if he'd come up against Adam back in the day. He'd more than likely been run out of town on a rail, maybe tarred and feathered to boot."

"Julian's there in Walnut Hollow. I think Oldsmar will meet his match in him, especially now."

"I don't know much about Julian; he's kept to himself over

the years, but I hope you're right. Anyway, I'm headed up to Edna's now. I'll let you know if I hear anything else."

Ben walks away, and I decide to stroll along the creek, having lost my enthusiasm for hewing bowls at the moment. Two deaths within a week, Buzz Griffin and Adam Runnion separated by a thousand miles, and yet the lives of both men affected in a negative way by Lawrence Khan. How many thousands or millions of lives have been disrupted or ruined by the avarice of this one greedy man?

Hasn't history taught despots like him anything? People will only be kept down for so long before they rise up and fight for their rights, and if enough do it at the same time, his wealth and power will mean nothing.

I meander along the path, searching among the rivulets in the water for answers. Before I reach the poplar tree, the hearse, cruises by on its return trip. Adam Runnion's struggles in this world are over and I suppose that he's fortunate in that he will not have to deal with the trouble that's come to Walnut Creek.

29

The Walnut Creek funeral home has a chapel within the building, and I'm sitting alone in the next to the last pew of about fifteen rows. Adam Rector's body is lying in a casket at the front, next to the pulpit. I can't see him clearly from this angle except to note that he's wearing a suit too, something that I suspect is as unusual for him as it is for me.

And such apparel is probably even more uncommon for Julian who's wearing a jacket that appears a bit tight, making him seem stiff and uncomfortable. He's sitting in the first pew, Cody is on his left and Patricia is sitting to his right, dressed in black, her head bowed down.

I've only spoken to her briefly since her father's death, the day after, when I went to the Runnion farm to offer my condolences. There were a number of people there, mostly family, and she was busy and distracted. Some of those people I recognize here today, seated on the right side of the chapel in the pews behind Adam's children.

The pall bearers are seated on the left, a mixed crew of men of whom Jerry Dale and Lamont Greely are the only ones I recognize.

The last funeral I attended was in Afghanistan, and that was for Mahmud's family: his son, Habib, his sister Parisa, and his father, Abdullah. Funerals are not so drawn out or elaborate in that country as they are here, and there's no viewing before the

176

funeral.

In accordance with Islamic law, the bodies are washed, wrapped in a shroud and buried as soon as possible. In the case of the Safi family this was the day after the ill-fated wedding. The burial site in the cemetery outside of Gardez was marked simply by three mounds of earth, topped with smooth, round stones.

The funeral director asks that we form a line, leading to the front to pay our final respect to the deceased and to offer our condolences to the family. I take my place after the line is well formed, and as I shuffle toward the front, I make the most of it, observing the other participants in this sad drama.

It's not a capacity crowd but a good turnout for a Wednesday afternoon in July. Old and young, male and female, all simple country folks, taking time out of their lives to observe the passing of their crusty old neighbor from Walnut Creek.

When I come up to the casket, I note that Adam looks quite dead, but he also appears peaceful and at rest, in spite of the suit. I share a firm handshake with Julian and a gentle one with a tiny woman beside him, Adam's older sister who has lived in Florida for many years.

When I face Patricia, I'm struck with how thin and fatigued she looks, and yet at the same time, how pretty she is. I hug her and she pulls me close, hanging on for a moment. She whispers to me before we let go.

"Ira, are you going to the cemetery?"

"I hadn't really planned on it. I thought that would be a family thing."

"Please do go. I want to ride with you."

"Okay, then I'm planning on it."

Patricia attempts to smile, but she can't unmask the sadness and anxiety. I actually hadn't even planned on staying for the service, but return to my seat now as the last of the mourners files past the casket.

Willard Lacey, the pastor of Walnut Creek Baptist Church moves to the pulpit while an organist plays the opening hymn,

Blessed Assurance. I remember this wonderful old tune from those summer days when I went to church with my relatives. The scripture passage that follows is familiar to me, too, and Pastor Lacey recites it without looking down at his bible.

"For I am convinced that neither death nor life, neither angels nor demons, neither the present nor the future, nor any powers, neither height nor depth, nor anything else in all creation, will be able to separate us from the love of God."

Another hymm follows, *Amazing Grace*, listed in the program as a hymn of comfort, and indeed it is to me. I can still hear Grandmother and Aunt Emma singing the words:

> Through many dangers, toils and snares
> I have already come;
> Tis Grace that brought me safe thus far,
> and Grace will lead me home.

In his eulogy, Pastor Lacey does his best to make a case for Adam's entrance into heaven, not such an easy task considering that he hasn't been to church since his wife died, and from what I've heard, could be quite scornful of the Walnut Creek Baptist Church. I listen for a few minutes and then let my thoughts drift, gazing out an open window to the hillside behind the funeral home. The foliage is in full bloom, and the aroma of summer is intoxicating.

I drift back to those summers when Amy and I would pass many hours of the day, playing in the woods near her house. All children should be so fortunate as to pass so many hours of their youth in the woods of Madison County. I awake from my reverie when the organist leads into the final hymn, another old favorite: *Near the Cross.* After all the years, I still know the words.

When the service ends, Julian, Cody, Patricia and the rest of Adam's family move to the lobby to speak with people as they exit, so I linger until last. When I enter the lobby, Patricia approaches me and takes my arm in hers. She breathes out a melancholy sigh as we exit the building, and I place my hand on hers in response. We make our way through the parking lot and heads turn as we pass. Those who are unfamiliar with the situation might presume we're a couple, a married couple, even.

I've wondered in these latter years what it would have been like to have lived a normal life. That is, got married in a traditional fashion to someone like Patricia, raised children, and pursued a conventional occupation. Such thinking has particularly crossed my mind since I've returned to Walnut Creek and pass so much of my time in reflection.

I wonder if I lost more than I gained by wandering out into the world, seeking answers to life's questions. Sometimes the answers I came up with were more complicated than the questions.

I maneuver the jeep into line, and move with the procession out of the parking lot, turning east onto Main Street. The windows are down and the temperature is ideal. Patricia stares out her window, seemingly absorbed in the scenery until she turns to speak, surprising me with what she's thinking.

"Ira, I'm worried about Julian. I haven't seen him like this in a long time. He blames Oldsmar for Dad's death. I'm afraid he's going to do something crazy."

"Like what?"

"Like beat him up. He'll do it. He did time once for fighting. He was younger then, but I haven't seen him this mad in years. Julian has a bad temper, all the Runnion men do for that matter. The difference with him is he holds things in and lets them fester until he blows up. Then he's likely to kill someone. I think that's one reason he keeps to himself, so that people can't aggravate him.

I'm just glad that Oldsmar didn't pull some fool publicity stunt like showing up at the funeral and making like he cares about what happened to Dad. Julian would have taken him apart and probably be on his way to jail right now."

"No, that wouldn't help at all; it would play right into their hands in fact. Oldsmar would have a legal team waiting in the wings that would rake Julian over the coals, and they'd probably get Walnut Hollow in the end.

I'll talk to Julian, if you think it will help."

"Ira, I'm sure it would help. Julian respects you and he trusts you. You could have lived anywhere you wanted to in the world, but you came here to Walnut Creek because you like it here. And you didn't build a fancy house on a hill, like Oldsmar. You bought a little house in the valley, a house that once belonged to people we knew and liked.

You're not here to change Madison County; you came to be part of it. Julian values that even if he doesn't think of it that way or say it out loud."

"Thank you for telling me, because I didn't really think of it that way either. I just did what felt right for me, and I'll do my best with Julian. There are other ways to deal with Oldsmar and his kind besides fighting."

The motorcade, meanders along Walnut Creek Road, in the direction of the Runnion property, slowing the usual road traffic to an appropriate and respectful speed. Familiar sights seem different from the viewpoint of a funeral procession, something I sense even in looking over my own homestead as we pass by.

Buddhism teaches that existence is transient, that all possessions are impermanent, and it's our attachment to life and property that causes unhappiness. A funeral gives us the perspective to see the truth in this concept.

We turn left onto Runnion Lane, and soon pass the stone house, where the fallen patriarch of the family will abide no more. The procession makes another left onto the trail that leads to the cemetery and to the grave that awaits Adam, between his wife, Florence, and his son, Samuel.

The hearse pulls up near the gate, and we park in a semicircle in the pasture nearby. At the other end of the field, cattle scarcely look up from their grazing, seemingly unperturbed by this unusual occurrence.

Bible in hand, Pastor Lacey walks ahead of the coffin as it's carried to the gravesite. The pallbearers place it within a chrome tubular frame, upon taut straps that span the grave. A push pole tent shelters the area, and folding chairs, placed in two rows alongside the grave, seat the immediate family and elderly members of the assemblage. The rest of us file in behind, I at the rear with the pallbearers, our backs toward Walnut Creek Road.

Pastor Lacey welcomes us from the other side of the grave with a benevolent smile and opens his bible. The passage he reads is appropriate to the occasion as well as the setting.

"The Lord is my shepherd; I shall not want. He maketh me to lie down in green pastures, he leadeth me beside the still waters."

Pastor Lacey pauses, allowing us time to consider the pertinence of his words. A sudden breeze bends the meadow grass and stirs the leaves of the overhanging boughs. In the stillness that follows, the sound of truck engines can be heard emanating from somewhere down the valley. As the pastor begins to speak again, the sound increases in volume, until it's enough to be a distraction.

Judging by the noise, a number of large vehicles are moving along Walnut Creek Road. The road is visible from our vantage point, and although a quarter mile away, when the convoy comes into view, the commotion causes heads to turn, and compels Pastor Lacey to pause in his speech. I turn to see trucks on the road, two of them are enormous and laden with what looks like parts of a drilling rig. The others are loaded with pipe.

What bad timing, for this particular fleet to go by, just as Adam Runnion is being laid to rest, and to interrupt his funeral, no less. One could almost construe it as a bad omen for the future of Walnut Hollow, following the death of it's patriarch.

A dozen trucks go by and before they are out of sight, engine brakes add to the din, which seems unwarranted considering that the convoy is moving slowly, and Walnut Creek Road runs straight along this section.

Would Oldsmar have orchestrated something like this to annoy the Runnion family at a time when they are most vulnerable? Is this a case of bad timing or devious planning? I can't let myself

181

entertain such a notion. My anger would know no bounds if I were convinced of it. As the final truck rolls past and the noise is receding, I put such thoughts out of my head and focus on the reason we are here.

After the interruption, the faces of the crowd reveal a variety of emotions, from confusion to anger. Pastor Lacey speaks again in a calm, measured voice, trying to restore dignity to the occasion. Patricia's eyes are closed as she listens to the clerics words, and her expression is calm and pensive.

I look past Patricia to her brother who is staring straight ahead, eyes fixed on his father's coffin. His face is red and his jaw is set. I presume that he's struggling to suppress the same emotions as I am except to a greater degree, and as his sister warned, holding them in, letting them fester, until he blows up.

30

Tommy Gosnell reminds me of Ahmad Shah Massoud. The curiosity in his eyes as he listens to what I say and the concentration on his face while he speaks is reminiscent of that extraordinary Afghan commander.

"America is a house of cards built on a house of cards, and it's only a question of time before it all collapses. It may not happen all at once, but it's going to happen. Let's face it, it's already happening. The last recession, the so called, *Great Recession* was a symptom of the collapse.

People can't find good jobs, they're getting further in debt all the time, and losing their homes to foreclosure. Meanwhile, the billionaires globetrot in their private jets and hobnob with the politicians they've bought and paid for."

Tommy is holding up a walnut bowl and studying it intently as he speaks. He showed up unexpectedly, wearing his *Old Tom* garb, and we hadn't been talking long when he began to articulate his politics.

"Used to be, common people had some measure of prosperity and liberty, but now the greed of the wealthy knows no bounds; they want it all. There's a great money grab taking place, encouraged by the way the bankers fleeced America with their mortgage scheme. They not only got away with it, but were rewarded for it with government bailouts.

We're in the age of billionaires, all psychopaths as far as I'm concerned. They have no regard for the wellbeing or rights of common people because power and money is all that matters to them. They don't care if people are dying in the streets, so long as they're not doing it too close to their gated community."

"Now, Tommy, not all billionaires are so bad. Some give a great deal of money to philanthropic causes."

"Bullshit, all they do is brush some crumbs off their tables, from time to time, to the masses down below. Compared to what they've got, they're not giving anything. The investment banker or the coal baron donates a portion of the money that's been swindled from the public and we're expected to kiss their feet and name a library after them.

We've been pretty much left alone over the years, but now they're here in Madison County to swindle us. The easy energy reserves are used up, so now they're blowing up mountains to get coal, and cracking shale a mile down to get gas.

I read your article in the Herald, by the way. I like it, like it a lot, and I learned a great deal. I hope everybody in the county reads it." 'Fracking', I heard the word before, but didn't know exactly what was involved. I never worried about it because it wasn't happening here."

"That's the word all right, Tommy, hydraulic fracturing, the darling of the industry. It spread out of Texas like a cancer, devastating Colorado and in recent years, has turned rural Pennsylvania into an industrial zone. Now it's coming here.

Other countries get invaded with soldiers and bombs; in this country we're invaded by corporations and their lawyers. The end result is the same, the local people end up losing while corporate suits and their lackeys make out like bandits."

"Yes, bandits, that's exactly what they are. Would you believe their mouthpiece, the white-haired guy on the hill, makes a million bucks a year, doing what he does?"

"Don Oldsmar, you mean?"

"Yes, Oldsmar, a million dollars a year for hoodwinking people. There are hardworking farmers in this valley who don't make fifty thousand a year, and that son of a bitch makes twenty times that with just cheap talk."

"How do you know that, if you don't mind me asking?"

"He's a big mouth and so are some of the people around him. Whether he knows it or not, everybody's listening and eventually word gets back."

"Hmm, that makes me wonder what word has gotten back about me."

"Ha ha, nothing that I didn't already know. I feel we're fortunate that someone with your reputation and skills came here at a pivotal time like this."

"Well thank you, I appreciate that. What makes this time pivotal, the arrival of Blue Ridge Energy Corporation?"

"Yes, the gas company, encroaching on our lives is the problem, and the government backing them up is an even bigger threat. With this eminent domain thing they pulled on Adam, the government is acting on behalf of Blue Ridge Energy, not on behalf of citizens.

We don't live in a democracy. Our political system is legalized bribery, a system that serves the wealthy, while the rest of us get handed a bunch of propaganda and lies. But I don't need to tell you this; you know better than I do. I've read what you've written."

"I know what might happen here, and I admit, I don't like the looks of things so far, but it hasn't happened yet. If we're vigilant and proactive, and I keep as many people informed of the truth as possible, I believe that most people will sympathize with our situation.

Hopefully that sympathy will translate into the public standing with us. If enough people are willing to say no than there isn't a corporation or government that can exert it's will, no matter how much money or power they have behind them."

"I agree, and that's why I'm glad you're here. If anyone can bring people together on this, it's you. I hope that's what happens. But the problem is, it takes time to get people together, and Blue Ridge Energy is moving hard and fast. Some parts of the county don't even know they're here yet, and up the road they're already setting up rigs. Julian learns what fracking is one day and within weeks their claiming a right-of-way through Walnut Hollow.

If we can't gain public support soon enough to stop the drilling, then we'll stop it our way."

"What do you mean by that, physically deter them?

"They push, we push back."

"You're prepared to do it?"

"Yes, we can do it. I have a well trained army under my command and I have good officers around me."

"But how far are you willing to go if trouble comes? Are you talking about resistance, a standoff, or an actual military confrontation?"

"I hope that resistance is all that will be necessary, but we're prepared to go all out if it comes to that. When I first took over the militia I saw it as a carrying on a tradition of my ancestors, and it was a way to help me come to terms with what happened in Vietnam. I never thought we would need to defend our rights or our land against the government.

After what happened at Ruby Ridge in 1992, I thought differently. That's when I intensified the training and began preparing for a fight with the government."

"I know the basic story of Ruby Ridge, but I don't remember the details anymore."

"Randy Weaver was set up on a weapons charge by an undercover ATF agent. When they came to arrest him, there was a siege and his wife, his son, and the family dog were killed, along with a federal agent.

"ATF, the Bureau of Alcohol Tobacco and Firearms, right?"

"Yes, they started it, set Randy Weaver up, then the FBI and Federal Marshalls took it from there.

Then, even as the Weaver trial was under way, the holocaust in Waco, Texas happened. Remember Waco, David Koresh and the Branch Davidians? Eighty people died, including twenty-six children. The lead agency in the assault was, you guessed it, the Bureau of Alcohol Tobacco and Firearms. Once again, the FBI, determined to make an arrest with a show of force, ended it.

Both were initiated by the ATF, based on weapons charges, and in both cases the FBI deployed military equipment against American citizens."

"And you think that could happen here?"

"I think it could happen anywhere. I was no fan of David Koresh and I wouldn't want Randy Weaver over for dinner, but they were American citizens, minding their own business on their own land, and they didn't deserve to be attacked and killed by the government."

Tommy returns the bowl to the pedestal and picks up a cherry bowl, hewn from the wood that Julian and I retrieved from Walnut Hollow. At some level, I can't believe what I'm hearing, but I have no doubt that the Field Commander is serious about what he's saying.

As I study his face in profile, I'm struck again with the resemblance between him and Massoud. As he raises the bowl to study it near the window, he turns and meets my gaze.

"Why are you looking at me like that, Ira. You think I'm a madman, don't you?"

"No, I don't think you're a madman. You remind me of someone I once knew, Ahmad Shah Massoud, a Mujahedin commander in Afghanistan."

"I know of him. I remember when he was killed, because it was right before nine-eleven. Is that right?"

"Yes, on September 9, 2001, Al-Qaida operatives, posing as journalists, set off a bomb, hidden in a camera, and killed Massoud. Osama Bin Laden once said that as long as Massoud lives, the war cannot be won. Two days after Massoud was killed the United States came under attack.

"And you knew Massoud personally?"

"Yes, I spent some time with him the year before his death, when he was fighting the Taliban. He was already famous by then because of his nine year fight against the Soviet Union. Many analysts believe that it was his resistance that ultimately ended that war. Despite being outnumbered and outgunned, throughout the entire campaign, Massoud consistently managed to win against long odds.

He was known as the Lion of Panjshir, after the Panjshir valley where he was born and where he fought."

"And he was fighting the Taliban when you were with him?"

"Yes, he served as the leader of the United Islamic Front who rejected the Taliban's fundamentalist interpretation of Islam. Massoud hated the extremism of the Taliban as much as he did the totalitarianism of the Soviet Union.

I was fortunate to have spent time with Massoud and the experience has affected me ever since. He once said to me, 'we're not only fighting for a free Afghanistan but for a free world'."

"My goodness, what a man he must have been. I need to learn more about him. It must have come as a shock to you when he was killed."

"Yes it was. I think about it still. I was in Paris when I heard the news of his death and I called a friend of mine, a photographer named Aamir Sadi. Aamir knew Massoud well because he spent time with him during the war against the Soviets, and he was there again in 2000.

I said, I'm calling because I hope to learn that this news isn't true. 'It is true', Aamir said, 'but it's okay. Now we are all Massoud'."

"*Now we are all Massoud,* I like that. And I can relate to what Massoud said to you, that he was not only fighting for a free Afghanistan but for a free world. That's sums up the way I feel about Backbone Mountain Militia. We're ready to fight if our freedom is being threatened, but in a way, we're making a stand for everyone who wants to be free.

Anyway, Ira, I've taken up enough of your time and need to be moving along. Thanks for the conversation; I've learned a lot.

I like your shop and your work. If I didn't know better, I'd swear you had always been a bowl maker instead of a writer, but, I'm glad you're still a writer, too. I'm going to make your article in the Herald required reading for all the men. I'm glad you're here, Ira."

"Thanks, Tommy. I'm glad I'm here, too.

31

"**A**re you kidding me; you've never hung drywall before? I thought all guys hang drywall."

"Nope, not kidding. I guess I'm one of the few guys in the world who doesn't. I never really had a place before to hang any. I've lived mostly in apartments or motels. How did you acquire your building skills?"

"Right after Donny and I were married, we bought a house that needed lot's of work and we did it ourselves. Then we added on to it over the years. Donny's family has as many builders in it as farmers, so we had plenty of help and advice when we needed it. I would never have taken on this project if I hadn't done that with him."

Patricia and I are working on the log house in Walnut Hollow, her great-great-great-grandparents house. When she informed me that she had put her home in Tennessee on the market and was moving to the family farm full time, I volunteered my services. Now I'm learning to hang drywall under the tutelage of a very patient instructor.

"So, Ira, how do you like living here in Walnut Creek, now that you're well settled in?"

"I like everything about it; living here is everything I had hoped for. The only problem is this Oldsmar character and the gas drilling operation. Everything was looking good until he entered the picture. I sometimes wonder how I was so unlucky that this would happen just after I move here. Then other times, I think that maybe it's why I arrived here now, to use what skills I have to help fight it.

Throughout my career, I tried to remain as objective as possible in describing the events I was observing. I can't say I always adhered to that policy, but I did my best. Believe me, there were many occasions when I wanted to take sides, even to the extent of picking up a gun and joining the fight on the side I believed in."

"And now you can."

"Yes, now I can."

"Well, I hope it doesn't come to that. I don't want to fight, and I don't want you to fight. But if there is one, I hope it's just with words and at the worst, in court.

I've known about Backbone Mountain Militia since I young, but I never really imagined them actually fighting. To me it was just an extension of the hunting club, a bunch of guys that got together and trained, to carry on a tradition. I do know that it changed when Tommy took over. In fact Tommy changed a lot of things on The Land, besides the militia."

"Really? He told me that he reformed the Militia but we didn't discuss much about The Land in general."

"He really just changed things back to the way they used to be. That's what my father always said, and Dad, by the way, was behind Tommy's ideas, one hundred percent.

The Runnions that first settled here were self sufficient, which was fairly typical back then, especially in places like this. As times changed, most goods could be bought and jobs away from the farm became more common, but the Runnions didn't change with the times. The more they relied on the outside the less independent they were, and staying independent was more important, even if it meant having to work harder for less money.

Grandpa Julian epitomized that way of thinking best when he planted the walnut trees in the hollow. They were planted to ensure that we could always have a way to make a living right here, with our own two hands.

But in recent generations, people let go of the old ways, and became more dependent on machines and supermarkets. For whatever reason, because of what happened in Vietnam or from all the books he reads, Tommy started pushing for reviving the old ways and making The Land self sufficient.

Nearly everybody farms to some degree and what's grown or what animals are raised is planned ahead so there's not so much overlap. What's produced can be shared or bartered for, and any excess is given to the older folks or people that can't farm for whatever reason."

"What you're describing to me sounds like a communal type arrangement. Is that right?"

"Y-yes, I've thought that myself, especially in recent years, although that's never how it's talked about here."

"Tommy didn't mention any of this."

"He probably didn't want to lay too much on you at once. Backbone Mountain Militia was enough. Were you surprised when you found out about it?"

"Yes, I certainly was, especially when I found out it was right up the road from me. If someone had given me that information before I moved here, I might have reconsidered this location. I didn't move here for that; I moved here to get away from that.

But am I surprised that people are prepared to protect what's rightfully theirs? No, I've experienced it before. Sooner or later it happens anywhere. However, based on my experience in other countries, I hope that all this militia will ever do is train."

"I agree, but I can't say I really see the point of all the training. What threat would require that kind of preparation?" Do you think what's happening now, with Blue Ridge Energy Corporation, has the makings of an armed conflict? These days, something like this is settled in court, not by guns."

"Yes, that's the way it should be, but suppose the courts are corrupt, bought out by the corporation and the local law enforcement is on the take, too. What if it comes to a point that they try to take The Land by force."

"That couldn't happen here."

"Sooner or later it happens anywhere. Let's just suppose that's the case."

"Then I don't think it could be stopped by force. I don't care how much Tommy and Julian train, this is the real world we're up against now. They wouldn't stand a chance of stopping something like that with guns."

"Patricia, I admit, the odds would be long, and there's no way they could win an all out fight, but they wouldn't have to win. The corporation and the government would have to win because they would be the aggressors. All Backbone Mountain Militia has to do is resist, just hold their ground and let public opinion build in their favor."

"And would it."

"I believe it would, if people are properly informed. And that would be my job, to see that they are."

"I think I understand, but I don't entirely agree. Let's not talk about it anymore. I just want to work on the house today and have fun. We'll worry about the war later, okay?"

"Okay, I agree. I'm shutting my mouth and focusing on drywall. How am I doing boss?"

"Good, especially for a beginner. I say we finish this corner and then break for lunch."

"Agreed."

High up the slope behind the cabin in an open area that affords us a view of the surrounding countryside, we spread a blanket alongside the remains of an ancient rail fence, almost hidden amid the vegetation. Patricia packed lunch in a wicker picnic basket that she said has been in her family as long as she could remember.

I gaze about a sunbathed landscape, enjoying uninterrupted vistas that are impossible from my homestead in the bottom land. Patricia points out the location of the cemetery, which from this distance looks like any other tree-covered hill.

"When I was little, my cousins and I loved to play in the

193

graveyard. We were never scared even though sometimes we purposely tried to scare ourselves. I think it was because we knew they were all family and they would never do anything to scare us or hurt us. Mom and Dad seemed to like us being up there, too. It was easy for them to keep tabs on us and yet we were at a distance, so they could still get some work done."

"There's something charming about children playing among the graves of their ancestors. I think the deceased would love it."

"Do you have a family cemetery, Ira?"

"Oh, no, there aren't many of those in Charlotte. My family has a plot in a huge cemetery, acres and acres of graves in all directions. We had no desire to play there as children, and it even spooks me now when I go back there. I plan to be cremated and that place helped me come to the decision."

"What will you have done with your ashes?"

"I don't know. I haven't really decided yet, but nothing fancy. Maybe my ashes could be used for some practical purpose like adding them to a compost pile. Actually, I haven't given it serious thought, although I guess I should start thinking about it. And what are your burial plans, Patricia, if I may ask?"

"Actually I have been pondering that very question, lately, and I've decided I want to be buried here with my family, next to Mom and Dad and Samuel. I always thought I would be buried with Donny, but I also assumed that we would grow old together, not that he would die so many years before me. And I also felt that our children would stay closer to home, that there would be grandchildren one day, but that hasn't happened.

I guess in my mind, Donny and I were to be the founders of a new family and rest at the center of our own family cemetery, with great grandchildren laughing and playing among the tombstones."

"Where are your children, Patricia?"

"Jesse is in Davis, California and Laura is in Washington, DC. They both flew from the nest early and never looked back. I don't know if that would have been any different if there father had lived, but at any rate, I find myself living in a town where my only family are in-laws. We all get along well enough and I'm actually very close to one of Donny's sisters, but it's still not like family. As cranky as Dad could be at times and as stubborn as Julian is, I still felt a pull back to the farm.

But that's it, I'm going to stop talking."

"No, don't do that. I like hearing you talk."

"Yes, but neither of us are eating. I prepared this potato salad the way my mother taught me when I was young and the ham in these sandwiches is from our hogs. Julian cured it last fall."

"Then let's eat. I'm actually quite hungry. This drywall hanging is hard labor; it really works up a workman's appetite."

"You're doing well. I think you're a natural at it."

"Really?"

"Uh, no, not really, but you're better than average. I'm on a budget here, and you get what you pay for."

"Oh is that so? And what's the pay?"

"Homemade potato salad and ham sandwiches."

"Ha ha, okay, it's a deal. Let's eat."

Patricia starts to spoon potato salad on to a plate and then turns toward me with a wistful expression.

"Ira, do you think you'll stay here in the valley, in spite of the drilling, I mean even if there is trouble?"

"If you're staying, I'm staying."

"Good, that's what I wanted to know."

32

The slow, winding, drive along Walnut Creek Road is particularly enjoyable on summer days such as this when I have the windows down and take in the scents as well as the sights. Of course, I only have to travel a few miles either way. Those who live further up the valley don't seem to find a slow, unhurried ride so enjoyable and rarely adhere to the designated speed limit of forty-five miles an hour. They're anxious to get to a job or in a hurry to get home from one and rush up from behind to disturb my reverie.

Experience and observation have taught me, however that there is a lull in traffic in the hours just after lunch, and that is when I venture to the grocery store. This strategy nearly always works and it has today for most of the journey. I made it all the way to Robinson's with no one coming up from behind, and I'm nearly home with no interruption.

I'm lost along the way, in thoughts of my drywall tutelage. Since Patricia has moved to Walnut Hollow, my life has been enriched in every way. How I love her! I thought I was too old and cantankerous to feel this way again.

The problem, seeping into the valley were easily held at bay while we leaned against that grand old maple tree, holding each other, reveling in the moment. Now I'm more determined then before to tackle this problem, and to do so in a peaceful way, with the pen, not the sword.

I'm not going to let these outsiders spoil this valley and interfere with the lives of we who live here. I must become more proactive in my writing and reach a wider audience, nationwide and worldwide. The trick is to stay ahead of them, and be prepared to thwart them at every turn.

Damn it, look at this coming now. A quarter mile to go, and a truck, racing up from behind. I no sooner spot the vehicle and it's already catching up with me as I turn into the driveway. The driver is not even slowing down to let me pull in, but is moving to pass despite double lines.

Then brakes are applied with force, the truck screeches to a halt and backs up to my driveway. Lamont Greely exits the vehicle, leaving the engine running. He's not wearing his characteristic grin, but instead exhibits an angry, worried countenance.

"Lamont, what's wrong?"

"Ira, goddamn it, there's a standoff in Walnut Hollow. Cody called me. Some boys come down the hill, surveying a route for a pipeline, and Julian stopped them with a shotgun. Some of them are carrying guns, too. You want to come up with me?"

"Yes, I sure do. I'll just grab my camera here and let's go."

I take the camera from the seat of the jeep and hurry to Lamont's truck. As soon as I shut the passenger door, he accelerates and races along Walnut Creek Road. At Runnion Lane, he slows out of necessity, but speeds up again after we cross the bridge, kicking up gravel in the vehicle's wake.

Adam Runnion's house appears vacant and forlorn as we drive past with no dogs appearing to greet us, the pack having been dispersed among family members. Patricia's car is not at the log cabin as we race by, but her house is vibrant and alive, with flowerbeds abloom and potted plants lining the porch.

Fifty yards past Julian's cabin, a number of vehicles are visible within the walnut grove. Lamont goes off the road toward them, and I see a group of men, just beyond the trucks, standing near Runnion Branch. I recognize Julian, Cody, Jerry Dale, and Tim

Ramsey, but there are a number of faces that aren't familiar to me.

As Lamont and I walk toward them, Julian is talking loudly to the other men, all of whom exhibit consternation on their faces to varying degrees. Only Jerry Dale seems unruffled in the face of whatever took place. He has a composed, almost businesslike expression as he listens to his cousin.

"I'll be goddamned if they're going to just walk on in here and mark off part of Walnut Hollow for a pipeline."

"You knew they were coming Julian, you saw that letter they sent your dad."

"I know I saw that letter, Jerry Dale, but I guess I couldn't believe that something like this could really happen. Hey, Ira, Greely, welcome to the party."

"What happened, Jules?"

"Survey crew come down over the hill, marking a path for a pipeline. I seen them from my front porch while I was sitting there putting my boots on. I grabbed the shotgun and stopped them right here. Turns out, a couple of them had guns, too."

"Do surveying crews usually carry weapons?"

"No, Ira, usually never, maybe somebody carrying a pistol for protection against animals if they're way back somewhere. These guys seemed a little hesitant to use theirs, especially with a shotgun pointed at them. And when Jerry Dale and Tim pulled up, they got that look of a deer caught in the headlights.

They said they were just doing their job and I told them right back that I was just doing mine, too. A couple more trucks pulled up at that point, Jake and Kenny here, and we had them outnumbered and outgunned. They backed off, same way they came down. What's the camera for, Ira?"

"I was hoping to get some pictures of the surveying crew."

"Why's that?"

"Because I've been doing some thinking about this and we have to let more people know what's happening here and let them know soon. We need as much support as possible if we're to have any hope of standing up to these people, and nothing tells the story better than pictures."

"Well, hell, I wish I'd a known. I would have had them wait and pose for you."

Julian grins and a few of the other men chuckle, then Cody comes up beside me, holding his phone."

"I got pictures, Mr. Stone. I took pictures of them from the time they pulled their guns until they walked back up the hill. Here, look."

"That's great Cody. Let's see here. Wow, good shots, and this one clearly shows that they were armed. I wouldn't be surprised if these two with the guns were hired for that very reason. We need to get this out on the internet so people will take notice. Maybe somebody will even know these guys."

"What about Facebook?"

"Yes, social media is an avenue I had in mind, but I have to admit, I'm not as knowledgeable about it as I'd like to be. What about you Cody, are you familiar with Facebook?"

"I know some, but I haven't fooled with it, since my girlfriend and I split up. Do you have a computer?"

"That I do. If you want to come by, we can get the ball rolling."

"Why do you think that's so important, Ira."

"Because, Lamont, we have to let as many people as possible know what's happening here. The man behind this thing and his cronies, own the news outlets, so they can paint whatever picture they want. Defending your own property like this can be twisted around to sound like an act of domestic terrorism. With social media the press is bypassed and people will receive the information unfiltered.

The news outlets I publish through reach readers who will be sympathetic to our cause, but it's a small audience, and in a sense, I'm preaching to the choir. We need to reach everyone across the spectrum and let them know what's happening. This isn't about left or right, this is a class war, billionaires infringing on the lives of

199

regular people. Today it's us in Walnut Creek, being oppressed, and unless we can make a stand here and now, everyone will eventually face the same thing in their community."

"Hell yeah, makes sense to me. I think it's a good idea. It's like the way that pamphlets were used in the American Revolution. The internet is the pamphlets of the 21st century. Cody why don't you give Ira a ride back to his house, and you two can talk about it, maybe get the ball rolling."

"Okay, Dad. Last I looked, I had about a hundred and fifty friends on Facebook, so I guess that's a start."

Cody turns into my driveway and parks his truck, a white Chevy Silverado that is obviously an older vehicle. But it runs well, smooth and steady, and the interior is neat and clean, unlike my jeep.

As we enter the house, Cody glances from side to side, surprised, as most people are, at how sparsely furnished it is. My living room furniture consists of a couch, facing the fireplace, a reading lamp, and a small, wooden statue of a hooded monk, resting on a pedestal beneath the lamp.

The room I use for an office is a bit more cluttered, with filing cabinets and the computer desk, taking up half the floor space, while bookshelves and maps line the walls.

Cody takes this all in, but soon focuses on my aging Hewlett Packard. Within minutes he becomes comfortable with the device such that by the time I pour two glasses of tea and pull up a chair, he begins questioning me about how I think a Facebook account should be set up.

"What kind of page do we want? These are the choices, and we need to choose one."

"Hmm, I think this category best describes it: Community or Cause. What we're doing is for both. Don't you think?"

"I guess. What's the name of our community or cause?"

"Let's see, even though our immediate goal is to stop the gas company from constructing a pipeline through Walnut Hollow, I think we should paint a bigger picture here. Ultimately we want to stop gas drilling in the entire valley, so my instincts tells me that we should choose a name to attract a wide audience. How about *The Battle of Walnut Hollow*?"

"Uh, it wasn't exactly a battle."

"No it wasn't, at least not in the sense of an armed conflict, but 'battle' can also be defined as a struggle to achieve something or overcome something, like say, the battle against malaria. What happened today was just the beginning. There are more struggles to come."

"Yeah, you're right. And *struggle to achieve something* doesn't sound too exciting."

"Ha ha, no it doesn't. Headlines are important, and we don't have time to be subtle here. No matter how good the content is, it doesn't amount too much if you don't get people to read it."

"Do you think this will work, I mean to stop them from digging up Walnut Hollow?"

"Social Media can't win causes, Cody, only people can, brave people who stand up for their rights. However, communication through digital channels gives people the ability to communicate, organize, and plan at a level that was unimaginable, in the past. Social media gives us the means to reach a lot of people fast, and this in turn gives us a better chance at stopping them from digging up Walnut Hollow."

"Okay, The Battle of Walnut Hollow it is. What about a description?"

Drawing from articles I've written, I propose a statement about the impact of gas drilling on Madison County, focusing on the surveying incident as a harbinger of what's to come. Cody types as we refine the description to our satisfaction and post it.

For a header image, Cody suggests a picture that was actually an errant shot, taken as he maneuvered his phone to photograph the survey crew. The view is up through the walnut tree canopy, a dark framework of limbs, supporting a luxurious crown of green foliage against a sunlit sky.

There's no hint of the human standoff on the ground below, instead, the image of the sun shining through breaks in the leaves suggests a principle beyond such conflicts.

Cody crops the photograph to the appropriate dimensions, positions the sun above and to the left of the title, and sharpens the image until we're both pleased with the results. After uploading a selection of photos of the armed, survey personnel, I provide captions, describing the face-off in Walnut Hollow. I express disbelief that this can happen, and hope that our efforts will elicit a similar response from the audience.

Cody publishes the page and then logs onto his personal Facebook account to post an entry, which includes a photograph that's linked to the newly constructed page, *The Battle of Walnut Hollow*.

Encouraged by our progress, we proceed to set up a Twitter account. Cody isn't as familiar with the format, but he has little trouble working through the setup.

"Why do you prefer Facebook over Twitter, Cody, if you don't mind me asking?"

"Um, I guess because Facebook is more about keeping up with friends and family, people that you want to keep in touch with. Twitter is more about what you're talking about than who you're talking to. The conversation is about what's happening right at the moment, while Facebook is more of a conversation that can go on for hours or days, and that suits me better. Does that make any sense."

"Yes, I think I understand what you're saying, and I can see the value of both formats for what we're trying to do. From what I've learned so far, I'm more convinced than ever that social media is a route we need to go here. The more people that are aware of what's happening and are getting information as it happens, the less likely we will be misrepresented."

"I just hope it's enough to stop the trouble."

"Any conflict can be averted if enough people stand up and say no at the same time. And that's our best option here, stopping the trouble before it starts. Once back and forth skirmishes get going, even the coolest heads can get drawn into a fight, and things have the potential to spin out of control quickly."

"Were you ever in a fight, Mr. Stone, I mean in a fight where you were shooting at someone and they were shooting back?"

"No not exactly, but I did pick up a gun once and I shot at a helicopter."

"Whoa, was this in a battle? Who were you shooting at?"

"Not a battle, really. I've told few people about this, Cody, so please don't spread it, because I'm not proud of what I did. It was at a wedding celebration in Afghanistan and some good friends of mine were killed by Hellfire Rockets, fired from a helicopter."

"I heard about that. Dad told me about it."

"Oh, okay. Well, I usually leave this part out. I was so enraged about what happened that when the helicopter circled around, I grabbed a gun and shot at it."

"Did you hit it?"

"No, there wasn't much danger of that. It was an old Lee-Enfield rifle that was there as part of the wedding celebration, and I'm not much of a shot anyway. But I tried to hit it; I wanted to. If there had been a rocket launcher, leaning against the wall, I would have grabbed that.

The air strike on the wedding was claimed to be an accident. The military said that they were targeting suspected Taliban militants. Apologies were made; reparations were paid. I suppose it was an accident. But in the heat of the moment, nothing mattered to me except shooting that helicopter out of the sky."

"So you were shooting at Americans? Did you get in any trouble?"

"Ahem, a little. I *was* shooting at Americans, but not military. They were contractors, mercenaries, so making a case against me was a little more complicated. And like I said, I wasn't really a threat to the helicopter with that little gun, it was more the principle of what I did, and they had video to prove it.

There was a stir about it, some mention in the press, and I

was questioned by the military, but no charges were filed. Some of my detractors in Washington and pundits on Fox News wanted my head on a platter, but within weeks, all talk about my role in the incident was snuffed out. I'm still not entirely sure why, but I think it was to avoid having me testify as to what really happened that day."

"Did you?"

"No, I left Afghanistan, so I haven't testified, not yet. I didn't want to talk about war anymore, I wanted out. And I never wanted to feel that way again, so angry and bitter that I wanted to kill someone else in retaliation.

So anyway where were we here?"

"Talking about things spinning out of control."

"Yes, and it won't happen here, Cody, not with you at the keyboard, keeping the world informed."

Cody shrugs and turns his attention back to the computer. We set our Twitter account to follow organizations that are most likely to help spread awareness of our dilemma. I'm fascinated with the process, the idea of composing significant content in one entry with the mandatory limit of one hundred and forty characters. Our first tweet was to ask the Twitter community to follow our organization's account for updates.

Cody leaves at six o'clock turning down an invitation for dinner because he and some friends have plans for the evening. I'm not hungry yet and decided to work on the Twitter account a bit longer. I feel like a kid with a new toy.

I find working and talking to Cody quite enjoyable and look forward to doing more of it. He asked me if I would mind if he would come over and use my computer for personal reasons, and I told him that it was at his disposal, so long as he was willing to continue as a social media consultant. Cody grinned at first, but when he realized I wasn't kidding, he became serious and nodded.

When I do break for supper, I'm upbeat and more hopeful about our prospects than I have been in weeks. Already *The Battle of Walnut Hollow* has received several comments and numerous likes. Tweets are starting to come in from around the country. I can see that digital media is an avenue to a broad swath of the public, left, right, hippies and rednecks. This is what I was hoping for. We're all in this together.

I feel a thrill for journalism that I thought was extinguished. I believe that if we get enough support, the people here in Walnut Creek can make a real stand against Lawrence Khan and aggression need not be part of the picture. If I was indeed drawn here by fate then I want to believe that this is the reason why.

33

"Say, I read your article in the Herald and I thought it was real good. The facts speak for themselves as far as I'm concerned."

"Thanks, Barney. I was hoping that would be the case, but it's good to hear that from you."

Barney Flynn hands me my mail through his open car window. I was sweeping the front porch of the shop and the mailman pulled into the parking area. In spite of my enthusiasm over our digital media efforts, I'm glad to know that my words are getting out the old fashioned way.

"I'll warn you though, there's some people who don't like it so much. I don't want to mention names, but, as you might guess, it's mostly the people that stand to make money from the drilling."

"Well, that's to be expected. I can understand their decision, but it's not right to disrupt the entire community just so a few can benefit."

"I agree, and I'm one of those who isn't going to benefit; I just lose. They're drilling now on the Rathbone farm, up above me. I get noise, diesel fumes, bright lights, and no doubt will have a contaminated well in the end, but no royalty checks. So more power to you if you think you can stop this. I'll raise my voice, use my vote, whatever I can do."

"Thanks, Barney. If everyone did as much, we can stop this."

Barney crosses the road, delivers Ben's mail, and drives on.

I thumb through the letters that he handed me, and stop at a curious envelope, addressed to Wooden Bowl Shoppe, written in a penmanship that is familiar to me. Even without a return address, I know the letter is from Justine, but I'm puzzled by the fact that it was postmarked in Asheville. I open the letter as I enter the building and sit at the hewing bench to read.

Dear Ira,

Please excuse the secrecy, but I feel it's necessary for your sake and for mine. A friend was passing through your area and I ask her to drop this in a mail box near Asheville.

You're drawing attention to yourself there, dear man, with your stand against gas drilling. This information isn't public knowledge; I obtained it through people we know. You've been placed on a domestic terrorist watch list! To me it seems a bit absurd or at least, premature to tag you with that title, but it doesn't take much these days to qualify for the distinction. And, of course, in your case, you do have a history that would prompt such a conclusion.

I know this isn't the first time you've been monitored, but I have an uneasy feeling about it this time. You know the drill, watch your phone calls, emails, and computer searches, because you can assume everything's being scrutinized. Don't write back, please. No more letters after this, but I'll contact you as soon as I learn more.

Love,
Justine

P.S. Hey, I thought you were retired.

I fold the letter and return it to the envelope. Striking a match, and lighting one corner, I hold Justine's note until it's engulfed in flames, and finally toss it into the wood stove. What did I expect? Even if I would have come to Walnut Creek and quietly hewn bowls for the rest of my days, they would still watch me. From the moment

I became a critic of American foreign policy, I've been on their damn lists.

I'm hyped up now, in a mood to write. I'll give them a good reason to put me on a list. First I'll go to Robinson's, to buy something quick for supper and a bottle of wine for later. It's time to write an article for general release and spell out what's happening here, this time, stating my opinion, in no uncertain terms.

As I approach the market, a white pickup truck is on my tail, which is not so surprising, except that this one is riding me unusually close, and it seemed to come out of nowhere. It's only a few feet behind as I slow to turn, and looks all the more menacing because tinted windows give no hint of the occupants.

The truck follows me into the lot, but parks just inside the entrance, while I drive on to the center aisle. Glancing over my shoulder before I enter Robinson's, I see that no one has emerged from the vehicle. Once inside, I convince myself that I'm just being paranoid, and by the time I'm perusing the selection of wine, all but forget about the incident.

As I exit the store, I see that the truck is now parked alongside the jeep. There's a tall man dressed in denim clothes, leaning against the tailgate, reading a newspaper. As I walk toward my vehicle, another person exit's the passenger side of the truck, a neighbor, Don Oldsmar.

"Ira, good to see you again. Funny we keep bumping into each other here at the market. There's something so small-town-like about it. Don't you think?"

The man leaning against the truck snorts at this and begins folding the newspaper.

"You two haven't met, have you? Ira Stone, this is Scott Hagan. Scott works for Blue Ridge Energy, like me. Scott, I'd like to introduce you to Ira Stone, world famous journalist, a Pulitzer Prize winner, no less, and now, he's a just a simple country bowl maker. At least that's what he told me. There, with introductions out of the way, we're just some good old boys, being sociable."

Oldsmar steps aside, leans over the bed of the truck with his back to us, and gazes toward the road, while Scott approaches me holding the folded newspaper against his chest. I recognize a picture I took of a drilling equipment convoy, going by on Walnut Creek Road, a photograph I submitted with the piece I wrote for the Herald. The newspaper has been folded to frame my article.

"I heard you were retired from writing. Isn't that what you told Don, Mr. Stone? You said you just wanted to be a bowl maker. He took you at your word. What's this then, this drivel in the newspaper? This isn't about bowl-making. From what I read, this is an attack on my livelihood and the livelihood of the people that I work with."

"I *am* retired, in the sense that I no longer write for a living, but I made no claim that I would give up writing. I wrote an honest article about hydraulic fracturing because it's information that people in the county should have, and I wrote it on my own time.

What you do for a living is your business, and if you interpret my article as an attack on your livelihood, than there's nothing I can do about it. Sometimes, the truth hurts."

"Well, listen to that. Don. You never told me he was a hard ass, too. Now I'll be as nice as I can be with you, Stone. I want you to back off with your fancy words, and I mean soon, or there will be consequences. You understand me? You may just find out first hand, how bad the truth hurts."

Oldsmar doesn't face us, but shifts in place at his companions words, as if he's not altogether comfortable with them. I can scarcely believe that I'm hearing such a blatant threat from this man, but I've been in similar situations, and I'm not intimidated.

This Hagan reminds me of a Taliban commander who got in my face because he didn't appreciate what I was writing about him either. I suppose he saw me as a threat to his livelihood as well. That confrontation was in an undisclosed location in the Hindu Kush Mountains, and I lived to tell the tale. If I keep my wits about me, I should be all right, in the middle of the parking lot at Robinson's

209

Market.

My mind races for words that might diffuse the situation without giving the impression that I'm giving in to his demand, but Hagan steps uncomfortably close and begins to speak again, giving me little time to develop a diplomatic refrain.

"So what'll be, Stone? Do we understand each other?"

"I understand what you're saying, but you apparently don't understand me. I will write what I believe should be written and publish where and when I desire to. If you don't like it, that's your problem."

Oldsmar turns at that and by the look on his face, he's shocked at my response. I believe his companion is surprised as well, but Hagan doesn't hint at backing down and in fact, seems all too ready to act upon his threat.

As he leans toward me, I hear the screeching of tires on pavement and look past him to see a flatbed wrecker pulling into the parking lot. Hagan and Oldsmar are distracted by the commotion and turn as the truck straightens out and rolls toward us.

The driver breaks to a halt twenty feet away, and exits the vehicle with the door left ajar. He's a tall, portly man, with a short beard and a ball cap pulled low over black hair. He walks directly toward us and speaks in a loud voice.

"What's the problem here? Which one of you called?"

"N-no problem here. There must be some mistake. My friend Scott here and I were just talking . . ."

Oldsmar is interrupted by the sound of a loud, rumbling engine, coming from behind. We turn to see a blue pickup racing toward us and watch in silence as it pulls up within feet of the wrecker. When the driver exits, I recognize a familiar face, and so does the operater of the wrecker.

"Hey Jerry Dale."

"Vinny, what's up?"

"I was just trying to figure that out, myself."

"Uh, I was just saying that my friend and I . . . Oh, by the way, I'm Don Oldsmar. I'm with Blue Ridge . . ."

"I know who you are and I know who you work for. What I want to know is what you're doing now. Are you looking for trouble?"

As Jerry Dale speaks, he keeps his eyes on Hagan, as if he anticipates a move from the man and is watching to counter it. Just then another truck speeds across the parking lot and stops an aisle away. Lamont Greely and a man I don't recognize exit the vehicle, both with tense, gritty expressions. And yet another pickup races toward us from the south entrance and stops just behind my jeep. Augustus Ramsey emerges and addresses Jerry Dale as he eyes the provocateurs.

"What the hell's going on here, Jerry Dale? Lavina called me, told me there was trouble."

"We got the situation under control, Gus. These two boys made a mistake, and now they're going to turn tail and leave. Right?"

Oldsmar looks at his companion but says nothing. Hagan glances at the men surrounding him, eyeing Jerry Dale last, a man about his own age, and equal in size and demeanor. He gestures toward Oldsmar, and then walks past him toward the white truck. Oldsmar follows and they enter the pickup without a word.

We watch as they back away from us, turn and cruise toward the exit. As the truck eases onto Walnut Creek Road, Jerry Dale turns to me.

"What happened, Mr. Stone, you pick a fight?"

"Jerry Dale, I just came here to get supper and . . ."

I stop talking when he smiles, realizing that he's joking. A chuckle from Greely and grins from the rest of the men affirm that. He looks from side to side and then speaks in a serious tone.

"I know what happened. They're trying to lean on you because of the stuff you wrote about them, huh?"

"Well yes, that's exactly what happened. But tell me, how did all of you know what was going on?

"My sister-in law is manager at Robinson's. She knows you and she knows about Oldsmar. She called me when she saw what was going down. I made some calls on the way here, first to Vinny, since

211

he's right across the road. I see he didn't mess around. He brought the heavy equipment."

Vinny shrugs and introduces himself. Jerry Dale stares past me, toward the supermarket, and I turn to see a tall woman with short, auburn hair, presumably Jerry Dale's sister-in law, staring at us. He waves and she reenters the store. Jerry Dale addresses the men as they begin to disassemble.

"I say we best be real watchful from now on. This won't be the last time something like this will happen. But you see how it works, we stand together and come right back at them."

The men nod in agreement and depart in various directions while Jerry Dale remains beside me.

"Do you have a gun, Mr. Stone."

"No, I don't. I used to carry a gun, and I'm familiar with firearms, but I quit carrying one years ago."

"Well, I think you ought to consider carrying one again. I'm not worried about the white-haired guy. My opinion is he's a coward and a punk. But that other guy, he's neither of those, and he'll be back, or somebody like him will come around instead. I'd consider real strongly about getting yourself a gun."

"I'd really prefer not to. These days, I want to believe that conflict can be settled without guns. After all, this incident was settled and no guns were in the picture."

"No there weren't, but I can tell you this much, had one of those boys pulled a gun, there would have been half a dozen in the picture real quick, pointed right back at them."

34

"What's wrong, Ira? You seem distracted, and I'm doing all of the talking. Is it about what happened at Robinson's?"

"Oh, no, well yes, in a way, that's part of it. I'm sorry, Patricia. I was determined to enjoy a pleasant walk with you, and keep the problems at bay for a while."

"It didn't work, huh. I'm sorry, and I can see why. It's hard to believe Oldsmar would pull a stunt like that at the supermarket. Julian was furious when he heard about it. It was all Cody and I could do to keep him from going after Oldsmar. He still blames him for Dad's death. Julian has a crazy streak in him Ira, and when he gets mad enough, there's no telling what he'll do."

"You mentioned that before and I must say, I would never have guessed that."

"Trust me, he will only take so much. And he's not feeling well, either, which makes him grumpier than usual. He's not taking care of himself like he should."

"I'll try to tone it down when I see him. I don't want to give him anything more to worry about.

Are you worried, Ira?"

"Yes, of course I am, but I've been in similar situations. I just never expected such a state of affairs here in Walnut Creek, so I'm angry as much as worried."

"Do you have a gun?"

"You know, both your brother and Jerry Dale, asked me that same question, and the answer is that I don't. I hate to admit it, but lately the thought *has* crossed my mind that maybe I should carry one. Isn't that awful?"

"No, I don't think so. I have a gun, and I wish you would take it. Dad gave it to me years ago, when I left for college. He was worried about me going to live in a city."

"What kind of gun do you have?"

"A Smith & Wesson three fifty-seven magnum."

"My goodness, you *do* have a gun."

"Yes, one that I haven't shot in years. In fact, I was considering giving it to Julian or Cody. I'd feel better knowing that you have it now. There are certainly enough guns around here, so I don't feel like I need to be armed. I want you to take it."

"Patricia, I appreciate your offer, but I don't think I should. You see I decided years ago, that I wouldn't carry a gun in my profession."

"But your not a war correspondent now. You live in Walnut Creek and you're being threatened. Ira, please take it, just until this trouble is over. I'll feel better knowing you have it, and I know I'll never use it. Like I said, I'm safe enough here."

"All right, I'll take it, if it will make you feel better."

"Good, it *will* make me feel better. I have to admit, though, I never thought it would come to something like this, that I would worry about this kind of trouble here. This is a place where I always felt safe and if anything, overprotected."

"Well, I'm afraid we're getting a taste for what it's like to run up against money and power. We're standing in the way of profit, which is unacceptable. Wars are being fought right now in other parts of the world for the same reasons that we're being harassed here, and most likely instigated by the same people. The only difference is it doesn't often come to open warfare in this country like it does in other parts of the world."

"Do you think this could become an actual gunfight here?"

"I, I think it's a remote possibility in this case, but not out of the question. Unless people here go along with what Blue Ridge Power Corporation wants, yes, there *is* going to be a fight. It's just a matter of what form the fight will take: verbal, legal or physical."

"So what do you really see happening?"

"I hope that it can be resolved through discussion, and, at the very worst in the court system. But the basic problem will not go away; it'll emerge again in another form. A profit driven system is the problem and as long as there's money to be made, the machine won't stop."

"But this isn't how it should be. We're Americans, we live in a democracy, this shouldn't happen."

After walking a circuitous route on trails through the woods, we've reached the cemetery. Patricia knew the trail well, while I was lost most of the time. I place both hands upon the fence and she leans against me, her hands cupped over my shoulder.

I pause and study Patricia's face before speaking. I don't want to risk, sounding like the old political curmudgeon that I've become, but I owe it to her to give my honest opinion.

"Patricia, we really don't live in a democracy. That's a myth, and if it ever was true, it certainly isn't anymore. We live in a society that is more accurately described as a collective dictatorship."

"A collective dictatorship?"

"It's not my terminology. 'Collective dictatorship' was coined by a friend of mine, Buzz Griffin. He used it to describe the United States government in an essay he wrote, that compared it to totalitarian regimes such as Nazi Germany and the Soviet Union under Stalin."

"Oh come on now. I don't care how bad it seems, our government can't be compared to the Nazis or the Soviet Union."

"No, not on the surface. That's because a collective dictatorship doesn't revolve around a charismatic leader, like Hitler or Stalin. It's controlled by a collective of the wealthiest individuals, the billionaires. It's no small coincidence that the president of the United States and half his cabinet are billionaires.

They profess to honor elections, freedom of the press, and

the guarantees of law, but at the same time, manipulate the courts, the press, and the electoral process, making true participation impossible."

"What about the Constitution? Even billionaires can't rewrite the Constitution."

"No, the Constitution hasn't been rewritten, but it's been so weakened through judicial and legislative interpretation that it's a shell of democracy with a totalitarian core."

"Ira, if you really believe this, then why are you here, why do you even live in the United States, let alone Madison County?"

"I spent my career on the front lines of conflict trying to provide the world with the truth about war. My hope was that when people knew what war was really about, it would affect a change in foreign policy for our country, and for all countries. But the fact is that during the course of my career, things got worse not better. Last I checked, there are ten official wars and dozens of other military conflicts in progress.

So I decided to try something different with the rest of my life, an alternative lifestyle to the profit-driven, winner-take-all mentality, which is really the root of war. I'm trying to fashion a life that is fulfilling and productive, and as much as possible, not dependent on fossil fuels."

"So you won't have to buy what their selling, like you said before."

"Yes, exactly. If we don't buy it, they won't make it. Madison County, seemed like a good place to undertake such a project because it's still relatively unspoiled, with good people who work hard and have lived here for generations. I didn't come here to change Madison County, I came here to be inspired by Madison County.

What I never could have guessed is that I would come face to face again with the *root of the evil* so soon. I just got here; I'm just getting started. It's almost like trouble followed me."

"Oh, Ira, don't be silly. It's just an unlucky coincidence. But now that it's happened, why not go somewhere else where you can carry out your plans and not have to fight at the same time?"

"There's no place left to go. If it can happen here, it can happen anywhere. Eventually it *will* happen everywhere. Sooner or later the machine has got to be stopped, before we are all just subjects of the wealthy. "

"So you're saying that we need to fight here?"

"Yes, I don't mean a gunfight, but we need to work this out and do it without backing down. Every avenue to reach a compromise must be looked at to avoid violence, and that's where I believe my experience can help."

"And if compromise doesn't work?"

"In that case, I think that armed resistance is a possibility. I believe that humanity is at a tipping point in history, when greed is reaching a self destructive extreme, leaving people no choice but to fight back for their own survival."

Patricia stares at me with an uncertain look on her face, but that gives way to a smile. Then she reaches out and takes my hand in hers.

"Lets not talk about it anymore. It's too nice a day, and I want to enjoy the walk back.

The wood frame screen door slams behind us, bangs open a few inches and then shuts. Patricia backs me up against the door and kisses me on the lips.

"You're trapped, Mr. Stone. You look surprised. You're not nervous, are you?"

"Yes, I am, but I'll get over it."

I encircle Patricia with my arms, pull her close, we kiss again.

"Wait, I want to get this for you now, so I don't forget."

Patricia leads me into her bedroom and withdraws a gun, sheathed in a leather holster, from a chest at the foot of the bed. She closes the chest, places the gun on top, and comes back to face me.

"Please don't forget to take that. I'll feel better, knowing that you can protect yourself."

"I will do that."

"Good. And I've been thinking about what we talked about at the cemetery, and I like your plan of trying to change things by the way you live. It's really not so different from what I want to do here, but I never thought of it as a way to change the world.

So, now that you put the idea in my head, maybe we can work together on it, between your place and mine. You can come here to work sometimes, and I could come over to your place and help with the gardens. Maybe we can change the world and still have fun at the same time."

"Patricia, what can I say? I couldn't ask for a better proposition. And Cody could be part of it, too. He's looking for direction now and he seems receptive to what I'm doing. We've even talked about him learning to make bowls."

"Oh, I think that would be wonderful, Ira, and what a coincidence that you should say that. Cody and I were just talking about career possibilities and one idea he's been mulling over is starting an organic vegetable farm here. He said that he knows a couple in Weaverville that have one and they told him there's a ready market in Asheville."

"Wow, this is sounding better all the time."

"Yes, dear Cody, he's such sweet guy. He's not a fighter. He's a thinker and a farmer, so I think this is a wonderful idea."

35

Two hundred and ten 'likes' already and our Facebook page has only been up for three days. It's fascinating to see from whom or what organization the 'likes' are coming. Eleven of them are from citizen militias, and they not only offer moral support but want to know how they can help, either physically or with supplies.

I'm anxious to share the news with Cody, and also to talk to him about what Patricia and I discussed. I wonder where he is, because we had planned to work at the computer this morning. No big deal, I'm in the mood for physical work now, bowl making to be exact.

I believe the large walnut bowl I started yesterday has the potential to be the nicest I've ever made. With a sense of optimism and hope for the future, taken to new heights after time spent with Patricia yesterday, I refill my coffee mug and make my way to the workshop.

Seated at the bench, I position the rudimentary bowl, take several swipes with the adze and then pause to finish my coffee. Walnut Creek is running clear now, after several days of rain, and the soothing sound of it's water makes me forget for the moment, the tide of trouble that is rising in the valley.

Everything passes, and we will get through this. This quiet moment with the sound of the creek behind me and a fine piece of walnut in front of me is why I'm here, and that's what I'm going to focus on.

Every chip removed is progress. That's how a bowl gets finished, chip by chip, a slow, determined process, focused on the present, but with an eye to the larger picture. That's how a life is enhanced and a civilization is improved, by slow, measured steps. With such lofty thoughts in mind, I wield my adze again, determined to create the finest bowl I'm capable of.

As I take another swipe, a vehicle pulls into the parking lot, causing such a scraping noise in the gravel that I start up from the bench. The driver is obviously moving fast and brakes with force. I'm roused from my meditative mood, startled, and suddenly feeling threatened.

Patricia's gun is at the house, and I wish at the moment I had it in my hand. Stepping to the back door and peering toward the road, I'm relieved to see Julian come around the corner, of the building, but alarmed by the angry expression on his face.

"Goddamn it, Ira, Cody got busted. Sold a sawed-off shotgun to a guy he met at the bar. Turns out it was an undercover cop, a federal agent. What the hell was he thinking? They got him downtown. I'm going now to bail him out."

"Oh no, was it Cody's shotgun?"

"It was his alright, but it was legal. Says he needed the money to pay his truck insurance and didn't want to ask me for it. But he swears he didn't shorten the barrel for this guy."

"Well maybe he didn't, Julian, and I don't like the sound of this one bit. How is it that Cody bumped into a federal agent at a bar in Walnut Creek, anyway? Do you want me to go down with you?"

"Yeah, would you, Ira? I'm so mad that I'm afraid I might make things worse. Never have been too friendly with the guy that's sheriff now, and he had a hand in this. Joel Pettit's his name. I went to high school with him. And get this, Greely says he sees him in town talking with Oldsmar sometimes. I don't trust Pettit as far as I can throw him. He always been a back-stabbing son of a bitch."

"Humph, now I *really* don't like the sound of this. Let's go then, and my advice is be businesslike and say as little as you have to. This may well be a setup and they're after something else here, and for you to go down there swinging might play right into their hands."

"Okay, Ira I'll do my best."

On the way, Julian is agitated, working the stick shift aggressively. I'm tense as well, trying to convince myself that this isn't related to the confrontation with Blue Ridge Power Corporation, but my instincts tells me it is.

"I don't need this now, Ira. Between Dad dying and this gas drilling thing, I got enough to think about. Goddamned boy, why would he sell a gun to someone he doesn't even know? But I'll tell you this much, as far as it being sawed-off, Cody's knows guns better than anyone and he'd never cut a the barrel down below the legal limit. And he ain't a liar either."

"Cody might have been set up. Like I said, they might really want something else.

"Like what?"

"This may be tied into the gas drilling. This may be just the latest tactic to bully your family, right in line with the fireworks on the hill, the convoy going by at your father's funeral, and the pipeline through the hollow."

"God damn it, and the thing with you at Robinson's."

"Yes, what's happened so far can't be just random events. It's more likely a coordinated pattern of intimidation. Cody's arrest may be more of the same, except taking it to another level by bringing in the legal system."

"Well that's just great. I hope you're wrong, Ira."

"I hope so, too, but I'm probably not."

The town of Walnut Creek is quiet on this August morning. A few heads turn from sidewalk tables at the Riverside Café as

Julian and I ascend the courthouse steps. We're met in the lobby by Jim Sorrels, a bail bondsman who is introduced to me as a cousin of Julian, on his father's side. Jim gives me a firm handshake and knowing smile, saying that he's heard about me. Then he quickly turns his attention to Julian.

"Something's weird here, Jules. Nobody's being too friendly and even the people that are, aren't saying much. All Cody did was sell a sawed-off shotgun, right? They got anything else on him?"

"N-no, I don't think so, Jimmy. He would have said it if there was."

"The bail is ten thousand dollars, which isn't out of line, but I have a feeling something else is going down here."

"What're you saying Jimmy? We come to bail Cody out, and we got the money. What the hell's wrong?"

I understand the bondsman's concern, because I feel it too, tension in the room. The clerks behind the glass in the billing department glance our way, but don't make eye contact. Then everyone goes silent when the sheriff appears in the hallway.

Tall, slim and odd are the words that best describe Sheriff Joel Pettit. With his jet black hair, slicked to one side, and pasty complexion, he reminds me of a villian in a play.

I knew about the sheriff before now. Joel Pettit came out of nowhere in last fall's election, with lot's of money behind him and steamrolled past Billy Harper, the county sheriff of many years. Sheriff Pettit walks toward us paying little attention to me or to the bail bondsman.

"Julian Runnion, you're under arrest for criminal trespass and threatening with a firearm."

"What the hell are you talking about, Pettit?"

"Sheriff Pettit to you, and what I'm talking about is you obstructing a legal right of way and threatening the rightful owners of that right of way."

"Let me ask you again, what the hell are you talking about? That is you, behind that badge, isn't it?"

"That's enough, Runnion, you're coming with me."

"The hell I am. I came here to bail out my boy and that's what I intend to do."

"What *you* intend to do makes no difference. You're coming with me."

A deputy sheriff walks out from a doorway and takes a few steps toward Julian. At this Jim Sorrels comes up behind, and places a hand on his cousin' shoulder.

"Go along with him Jules; you'll just make it worse if you resist. I'll take care of Cody and then I'll come back for you."

Julian's eyes are flashing with anger, but the bail bondsman's words have a calming effect, and he steadies himself between the sheriff and the deputy. When the deputy touches Julian's elbow he nudges the hand away defiantly and then turns toward me.

"Ira, Cody can drive you back. Tell him to stay on the farm until I get there. And let Jerry Dale know what's happened."

Cody is quiet as he's led through the bailout procedure, only answering questions, and he says nothing as we walk to his father's truck. Driving up Main Street, I catch sight of Don Oldsmar, standing outside the café, talking to the character named Scott Hagan who I was introduced to in the parking lot at Robinson's. They look toward us as we pass, and while Scott is expressionless behind dark glasses, I can't help but notice a smirk on Oldsmar's face.

Not until we crest the hill and are descending into the Valley, does Cody emerge from his quietude. In fact, he becomes loud and animated, watching the road only as much as necessary, and glancing over at me with every other sentence. His tone of voice and angry expression remind me of his father, his Runnion side showing through.

"I did not sell that son of a bitch an illegal shotgun. He wanted one and I told him I wouldn't do it. I had a shotgun to sell and I needed the money. If that gun's short now, than he did it or somebody else did."

"Cody, how did you meet this guy?"

"Just someone who started hanging out at the Tavern. Darrell Rogers he said his name was. Rode a Harley from Atlanta and was staying in the area to ride the roads around here. I can't believe the asshole lied to me like that."

"Don't be too hard on yourself, Cody, it's what he does for a living. What else did he talk to you about?"

"Bikes, sports, but mostly guns. Said he'd really like to get his hands on a short-barreled shotgun that he could take with him when he's on his bike. That's how he brought it up. Said he runs into some rough characters where he's from, and that's why he wanted the gun."

"Well, I hate to say this, but I'm nearly certain that getting you on a weapons charge wasn't the main objective here. This Darrell character and the people behind him are after something else."

"Like what?"

"I don't know, but it could have something to do with the drilling, maybe to get some leverage over your father."

"Are you kidding me?"

"No. The fact that the sheriff was waiting to arrest your father, on the day that you are bailed out, was no coincidence. It was a way to get him on their own terms, away from The Land. Did this Darrell guy happen to say anything about the drilling, or anything suspicious?"

"No, nothing about drilling or The Land, but now that you mention it, he did ask me about militias in the area."

"About Backbone Mountain Militia?"

"No, not straight out about Backbone Mountain Militia, just ask if I knew of any militias that were in this area."

"Why, how did he happen to bring that up."

"He said he'd been interested in joining a militia for a while, and had been looking into it around Atlanta. And then he said he heard there was one in this area."

"What did you tell him?"

"I said no, I don't know anything about any militias. That's what I always say; that's what everybody says. I've been taught that since I was born. Darrell seemed like he really didn't believe me, but, like he was cool with that, like he understood that I didn't want to say. You know what I mean?"

"Yes, I know exactly what you mean. That's an old tactic. Well, Cody, it's good you didn't mention Backbone Mountain Militia, that was quick thinking on your part."

I stop asking questions, although many more come to mind. I don't want to add to the stress that Cody is feeling, but I have to assume that this Darrell character and the people he works for know about Backbone Mountain Militia and now that they've got something on Cody they'll use it to bargain for more information.

Cody turns into my driveway, stops the engine, and stares straight ahead, with a somber expression. So I tell him about the activity on Facebook and Twitter, the accounts that he set up, and his humor improves. I ask him if he's hungry, and before he can bow out of dinner, I inform him that I have half a pizza in the refrigerator and some cold beer.

Cody uses my phone to call Jerry Dale, while I heat lunch, and we meet on the back porch. I get Cody to laugh a little by telling him of Ben's latest exploits, of how he got his lawn tractor hung up on the bank of Walnut Creek, trying to cut too close, and we had to pull it off with a chain attached to the jeep.

Cody soon turns solemn again and gazes toward my garden area. He stares toward the statue of Buddha, which now looks quite at home on my lawn. We both observe the statue in silence for a few moments until Cody speaks.

"Are you worried about what's happening, Mr. Stone?"

"Hmm, yes, but you know, Cody, I've been worried about what's happening for a long time, practically ever since I became a journalist. I wasn't much older than you then. The trick is to channel the worry into awareness and readiness, make it a positive thing. You have to put it into perspective and go on with your life, and then you have a chance at beating the problem. If you let worry consume you, then there's no chance."

"I guess. I wish I was like that statue out there, you know, just sitting peacefully, letting all the problems in the world go by."

"Hah, don't we all wish that."

"Well, I better be heading up to the farm and feed Wagon. He's probably okay, though. My guess is he's hanging out with Aunt Pat."

"Smart dog. That's one of my favorite people to hang out with, too."

"Ha ha, do you think you and Aunt Pat will get married?"

"Whoa, not so fast. Your Aunt and I have just met."

"It seems to me that you've met pretty well, as much as I see your jeep there."

"I'll have you know, young man, that your Aunt Patricia is giving me lessons in building techniques."

"I hear you, Mr. Stone. I'm just teasing anyway. Thanks for lunch."

36

Waving his hands and clenching his fists for emphasis, Julian paces as he talks. Jerry Dale picked up his cousin after he was bailed out by Jim Sorrels, and soon after, word came round that we would meet at the hunting camp. Along with many new faces, the same men are present that were in attendance the first time I came here. Needless to say, the mood is not so mirthful at this meeting. Julian is animated and angry as he speaks.

"Fuck them; they're playing with us. That Pettit's a piece of shit, and if it wasn't for that badge that the gas people bought him, I would have dealt with him like he deserves."

"I would like to see that, Jules. What the hell is Madison County coming to when Joel Pettit is the sheriff? He always was a punk in my book."

"Tell me about it, Greely. The man's full of himself, too. You should hear him, like he earned this, when all he did was jump in bed with the gas people. And get this, they charged me with trespassing on my own land. Blue Ridge Energy Corporation, owned by someone in Texas, claims a right-of-way through Walnut Hollow, *my family farm*, and now the state says I trespassed because I stood in their way.

I'm defending my home, where my family has lived for hundreds of years. Outsiders come in who are looking to make a buck, and the government is taking their side on it. I'll be damned if they're going to build a pipeline through Walnut Hollow. If they do, it'll be over my dead body.

And Cody, here, as far as I'm concerned, he was set up, plain and simple. He said he didn't cut that gun barrel down, and I know he's telling the truth. They set him up like a bowling pin and now they're trying to knock us all down at the same time. Ain't going to happen. I won't tolerate it."

I listen to Julian with a mixture of surprise and admiration. I would never have guessed that he would take center floor like this and argue his case before a crowd. He's making his point well, and to a receptive audience, with none more approving than Jerry Dale who echoes his cousin's words at times and adds bellicose innuendos of his own.

While agreeing with Julian's reasoning and even finding myself somewhat stirred by his belligerence, I'm fearful at the same time, fearful that these men don't really understand what they're up against.

Tommy Gosnell is one person in the room I suspect does understand. He's standing off to the side, one foot on a chair, arms crossed over his knee. The Field Commander is giving Julian his unwavering attention, but he is one of the few who remains silent.

"I feel it's time to make a stand against these jackals. They're not going to run that pipeline through my family property. My dad wouldn't have allowed it, and I ain't going to allow it."

A rush of consensus emanates from the crowd with this statement, while Tommy continues to watch in silence. When the forum becomes more of a group discussion, he walks over to the corner that I'm leaning in and comes up beside me with a wry smile.

"Ira, why are you and I the only ones not talking here?"

"I'm not talking because I'm old and wary. Not that I don't agree with what's being said. It's just that I worry about where such talk can lead."

"Right, it's not something to fall into lightly, pushing back against the government. But sooner or later it becomes necessary."

"Is that where we are?"

"Hmm, I don't know. That's one reason I'm not adding to the conversation. I can learn more at this point by listening, and it's a way for me to find out about the men under my command.

Julian I know well. He has a temper, but a temper isn't necessarily a bad thing as long as it's kept under control. Right now, the best thing I can do for Julian is to let him vent. He'll eventually settle down and think things through clearly. Then, he and I, and the other officers, will talk this over and decide the best course of action. I'd like you to be there, Ira, if you don't mind. You're input would help."

"Sure, I'll be there, for whatever I can add to the conversation. Tell me, Tommy, does Jerry Dale have a temper, too?"

"Nope. Sometimes, I think he has ice flowing in his veins. He can stay calm in any situation, and will most times avoid a fight. Jerry Dale *will* fight if it comes to that, *believe me*, but when he does, the fight will be on his terms."

"That's interesting, because I would have sooner guessed that he would be quick to anger as opposed to Julian."

"No, not quick to anger, but hard to stop once he is angry, which isn't a bad thing either, as long as it's kept under control. He's a born soldier and a natural leader. Jerry Dale is the future of Backbone Mountain Militia. You should see him running drills with the men."

"So you drill like an army would?"

"Yes, I run the militia like any modern army, and I work the soldiers hard. If we're going to do this at all, and truly have a chance to hold our ground against the government, then we've got to be prepared like a true army."

"That's what you train for, to fight the government?"

"No, not necessarily the government, but anyone who would infringe on our rights. As I see it, the government would present the greatest challenge, so that's the standard by which we gauge our capabilities.

But I don't want to give you the wrong impression. We train hard, but we're not looking for a fight. In fact, our policy is to always have good relations with everyone, but we never accept being oppressed by anyone and that includes the government."

Patricia's house stands out like a lone star in the darkness of Walnut Hollow. I slow alongside, and see her sitting on the wicker porch swing that we hung earlier in the week. She tilts her head to one side as I pull over.

"I was hoping you would come by tonight, but I thought it would be from the opposite direction. You obviously didn't get my message at your house since I just left it half an hour ago."

"A phone message, no. I just sensed that you wanted me to stop, I think it's a telepathy type thing."

"Hmm, not to mention that you had to come this way to get off the farm."

As I reach the top step, Patricia stands, takes my hands in hers and gazes at my face. Then she pulls me close and hugs me.

"Where were you, at Julian's cabin?"

"No, at the hunting camp."

"Ah, the mysterious hunting camp. I haven't been there in years. I would like to think that you were there for fun, to sip moonshine and tell hunting stories, but my guess is it had something to do with Julian and Cody and the trouble they're in. Was Cody there? He and I talked earlier and he filled me in on what happened."

"Yes, he was there, but he didn't say much. Julian held the floor for the most part and seemed to speak for everybody. The talk was mostly about he and Cody's arrest, but the general consensus is that it's all tied in with the gas drilling."

As I say this a look of concern comes over Patricia. She leads me across the porch, never letting go of my hands, and then seats me on the porch swing beside me. She rests her head on my shoulder and sighs before speaking.

"Ira, what do you think is going to happen? I mean is there going to be a fight here?"

"I don't know, to be honest with you. A real fight, like a gun fight, the chances are still slight, I think, but I can't rule it out. One thing I'm sure of, a man like Lawrence Khan will stop at nothing until he gets what he wants. Whether he disrupts people's lives or ruins a community means nothing to him."

"But what motivates people like this? Why does he need so much money?"

"He doesn't need money. Khan has never needed money; he was born wealthy. Lust for money is an addiction like any other addiction. The quest for wealth never ends for him and his kind. Born into millions, they strive to make billions, and next they'll want trillions. Separate Lawrence Khan from his wealth, and there's nothing outstanding about him. He's no better than most people. In fact, he's not as good as most people.

When you think about it, it's all so stupid and meaningless. Some people, like Khan, have lots of pieces of paper that the government says are worth money, and they *are*, as long as everybody respects the system. And despite the fact that most people don't have lots of those pieces of paper, they are still bound to respect the system. The police and if need be, even the army is ready to back up Lawrence Khan and his pieces of paper.

But the truth of the matter is, if enough people rise up at once and reject the validity of those pieces of paper, then the system falls apart and Khan is powerless. It's happened many times throughout history and I've personally witnessed it happen in other parts of the world.

"Do you think there's any chance that it could happen here?"

"I feel that it's very unlikely, but I do believe it could happen anywhere if the conditions are right.

"And you think we're at that point?

"Uh, no. Well, maybe."

"You sound like you hope we are."

"I do and I don't. I came here to get away from such thinking, to explore a different path to change the system, but sometimes I worry that we've run out of time for a slow, methodical change. I fear that revolution, may be the only hope for real change."

"Ira, would you like a glass of wine?"

"Yes, maybe that will shut me up."

"I'm not trying to shut you up, just maybe change the direction of this conversation. But I wish you would have answered a clear no to my question. I don't want a fight."

Patricia smiles as she gets up, but she has a sad and weary air about her. I grow warm, sorry that I ranted on like I did. Patricia returns with two glasses of chardonnay and sits close beside me. She sips her drink in silence for a moment and I do the same. She puts her glass down and takes my hand.

"Ira, I came back here because I wanted to start over again, to retire on my family farm, not to fight in a revolution. I love Walnut Hollow and I respect my family for preserving it, but at this stage of my life, I'm not willing to fight for it. I'm nearly sixty years of age, I have grown children, I've lost a husband already. I just want to live and grow old gracefully. I don't want to fight."

She sighs, and leans against me. I resolve to change the conversation, to speak of simple, positive things, and enjoy a glass of wine with this lovely lady. Patricia smiles as if she senses my resolution and on impulse, I lean towards her and kiss her. She seems surprised at first, but her smile widens.

"Ira, why in the world did you come back to Walnut Creek?"

"To meet you."

"Okay, that's a good answer, and I hope you never regret it."

37

With trucks, rolling past the house before daylight even, coffee on the back porch has lost much of it's appeal. I abort an alternative plan, to breakfast at Riverside Café, when I see Don Oldsmar's car parked outside. Interacting with him would serve to make worse, a day that is already off to a bad start.

I park the jeep a block away and cross the bridge to Island Park with the intent of walking off my irritation, while awaiting businesses to open.

Along with my annoyance, I'm wrestling with embarrassment, recalling my talk of revolution with Patricia yesterday evening. The lifestyle I've adopted seems to be only a veneer at times, and the old Ira Stone still shows through. Fortunately, Patricia is deft at redirecting me before my rhetoric clouds an otherwise pleasant occasion.

Buddhism teaches that one should not be an aggressor for any reason, not even if it's to protect Buddhism. Can I ever be like that? Regardless of what has occurred or what may come, I need to stay centered on the ideals that brought me here and not get caught in the drift toward a fight. My experience and literary skills can best be used to advocate for a peaceful resolution to this conflict.

The notion isn't so difficult to imagine in this peaceful setting with the timeless waters of the French Broad River, flowing past me. A gentle lapping sound of water against the shore, serves to focus my thoughts.

The path around the island is half a mile long and as I complete the first circuit, my mood has improved to such an extant that I decide to go around one more time. Upon reaching the northern tip of the island, where the walking trail crosses a gully on a plank bridge, I become aware of a black vehicle, slowly moving into the graveled parking area on the other side of the park.

This would not be so unusual except that in an empty parking area, the driver pulls to the very end of the lot and leaves the engine running. It's some sort of sport utility vehicle with tinted windows, and it seems out of place here in the park. The car stops such that it's pointed directly at me and I slow my gait, wondering if there is a purpose here.

The sight stimulates a flashback to a similar scene. I was in Quetta, Pakistan, searching the background of a suicide bomber who had attacked a consulate in Afghanistan. I came home late one evening and saw a vehicle, similar to the one that I'm staring at now, parked near the hotel where I was staying.

An hour later, three men broke through the chain lock on the door and entered my room. One of them spoke English and seemed to be in charge, and as I soon found out, the other two were the muscle. They seized my computer, notebooks, and a cell phone, and when I protested, one of the men punched me in the face, knocking me to the floor. That's how they left me.

When I related the story to a Quetta journalist, he shook his head and assured me that the intruders were plainclothes agents with the Directorate for Inter-Services Intelligence, and that were it not for the fact that I was an American, I probably would not be alive to tell the story. He said that journalists in Pakistan can smell ISI cars a mile away, and that in my case, he would have walked right past the apartment and stayed somewhere else for the night.

With that thought, I face forward and walk on, trying not to assume too much and spoil the moment with undue caution. However, just in case this intrusion does have something to do with me, I make an effort to get closer to the town museum where there is usually somebody present.

The suspicious vehicle is still in place a minute later when I emerge from a stand of spruce trees near the building. I can't seem to shake the feeling that I'm being observed and welcome the chance to slip out of sight again when the trail circles behind the museum. As I come around to the front, I'm so preoccupied that I don't notice a woman, descending the stairs until she speaks to me.

"Mr. Stone, I thought that was you. You're getting a morning walk in, like I ought to be doing."

"Oh, hello Susan. How are you? Yes I'm getting in my morning walk and daydreaming session. I didn't expect to see someone I know."

"I'm here working on the county quilt project. I don't know if you've heard about it. We're putting large wooden paintings of traditional quilt patterns on the barns in the county, so people can drive around and learn about the history of quilting in this area. I'm in charge of Walnut Creek Road, picking out the patterns and lining up the barns."

"What a great idea. Makes me wish I had a barn. And I assume the paintings are being made here."

"Yes, and I just turned in the patterns that will be on our road. Where's your jeep? I know you didn't walk all the way here from home."

"No, not quite. I'm parked over in town."

Well, that's still a good piece away. I'm heading that way, if you want to cheat a little. My car is right here."

"You know, I think I'll just take you up on that, Susan. The right hip's been bothering me a little."

I decide not to trouble Susan with the actual reason why I accepted her offer, and I'm relieved as we leave the park and cross the bridge. I'm not certain how much she knows of the escalating trouble with the gas company, and I don't want to cloud her cheerful mood with what might be just my paranoia. We talk about the quilt project a bit longer, and we discuss her children. I congratulate her when she tells me that she and Michael just celebrated their wedding anniversary, but I find myself distracted and only half listening.

I thank Susan for the ride and linger outside the jeep until she's out of sight. Moving along the sidewalk until an opening between buildings affords me a view of the island, I can see that the black vehicle is gone.

Climbing the hill out of Walnut Creek, I'm warm and angry about a morning that has been very much disrupted. I'm also a bit confused about what just happened. If the purpose was simply to keep an eye on me, the operation could have been handled much more discreetly. If the vehicle was indeed there on my behalf, then the intent was not just for surveillance, but to let me know I'm being watched. Was it another effort to intimidate?

My property comes into view and I'm startled to see a black pickup parked in the driveway, another dark vehicle with tinted windows that belongs to no one that I know. I pull in, within inches of the rear bumper, and upon exiting the jeep, I catch sight of two men walking together at the end of my field, near the big poplar.

Owning land is a relatively new experience for me and I'm not a territorial person in that regard, certainly never one to get angry about someone harmlessly traversing a parcel of land that I happen to own. But these intruders with their overbearing truck, so eerily similar to the vehicle I just encountered at the park, and so deliberately parked in my driveway, infuriate me. I don't see this as an innocent happening, but a calculated extension of the bigger trespasses that the whole valley is experiencing.

They notice me and begin to walk toward the house, but I turn and go inside rather than wait for them. I'm tense, fuming, not prepared to deal with this imposition so close on the heels of the incident in Walnut Creek. Another coincidence? I think not. I wouldn't be surprised if there is communication between these interlopers and the vehicle on the island.

My hands are shaking somewhat, as I'm hanging my coat in the hall closet. I spy Patricia's gun, on a hook just inside the door. On impulse, I remove the pistol from the holster and nest it in my right coat pocket and then put the coat back on.

When I hear a knock on the door, I remind myself to stay calm. A second knock follows, more forceful, almost demanding, so I take a deep breath and open the door.

A man faces me on the stoop, another stands a few yards behind, looking idly across the road. They're both dressed in work clothes, crisp and new with little evidence of much work being performed while wearing them. The man at the door is about my age, with a weathered face and a businesslike expression; the one behind is much younger and looks annoyed when he turns toward me. I can see a holstered revolver at his side, hanging just below a suede vest.

"Say, would you mind moving the jeep, so we can get out of your driveway. We don't mean to impose, really didn't plan to be here long. I'm Paul Timmons and this is Sam Hillman. We're with Blue Ridge Energy Corporation and we need to map out a route for a pipeline along the valley. If we decide to go through here, you can make yourself some money."

"I don't need some money. I just need some privacy and some respect for my property rights. Do you people ever consider asking permission before you come on someone's property?"

"Well, I, uh, figured you had been notified, but anyway, I thought everyone knew we were in the area, and what we're doing. Most people seem to welcome the opportunity . . ."

"No, not most people. A few people do, people that *do* need some money, and many of them regret their decision before it's all over. And I don't think it matters to you if you're welcome or not. You people work with impudence, like property rights don't apply to you, like your plans for this valley are more important than the lives of people that live here.

"Now hold on mister. I'm just trying to do my job. Somebody

forgot to call you, but that's no reason to make something bigger of this."

"Humph. Maybe, maybe not, we'll see. I'm going to move my jeep and then I want you off my property. And don't come back. Next time, I'll prosecute for trespassing."

I believe that Paul Timmons is telling the truth, and he seems to be caught in a situation that he's not comfortable with, but I can't accept that the presence of the two men on my property is an innocent misunderstanding.

Timmons is trying to be somewhat of a facilitator here but I suspect that this Hillman character is an agitator and quite comfortable in that role. As I walk past him he backs up my assumption.

"Look here, buddy, do you know who you're messing with?"

When I turn, Hillman gives me an ugly sneer, arms folded, making his gun all the more obvious.

"Sam, no, let me handle this. We're on our way, Mr. Stone. That's your name, right? I thought you were notified that we would be out here. If you'll move your jeep, we'll be on our way, but I can't promise you that you've seen the last of us. Like I said, I'm only trying to do my job. Let's go Sam."

"Move out of our way, old man, so we can go. But like he said, you haven't seen the last of us."

To such nonchalant belligerence from a man who looks half my age, I don't know exactly how to respond. My better judgment tells me that I shouldn't at all and yet I feel his insolence demands a response. He's standing uninvited, on my property, armed, and attempting to intimidate me. I finger the pistol in my coat pocket, and for an instant entertain the notion of sticking it in his face. How confrontational would he be then?

A pickup approaches from the east, brakes as it goes by, and pulls off the road in front of the shop. Lamont Greely steps out, and walks toward us with a somber expression.

"What's going on, Ira?"

"I came home and found these two, staking out my property for a gas pipeline."

"What, here along the creek? That doesn't make sense to me."

"It doesn't make sense to me either, but I'm sure it does to them. Do you have your phone, Lamont?"

"Yeah, right here."

"Would you call the state police. Tell them I'm being threatened by two men I caught trespassing on my property."

"Yeah, yeah sure, Ira, I can do that."

Greely steps away to make the call and Timmons is visibly unnerved by this turn of events.

"Threatened? Now hold on Mr. Stone. We said that we're leaving. You don't need to make some big scene out of this."

"No, that's exactly what I need to do, make as big a scene as possible. I'm going to charge you with trespassing, and you can thank your tough friend here for that."

"Police are on there way, Ira."

"Good. Can you do me another favor? Take pictures of these two, so we have this encounter on record."

"No, there's no need for that."

Greely snaps several pictures in spite of Timmons' plea, and gives me a thumbs up.

"Did you get the gun, Lamont?"

"Got it."

Timmons turns toward his partner with an angry look that prompts Hillman to adjust his vest so that the weapon is no longer visible. Then he looks back with a conciliatory expression.

"Mr. Stone, look, there's just been a misunderstanding here. Right before you came we decided that this wasn't a good route for the pipeline, so we're done. Why don't we just forget this before it leads to any trouble."

"There's already trouble, but I'll make a deal with you: no pipeline here and no pipeline through the Runnion farm, and we forget this."

"Now hold on, what's happening up the road has nothing to

239

do with this. That's a whole different . . ."

"It has everything to do with this. All the activity in this valley is part of one big project that's being orchestrated by the same company, right? You ultimately work for Lawrence Khan, don't you?"

"I, I don't know what you're getting at exactly. I know who he is, but I don't take my orders from him. I've never even met the man."

"I know who he is, too, mister, and you better not mess with him. If he wants to, he can buy and sell this whole valley, you included."

"Sam, shut the hell up."

Timmons turns in response to the sound of a siren, and then looks back at me with a pleading expression.

"Look, I'll do what I can. I just work for the company, and I'd retire tomorrow if I could. I don't have much say in these decisions, but I'll do what I can, you have my word, all right?"

Timmons strikes me as an honest man caught in a difficult situation that's not of his making, and I choose to believe him. I glance at Lamont and nod just as a state police car, flashing blue lights, rounds the bend and crosses the bridge over Walnut Creek.

The cruiser slows as it nears us, and pulls off onto the grass. The lights remain flashing as a police officer emerges, a young man, tall and angular, who reminds me of a soldier in dress uniform.

"What's the problem, gentleman? Which one of you is Lamont Greely?"

"I am officer, and I'm sorry to have bothered you, but the situation seems to be under control now. These men made a mistake, but we worked it out, and they were just leaving."

"I have no problem with that. I'd rather come and see things worked out than see someone pointing a gun at someone else. Who's the owner of the property?"

"I am, officer, Ira Stone."

"I'd like to ask you a few questions, Mr. Stone."

"Certainly."

The young officer pauses, and then turns to Timmons and Hillman. He asks them for their names and who they work for, but writes nothing down.

"You men can go on your way. I just need some information from the property owner to file a report—earn my pay."

Timmons is obviously uneasy as he ushers a still insolent Hillman toward the truck. I back up the jeep and pull it to the side, and watch in my rear view mirror while their vehicle pulls out and drives away. As I exit the jeep, I'm surprised to see the police officer grin and turn toward Lamont.

"What happened here, Lamont, you causing trouble again?"

"Not me, Bob. Guys from the gas company, we've already had a couple run ins with them."

"Yeah, I know about that."

"Well this is more of the same. Ira come home and found them behind his house staking out a route for a pipeline. Seems they got testy with him. That's when I drove up."

"Well this isn't the first time I've had a call about the gas people, and I'm afraid it won't be the last. Ira Stone, nice to meet you. I'm Bob Queen, brother-in-law to this hooligan here. I had a meeting with the district attorney at one. I was early, hoping to grab some lunch at the café. Now my stomach will be growling through the meeting, thanks to you, Lamont."

"Sorry Bob. I'll make it up to you. Glad you were in the area, though."

"Me too, but I got to get to the court house right now. I know what's going on around here, Mr. Stone, and well, I can't take sides on this, but I can at least say that I'm not on their side. So, don't hesitate to call if those guys come around again."

"Will do. Thanks, officer."

Before the police cruiser rounds the bend, Greely is backing toward his truck.

"I got to run too, Ira. I'm on my way to pick Julian up at Mission Hospital in Asheville. There's no way I'll make it when I said

I would, but he'll understand when he hears what happened."

"Why, what's wrong with Julian, is it his diabetes?"

"Yeah, got damn foot ulcers now, makes it hard for him to even walk sometimes. Doctor says they might have to amputate some toes or maybe his foot. Julian won't hear of it. I don't know what to think."

"Damn, sorry to hear that. I knew about the diabetes, but I didn't realize it was so bad."

"It's bad, believe me, and I think he's starting to know it, even though he won't admit it to anyone. Anyway, I got to run. Watch yourself, Ira, you hear."

"I'll do my best, Lamont".

38

What have I gotten myself into here? I moved to the Blue Ridge Mountains, where I envisioned the polar opposite of Afghanistan. I came here to remake myself, or as I prefer to think, let my true nature express itself. I'm not a fighter; I don't want to be a fighter. I'm an observer, and I'm a bowl maker. I came here as an advocate for peaceful change.

I reach the grand old poplar and find it still impassive and firm despite the interlopers who trod upon its roots. I only wish I had such resolve, rather than being swayed so easily. *Was I really considering, pulling that gun from my pocket?*

I pause to rub the rough, furrowed bark of this aged sentinel, and reaffirm my goals in coming to Madison County: self sufficiency, spirituality, and peaceful change. It's a good plan, it's the only viable path, and I must not lose sight of it again, no matter what the outward circumstances. The gun is safely back in the closet, the pen is once again my weapon of choice, and this afternoon, I will realign my thoughts by hewing the finest walnut bowl I'm capable of.

As I walk toward the house, a vehicle, slows on Walnut Creek Road, and Patricia's car pulls into the driveway. My outlook on life improves even more so at the sight of this, until I see the expression on her face as she exits the car. Sensing urgency, I hasten along the path, and meet her halfway around the house. Patricia looks frantic, frightened, and begins to speak as soon as we're close.

"They're coming for Cody."

"What, coming for Cody? Who, why? I thought everything was worked out for now."

"No, I just got a call from a friend at the court house and he said they're going to arrest Cody because he failed to appear for a hearing. I thought he was scheduled to appear a week from now, so I don't know what this is about. And it isn't like Cody to just forget something this serious.

I didn't want to bother you, Ira, but I'm so upset. I was hoping I would find Cody here or Julian. Do you know where Julian is? His truck is at the cabin, but he's not around."

"He's at Mission Hospital. Lamont went to pick him up. Did you know Julian was there?"

"No, I'm always the last one to know. It's his diabetes again, isn't it?"

"Yes, it seems to be related to that. He's having problems with his feet, ulcers."

"Oh my God."

"Yes, it's bad, but let's deal with one thing at a time here. Why don't we go back to your place, and work this out. First, we need to find Cody as soon as possible and stationing ourselves there is probably the best bet. Why don't you go ahead so we don't miss him, and I'll leave a note on my workbench in case either he or Julian come here first. Oh, and I think we should contact Tommy."

"Tommy, Why Tommy?"

"I, uh, just think he needs to know this. I don't want to be an alarmist, but I don't believe there's been a mistake. This may just be the next step in a plan, and as far as I'm concerned, if they're coming for Cody, they're coming for all of us. Tommy should know; he's the Field Commander"

"All right, I'll call him when I get there. I'm sorry, Ira, I didn't mean to ruin your day with this.

"Don't worry about ruining my day. Blue Ridge Energy Corporation already had a hand in that. I'll tell you about it later.

I'll be right behind you."

A sense of relief comes over me as Cody's truck comes into view, and I inform Patricia of his arrival through the screen door. She joins me on the porch, and we walk out to intercept him. He had been turkey hunting with his friend, Joel, and was unaware of the proceedings against him. Apparently Tommy sent word out to find Cody, and he and Joel were tracked down in the woods.

Cody is somewhat shaken by his predicament, and as Patricia and I attempt to bolster him, we notice Tommy's truck approaching from the opposite direction. He steps from the vehicle, nods to us, then addresses Cody.

"You alright?"

"Yeah, but I think I'm in trouble."

"Ah maybe, maybe not. Everybody's in trouble these days. Pat, did your friend know any specifics about this arrest, such as when?"

"No, he wasn't even in the courtroom. The deputy clerk tipped him off and he stepped outside the court house to make the call. He didn't know about a time, just that a bench warrant had been issued because Cody failed to appear in court."

"They set me up again, Tommy, They must have changed the date. I've checked my email every day, and I didn't get any phone messages either. They set me up."

"What did your attorney say?"

"I called her and left a message, sent her a text, too, but she hasn't gotten back to me."

"Her? I assumed Dale Burnside would be your attorney? He's always done good work for us."

"He retired or something. His daughter, June, has taken over the business."

"I knew his daughter worked with him, but I didn't know Dale was out of the picture. What's she like?"

"Miss Burnside, she seems all right, typical attorney in some ways, and she seems like she really wants to help me."

"So you've sat and talked with her?"

"Oh yeah, we talked for over an hour. She wanted to know everything that I talked about with Darrell, the guy at the bar. I told her what happened more than once, but she just kept asking more questions, even about things that didn't really seem to have anything to do with selling the gun."

"Like what?"

Things about The Land, and about Dad. Miss Burnside said that the more she knew about me the better picture she could present to the judge."

As I listen to Cody's portrayal of his legal counsel, a sense of unease comes over me, a concern heightened by the fact that Attorney Burnside seems to be not responding at a crucial time.

"Excuse me, Cody, Did she ask anything about me?"

"Well, now that you mention it, she did ask if I knew you, Mr. Stone, and I told her that I did. She said it was just that she's read your article in the paper and knew you lived near me. That's why she was asking."

"Uh huh. What did she ask about The Land?"

"Just if this is where I live now, and if I work here. Oh, and she asked how many people lived here. I said I didn't know, because I'm not sure, but I wouldn't have told her anyway."

"Nothing about the militia, then?"

"N-no, not about here, anyway. But she wanted to know everything that Darrell and I talked about, so I told her that he asked about any militias in the area."

"What was her reaction to that?"

"She didn't seem surprised at all. And I told her my answer: that I didn't know anything about any militias around here. Miss Burnside kept bringing it up though, saying that the more she knew about what Darrell and I talked about, the more it would help my case. But I don't know why that would help. Seems like it would look bad for me to be talking about militias, considering they've got me on a gun charge."

Tommy turns away, looking from side to side, eyes elevated,

seemingly studying the treetops. I would guess that he's drawing the same conclusion as I have from Cody's revelations, that not only does this incident entail more than a sawed off shotgun charge, but may even go beyond the conflict with the energy company.

"Tommy, I didn't miss any appointment. They changed the date. I check my messages every day."

He turns and addresses Cody, compassion in his voice and calm in his demeanor.

"That's okay. I know you didn't, Cody. It's not your fault. But let's lay low for a while. Don't go out in the open, especially into town. In fact, it's probably best to stay on The Land for now. We'll make them come here to look for you, okay?"

"I guess so. I'm sorry about this., Tommy."

"Don't be hard on yourself, just take it as it comes and learn from it."

The somber mood is interrupted by a burst of enthusiasm as Wagon charges Cody from some unknown location. Cody smiles and stoops to greet his dog as the exuberant animal hovers about him, tail wagging furiously, as if his master has been away for days.

"Let's go up to the cabin, boy. I'll get you something to eat."

As Cody and Wagon turn to go, Patricia intervenes. I hear an offer of dinner, to which he declines, and then in a hushed tone, she talks to him. Cody opens the truck door and Wagon jumps onto the seat. As he passes us on the road, Tommy steps up to the truck to have a few more words with his cousin. Two hands encircle my waist from behind and Patricia rests her head on my shoulder.

"I'm going inside now. Do you want to stay tonight?"

"Yes, I'd love to. I'll just need to go home to do a few things, and get my toothbrush and pajamas."

"Ha ha, okay, I'll be home. There's something I want to talk about."

Patricia releases me and turns toward the cabin. I detect a note of sadness in her voice, and as I watch her walk away I'm left wondering what that *something* she wants to talk about might be.

When Tommy rejoins me, he's silent for a moment, but I

know he has something to say. He scrapes the dry, stony surface of the road with his boot heel as if he's organizing his thoughts, so I take the opportunity to speak first.

"Do you think this is good idea, Tommy, having Cody just stay here? This may be playing right along with their plan."

"I don't think it's a good idea, Ira, but they've forced our hand. It's the best idea I can come up with at this point, and I'm sure Julian will agree with me. It was going to come to this anyway, sometime, for some reason, they just happen to be using Cody now.

"Maybe we should go to the court house and try to sort this out, or maybe consult with a different attorney."

"If we *would* sort it out this time, they'll find another reason to drag one of us into court. And what attorney can you really trust? Next Julian's court date will get switched, or you'll get arrested, or Greely."

"Do you think that Cody's attorney is cooperating with them?"

"That's my bet. Her father was a good man. He wouldn't do this, but they've gotten to her. When Cody wouldn't play ball, he was set up to miss a court appearance to add to what they already have on him. And this sudden interest in militias is no coincidence. We would be naïve to not assume it's Backbone Mountain Militia they want to know about.

"How do you think they heard about it?"

"That's what they do, monitor everybody and everything, and they keep an eye on militia groups in particular. If you heard about us through your contacts, then the government's known about us for a while.

That's no surprise. I've always assumed as much and have operated accordingly. We keep a low profile and mind our own business. No bragging about what we do or ranting about the government like some militias do."

"Why the interest now, because of the gas drilling?"

"Probably, or else the gas drilling is here now because the

government wants to draw a bead on us. Who's to say? Business and government, two side of the same coin as far as I'm concerned. Haven't big business and government always gone hand in hand?

But whatever they're after here, I feel the time has come to make a stand; the time has come to push back. Cody was framed as a way to get to us. If the government comes in here and tries to take Cody by force, they'll find out what it's like to step on a yellow jacket nest.

Yellow jackets build nest along the path to my garden, and if I leave them alone, they leave me alone. But I know well that if I step on a nest, the yellow jackets will defend their home and I *will* be attacked.

Should we let them take Cody for something he didn't do? They'll wreck the life of a good young man, trying to get him to sell out his family. I don't care who we're up against, Blue Ridge Energy Corporation, ATF, FBI, or the county sheriff, if they're wrong, they're wrong. And if they mess with us, they'll learn what it's like to step on a yellow jacket nest."

Tommy turns as a vehicle appears, and we watch as Greely's truck drives up to us. I'm thankful to see Julian with him, and as he and Lamont exit, Tommy walks over to them. I welcome the chance to ponder the words of the Field Commander because I'm having a hard time believing what I'm hearing.

Tommy is ready for a fight, even with the United States government if need be, and he seems confident that Backbone Mountain Militia is capable of doing just that. He has not once given me the impression that he's rash or reckless, but instead has impressed me as a calculating and sensible man. Yet his defiant words conjure up a possible scenario that seems outrageous to me.

But why is that so? Haven't I been witness to just such a chain of events in the past, and stood beside other people making a stand for similar convictions? My disbelief stems from the fact that I'm in the United States and still hold on to the popular notion that something like this can't happen here.

I was present in other countries, where the conflict was raw and blatant, and now I'm here where it is veiled and stealthy. But the same forces are behind it, the same corporations, billionaires, and politicians, the same insatiable lust for power and wealth.

In this quiet valley, I wanted to believe that change can happen from within, beginning with me, and the system might be changed without confrontation. But it's not to be. Karma is catching up with me.

"You and Cody stay alert, Julian. I doubt they'll come in the dark, but if Wagon barks, take it seriously. I'll be at camp if anyone's looking for me. Ira, be careful. Keep your doors locked and your gun loaded."

"Will do, Tommy."

The Field Commander walks at a brisk pace to his truck. I watch him grind up the road past Julian's cabin and disappear around the bend. Lamont drives off in the opposite direction as I approach Julian.

"Are you all right, Julian?"

"No, I ain't at all. Guess you heard, my feet are all fucked up. And that's bad enough, but I feel so tired and light-headed anymore. Sometimes I can't see real clear, things are blurry. Guess I'm breaking down at both ends."

Julian turns toward Walnut Creek Road as he grasps at his shirt pocket. He lights a cigarette, takes a drag, and tilting his head back, he exhales the smoke into the evening sky. Then he turns to me with a look of weariness and concern.

"Hell, Ira, where'd all this trouble come from? It started with Oldsmar, didn't it? Ever since that son of a bitch moved here, things have been changing for the worse. All the while he smiles and shakes hands, acting like he's doing everyone a favor. I can't stand the bastard. You suppose if we tarred and feathered him, run him out of town on a rail, it would solve our problems?"

"Right now, I wish it were so easy. But Oldsmar is just a part of it, Julian, a cog in a big machine. The real culprit is Lawrence Khan, he's the one that's ultimately pulling the strings."

"As big as he is, do you think he even knows what's going on here?"

"Actually, I would guess he does. From what I've learned, Oldsmar is one of his golden boys and Khan is grooming him for bigger and better things."

"Well I'd like to talk to this Khan, face to face, if he ever comes here to check on his golden boy."

"You would? What would you say?"

"Ask them why he wants it all. With all the money he's got, why is he grabbing for more, even if it means messing with my boy's life. What good is all that money going to do him in the long run, anyway? He's going to get old and die just like you and me.

And I'll tell him that I ain't got a lot of money, all I got is my family and this land. Walnut Hollow has been ours for hundreds of years. My great-great-great grandfather planted the walnut trees. I'll ask him why he can't respect that and let us live our lives the way we want to. What do you think he'd say?"

"I don't know how Khan could give you an honest answer without exposing himself for the fraud that he is. My guess is he would spout off the usual rhetoric about free enterprise, job creation and energy independence, like it's a duty he performs for society. He may actually believe that at some level, but it's all about money in the end. In a system driven by profit, the desire for money supersedes any genuine motive.

Unfortunately you'll never get to ask Khan those questions, Julian, as much as I wish you could. I'd guess that the closest contact he has with any of the people whose lives his business affects is at the level of Oldsmar, and you can be sure Oldsmar won't pass along any of those questions."

"Well, that's too bad. Dad always taught us that the best way to work out a problem with someone was face to face. I've avoided more than one fight that way."

"Let me ask you a question, Julian. If worse comes to worse, do you really think this is going to come down to a fight, an armed standoff?"

"I would guess so, from the way Tommy's talking now, I'd say

251

there's about a fifty-fifty chance, depending on what they do next. To be honest with you, Ira, I can hardly believe I'm saying it. Even though that's what we've been training for all these years, I guess in the back of my mind I never thought it would come to this.

Even though Tommy's warned about it since he came back from Nam, I never thought I'd be threatened by the government on my own land. We've always been left alone back in here. So, yeah, I think this could come down to a fight. I won't stand by and let them do this to Cody, and they ain't going to put me in jail for trespassing on my own land."

"Then my next question is, if it comes to a gun fight, do you think Backbone Mountain Militia has a chance?"

"Hell yeah I do. If they attack us on this property, they're going to lose. The way I see it, if we don't make a stand now, we'll have to further down the road, and by then we may have lost our advantage. We're not alone in this. Tommy has connections, believe me. And with you and Cody spreading the word on the computer, I know others will join in once there's a fight."

"So we're not just talking about a standoff here, or a skirmish to make a point. If it comes down to it, Backbone Mountain Militia is prepared for a battle."

"Yes sir, it's not what I want, or what any of us want, but it's what we train for. No sense even starting, if you don't plan to go all the way."

"Hmm, well thanks for telling me, Julian. I respect you, and all of you, for your conviction but it worries me, too. I've seen too many battles, and no matter what the cause, or who is right, everybody gets hurt. If there's any chance of working this out, face to face like your father said, we should take it.

I'd be willing to go talk with Oldsmar and see if there is any chance of that. It's a long shot, and I don't relish the thought of negotiating with him, but I think we should give it a try."

"Well Ira, that's up to Tommy. I agree with what you're saying because I don't really want a fight, but I can't make that call. At a certain point I follow orders, and we're past that point, now."

"I'll discuss it with Tommy, then. It won't hurt to talk to Oldsmar. I would think it's in his best interest to avoid a fight, since no matter what the outcome, it will reflect badly on him and his employer. He's supposed to be the facilitator here, making the concept of gas drilling acceptable to the public, winning over hearts and minds, not bullying people who won't cooperate.

At the very least, I can pick his brain and try to learn what their next move is. Like I said, I don't like the guy and I don't want to talk to him, but I've dealt with many unsavory characters over the years. It's just part of the job."

39

"**B**ut who are *they*? Are you saying that the gas company, the sheriff, and the government are all in this together, all out to get us?"

"For the sake of our own security, we have to assume that. In one way or another, they're all part of the same system, and that system is rigged for the wealthy. And in our case the one that's pulling the strings is Lawrence Khan, one of the wealthiest people in the world. The system has been rigged in his favor since he was born. He know no other way to play."

Patricia stares at me, expressionless for a moment, and then smiles. I've been rambling again and we both know it.

"Did you eat anything for supper?"

"Uh, no, I didn't even think about it. I was too mad about everything that's happened, especially what they're doing to Cody. I stomped around the house, checking doors and windows, cursing Oldsmar and Lawrence Khan and never even opened the refrigerator. But you don't have to . . ."

"No, it's no problem, and I want to. I made lasagna earlier today and all I have to do is reheat it. Why don't you pour us each a glass of wine while I do that. Oh, and why not light a fire. That would be nice."

I pour two glasses of Chablis and place them on a low table that fronts the fireplace. The stones of this elegant hearth, like the logs of which the walls are constructed, were acquired here on the

Runnion Homestead. On one of our walks, Patricia showed me the small quarry where they were excavated.

Today, at my own homestead, everything looked different to me, as if I'm no longer part of it now. The walnut bowl sat on the hewing bench unfinished, and the raised bed gardens were in need of care. I stood on the porch for a moment and longed to go back six months to when I was just starting out here in Walnut Creek.

I'm impressed by how organized Patricia is about her fire materials, with sticks of varying dimensions, arranged neatly in wrought iron holders, making it easy to build a fire. This orderliness and attention to detail characterizes her approach to renovating this grand old house. Memories of working alongside her this summer hang pleasantly in my mind and help me forget for the moment, the trouble outside the door.

I soon have a crackling blaze, and place several pieces of wood on the flaming kindling as Patricia enters the room with a plate of food. I didn't realize how hungry I was until the aroma of lasagna wafts about me. I move to the couch at her direction, and she sits next to me, sipping her wine and watching as I eat, a smile playing on her lips.

"Poor man, you're really hungry. There's plenty more, so eat up."

"I'm sorry. Am I being that obvious?"

"Don't be sorry, just eat. After all, I played my part to throw off your schedule, so I'm happy to help get something back in order."

"Patricia, it's never a disruption to see you, no matter what the reason. In fact I'm glad that you came to my place today so I could help. But tell me, you said earlier that you have something you want to talk about. I could tell by the tone of your voice that it was no small topic. So please say what you have to say. I've been wondering about it."

"Well, okay, here goes. I've been doing a lot of thinking, and I've decided to move back to Tennessee. The house up there hasn't sold yet, and I still have furniture there. I could move back in anytime. This isn't my fight here. If my father were still alive, it would be, but he's not, and I didn't come back to Walnut Hollow to fight.

I had an old fashioned dream of coming back and growing old on the home place. I even imagined grandchildren coming to visit and playing in the woods and scaring themselves in the cemetery, like we did when we were kids.

But I know that's not going to happen now. I spend too much of my time upset, worrying about what might happen next. My life in Tennessee wasn't perfect, but at least I know what I'm going to have to deal with the next day. Do you understand?"

"Yes, I understand. I'm surprised, but I understand."

"Okay, since you understand, then I'll ask you another question and surprise you even more. If things go from bad to worse, with the trouble, I mean, would you consider joining me in Tennessee?"

"Leave Walnut Creek? I don't know, Patricia. This fight, if it happens, it's not what I want either, but I feel it's one I need to fight."

"Why? You're not from here; you don't have family here."

"It's hard to explain, but in a way, Walnut Creek has always been home to me, wherever I was in the world. I wasn't born here, I wasn't raised here, but in a sense I grew up here. The basic values that I've adhered to over the years were instilled in me here.

But it's not just that. I can't escape the pull of my past. Since the beginning, covering the Vietnam war, I've felt an obligation to write the truth, expose, hypocrisy for what it is, even if it was about my own country. It's what I do, what I've done for decades, except in other countries, and in other people's fights. This is basically the same fight, and it's in the place that's home to me.

At this stage of my life, I wanted to make a difference by example, with my two hands, more so than with words. I wanted to make wooden bowls, and work my gardens, but I can't let go of who I am. When this gas drilling problem arose, I was angry because I finally made it back here and then something like this developed. But now I believe this is why I came back, to do what I can to stop it."

"I understand, Ira, and it's really what I expected you to say. I have children whose lives I want to be involved in, and if grandchildren come along, they'll never know the difference. They'll be a generation removed from Walnut Hollow and the farmhouse in Tennessee will be the home place to them. Please don't judge me for wanting out."

"I would never judge you for leaving or for anything, Patricia. In fact, I'm glad you made this decision. I don't know what's going to happen here, but from the way your brother and Tommy are talking, there's a possibility of real trouble. As much as I don't want to see you go, I'll feel better knowing you're out of here. I don't want you to get hurt or have your life compromised."

"And I don't want you to get hurt, either."

"I'm already hurt; I came here hurt. I've seen too much of war, and I don't think I'm destined to ever settle into a normal life."

"No, I don't believe that. If you want to, you can."

"Maybe, but not yet. Perhaps I'll try again some day, but for now, I feel I need to be part of this. I want to be part of this."

Patricia stares at me for a moment, moves closer, and kisses me. She takes my hands in hers and rubs them gently as she speaks.

"I have to go, Ira. I *don't* want to be part of this."

"I understand, and I think you should leave as soon as possible. Conflict is unpredictable; things can spin out of control at any time. As much as I'll miss you, I'll feel better if you're away from here, and I wish you could take Cody with you."

"Could I?"

"Oh no, you can't do that. However it plays out with Cody, it has to happen here. If he runs, there's no doubt how it will play out. And who knows, Patricia, if trouble starts, you'll probably be more help to him from the outside."

"Okay, Ira, I'll leave at the end of the week. It'll take me a little time to pack and make the arrangements. You can stay here at the house if you want to. I'd feel better knowing you were here. And please keep the gun."

"Thanks. I may take you up on both counts. And thank you for dinner. I haven't eaten lasagna in years, and I've never eaten lasagna that was so good."

"That's nice to hear. Lasagna was one of Donny's favorite meals, so I worked at it.

Ira, you know what I would like to do now? I'd like to just sit in front of the fire and forget about trouble for the rest of the evening. Let's just be two old folks, watching the flames and enjoying each others company."

40

The sun appears through treetops as I drive up the last incline to the hunting cabin. Rounding the bend, I see a horse, tethered near the door. Julian told me that Tommy is at the hunting cabin most of the time now. As I might have guessed, it's also the command center, and was built on top of Backbone Mountain because it's hard to reach, and easy to defend.

Julian arranged the time of the meeting, and has briefed the Field Commander on its purpose. I'm a little apprehensive as I knock, wondering if I'm stepping out of bounds with this proposal, but I'm put at ease when Tommy opens the door and smiles.

"Come on in, Ira. Have a seat. Coffee?"

"Yes, please. That's just what I need. This is a great setting to drink coffee and watch the sun come up."

"It is, but this morning I've kept my face to the computer. I have dispatches to get out."

"Email?"

"No, old fashioned letters, except for the fact that I'm writing them with a word processor. No email for me, or cell phones."

"I think that's a good idea. That's long been my policy for anything I want to keep private.

So, Tommy, Julian has told you about my proposal. What do you think? It's just a suggestion and I'm not trying to push my own agenda. Believe me, there are few people in the world I care less to talk to than Don Oldsmar. Since you opened the door and let me in, you mustn't be totally opposed to it."

"No, not opposed, I have mixed feelings. But I trust your judgment, and I know you're with us. I don't want to show them our hand, but maybe we can call their bluff and see what they've got in their hand. How far are they willing to go with this, that's the question. Are intimidation tactics and legal tricks as far as they take it or will they resort to force."

"I can't imagine military action to arrest Cody."

"Hmm, I don't know. It's not just about Cody, you know that. It's more about Julian, someone who won't bend to their will. And, it may be about all of us, armed citizens who don't play by the rules. I think anything is possible here, so we have to be prepared."

"If I may ask, Tommy, just how prepared are you to stand up to this? I've only seen a handful of men at any one time, that's hardly the makings of an army."

"There are many more; I can muster two hundred soldiers at a moment's notice. These are men who have trained hard in these woods and who are just as determined as I am not to be invaded.

"But that's still a paltry number compared to what you would be facing. When you take on the state, you're defying an empire and it could bring more arms to bear than anyone here has ever imagined."

"Once trouble starts, more troops will come. Some years back, I helped formed a citizen soldier alliance, a partnership to coordinate militias across the country to respond to aggression against any one group. That's what I was doing when you came in, preparing a dispatch to update the others on our situation here.

Presently there are over four hundred active militias in the United States. I contact a hundred of them directly, and the rest will get the message from the ones I contact. So you see the number of troops adds up quickly. The Michigan Militia alone has ten thousand members."

"And you just contact them by regular mail?"

"Yes, in plain envelopes, without return addresses. An employee at the post office makes certain they get distributed throughout the day's mail, and sometimes staggers their release, so that they don't get noticed."

"An employee at the post office is part of this?"

"Yes, more than one in fact, but the one I'm speaking of is Amy Caldwell."

"Amy, my cousin, she knows about Backbone Mountain Militia? You're telling me that you take this correspondence to the post office and Amy helps distribute it."

"No, the mailman takes the letters down. I meet him at the end of my lane, and he takes them to Amy."

"Barney's involved, too?"

"I wouldn't say he's involved. Barney and Amy and other people in the county are what might be called sympathizers or collaborators. They don't know all the details or exactly who we all are, but they identify with the cause, and help however they can."

"Whew, this is much more involved than I thought. Okay, so tell me this, are you confident that these other militias will come in the event of a fight?"

"Oh they'll come, and come silently from every direction. Just when the feds think they have us figured out, guns will be pointing at them from behind every tree. And some of the groups have their own actions planned to show support. If the government strikes here, they'll find themselves facing armed disruptions all over the country soon after. You might say it's our own version of the Tet Offensive."

"You know, Tommy, what scares me is I know your serious. You're talking about revolution."

"I don't think you scare that easily, and you, yourself, said that at some point revolution is the inevitable outcome of a dying capitalist system. Maybe not in those exact words, but you made that point in more than one of your articles."

"Hmm, I guess I can't argue with that then. Let's hope it

doesn't go that far, which brings us back to my meeting with Oldsmar."

"Right. So what exactly do you plan to propose to him?"

"I don't really plan to propose much. I know the man, somewhat, and he's an egotistical sort, to say the least. Julian got under his skin and no doubt some of this is about payback. But in the end, money and control are what matters most to his kind, and trouble costs money and makes control unpredictable.

Maybe I can convince him that it's in the best interest of his boss, and thus in his best interest, to diffuse the situation and avoid the cost of trouble. After all, he'll eventually be moving on to do this in another place, so why get mired down here.

What I thought I could do is hint that there could be much more trouble than he imagined, without being openly threatening, or telling him too much. In fact, I want to come across as sharing with him some inside information, from one outsider to another.

Maybe if I can get them to back off a little and talk to us, we can get the charges dropped against Cody and Julian, diffuse the immediate crisis. At the least I might buy some time to let the word get out."

"Okay, Ira. Sounds like a plan to me. I have my doubts, but if Oldsmar goes for it that would make my job easier. I'm not looking for a fight, but as the commander I have to know when to make a stand before we lose too much ground. Like I said, I trust your judgment on this."

"Thanks, Tommy, I'll do my best."

41

I can see by the court house clock that it's nearly time for our meeting. What do I say to this Oldsmar character? I have little optimism that discourse between the two of us will avert conflict, but I must try at least.

Out of the woods, away from the aura of the Field Commander, my discussion with the man seems surreal to me. Backbone Mountain Militia has no chance in a confrontation with the government. Like it or not, I've got to talk to Oldsmar.

A Porsche pulls to the curb on the opposite side of Main Street and Oldsmar steps out. He grins and waves to a woman who is walking up the courthouse steps such that he doesn't notice my approach. As I enter the café, Oldsmar is at the counter and turns to the sound of the door chime.

"Ira, just in time. I'm having a Chai latte. Do you want one?"

"No, coffee's fine, black."

"Okay, that's simple enough. We can sit out on the deck. More private out there, and we can watch the river go by."

Oldsmar is trying to be friendly, smiling and being polite. He chats with the waitress as she prepares our beverages, and it's obvious from the conversation that he's a regular here. I follow him out the back door to a long porch running horizontal to the river. He stirs his latte with a cinnamon stick, while I sip my coffee, both of us distracted by the sight and sound of the river, swirling and

263

frothing as it wends it's way north to Tennessee. Oldsmar takes a resolute swallow of his beverage and turns toward me.

"I'd like to think that we're here because you've had a change of heart and want to do some writing for Blue Ridge Energy Corporation."

"No."

"Too bad. That would have been a lot more fun. Then my guess is that you want to discuss what's happening in the valley. I don't think I'm being presumptuous by assuming you've come in the role of ambassador for the indigenous people. Anything in particular you want to chat about, Mr. Ambassador?"

"*Everything* in particular: the fireworks on Memorial Day, the engine brake salute during Adam Runnion's burial, Cody's arrest, Julian's arrest, what happened in Robinson's parking lot, the two men . . ."

"Whoa, what makes you think all those things are related?"

"Aren't they?"

"Maybe they are, but I can't say for sure. I just do my end of the job and that is to buy and lease land, prepare the way for this project to go forward. As far as what happened at Robinson's, I was there to introduce you to Scott Hagen. We're associates, but he works independently of me; he has his own part to play."

"And that is?"

"Hmm, I guess you could say he does whatever needs to be done to keep things running smoothly. While I'm preparing the way, Scott deals with obstacles that get in the way."

"The muscle, eh"

"No, the facilitator. But speaking of muscle, it looked like you had a little muscle of your own, Mr. Ambassador. I was impressed. Scott wasn't though, and that may be why . . ."

"What about the ATF, why bring them into it?"

"Who, what, the ATF? Nobody brought them into it; they were already into it. Your friends were already on their radar."

"Lot's of people are on their radar, but my guess is someone used a little political pull to make the Runnions a priority."

"I'm not saying that's what happened, but I wouldn't be surprised if that's what happened."

"But why these tactics; why such a tough and underhanded approach from the start? These are decent and reasonable people that you're dealing with here. Why not try to find some common ground and avoid trouble?"

"Takes too much time, and time is money. And these tactics work. We move in quick, get the job done and then move out. Lawyers and accountants take care of whatever trouble is stirred up in the wake."

"But is money all that matters to you? You're tearing apart a community, disrupting lives."

"I told you, my job is to buy and lease land and prepare the way for this project to go forward. I have to do what I have to do. Let's face it, in any big operation, there's always some collateral damage."

"Collateral damage, eh? I've only heard that expression in reference to a military operation. Is that the way you view your business here, like a battle in a war?"

"If you consider war in the sense that one side is determined to get something the other side has, with whatever means is necessary, then yes."

"What you're saying then is that since your side has the money and the power you can just take something that belongs to somebody else."

"Um, yes, basically that's what I'm saying. The big picture is what counts, and we can't get slowed down by details. This is how the world operates, Stone. You know that. And you had your chance to be part of it, to retire in real style. Instead you choose to be the social crusader, fighting for a hopeless cause. As such, you and your career, *or what's left of it*, will be part of the collateral damage."

"Oh, you think so? Well our discussion here is over then. Sorry to have wasted your time, and even more so to have wasted mine."

I'm enraged. I didn't expect much empathy from him but I'm surprised at just how arrogant he is when the façade comes down. I get up and start to walk away, so that I don't vent my fury with careless words, but at the door, I collect myself and turn back to face Oldsmar.

"I'll tell you one last thing, not that it will matter to you. These are good people here whose lives you are toying with. They're not details in a business plan. They don't have a lot of money, but they work hard and are proud of what they do have. Someday this will come back to haunt you."

"Hah, I don't think so. Don't give me that comes around goes around bullshit. I don't believe in karma and neither do you, Stone. Just sticking a Buddha in your yard doesn't change who you are."

"And how do you know what I have in my yard? I don't recall having you over for tea."

"We know a lot about you, especially your time in the Mideast, *consorting with the enemy*. We'll see whose past comes back to haunt them.

And as far as these so-called good people you're associating with now, we gave the Runnions a chance to be part of this, to make some money for once in their miserable lives, and they turned it down. And tell me this, if they're such good people, why do they have a private army in their backyard?"

I know this is no offhand remark, but a card Oldsmar was waiting to play. Like a cat, he watches me, with an expression of superiority and self-satisfaction. As much as I loathe this man, I must choose my words well and not play into his hands. Fortunately I have decades of experience, dealing with such offensive personalities.

"An army in their backyard? I assume you're referring to the hunting club. They're a handful of men that go out and play army on weekends."

"What fun. I'm surprised you haven't joined up with them."

"I came here to get away from that, to start a new life. I

don't want to play army with them anymore than I want to play journalism with you."

"Well that's good to know, Stone, that at least you won't be taking up arms against us. And I'm glad we had this talk, I mean that. I'll be sure to pass the information along."

Oldsmar grins, as if satisfied with what he's learned, and I decide to end our conversation by walking away from him.

I drive slowly along Walnut Creek Road, talking to myself, trying to settle down. Oldsmar is a more sinister character than I even imagined, and I know too well now that further discussion with him is futile.

The Wooden Bowl Shoppe comes into view, and the sign looks so inviting as I round the bend that I pull into the parking lot. I enter by way of the workshop, leaving the front door locked. Positioning myself on the hewing bench, I pick up the bowl adze, and tap it gently against the walnut bowl that has been lying in place for over a week, rough and unfinished.

With my left hand, I brace the bowl and hew a few chips from it's interior. Laying the adze down I close my eyes, and drop my head. How could I ever have imagined the events that are unfolding around me? And now Patricia is leaving.

"What's going on in here young man?"

I'm startled by the sound of Ben's voice and turn to see him staring at me through the open door. He places his hands on each side of the frame and pulls himself into the shop.

"Hello Ben. How are you?"

"Good as I can be. I just came over to see why I don't hear too much chipping these days. Are you on strike?"

"Ha ha, no, just distracted. There are some things happening now and . . ."

"I know what's happening."

"You know about the trouble with the Runnion family?"

"Yes, and I know of that Oldsmar fellow, too, and what he's all about."

"Funny you should say that, I just had a meeting with him downtown, hoping that a face to face talk might prevent trouble, but now I know better. He wants trouble."

"Humph, I don't doubt that. What time was the meeting?"

"Right at noon, I just got back from it. Why?"

"That's just about the time a black Suburban pulled up to your place. A man got out and went around behind and wasn't there long before he came hurrying back to the vehicle. I tried to get the license number, but couldn't quite make it out from inside my house."

"Well, what do you know. I'm sure that wasn't a coincidence, and I have no doubt that Oldsmar knew about it."

"What do you suppose the guy was doing here?"

"Who knows, but I'm sure it wasn't just a house call. Maybe he bugged the place."

A truck pulls into the parking lot and seconds later, Tommy walks through the door. He grins when he sees Ben.

"Hey, Ben, how are you?"

"Good, Tommy, you know me, still at it."

They shake hands and Ben puts a hand on Tommy's shoulder as he turns to me.

"I've known this man since all the way back when he was riding the school bus."

"That's right, when the bus would break down, we hated to see Ben come along because he'd get it running again, and then we'd have to go to school."

"Ha, ha, I remember that, and you were one of the ones that complained the loudest."

"Is Edna well?"

"Yep, doing fine. In fact that's where I'm heading now for lunch, so I better get back across the road. And I'm sure you and Ira have things to talk about. Come and see me Tommy."

"I'll do that, Ben."

Ben steps out and Tommy turns to me.

"So how did it go with Oldsmar?"

"Not good. He wouldn't even consider compromise."

"Well I thought that's the way it would turn out, but I was hoping to be proven wrong."

"And once the fake smile comes off, he's a more sinister character than I suspected. Unfortunately, I can't say I gained much knowledge as to what their next move might be or how far they're willing to go, but one point of interest came out right at the end of our conversation. Oldsmar mentioned the militia."

"He did?"

"Yes, not by name, but he alluded to it as the private army the Runnions have in their backyard. I'm not sure what he knows, but my guess is not much. He may have been trying to find out more, because he seemed to be trying to catch me off guard. I told him that the militia isn't much more than a hunting club, a handful of men who go out into the woods and play army."

"Do you think he believed you?"

"Hmm, I can't say for sure, but probably not."

"If he did, you played him well."

"He played me, too. Ben just told me that a man showed up here right about the time I was meeting with Oldsmar. He went around my house then came hurrying back to his vehicle and took off."

"That doesn't sound good. You know Ira, maybe you should consider moving onto The Land. I know you've put your heart and soul into this place, but I don't like the way they keep targeting you. Alone here, you're a sitting duck. Ben's watching, but I don't think he'd be enough help if there was real trouble."

"That's interesting that you would say that. Patricia offered me her place just yesterday. She's moving back to Tennessee. Did you know that?"

"No I didn't."

"She doesn't want to be here if there's a showdown."

"Well I hate to see her go, but I can't blame her. I'd take her up on the offer though. That house is in a good spot, well off the main road, and with Julian right there behind you. You can still come back here during the day, but I would come with someone else or at least make sure others besides Ben know you're here."

"Does Ben know about the Militia?"

"Oh yeah. We call him the gatekeeper. Anything that happens at this end of the valley that he thinks we should know about, he lets us know."

"How, he doesn't call you, does he?"

"Oh, no, he slips a note to Barney and it gets to me with the mail."

"I never imagined this, such a network and collaboration."

"Well, imagine it, Ira. People around here aren't going to be pushed around. We may not have a lot of money or political pull, but we have the numbers, and we stick together. That's what people like Khan don't realize. A man like him has lost all sense of community or cooperation, if he ever had it. The only kind of loyalty he knows about is the kind that's bought and sold.

Move onto The Land for now, at least until we see how this plays out. If nothing else it will make them wonder where you are."

"I'll give it some thought. I hate to give the impression that they've gotten to me, because, in a way, they have. Let me ask you something, Tommy, did you ever think it would come a showdown like this?"

"Yes, I always knew it would come to this someday. That's why I've been getting ready all these years."

"So you'll go all out, if necessary."

"A battle, you mean? I hate to say it, I hate to even think about it at times, but the answer is yes. Only as a last resort, of course, but combat has to be on the table. I believe we have no chance of holding our own against these people unless we're willing to see it through to the end."

The Field Commander leaves on that note. I move the jeep to the house, and sit in the driveway for a moment, feeling old and a bit overwhelmed by all I've learned today. In a sense, I've talked to leaders of the opposing forces in a potential conflict, and each in their own way are defiant and confident. A clash seems inevitable.

I have no reservation concerning the side with which I stand in this fight, the question that disturbs me is why I'm standing here again. Is it just bad luck, unwholesome karma, or am I the problem? Do I foment conflict with the very rhetoric that I hope is alleviating it?

I withdraw the gun from my pocket and enter the house, but see no sign that someone has entered. I'm relieved to see the office undisturbed and return the pistol to my pocket when I find the back door still secure.

Stepping onto the porch, the rock garden catches my eye. The statue of Buddha isn't there. As I look more closely, I see that the statue *is* there, but has been smashed into a pile of rubble.

42

"I will get your mail to you Ira, don't worry about that. Are you going to be okay?"

"I'll be fine, Amy. I'm just being careful."

"I don't blame you. There's some funny things going on around here, except they're not funny. If you need anything, just let me know."

The door chime rings and Amy looks past me as a man and woman enter the lobby. Another man is approaching the door, and I elect to end our conversation and go. I don't want to linger in town for long. I give Amy a reassuring smile and promise her that I'll be in touch.

Exiting the post office, I glance up and down Main Street and see only few pedestrians, and these are at the next intersection, near the court house. I look toward the hardware store, and wish I were going there next to buy supplies for my various projects, but I make straight for the jeep. I've got other work to do now.

I've had enough, and I'm tired of being a target. Oldsmar knew what was happening at my place even while we spoke. He mentioned the Buddha, knowing that I would find it destroyed shortly after our conversation. Was his intent merely to mock me or to demonstrate how easily they can get to me? And what else do they know about me, of my support for Massoud, of my friendship with Mahmud? Do they know about the wedding, about Bamiyan, even?

Just as I turn to fasten my seat belt, the passenger door opens and a man gets in beside me. With a hand that's inside his coat pocket, he motions forward and tells me to drive. I assume he's holding a weapon and when I hesitate to follow his directive, he reaches across, pats my jacket and deftly removes Patricia's gun from the pocket.

"Drive, Mr. Stone. I mean no harm. I just want to talk. Take a right at the light and head toward River Road."

Aside from the sudden imposition, I sense no malice in his tone or demeanor. The man is younger than me, but not by much. He has a tough, weathered face, thinning auburn hair that's smoothed back behind his ears, and a neatly trimmed, mustache. If I were to judge him by his dress, I would assume he was a vacationer, passing through Madison County, or a retiree, recently moved to the area.

I ease out of the parking lot, turn south on Main Street, and drive out of town along the French Broad River. My passenger studies the side mirror for a moment and then turns toward me, placing the Smith and Wesson on the seat between us.

"You should wear this in a holster, Mr. Stone, over your left shoulder."

"I guess I should. Have we met before?"

"As a matter of fact, yes, fifteen years ago in a hotel room in Pakistan. I was in the company of two disruptive companions, who relieved you of some of your possessions."

"I remember that well. In fact I just thought about it last week. Who were you working for? I've often wondered about that."

"It doesn't matter. I don't work for them anymore."

"Was that you in the park, the vehicle on the island?"

"No, but I know who it was, and you were in no danger. They were there for your protection."

"What's this about then? We're both a long way from Quetta."

"Yes, we are, and like you I've never forgotten that night. It

273

was the beginning of the end for me, when the notion that I might be on the wrong side got into my head. You were doing your job, doing what was right and willing to risk your life for it. *You have no idea how close you came to losing your life that night.* And in the face of it you were defiant, unwavering. You seemed sure you were on the right side, and I, somewhere deep down, knew you were on the right side, too.

But enough of that. I have some things to tell you, and you'll have to fill in the details because I must be brief. We can't be seen together. You're in danger, Mr. Stone. Do you realize that?"

"You mean with regards to the gas drilling? I know the situation has become volatile, and I'm taking necessary precautions, but I really didn't . . . You mean as if my life is in danger?"

"Yes, that's exactly what I mean. The dirty tricks are just a prelude to get you to mix it up with them, then they'll take you out."

"But why, because of what I'm writing?"

"Yes, because of what you're writing, but even more so, because of what you've written. Your words have always hit too close to home, and influence too many people. That's why you're a target now; that's why you were a target in Quetta. It was no chance encounter that night and neither is this."

"What are you saying?"

"Just what I said. With your essays and books, you've been a thorn in the side of the power brokers for decades. Even in retirement you're a threat. So long as you're alive and still writing, you're a living testimony to what you've said and done in the past. *And* there's an element of retribution here, key players that you've crossed along the way sense an opportunity now."

"Are you telling me that Blue Ridge Energy Corporation is in Walnut Creek because of me?"

"The power and authority that Blue Ridge Energy represents is everywhere now, all pervasive. The gas drilling is just how it manifests itself to serve this purpose. You being here influenced the decision to undertake a larger and multifaceted operation, but you're not the only reason.

Backbone Mountain Militia have been monitored for some time now, and of particular interest is the individual known as the Field Commander. Sooner or later they were going to move on him and the militia he commands, just as they were going to move on you. For whatever reason you two ended up in one place, it opened up an opportunity that can't be passed up.

"Then what's your message, that I should get out of town, for everybody's sake?"

"No, it's too late for you to get out of town. My message is that you're not alone here, and the odds aren't as long as they might seem. The American empire is coming to an end, Mr. Stone. You know that as well as anybody, but I don't think even you would guess that the end is so close.

A government seems to have control right up until it collapses, and that's because the system rots from within. It comes to an abrupt end when the enablers: the police, the armed forces, and the security services will no longer support it, when they realize they're on the wrong side."

"And you think we're at that point?"

"It's impossible to say for sure, but from the information I'm receiving, I think we are. Besides that, citizen militias are mobilizing all over the country. Something is amiss. We've never seen anything like this before. All that's needed is a flashpoint. That's why you and I are talking now.

The government is tripping over it's own hubris and little wonder: a puppet president, a cabinet of billionaires, and a complacent congress, most of them beholding to Lawrence Khan, the man who wants to be king. You know Khan's gearing up for a run at the presidency in 2020, don't you?

Oh, uh, take this left up ahead and pull over at the top of the mountain."

Slowing to turn, I glance at the rear view mirror and see a blue car about a hundred yards behind. Halfway up the rise, I look back to see that the vehicle made the turn as well and closes the distance between us. The wooded road is unfamiliar to me, and we pass no structures before reaching the crest of a mile long slope.

The area to pull off is obvious and large enough for two vehicles. The trailing car pulls in behind, some sort of convertible, shiny, metallic blue, with a black, fabric roof.

"Is this your ride?"

"Yes. I doubt we will speak again, so I urge you to heed my words. Take no chances. Trust your instincts and experience, even over what seems to be common sense. Do what you do best Mr. Stone, and I'll do what I do best."

"Wait, one more question. Why here and why now? If I'm that much of a threat, why didn't they take me out before now?"

"You've had some help, some resistance from within. I like to think it's a sign that the foot soldiers are starting to turn. Your well known in political circles, not to mention, a Pulitzer Prize winner. They want to take you out on their terms and be careful not to create a martyr. If it can be made to appear that the action is warranted, then your legacy will be tainted as well."

"Warranted, for journalism, for writing the truth?"

"What's true doesn't matter, as long as the public goes along with the popular narrative. If the story is that you're consorting with terrorists then no one will feel sorry for you."

"Consorting with terrorists, here in Walnut Creek?"

"It all depends on how you define terrorism. The fact is, an attempt was made to take you out in Afghanistan and for that very reason, but they missed. I need to go. Take the next left, a gravel road. It winds around for a few miles and comes out on the other side of Walnut Creek. Good Luck, Mr. Stone."

The man gets out and walks at a brisk pace to the waiting car. As soon as the passenger door shuts, the vehicle makes a U-turn and descends in the direction whence it arrived. Despite my astonishment at this encounter, instinct warns me against lingering here to think about it. A quarter mile along the road, I make the recommended turn, and welcome the wilderness that engulfs me along a route that is obviously little used.

What am I to do with this information? Do I have any right to remain in Walnut Creek if I my presence puts others in danger? How could I have been so naïve as to think that I could leave the fight behind in Afghanistan. This is a clash that has no borders.

They missed me in Afghanistan, eh? What terrorist group was I consorting with? Was it the Northern Alliance? Massoud was battling the Taliban when I was with him, and at the time, *they* were the terrorists.

After Massoud was killed and the United States invaded, I made an effort to remain neutral in my interactions and writing, and I don't see how my associations during that period could have been interpreted as consorting with terrorists. At any rate no attempt was made to kill me that I'm aware of, unless I didn't notice amid the usual violence.

He casually made the statement that they missed me, which implies that he's referencing a specific incident. But I can't recall an occasion . . .

Oh no, how can fate be so cruel. Why didn't I see it before, amid the guilt that I can never seem to dispel. Goddamn them a thousand times. Habib's wedding, those rockets were for me.

43

"Federal Marshals ask you to talk to us? You got to be kidding me."

"I wouldn't kid you, Julian. People told them that I lived here for a while and how I got along with you and your folks. Figured there'd be no trouble this way, I guess."

Julian grins. "Why didn't they send the sheriff, isn't that his job? And don't tell me they drove back to your place? They're likely to have got shot."

"Nah, sent Billy Hunter back to fetch me and I met them at the Community Center."

Such an interesting character, this man who pulled up to Julian's cabin in an aged Ford pickup, painted in a camouflage pattern. Julian greeted him with loud exclamation, and called him Josiah. At first sight, he reminds me of Julian, although he's at least a decade younger and sports a beard that's longer and more unruly.

The two of them seem to know each other well. They stand close and half smile as they speak, suggesting they share some inside joke. The fact that Josiah was allowed to drive to Julian's doorstep indicates that he's a trusted acquaintance.

"Ira, this is Josiah Johnson, a friend of the family. He lives way at the end of Heck Creek Road. He used to work here on the farm some years back, but we don't see him much anymore. He only comes out of the hollow a few times a year. Josiah, this here's

278

Ira Stone. He's a bowl maker and a writer."

Josiah steps forward and shakes my hand.

"Ira, nice to meet you. Don't believe what he says about me. If it ever was true, it isn't anymore. You're set up down in the old Ramsey store, right?"

"Y-yes, I'm not there so much lately. I'm kept pretty busy with what's happening around here."

"Yah, I bet. Things are getting worrisome for sure."

"So what did the Feds send you here to talk to us about? Did they bribe you or blackmail you into it?"

"No, they're pretty nice guys, a little uppity, but all right. The guy in charge told me that they're the law enforcement arm of the court and it was their duty as US Marshals to bring in the fugitive named Cody Runnion."

"Who, Cody? Cody's a fugitive?"

"That's what they called him. Said he failed to appear for a court hearing and the The Bureau of Alcohol, Tobacco, and Firearms passed the case on to them."

"He didn't know anything about that hearing. The date got changed on him."

"Well, I don't doubt that a bit, but according to them a letter was sent out, and since Cody didn't show up, they have to bring him in. They said they're prepared to do it one way or the other and the easiest way is if he surrenders."

Julian sighs, pulls a cigarette from his coat pocket, and lights it. He gazes at the ground for moment, then back at Josiah.

"How many of them are there, Jo?"

"More than a few. Sheriff Pettit was there, but he kept his distance from me. A couple state cops and then the people I talked to, the marshals."

"Any guns?"

"Hah, for sure. I saw lots, and I'm bettin' there's more I didn't see. What do want me to tell them, Julian? I ain't supposed to bring him in, just see what he wants to do. I better get back down there in a timely fashion or they'll suppose I joined up with you."

"Joined up with us? Hell, you're more dangerous than we are, they should know that."

"Ha, ha, but I ain't like that anymore."

"Uh huh, I hear you, Jo. Let's see, how about if you tell them Cody needs a little time to think it over?"

"All right, how's this? I'll tell them I think the Runnions are coming around, but they have to talk it over first. How about if I come back in a couple hours?

"That sounds good."

"Tell me, just between us, will you let them take Cody?"

"No, not a chance."

"Damn, I didn't think so. Can't say I blame you. Okay then, I'll be off."

"Thanks Jo."

As Josiah Johnson's truck squeaks and bumps away from us, Julian turns to me and sighs.

"I best go talk to Tommy about this, even though I know what he'll say. Last I talked to him, he seemed well dug in for a brawl."

The Field Commander listens, his elbows on the arms of the chair, his chin resting atop folded hands. When he hears that Josiah Johnson is the messenger, a smile plays on his lips. He shakes his head from side to side and stands.

"I swear, wild Jo, it would take something like this to bring him out of that hollow. Doesn't that beat all. I can see why they'd send someone we know back here, but I wonder why they asked Josiah. There are other people who would better fit the bill. Anyone who knows Josiah would suppose he'd be on our side.

Anyway, as far as a response, I've been doing a lot of thinking, and I'm even more convinced that we have to make a stand here and now. We're being provoked, our rights are being encroached upon. I say it's time we hold our ground by not turning Cody over to them. Where's Cody now, Julian?"

"He's working with Jerry Dale at the mill."

"Good, well tucked in. We got to keep him on The Land and away from the road. What do you think he'll want to do?"

"I already had this discussion with him and he says he's not going back in, no matter what we decide. My boy ain't naturally a fighter, but he's been tricked and lied to, and he's had enough."

"Alright, it's settled then. I'll send a dispatch out to our associates in the alliance and let them know what we've decided. How's the internet side of this going, Ira?"

"Good, real good. Thousands of people are behind us, and we have support all over the world. The numbers have grown considerably, even in the last few days."

"That's what I was hoping to hear. Well Julian, I think we should let Mr. Johnson know of our intention, so that he doesn't keep the Feds waiting. I'm going with you. I want a few words with Josiah."

Downhill, it's an easy walk to Patricia's cabin and just the exertion I need to clear my head. As I trudge down the dirt road, away from the hunting camp, I breathe deep the crisp autumn air, soothing my lungs as well as my spirit. Yet at the same time, the gray sky casts a melancholic mood, and the raspy cawing of crows seems to herald trouble.

How did it so quickly come to a standoff? Is it fate that I've crossed paths with Tommy Gosnell, a military hermit who's been preparing for this moment for decades. The stand he's taking seems hopeless, but so it must have seemed with Massoud in the beginning, when he chose to defy the Soviets.

The Lion of Panshir prevailed, the Soviets were defeated. Is Tommy an American Massoud, the Lion of Walnut Creek? If he is, am I really prepared to stand with him? Revolution has been hypothetical up until now, words on paper.

I round a bend to a long downhill slope and see a woman approaching me, and when she waves, I know it's Patricia. As I cross the distance that separate us, the thought enters my head that I'm a fool to not go to Tennessee with her.

"Julian told me you were walking back, so I thought I would head you off. My goodness, I'm out of breath. I need to get out and walk more."

"Or else plan your walk by a downhill route, like I did."

Patricia smiles and we embrace, holding each other tightly until I'm a bit out of breath, myself. In spite of the drama that has enveloped us, and the threat of greater trouble on the horizon, the present moment is perfect, like a dream.

"I made lentil soup for lunch. There's a pot on the wood stove, if you're hungry."

"Mmm, if I wasn't, I am now. I'll race you back."

"No thanks. I want to take a leisurely stroll with you while I still can. I've been thinking about you a lot today, and a question came to me. Was there anybody in your life all those years that you were traveling? I mean a woman. Especially the years in Afghanistan. You seem to have liked the country and people so much, I was just wondering. You don't have to answer if you don't want to. It's really none of my business."

"No, it's a reasonable question. There was always Justine, and I've told you about Justine, a complicated relationship from the beginning that only got more complicated over the years we worked together. For what it is, it works and we're still together in a sense.

There was no romantic relationship in Afghanistan. Well, I guess that depends on how you define a romantic relationship. The sister of my friend Mahmud, Parisa Safi, she and I were fond of each other. Parisa was in her forties and had never married, which is unusual in Afghanistan, but not surprising to me once I got to know her. Nothing amorous, I never held her, or kissed her, but I knew she liked me and she knew I liked her. We always gravitated toward each other on any occasion when we were both present."

"Did your friend, Mahmud, know about this?"

"I think he did, but I'm not sure. Such a relationship was out of the question so he may have just not acknowledged it, whether he approved or not."

"So what happened, did it end when you left Afghanistan?"

"Uh, no. It ended when Parisa was killed in a military air strike."

"Oh no, I'm so sorry."

"It was a terrible thing. It was the wedding of Mahmud's son, and was a most wonderful occasion up until the strike. Mahmud and I had just stepped outside to talk when the rockets hit the house. Ten people were killed, including Parisa."

"Oh, Ira, that's terrible. I'm so sorry I brought it up."

"Don't be sorry. It was an honest question with an unfortunate and tragic answer. It's something I've had to live with ever since, the death of Parisa and her family, a family that had taken me in, treated me like one of their own."

"Why would a wedding party be bombed?"

"Until recently, I believed it was a mistake, but now I know that, uh, that the answer is much more complicated. I've seen many terrible things in my years as a war correspondent, but this particular incident broke me. I knew I had to get out. I couldn't witness any more war."

"Then why not stay out? I know what's happening here is no comparison to what you've seen, especially what happened to Parisa and her family, but why take a chance? After what you've been through, you deserve a peaceful life, working in your garden and writing just for pleasure. Why stay here when you don't have to?"

"Because it's what I do; it's what I've always done. People need to know the truth, what's being done in their name. It's my job to tell them, whether they like it or not, or whether I like it or not."

"I'm still going to Tennessee, Ira."

"I understand that, and I think you should. Hopefully, after this is settled, we can pick up where we left off and get back to our many projects: your family home place, the gardens, the Wooden Bowl Shoppe, Cody's organic farm."

"And you think it's all going to just settle? Josiah Johnson is involved now. Do you know who he is? I saw Josiah and Tommy talking before I started up here and I know it wasn't just to make conversation."

"I only know what I was told about Josiah when we were introduced."

"Well you weren't told the half of it, I'm sure. Josiah is a crazy man, smart, but crazy, and his specialty is explosives."

"What?"

"Josiah was a navy seal. He was in the Gulf war and has medals to prove it, although he'd never show you."

"He mentioned that he once lived here. When was that?"

"His father died when he was a boy, and my father was a friend of the family. He took Josiah under his wing for a while and had him work here on the farm. Everyone liked him, especially Julian who was like a big brother to him. Josiah was always wild and his years in the service didn't change that.

He did some time in jail for blowing up a barn that belonged to some people from Florida that he had a run-in with. In recent years, he's kept to himself, out of sight and mostly out of trouble. That's why I was surprised to see him here. Julian said he was asked to mediate on behalf of federal marshals, but I can't imagine that."

"On the surface, the reason that they gave him seems plausible enough, but now that I know a little of his story, I have to suspect an ulterior motive, maybe to associate us with him. At any rate, this is getting interesting."

"Not for me. It's getting scary. I know my family, Ira, and they're not going to back down. There's going to be real trouble here for sure.

44

Early morning, lying with a beautiful women in the most serene of settings and staring into darkness. Patricia is asleep, at peace with her decision to leave, while I lie awake, resigned to my resolution not to accompany her. I get up, put on a coat, and slip out the front door. Fresh air is what I need, a session of quiet contemplation on the porch swing to reign in my thoughts.

After hearing about the clandestine passenger I entertained yesterday, the Field Commander was unwavering in his defiance. He expressed skepticism that I was the reason for the outside presence in the valley, and stated that even if true, it didn't alter the situation. He implored me to remain in Walnut Creek, and was adamant that I should do so here on The Land.

Tommy was not surprised that he and the militia are part of the equation. In fact, he seemed quite amused by that information. He instructed Josiah Johnson to use his moniker, Field Commander, in reply to the Federal Marshals. They know the name, and the message will be clear. Not only will Cody not turn himself in, but Backbone Mountain Militia will fight to prevent his apprehension. What form will the government's response take, and what sort of fight is the Field Commander prepared to engage in?

I've never pressed he or Julian on military specifics, but both men speak with confidence about the capability of their army. My assumption is that the arsenal includes more of the light arms I've seen, and their tactics would necessarily entail guerrilla warfare.

Certainly they have the capability to make a stand, to fight a battle, but battles become wars. I can't envision this mountain militia engaged in a prolonged campaign against such a formidable enemy. If the state decides to use even a fraction of the power at it's disposal, the fight will be over before it even starts.

And yet revolutions happen. I've witnessed it, but I never expected such a development in the United States. Even if the information I garnered in town is trustworthy, and the time is right for revolution, are these people prepared to be in the vanguard of such an uprising?

The cool autumn air is invigorating, and I find comfort in the whirring and chirping of myriad insects, as if they are on our side. They're small in size, but countless in number and unrelenting. The future is not fixed and I shouldn't fret the night away, worrying about how it might play out. If this is indeed that point in history, a time for revolution, than I must be strong and resolute. As I was advised, I must trust my instincts and experience, even over what seems to be common sense.

What of my retirement plans: hand hewn bowls, raised bed gardens, a peaceful little homestead in Madison County? Was I being foolish to imagine such a life for myself? Once violence starts, there is no going back. War is referred to as the last resort for a reason. Why am I not resisting then, with whatever power of persuasion I can muster? *Do I really want war, is that it?*

No, of course not. Why do I allow myself to drift in this direction? Every day dawns anew and all sins are forgiven. So what if the Buddha statue was destroyed. Let them break up a thousand Buddhas before I yield to belligerence.

I must come up with a new approach to this age old problem. My experience as a writer, coupled with the far reaching potential of social media will stimulate a revolution in thinking that will outflank this drift to battle. And Cody can help me. He's the future of the valley, the best of us all. Might I not be a mentor to him as Buzz was to me? I wonder what time it is. I can hardly wait to start again, and I will be relentless in this. Yes, there is still hope. This is the reason I came back to Madison County, to leave war behind. I must believe it. Karma be damned!

What's that? It's silence, sudden and total silence. The insect choir has stopped. The moon shines intermittently through ragged, fast-moving clouds, providing shady visibility across a dark blue landscape.

A dog barking, that's what I hear, and now someone calling. Something's happening here. Wagon, but why would the dog be out now? Oh no, gunshots. My God, somebody's shooting. More gunshots, somewhere beyond Julian's cabin. What to do here? Silence now, deafening silence.

"What is it Ira; what's wrong?"

"Patricia. Did you hear that?"

"No, I just woke up and wondered where you were. What did you hear?"

"Somebody's shooting. Something's wrong. I'm going to see. Call Tommy and tell him that someone's on The Land and there's gunfire."

"Okay Ira, I will, but please don't go out there."

"I have to. I heard Wagon barking, I'm sure of it, and Cody calling to him. They're out there, and someone is shooting."

"Do you have the gun?"

"Yes, it's in my coat pocket."

Off the porch, at a brisk pace, running now, in the direction of the disturbance. The moon hangs above the treetops in the western sky, my eyes adjust such that the entire theater is visible. Automatic weapon fire sounds as I approach Julian's cabin, accompanied by flashes of light from the creek bottom. Another volley of gunfire and sparks erupt from the shadows, followed by the sound of Julian's voice.

I run in that direction and spot him through the tree trunks, crouched over Cody who is motionless on the ground. He's speaking in an anxious tone, urging his son to lie still.

"Julian, it's me, Ira, coming in on your left. What's happening here?"

"Ira, help me. They shot Cody. They killed Wagon and when Cody fired at them, they shot him. I killed one of them for sure, but there's more out there.

I stoop beside Cody who is lying on his back, the moon reflected in his eyes. I can detect slow, labored breathing, but he seems unaware of my presence. I feel considerable wetness about his midsection and my hand stains dark as I feel for a wound.

"We have to get him out of here, Julian, he's bleeding badly. Let's get him to your cabin."

Julian pauses in silence for a few seconds, looking at Cody and me, then turns and rises to his knees, firing a spray of bullets in the direction of Runnion Branch. Before the reverberation has subsided, he crouches low and cups his hand under Cody's right arm.

"Let's go. Get his other arm and stay low until we get away from this spot. They'll be zeroed in on it now"

No sooner had Julian spoken, when a hail of bullets rips through the foliage above us. He and I push through the brush, dragging Cody behind until we descend into a small depression where we lift him and move at a faster pace. More bullets tear through the trees, but the sound is above us now and off to the right. I can only trust Julian's guidance as to the direction we're heading because I've lost all orientation in the shadows.

Cody is silent, seemingly oblivious to what's happening around him, a fact I find alarming, coupled with the knowledge that he's suffered a bullet wound somewhere in his midsection. His weight becomes more obvious as we start up a small slope and after another fifty yards, we pause to catch our breath.

I bend over Cody, and move my hand to his wrist to check for a pulse. When I detect no pressure, I reach for his neck, hoping in vain for some sign. Cody is as silent and still as the woods, and so he will be, forever.

"How's he doing, Ira? He's a tough boy. Hell, on a good day, he could drag both of us through these woods."

"J-Julian, I don't . . . He's gone, Julian."

"What, what the hell are you saying? No, he'll be all right."

Julian kneels beside his son; his head descends onto Cody's chest. He sighs, a long mournful exhale, acknowledgment of the grim truth.

Would it only be that this is a nightmare and I could awake, lying in bed beside Patricia, warm and secure. But this is no dream, it's bitter reality, and I must act accordingly. I've been in this situation before and know too well that to allow oneself to get overwhelmed with the moment can be fatal. Whoever did this to Cody could very well be in pursuit and will likely do the same to us.

"Julian, let's get him to the cabin."

"Huh, yeah, Ira, let's take Dakota home. Goddamn it, Ira, he didn't want to fight. He didn't want this trouble. Let's take him home, then I'm going out there and get every one of those bastards that did this to him."

Tommy turns from the front window as I enter the room, his expression is severe in the dawn light. He returns his gaze to the walnut orchard before speaking.

"How's Julian doing?"

"Not well, but I think exhaustion has caught up with him. He's asleep in a chair beside the bed. I don't think we need to worry about him, going back out."

"Good for now. We don't want to lose him, too. And what about Pat?"

"Inconsolable. She's holding up as best she can, no doubt for Julian's sake, but she's devastated. She and Cody had a special relationship."

"Damn it, Ira. I was afraid of something like this."

"Do you think they came on the property to arrest Cody?"

"No, my guess is that they were doing surveillance for a future operation, to either arrest him or to get all of us and didn't anticipate Wagon, sniffing them out. Here comes Jerry Dale now. He'll be able tell us more about what happened."

We exit the cabin and meet Jerry Dale at the road, an imposing figure, dressed in battle gear with a rifle slung across his shoulder. His nonchalance as he approaches suggests that there is no longer a threat in the woods from which he emerged.

"There were three of them, came down from the Ponder farm and went back that way. Didn't find the one Julian hit, but saw lots of blood. They must have carried him out. Wagon was there. He was shot twice. I formed a line along that border in case anyone else crosses."

"Good. If anyone does, shoot to kill. We're under attack now, Jerry Dale. They invaded The Land and murdered one of us, murdered a fine man and his dog, too. Shoot to kill."

"Yes sir."

45

I gaze into walnut trees, leaves turning brown, nuts dropping to the ground, not to be collected. For all our preparedness and posturing, we who brought on this fight, one of our best is lost, and with him, a promise for the future has died. I blame myself for Cody's death as much as I do the person who pulled the trigger, and I blame Julian, Tommy, and Jerry Dale, and all who choose to fight, here and everywhere.

Patricia, grief-stricken, heartbroken, works in the kitchen, preparing something for Julian to eat. What can I say to her? Does she blame me as much as I blame myself? Her departure for Tennessee is postponed until after Cody is buried, much to my dismay. Despite my worry, I make no effort to convince her otherwise. I plan to stay by her side, firearm loaded, until she is out of here.

We on The Land are consumed with Cody's death, and out there, those who instigated this tragedy are no doubt outraged over the loss of one of their own. We want retribution and they want retribution. The dogs of war are howling.

"I'm ready to go, Ira."

"Okay, I am too. How are you doing?"

"Not good. I can't think about it too much and I want to be strong for Julian's sake. This is likely to kill him and I can't lose him, too."

Driving slowly along the heirloom walnut orchard, I think

about the day when Julian and I procured the wood from the fallen cherry tree. What a happy time that was, working in the spring sun alongside Julian, and all the while, Wagon frolicked around us. Trouble was only a murmur on the distant horizon, like the sound of gunfire on Backbone Mountain. Now autumn is here and trouble engulfs us. A wonderful young man and his joyful canine companion are dead.

Jerry Dale's truck is on the road as we pull up to Julian's cabin. He's beside it, and Pete Rice is on the opposite side. The two of them stop what they're doing and walk to meet us as we pull up.

"Can I help you carry something, Mrs. Cartwright?"

"No thanks, Pete. I can manage. Are you guys hungry. I brought plenty of food."

"Oh no, we're okay Pat. Pete and I need to get going. I'm glad you're here because we hate to leave Julian alone at a time like this."

"You go on in Patricia, so you and your brother can talk. I'll be in soon."

"All right, Ira, but stay close, please."

We watch as Patricia enters the house, and Jerry Dale turns to me as the screen door shuts.

"We have Cody in the back of the truck, Mr. Stone. We're taking him to the Reams' Farm. Hazel and Jake Reams are preparing his body for burial. Julian wants to bury him tomorrow.

"I won't hold you up then. Anything else develop?"

"Nope, been quiet all day. We got soldiers out there where them others came across, and the Field Commander is calling more people up. He wants the border with the Ponder Farm sealed and everybody armed, too. Do you want a gun?"

"I have one right here."

I lift my jacket to show Jerry Dale that I am indeed armed, when an excruciating burning sensation jolts my shoulder. Warm liquid runs down my back as I stagger forward and go down, Jerry Dale easing my descent to the ground.

"Stay still, Mr. Stone. You've been shot. Looks like you took

292

an in-and-out to the shoulder. Hold onto it tight. There must be a sniper out on the slope somewhere. Do you see anything, Pete?"

"Nah, nothing. Must have a silenced gun, too, cause I didn't hear anything."

"Get to the radio. Tell Gus there's a shooter on the slope across the branch. My guess is somewhere high and east of where he is."

I feel nauseous, light-headed. I've been shot. In all my years of covering wars all over the world, I've never been shot before, and now it's happened. I lie bleeding on a battlefield in my own country.

A metallic creaking noise causes me to turn as Pete withdraws a field radio from the pickup and sits on the ground against the vehicle to relay Jerry Dale's message. The image of a soldier, taking cover from enemy fire while talking on a field radio, is a familiar sight to me, one I never though I would witness again.

A scraping sound, a wooden door opening this time, and Patricia's voice causes me to turn toward the cabin.

"Ira, my God, what happened?"

I attempt to rise, but Jerry Dale presses me to the ground as he gets up and moves toward the porch. Julian appears behind his sister with a rifle in hand. He grabs Patricia's arm, and pulls her back. Her eyes open wide, she goes limp and falls back towards him. Jerry Dale leaps onto the porch and helps move Patricia inside, closing the door behind them.

What has happened? I struggle to get up, rising to my elbows, but I'm too weak, too disoriented and lay back down, head swimming. Consciousness returns; I rise to a sitting position. Pete is beside me, helping me to my feet.

"Take it easy, Mr. Stone. I have you."

"What happened?"

"Sniper up on the slope. One of Gus's boys just got him."

"What about Patricia. Was she shot?"

"Uh, yeah she was hit. I don't know how bad it is."

I turn and stagger toward the cabin while Pete follows, imploring me to go slow and propping me up as needed. The door opens to tragedy with Julian on his knees, bent over the couch where his sister lies motionless. Head down, he sobs and utters deep disconsolate moans that tell me what has come to pass. I can see that Patricia has been struck in the chest and I know that she's dead.

My legs grow weak, I'm down on my knees, eyes shut, senses reeling. No experience from my past has prepared me for such a searing moment. Unbearable grief hollows me out and rage fills the void. I grasp the weapon at my side and struggle to rise, intent on using it against those who committed this murder. Oh the rage! How much rage can a person bear?

Blind with fury, I rise, stumble through the door and onto the porch floor.

"Stay down, Mr. Stone. You've lost a lot of blood. We got to get you some help."

"Let me go, Jerry Dale, goddamn it. I can't let this happen and live with myself."

"No, you need to stay down and you have to stay alive. We aren't going to let this happen, believe you me. The wrath of hell is going to come down on these people."

A radio sputters, "two more of them in the woods. We got them both". I'm light-headed again, trying not to black out. I gaze into the walnut grove and see a group of soldiers at the tree line. Then I make out more soldiers at a distance, walking in open pasture, all of them in military gear, and brandishing weapons. The scene grows hazy and I'm losing consciousness. I'm not so sure where I am now or what war I'm covering.

Awake, moving, the Field Commander driving. He informs me that Pete is behind us, driving Jerry Dale's truck, with Julian in the passenger seat and the bodies of Cody and Patricia in the bed. Jerry Dale remains behind to maintain a skirmish line along what is now the battle front. Tommy feels that the cabins in Walnut Hollow are too close to the front, especially for high priority targets such as Julian and me.

We are about half way to Backbone Mountain when the sound of an explosion, somewhere to the east, causes me to start in my seat. I look back to see smoke rising above trees in the distance. Tommy doesn't turn as he speaks.

"Josiah Johnson has blown up the bridge at the foot of Walnut Mountain. I asked him to do it. Now there's only one way into the valley on paved roads, which will make things a little more difficult for the invading army."

Although I can appreciate the strategy behind this move, I'm still surprised that such an action has been taken. But I say nothing, I don't want to talk and wish I could stop thinking as well.

As we near the camp, a group of soldiers falls into order, obviously aware of our tragic cargo. Tommy speaks with his charges in a hushed voice while Julian remains in the truck behind with his head hung low. I wonder if I should go to him and offer what consolation I can, but hesitate in my weariness and confusion. Tommy places a hand on my shoulder and gestures toward the door.

"I think it's best if we leave Julian alone for now, Ira, Trust me. I know him."

Another truck pulls up and a distraught driver announces that there are two more casualties in the bed, one dead and one wounded. Soldiers scramble to attend to their fallen comrades, and Tommy instruct them to transfer the wounded man to the field hospital.

I turn away, enter the cabin. A fire is burning in the hearth and I gravitate toward it, dropping into an overstuffed couch that fronts the fireplace. Focusing on the rollicking flames, I seek distraction from the sorrow, tormenting my mind and the throbbing ache in my shoulder. I reach up and realize that a dressing has been applied at some point. My thoughts drift, I doze off momentarily, awakened by the sound of the cabin door.

Moments later, I'm handed a glass that's half-filled with an amber liquid. Tommy walks past me and reaches for a poker, leaning against the hearth. Sparks dart in all directions and flit up the chimney as he prods the flaming logs into a tighter configuration.

"I've known Pat and Cody since they were born. You don't know how this tears me apart. And I know what they meant to you, Ira. I'm so sorry. The other man who was killed is Cameron Flynn, a good soldier, nice kid. He just got married this summer.

I went to high school with his grandmother. The only consolation For me in this is that none of they're deaths will be in vain. The government has stepped on a yellow jacket nest now, and they *will* regret it."

I have no response to that declaration. The Field Commander and I sip whiskey in silence for a brief moment that is interrupted by a knock on the door. Tommy places his glass on the mantel and steps onto the porch, shutting the door behind. I hear conversation, and when the Field Commander returns, he's animated, excited.

"Got to run, Ira. Word's gotten out about what happened and more soldiers are reporting in. Help yourself to the whiskey, get some rest. I'll have somebody up here to look at that shoulder, but it looks like a pretty clean wound to me. When I get back we need to talk."

I nod, the door closes, and I'm alone with my conscience. Somehow I feel it will not be good company. Did I in any way, through words, deeds, or else by silence or inaction, precipitate this disaster? Should I have seen this coming? My God, three people are dead, just like that. In the name of resistance, Patricia is lying dead in the bed of a truck, Cody beside her.

I walk across the room, lean against the window frame and peer out at the gloomy scene. Julian still sits stoically in the cab of Jerry Dale's truck, keeping his dark vigil.

Patricia will not go back to Tennessee or see her children again. She will never realize the dream of living out her days in the family home, and we will not grow old together, puttering around in our gardens and sitting on the porch swing. Cody will never start an organic farm or learn to hew bowls. Julian has lost his family.

I turn back to the fire, hoping to find solace in the simplicity of the flames. Instead the blaze crackles angrily and sparks fly, as if the logs are still reacting to the prodding of the Field Commander. His words have stirred me as well.

Why did the government hit so hard and so recklessly? I'm sure they don't know what they've gotten into. I stand and refill my glass then return to the fire. Federal marshals have been killed. Do we know what we've gotten into?

46

I awake to the sound of voices and the aroma of coffee. From light, filtering through the window, I know it's morning, and after a moment, realize where I am. The voices are from conversation on the porch of the command center; the coffee scent comes from a percolator near the sink.

The events of yesterday seep into my thoughts, and I'm filled with such sadness and apprehension that I don't want to get up from the couch, ever. I rise onto my elbows and look out the window, hoping that Jerry Dale's truck isn't outside with Cody and Patricia's bodies in the bed, and it isn't.

I recall various conversations through the night and vehicles coming and going, but by focusing on the fire and yielding to the whiskey, I was able to shut it all out. A soldier came and tended to my shoulder at one point, and someone covered me with a blanket after I dozed off. I wish I could pull it over my head and return to unconsciousness, but there's no retreating now.

Picking up my glass from the floor, I shuffle across the room, and rinse out a sticky brown residue at the bottom. Then I fill a mug with coffee, and sit down in a stiff-backed chair behind the computer. Although I don't really want to, I need to see how the world is reacting to yesterday's events. I steady myself before logging on to CNN's site, but the headline still makes my heart race: *Federal Marshalls Killed in Gunfight with North Carolina Militia.*

I skim the article quickly amid rousing anger, and stop at a particularly galling line: *Lawrence Khan outraged over the conflict in North Carolina. Calls the Runnions thugs and terrorists.*"

Anger wells up to surpass my shock and transforms my grief into rage, compelling me to respond. I'll give the world some headlines to put this event into perspective: *Innocent people were gunned down on their own property by . . .*

The door opens, the Field Commander enters, bearing a weary, careworn expression.

"How are you, Ira. You were sleeping so soundly, we crept out and left you here."

"I'm as good as can be expected, Tommy. Kind of numb; it still hasn't quite sunk in yet, but it will. Where, uh, where are Patricia and Cody?"

"They've been taken to the Ream's farm to be readied for burial. Hazel Ream is their aunt and she also volunteered to contact Pat's children. Julian and Greely took them over, and as far as I know, they're still there. I'm sorry, Ira, I hope that was okay with you. I know that . . ."

"No, that's fine. I want to remember both of them as they were. I learned long ago that it does no good to grieve over a corpse. I'll get over this in my own way. How's Julian doing?"

"Oh, not so good. How can we expect him to be after all this? He's talking a little again, which I guess is a positive sign, but it's like he really isn't there anymore. He's insisting that Pat and Cody be buried in the family cemetery even though I think it's far too risky to expose ourselves like that, so close to the road."

"Hmm, I agree with you, but I'm not surprised, that Julian wants to bury them there. When did he want to do it?"

"Today, this afternoon. They're building coffins now over at Andy Beale's woodshop. I didn't argue with him, but I'm hoping that after he thinks about it for a while, he'll change his mind.

Whether we like it or not, we're in the thick of it now and have to take every precaution. Killing federal agents will not go over well, especially with the world not knowing our side of it. I'm been told the news channels are going wild, stoking the fire, and we're definitely being portrayed as the villains. How's it look on the internet?"

"From what I've seen so far, it's like you've said. I just logged on, so I haven't checked the alternative sites or social media yet. My guess is that it'll be a different story there."

"Let's hope so. We need all the support we can get. Ira, I know this is hard on you, and this isn't your fight. I wouldn't blame you if you wanted to get off The Land now before it gets any worse. It can be arranged, you know. You can still help from outside by keeping . . ."

"No, Tommy, I don't work well from the outside. And this *is* my fight, too. It's the same fight I've been in most of my life. For my own part, I want to make a stand now, for Cody and Patricia and all the people I've known who shared their fate. Their deaths can't be in vain."

"No, we can't let that happen. Don't let me interrupt then. The computer's yours; that's why we set it up here. And I'm glad you're choosing to stay on; I feel much better about our chances. I can tell you this, that in spite of our losses, morale is good, and the headlines are just making everyone more determined then ever to hold their ground."

Tommy and I and turn to the sound of a scuffle on the porch. The door opens and Don Oldsmar is pushed into the room by Josiah Johnson. Oldsmar is disheveled, with scratches across his face, and has a wild, scared expression, while Josiah seems to be alert and poised as if he's engaged in a sporting event. Julian and two other soldiers come in behind them, as Josiah explains.

"This guy pulls up in a car, just as I blow up that bridge, and he was on the wrong side of the creek. He got out kicking and cursing, and when he took off on foot, I followed. I was close enough to hear him talking on his phone and eventually, I figured out who he was.

When I introduced myself, he starts telling me off and yelling and throwing threats around, saying I work for him, and that all of us are going to pay for this, especially Julian. So I thought I better march his ass up here and let him talk to Julian personally. He doesn't seem to like walking in the woods at night."

Julian circles to the front and faces Oldsmar. I hear Tommy exhale as he takes a step forward. The look on his face is a mixture of surprise and displeasure.

"You aren't going to get away with this, Runnion. The people I work for will squash you and your little band of assholes like the insects that you are."

"Shut up, Oldsmar. We *have* gotten away with it, in case you haven't noticed. Shut up or I'll strangle you."

Tommy speaks up as Julian takes a step toward Oldsmar. "Julian, no, you know the rules. We treat prisoners of war according to the Geneva Convention."

"Who, me, a prisoner of war? Are you kidding me?"

"Oh this is no joke Oldsmar. You and those people that you work for started this and my son and my sister are lying dead because of it. You think that's something to joke about?"

By the change in Oldsmar's expression, it's obvious that he was unaware of the deaths in our camp and also that he realizes the malice in Julian's demeanor is very real. There's a moment of tense silence, finally interrupted by Tommy

"Josiah, did you take his phone from him?"

"Yeah, I took it, Field Commander. Gave it a long toss in the woods. I hate those damned things, anyway. I hear they can use them to track a man anywhere, even when they're turned off."

"Uh huh, good thinking. Would you take him out of here for now, Josiah, so Julian and I can decide what to do with him. I don't want him to hear."

Josiah complies, accompanied by the two soldiers and Tommy turns toward Julian.

"I know what you're thinking, Tommy, but I'm glad he dragged that son of a bitch up here. After all the trouble he's caused he deserves to be roughed up a little. In fact, Oldsmar deserves a lot worse than that."

"Julian, remember our policy: we take no prisoners. We disarm captors and then let them go."

"But this isn't some foot soldier here, Tommy. This is the weasel that set the wheel in motion. If it wasn't for him, my family wouldn't be dead now."

"Yes, he *is* a foot soldier. In the end, he just follows orders, too. And besides holding him or punishing him will serve no good purpose. It won't get your family back and it's just going to hurt our cause. They probably already know we have him and will use it against us. We need to let him go."

"Now Tommy, I . . ."

"Julian, we let Oldsmar go."

"All right, Field Commander, sir, whatever you say."

Julian walks toward the door, and stops as he steps onto the porch.

"How do you want it done?"

"Let him get cleaned up and fed. Pick some soldiers to look after him, treat him decent. Later, we'll take him down to the front and he can walk out.

"When do you want it done?"

"The sooner the better, as far as I'm concerned, this afternoon sometime, maybe.

"Could we at least hold it off until after I bury my family. I'd feel better that way."

"Yes, that would be fine and appropriate, too."

Julian grits his teeth, turns and steps off the porch. Tommy turns toward me and speaks in a low voice.

"That's the problem with Josiah, you take the bad with the good. He thought he was doing the right thing for Julian, but we sure didn't need this complication now. If he hadn't crossed paths with Oldsmar, he just as well could have gone back to his farm and we wouldn't see him for another year. Josiah is like a wild animal, unpredictable. He's always been that way."

47

Bent over his desk, studying a topographical map, Tommy doesn't seem to notice the increased activity outside. Stepping out the door I see two women and a man, distributing food from the back of a pickup truck.

One of the women is dressed in camouflage and is introduced to me as Cindy Greely, Lamont's wife. Her companions are Cathy Hillen and Cathy's husband, Rob, from a farm on the southern corner of The Land.

I learn that the Hillen farm is where food is prepared, something that was decided well in advance of the current circumstances. Supplies have been stored on the premises and all excess food from garden plots is now channeled there. The Hillen Farm is also where livestock are slaughtered for food as is necessary.

Cindy watched news earlier and was filling everyone in on the latest developments when I came out. After introductions, she resumes.

"It's all over the news, in fact it's about all they talk about on every channel. You know how it goes with stuff like this, they keep repeating the same things over and over, while they interview expert after expert for their two cents worth. It's just weird to see them talking about us. One thing is for sure, everybody's surprised; they didn't expect much of a fight."

"Well they got one on their hands now, goddamn it."

The crowd turns to the source of this bold proclamation. An

elderly man, leaning on a long rifle, tips his hat and grins.

"I hear you, Joe Runnion," Cindy replies, smiling.

"Tell them the other thing Cindy, you know, about the head honcho coming."

"That's right, Rob, I didn't want to forget that part. Lawrence Khan, the man that owns the gas company, he's coming."

"Lawrence Khan's coming here?"

"Yes, Mr. Stone, sometime tomorrow. It's mostly because of that guy who works for them who they say we took prisoner. Khan said he won't stand for it, and he wants to be here personally to support his man and do whatever he can to free him from the terrorists, which is us, I guess. He's flying into Asheville on his private jet, and then coming here."

I'm stunned to hear this information and alarmed at the same time. If Khan is coming than he's determined to resolve this situation as quickly as possible and to make a show of it. I'm not so sure if his personal involvement is out of concern for Oldsmar or to bolster his own image in lieu of his presidential aspirations. He'll have it all staged to place himself in the best light, controlling the media while he pressures the government to act decisively.

What will their next move be? Federal agents have been killed. That's more than enough reason for the government to come in with overwhelming force, and I have no doubt that Khan will push for such a move.

At the moment, it all seems so unreal that I wonder if these people realize how deep we are into this fight. They mill about, talking in small groups, subdued in the knowledge of yesterday's losses, but showing no sign of cowering or backing down. Am I the only one who realizes what might lie ahead or am I the only one who hasn't accepted it?

Breakfast is served on tin plates: bacon, eggs, and toast, all prepared from foodstuffs produced on The Land. I sit on the porch steps and eat alone for a few minutes, until Julian and Josiah pull up. Josiah fills a plate, but Julian sits down with only a cup of black coffee in his hands. He blows across its steaming surface between sips as the mug trembles in his grip.

I start to speak when the sound of gunfire reverberates from the direction of Walnut Hollow. Tommy appears on the porch, looks that way, then turns to a soldier close by.

"Mike, go see what that's about and get back to me on it. If I'm not here, I'll be at the back gate. Report to me there."

As the young man pulls away on an all terrain vehicle, Tommy stoops next to Julian and speaks with a gentle voice.

"Julian, what time do you want to bury Pat and Cody?"

"This afternoon, Tommy. I stopped at Beale's on the way over and Andy just about has the coffins made. They're going to take them to the Ream's place to get Pat and Cody and then bring them over here. Pete and them are at the cemetery now, digging the graves, and Jerry Dale's moving the skirmish line to give us room. That's probably what the noise is about."

Tommy stares at Julian and nods in an approving way, but his features show obvious concern. I turn at the sound of hoof beats and see two riders approaching on horses, each dressed in combat apparel and carrying rifles. One bears an M16 and the other is carrying a long gun, modified in a way that suggests that the soldier is a sniper.

The riders dismount at the porch and one of them hands Tommy a note. He instructs them to go down to the cemetery to see if the troops there need their assistance. The two men remount, and twenty yards past the cabin, they guide their horses off the road and disappear into the trees.

"Julian, I have to go. Soldiers from the Piedmont Militia have shown up at the back gate. I was expecting them and I want to be on hand to brief them. I'll be back well before we're to go to the cemetery, but until then you're in charge here. Are you all right with that?"

"Yeah, sure, Tommy. I'm fine."

The Field Commander goes back into the cabin and emerges with a beret on his head and an M16 on his shoulder. As he passes by, he quietly asks if I wish to accompany him, informing me that the back gate is a hidden entryway onto The Land. I decline, stating that I would like a chance to talk to Julian alone. Tommy nods and pats me on the shoulder. I watch his truck pull away and turn to see Julian staring at me as if he knew my intent.

"Aren't you going to eat anything?"

"Nah, I ain't got much of an appetite anymore, Ira."

"You should try eating something, even if . . ."

"They killed my boy. They shot him dead, he and Wagon, and then they killed my sister, too. They might as well have shot Dad for what they put him through in the end. My whole family is dead just because some greedy bastard wants the gas underneath our land."

"Uh, yes, that's basically what happened here. There's more to the story than that, but Lawrence Khan is the one calling the shots. And apparently he's going to take a more hands on approach from what Cindy Greely just told us."

"How's that?"

"She learned on the news that Kahn is coming here to do what he can to gain Oldsmar's release."

"Kahn's coming here, just because of Oldsmar?"

"Well Oldsmar *is* one of his golden boys, but I'm sure there's more to it. I figure he's doing this as a publicity stunt, too, to show that Lawrence Khan is presidential material, a man who fights terrorists head on."

"Terrorists, how can they call us that? We're just protecting our homes. We're not out to gain anything. We're not trying to take anything from Khan."

"They can say it because Khan owns the media, and the media controls what the public sees and hears. Fortunately for us, he can't control the internet, *yet*. Our side of the story is out there now, and it's our best hope of beating this. We don't have the money and the power that Khan has, but if enough people get mad, we can make it up with numbers."

"I don't know much about the internet. I've always given computers a wide berth. That was Cody's department. Jesus, Ira, he's gone. My boys gone, and Pat, too, my whole family. I can't think straight. I feel like I'm already dead myself."

"I know what you're saying. I try not to think about it too much or I get so full of rage that I can't think straight either, and that will do us no good. The best thing we can do to honor them, and the other's we've lost, is to continue to resist. We can't let Khan win here."

"But he'll win no matter what. He's not coming here to fight; he has people doing that for him. Government agents or soldiers will get killed, and we'll get killed, but Khan won't suffer so much as a bruise. However it ends, he'll still be a billionaire and face no consequences."

"Y-yes, I'm afraid that's probably true, but someday, Julian, either here or somewhere, enough people will get mad all at the same time, and they'll bring down Khan and all the others like him. It's happened before and it will happen again."

"Hell, to do that you'd have to bring down the whole goddamn government."

"Probably, but that happens, too. It just hasn't happened in this country yet. There are reasons to think that things might be pointing that way though. Do you want to see some of the support we're getting on the internet? I think you'll find it encouraging."

"Nah, no thanks, nothing's encouraging for me now, except to . . . Uh, wait a minute. There is something I'd like to see on the computer. Do you think you could find me a picture of this guy?"

"Lawrence Khan, you mean?"

"Yeah, after all he's done to me, I at least want to see what this guy looks like."

Searching Khan's name yielded dozens of images. In most of them, he wears a suit or a tuxedo, and the occasions include a number of philanthropic endeavors: a donation to an art museum, the addition of a new wing on a library to be named after his father. Recent photos are more often at political gatherings, backing up conjecture of his presidential ambitions.

I can't discern how these images are affecting Julian, but I find them quite repulsive. The man's dress is lavish costume to me, masking his true nature. His smile is condescending and fraudulent.

"He don't look like much to me."

"He's not, Julian. He's just rich."

"And he's coming here, huh?"

"Yes, Cindy heard that it's sometime tomorrow. Let's see if the time has been narrowed down more."

I search different news sites and all cover the standoff in Walnut Hollow. At one site, the headline is 'The Battle of Walnut Hollow', the author borrowing the title of our Facebook account. Within the article is a link to another piece with specifics about Khan's decision to come to the front line of the confrontation. I bring up the page and Julian reads through it.

"Look here, Ira. It says that the FBI is using the Community Center building as a command center. Isn't that a slap in the face, using the building that ties the community together to help tear it apart. And look here, it says that Khan plans to meet with law enforcement officials there and then hold a press conference."

"That's not so surprising, a nice safe base where he'll be well protected, and surrounded by a sympathetic press who can document his bravery and commitment to freedom and democracy."

"I, I wish I could talk to him, Ira, I said it before. I'd like to talk to him face to face, to tell him my side of the story, to tell what he's done to me. Do you think he even knows what he's done?"

"Khan should know by now, but even if he does, I'm sure he's justified it somehow. I have no doubt that Lawrence Khan cares more about how his reputation or business might be hurt than about who he's hurt. And you could never talk to him face to face. He has no intention of letting anyone enter the safe little bubble he lives in. I doubt he ever steps out of it, even in everyday life.

But Khan can't keep public opinion out and that's how we can get to him, expose him to the world for what he is."

"Yeah, you're right, Ira. He ain't going to talk to someone like me. I'm just all screwed up in my thinking, I'm so light-headed anymore."

"Julian, have you been taking your insulin?"

"I'm out, Ira, but I think I'm getting more soon. Bill Stamey's wife, Chris, works at the clinic. She thinks she can get me some."

"She thinks she can? Julian, this is a matter of life and death."

"Oh is it? Well so what. It doesn't matter much to me anymore. Right now, it's a matter of life and death for all of us."

"Julian, listen. You need to . . ."

"Ira, I need to lay down for awhile, okay. Andy will be along soon with Cody and Pat. I need to rest some before we bury them."

48

In spite of the heartrending circumstances, the beauty of this autumn afternoon is stunning, a welcome distraction as our convoy makes its way down the slope, and away from the hunting camp. I'm riding in the cab of Tommy's pickup and Julian, at his insistence, is sitting in the bed between his son and his sister, who are enclosed in pine coffins.

Tommy drives in silence, answering what questions I pose with as few words as possible, but when we round the last bend, and descend into Walnut Hollow, he draws in his breath and voices dismay in a low tone.

"This is not a good idea, coming down in here, like this. We're sitting ducks with these vehicles. Our best hope is that they show some compassion when they see that we're burying our dead. But we owe this to Julian, to honor his wishes for his family. He's suffered more than any man deserves to. After this, we have to restrict vehicle travel, go by horseback or on foot. They won't know what we're doing then. Are you comfortable on a horse?"

"It's been a while, but I'll manage."

"That's good. We have trails crisscrossing The Land that no vehicle can travel. The roads can be blocked and booby trapped, if we have to. My strategy is to use our knowledge of these mountains to full advantage. The lay of the land will be our edge."

"What about the outside volunteers, the other militias, how will they fit in?"

"They'll fit in well, I think. They're ready to fight, I can tell you that. I'm having them ring the property for now, watching the borders, and with a simple command: don't let anyone cross. That allows us to operate inside and calculate our moves more freely. And there are more troops on the way, coming from all parts of the country. The military backing we're getting is even better than I expected. How does the public support look today?"

"Real good. By far the majority of folks the world over are behind us and want to help. People want to know what they can do as far as money, food, and letters to politicians. Many of them seem ready to fight, too.

"That's good to know. Have you mentioned this, then, the funeral, the people we've lost?"

"Yes, I did. I waited until Patricia's children and Cody's mother had been notified, but then I told the story in detail. The news outlets were one step ahead of us with the news about the agents that were killed, but the world is finding out our side now. They know now that people like themselves are getting killed by their own government. It wasn't easy writing, in fact, I think it was one of the hardest pieces I've ever written."

"I'm sure it was, Ira. I'm sorry. This must be very tough for you. I know that you and Pat were close. You seemed so happy around each other. You and Cody were close, too. I shouldn't even have mentioned it at a time like this, on the way bury them.

I know I may seem to be matter-of-fact about it, but I'm not, inside. I've known Pat and Cody since they were born and I loved them both. A part of me has died with them. But now that this has started, I have to stay focused and hold the course, whatever happens."

"I understand, Tommy. You don't have to make any excuses for yourself. I know the position you're in. And as for me, I've been here before. I can shut it out and do my job. It'll all come crashing down on me later and merge with the other memories that haunt me, but I'll be all right.

I'm worried about Julian, though. I think that what he's

going through would be more than I could bear. He's putting up a stiff front, but between this and his health problems, I'm afraid he's crumbling. "

"I know what you're saying. When I voiced concern about the risk of burying Pat and Cody in the cemetery, he became somewhat hostile, which isn't like him at all. He threatened to do it alone if he had to, and I know he meant it.

I'm thinking that after today I'll keep him away from the front and the threat of any more action. We got to take care of Julian and that begins with seeing this funeral through without mishap."

We pass Adam Runnion's house, and the cemetery comes into view. I see men within the fence, among the tombstones, and the dark outline of dirt mounds. We turn onto the grass lane and I reminisce about the first time I made this ascent only months ago, Patricia at my side, Wagon running circles around Cody who ambled along beside us.

At the cemetery, a group of soldiers approaches the truck, to carry the coffins. Jerry Dale is standing twenty yards outside the gate, rifle in hand, staring toward Walnut Creek Road. As we enter the cemetery, he looks over his shoulder and nods toward the Field Commander

The coffins are placed beside freshly dug graves and we stand in silence, glancing back and forth at each other, until Tommy speaks.

"Family, friends, soldiers, we gather here under the saddest of circumstances, to lay to rest two of our own who died in this fight that has been forced on us. May they rest here in peace now with their family. We bury them today, but we will keep them in our hearts every day, and do them honor as we continue this struggle.

I, uh, well, that's all I have to say. Let's all be extra careful now and look out for each other. Julian, do you have anything you would like to add?"

Julian's head is bowed and his eyes are closed. He looks up when Tommy addresses him, and I'm alarmed at how pale and lifeless his face is. He clears his throat and speaks in a quivering voice.

"Th-this is a good boy here, my boy, Dakota. He had his faults, like we all got, but he worked hard. He was honest and told the truth and that's what counts. My sister, Pat, she had no faults to speak of. She just wanted to live and let live and be happy. I'll miss them both until the day I'm dead, too."

Julian's head drops again and mine does as well. After a moment of silence, Tommy recites the Lord's Prayer and all join in. At the prayers conclusion, he gestures to the men who met us when we arrived. Each grave is crossed with two thick, pieces of hemp rope, pulled taut by a soldier at each end. The coffins are laid across the rope, which is then slowly let out, lowering them to the bottom of the graves. Tommy nods toward the soldiers and they begin to shovel in dirt.

Throughout this impromptu funeral, Jerry Dale has remained near the cemetery gate, gazing in the direction of the road. He looks back at us now with a concerned look and as I step away from the graves toward him, I hear a faint but familiar sound, the percussive thumping of a helicopter. Tommy moves past me and out the gate alongside Jerry Dale who hands him binoculars.

The sound grows louder and I spot the helicopter, at a distance, a tiny object, far off on the other side of Walnut Creek Road. I can't see an insignia, which would indicate a news helicopter. I have an uneasy feeling about this, something about the way the aircraft banks and turns is memorable in a negative way. When the helicopter lines up and flies directly toward us, I flashback to the wedding in Gardez, and I sense the worst.

"Get down, get behind something. Get down now."

All are surprised at my outburst, even the Field Commander, but he adjusts quickly and echoes my command. He and Jerry Dale rush toward us as the Blackhawk opens fire and we dive behind tombstones and trees. A young soldiers hesitates, shovel in hand, and he's raked across the chest by bullets, propelling him backwards over a tombstone. He lies with eyes wide open, a trickle of blood trailing from the corner of his mouth.

The helicopter passes, Jerry Dale rises from the ground, and watches the Blackhawk circle as he shouts into his radio. He rushes to Tommy, speaking excitedly, and the Field Commander nods. Tommy directs us to stay under cover as Jerry Dale runs along the fence row away from us. Two soldiers materialize out of the trees and run along with him to the southern tip of the cemetery. Jerry Dale scans the sky while the soldiers burst from the trees and run across the narrow span of pasture, leading to thick woods.

This seems insane to me, even suicidal. It's an attempt to divert the helicopter away from us, but the men will be cut down easily out in the open. Then as if to invite such an end, they intermittently turn and fire in the direction of the circling aircraft. The Field Commander shouts instruction for us to stay out of sight just as the ominous mechanical clatter of the helicopter overrides all sounds, and the upper branches of the trees that hide us, thrash in it's wake.

Gunfire bursts from the Blackhawk as the two soldiers near the woods. Just before they disappear among the trees, one of them staggers as if he's been hit. Like a huge mechanical wasp, the helicopter swoops low and hovers at the point where the soldiers entered the woods. Tommy emerges and moves toward the fence, where he watches, hands at his sides.

His nonchalance at this seemingly desperate ploy baffles me, until two resounding booms emit from the woods, and flashes are followed by bluish-gray smoke. The firing signal of a rocket launcher is unmistakable, and the result is predictable. The Blackhawk is hit with both rockets and responds by spinning to the left and flying in a wobbly line for fifty yards as the pilot tries to stabilize the aircraft.

Trailing smoke, the helicopter swings back and forth, fighting for altitude that just allows it to clear the treetops along Walnut Creek, while grazing the uppermost branches. The craft passes over the road and then loses power, plummeting to the ground with resounding impact that's followed by an explosion. I stare in disbelief until I'm roused by the Field Commander's voice.

"All right men, let's cover these graves, and move out of here fast. You see what we're up against. Mount up, no more vehicles on the road after this, and from now on, use the cover of woods at all times."

As the soldiers fall into action, Tommy comes over to me and in a low voice says he wants to talk to Jerry Dale before we go back to camp. With a turn of his head, he gestures toward Julian, who is sitting with his back against a tree, facing away from us. I assure Tommy that I'll look after him.

As I approach Julian he's methodically rubbing his ankles and appears to be talking to himself. When he's aware of my presence, he looks up and half smiles, but it looks to me as if he's been crying.

"Hey, Ira, we got em, didn't we; old Dave Barnwell got em."

"Who? You mean Dave Barnwell the electrician?"

"Yeah, he's an electrician too. The chopper got led into a trap and Dave's boys were waiting. Only thing is next time they'll send ten helicopters, or fifty, or as many as they need, and they'll kill us all."

"Well, Julian, let's not think about the next time. We got through this time and that's what matters. They'll think twice before they send a helicopter over these woods again."

"Then they'll just drop bombs on us. A few bombs will flatten Walnut Hollow. Then they can just bulldoze everything over and build their pipelines all over the place."

"Julian, let's head back to camp. This has been a long ordeal for you, but you did right by your family and buried them properly. Now maybe you can get some rest."

"Yeah, maybe I can at that. I'm not feeling too good, and my legs are killing me."

With difficulty, Julian rises to his feet and, with an unsteady gait, walks past me. He pauses at the newly covered graves and stares for a moment but shows no emotion. In silence, he continues to the truck, opens the door and plops onto the seat, his head

315

hanging low. I decide to give him a few moments alone and linger at the grave sites, awaiting the Field Commander's return.

I'm struck by how peaceful this spot is only moments after the sounds of gunfire and explosions subside. I inhale the aroma of freshly turned earth, fertile soil that covers two more members of a proud family that has been buried on this hill for generations. At the same time, the air is tinged with the acrid odor of a mechanical fire, from an attack helicopter brought down in a clash between citizens and their own country, a confrontation that has now reached a new level of violence.

I turn in the direction of the smoke plume that rises from the crash site, incredulous that the helicopter was brought down in such a manner and even more so that Dave Barnwell, the jovial, good-natured man who wired my workshop, orchestrated it's destruction. I underestimated the Backbone Mountain Militia's military capabilities, as sure as I did the electrician's political convictions. The Field Commander was obviously cognizant of both.

At the site of the ambush, I see the Field Commander, talking to a tall soldier with his arms crossed who from his posture and gestures, I recognize as Dave Barnwell. As Tommy turns and trots in this direction, I see soldiers emerging from the woods behind him. Several of them are on horseback and two of the horsemen have rocket launchers strapped across their backs.

The scene is reminiscent of what I witnessed with the Northern Alliance in the Hindu Kush Mountains in Afghanistan, but is one I never would have imagined in the Blue Ridge Mountains in the United States.

Tommy comes up to me, grimfaced and out of breath. When he sees that Julian is in the truck, he walks me a few paces away and speaks in a hushed tone.

"One of the runners took a bullet in the leg. Nasty looking wound, but I think he'll be alright once they get him to the field hospital. The soldier that got shot here didn't make it; died soon after he was hit."

"Damn it. I saw him go down after he was shot and I knew it was bad. He went right over a tombstone backwards."

"Did you see whose stone it was?"

"Uh, not really. Oh, wait, it was right here, this one. My God, it's Samuel Runnion's grave."

"Uh huh. Boy's name is Tim Martin. He's only twenty years old, the same age Samuel was when he died. Samuel died on the other side of the world, fighting for his country and Tim died here, on top of Samuel's grave, fighting against the same country."

49

"They were trying to take us out quick at the cemetery, Ira. I still can't believe they came in with a helicopter. They wanted us all dead."

"According to the news they acted in self defense."

"No, they can't say that."

"They have said it; I'm reading about it. Listen to this: the helicopter was on a surveillance run when it came under fire. The crew was returning fire when they were ambushed, and their craft was struck by two rockets, fired from the woods. Three crew members, including the pilot were killed in the ensuing crash and another remains in critical condition."

"Surveillance and self defense, eh. Is that what it was? They shot Tim Martin's chest full of holes, a man with a shovel in his hand, burying the dead. That's self defense?"

"Truth doesn't matter, Tommy. Perception is what matters, and we are at a distinct disadvantage in that department. The mainstream media has vast resources and a wellspring of talent to convey their message."

"And considering who we have, I see them at a disadvantage, damn it."

"That's right, Ira. I'm with Tommy. They mess with you, they'll get they're comeuppance."

Peering around the computer, I see Julian on his elbows and then he sits up on the couch and faces Tommy and me.

"That Lawrence Khan guy had a hand in this, didn't he, Ira, this helicopter thing?"

"Uh, possibly. The longer this drags on and the more support we receive from the public, the worse it looks for him. He may have used his influence to push the government to act decisively to end this."

"He may have or he did?"

"My guess is that he did."

"He's an asshole."

"Yes, rich and powerful, but an asshole all the same. Julian, why don't you try to get some more rest. You need to take it easy until we figure out a way to get you some insulin."

"I'm okay. I just have to move slow and keep my head straight, but I'll be alright. I can't sleep anymore. Josiah been around, Tommy?"

"Yeah, he checked in on you a while ago. I think he's still around."

"Got to talk to him."

"Julian, you need to . . ."

"Ira, I got to do what I got to do, you know that. Got to talk to Josiah. I'm the only one that can keep that man in line."

Julian looks at me and smiles, and after some hesitation, I smile in return. He gets up, stretches in all directions, and walks out onto the porch.

"I don't know, Ira. I wish we could get him some insulin. He seems out of his head to me. And as far as Josiah Johnson goes, I haven't seen so much of the man in the last five years as I have in the last forty-eight hours. Why he's hanging around now, I can't guess, but I'm not so sure I like it. Josiah plays by his own rules and nobody knows exactly what the game is.

I shouldn't have had him blow up that bridge, but nobody could do a job like that better. Not that it was a bad strategic move, but now we seem to be stuck with Josiah, which isn't a great strategic move. You never know what he'll blow up next."

I hear a vehicle start and turn to the window to see Julian's truck pull away. Moments later, the Field Commander moves to the window at the sound of another vehicle pulling up, and becomes agitated.

"Damn it, we've got to limit road traffic, even on this side of the mountain. I thought I told . . . Oh, uh, it's the food truck, Ira. Can't argue with that. Better get some breakfast and see what they know. I asked them to have news on full time in the kitchen, so they could fill us in on how the world is seeing us on the screen. You ought to get something to eat while you can. I expect we've got a long day ahead of us."

"In a bit, Tommy. I want to check a few more things online."

"All right, suit yourself. I'll make sure they save you something."

The cabin door closes. I'm alone with my thoughts, a whirl of emotions, almost making me dizzy. I return to the computer, hoping for some encouraging information to thwart a feeling of foreboding that's coming over me.

I believe my commitment to this cause will be my final stand as a journalist, that I will die here in Walnut Hollow, or live out the rest of my days in a legal quagmire. But after what's happened, particularly the death of Patricia, there's no turning back for me now.

I'm roused from my melancholy by a wave of support from all around the world. Facebook is surging with encouraging comments, and the top post may explain the groundswell, a message from Patricia's son, Jeremy, acknowledging his mother's death. His tone is outrage and defiance, and he posts that he's resigned his job and is coming to join us here.

On Twitter the outpouring of support is just as robust. Many wish to aid our cause by providing material support in the form of money, food, or even guns. Large crowds are filling Pack Square in Asheville, decrying the deaths here and standing in solidarity with our fight. The Asheville police have defied orders to disperse the crowds. Similar demonstrations are springing up in cities all over the country.

Is this the stirrings of revolution? Is the sleeping giant of public outrage waking up? I'm incredulous, but why should I be? This isn't just our fight in Walnut Creek, it's everybody's fight, all over the world.

What's this, my goodness, a tweet from Aamir Sadi. "I see you are still fighting the good fight. Deeply sorrowful over your losses, but . . ."

The Field Commander bursts into the room, slamming the door behind himself.

"Well, you weren't exaggerating about the news reports. We're definitely being portrayed as terrorists."

"That's just mainstream media talking, Tommy. People all over the world are behind us."

"That may be true, but they're not beside us here, eyeball to eyeball with the government. We need to turn Oldsmar over to them. They're using him against us, describing this as a hostage situation now."

"Oldsmar, I'd nearly forgotten about him. Where is he anyway?"

"Over at the Reams place, in a tobacco barn. He's been well taken care of, better than he deserves. But we never intended to take prisoners, in fact our plan was to make a point of not taking prisoners, or at least not holding them for long.

The idea is to present our side of the story, treat them like they're one of us, and then let them go, with the hope that they will either take our side in the fight or at least not want to fight against us.

Oldsmar is such a hateful character that it's easy to forgot protocol, but we have to let him go."

"You won't get an argument from me. If nothing else it will force the press to change the narrative on us. How will you do it?"

"Blindfold him, drive him to the front, and then point him in the right direction. Or even better we could have Josiah escort him back through the woods in the dark and leave him where he found him. That would keep Oldsmar confused about where we are and keep Josiah busy for a while."

"That's a thought. Any sign of Josiah out there?

"The food detail said they saw him and Julian down the road, near the ammo depot. They also mentioned that Julian didn't look good, said he was limping pretty badly. He must have been hiding that from us.

I just received a dispatch that a militia out of Kentucky has shown up, so I'm heading down the mountain to welcome them. While I'm down there, I'll talk to Josiah. You want to come along?"

"I better stay here, Tommy. The activity on the web is picking up and I have lot's of posts to respond to. The impression that I get is that people want to know if we are in this for the long haul. Is this a local fight about a particular issue or is it a revolution?"

"And what do you think they hope to hear?"

"Far and away, they seem to want revolution."

"I declare, I never would have thought it."

"So what should I tell them?"

"I trust your judgment, Ira. I know you'll word the response well. We have the lives of many people to consider here and must weigh our decisions carefully, but for my part, I've been preparing for revolution since the day I got back here from Viet Nam.

And what was it Massoud said to you? He was fighting not only for a free Afghanistan but for a free world."

"Yes, that's what he said."

"Couldn't be stated better. That's what I like to think this battle is about. We're fighting to save Walnut Hollow first and foremost, but in the bigger picture we're fighting for everyone in the world who wants to be free."

It's a coincidence you would bring up Massoud. Just as you came in, I was reading a tweet from Aamir Sadi, the photographer I worked with in Afghanistan when I was with Massoud."

"Yes, I remember you mentioning him."

"Let me read it to you. 'I see you are still fighting the good fight, my friend. Deeply sorrowful over your losses, but it will be okay. Now we are all Runnions.'"

"Excellent, that's just what I needed to hear. Yes, Ira, as far as I'm concerned, the Battle of Walnut Hollow is the start of the revolution."

The Field Commander exits the cabin, leaving me with even weightier thoughts to ponder. War is an awful choice, but the elite, in their lust for wealth and power will ruin the earth and turn us all into slaves if they're not stopped. As undesirable as it is, if war is the only chance to stop them, then we have to fight.

50

"The man is impossible to reason with."

"Josiah Johnson?"

"No, Josiah's gone. Supposedly he wandered off on foot to get back home, to do whatever the hell he does. It's Julian I'm talking about. He's come up with the idea that he should take Oldsmar down into the valley and personally deliver him to Lawrence Khan."

"What, he must be joking?"

"This is no joke, Ira. You can hear his reasoning yourself. He's not far behind me. Says he needs insulin or he's going to die anyway, and he says that he wants to talk to Khan face to face. He wants to be the one to tell him that we won't back down. Well, here, he just drove up. You can hear it from him."

Tommy moves toward the back window as Julian's truck pulls up to the front of the building. The Field Commander plants his palms on the sill and stares into the forest.

"Talk to him, will you, Ira. I need a moment to think."

When Julian sees me coming, he exits the vehicle and walks toward me, bearing a gritty expression, all the more dour against the gray hue of his face. He brings up the subject before I say a word.

"I'm the one to take the weasel down, Ira. Tommy wants him gone, and I ain't gonna be much good here anyway, as bad off as I'm getting."

"Julian, you'll be arrested immediately."

324

"So what. Maybe I can do some good for us on my way out. I don't have a whole lot longer, anyway, here or there. I ain't got nothing left to lose."

"Julian, don't talk like that. You just need medication, and with the right care . . ."

"No, no medicine will save me. My feet are black, Ira. Doctor will want to cut them off for sure, and I won't have it."

"So you're giving up on living?"

"I ain't giving up, but I aim to die on my own terms, on my own two feet, not in some white room, plugged into a machine. And I don't want to die with a whimper, curled up in a ball, so long as I can still do something worthwhile."

"But what do you think handing yourself over to them is going to accomplish?"

"It doesn't have to accomplish anything. I want to at least see the man who's behind getting my whole family killed. I don't have any fancy words to say. I just want to let Khan know about what he did. Then I want to stick my middle finger in his face and let him know we won't back down. After that, we'll see what happens. If nothing else, I can buy you and Tommy some time, give you room to work this out.

I ain't afraid of going down there, because I can't be hurt anymore than I already am. I've made up my mind. I'm going no matter what, and I might as well take Oldsmar with me to sweeten the pot. If nothing else, it will take away two reasons they have for attacking you.

"Julian, I understand where you're coming from, but I have to question your reasoning. Khan isn't going to talk to you. If he was a man, willing to talk to you face to face, then his company wouldn't be in this valley in the first place. Wealth and power is all that matters to someone like him, not honest and fair relationships with other people. I'm afraid he'll just use your surrender to his advantage, and the press and the rest of the establishment is just waiting to crucify you."

"Well, they crucified Christ, didn't they? And look how that turned out."

"Julian, look . . ."

"Trust me on this, Ira. Can you set it up, me and Oldsmar in exchange for a meeting with Khan? I think he'll go for it, and what he says goes. He'll get more than what he came here for. Besides coming to the rescue of his golden boy, he'll have brought in a dangerous hillbilly terrorist. He'll have saved the day just by showing up and be the next president for sure. Do this for me, Ira. If you go along with it then so will Tommy.

Let me go down there. I want to see this man up close. I know what, uh, I . . . Whew, I'm so dizzy all of a sudden. I need to sit down, Ira. I'm light-headed and my feet are a-throbbing."

Julian leans against his truck, opens the door with a trembling hand and eases himself into the passenger seat. He paws at his breast pocket, but never withdraws the pack of cigarettes nested there. Instead he drops his head back and closes his eyes with a weary sigh.

The Field Commander is seated behind his desk when I open the door, his back towards me. He swivels around to face me with a serene expression that belies the circumstances. One would never guess that an army under his command is on the brink of war with the United States Government.

"He's determined to go, eh?"

"Yes, Tommy, Julian's determined to go. He'll die here, you know. He's going to leave us one way or the other. If he has any chance, it will be out there with proper medical treatment."

"I can appreciate that, but what does he hope to accomplish by talking to Khan? I'd hate for it to seem that he's capitulating to that bastard."

"Maybe it's a matter of pride, Tommy. Julian will be giving them Oldsmar and surrendering himself but in a way, they'll have to give in to his terms."

"But will they? I doubt that Julian will be allowed within fifty yards of Khan."

"Oh, I'm sure Khan would prefer to see him squashed like a bug as soon as he appears, rather than lower himself to speak with him, but if I frame the proposal in the right way and with the whole world witnessing, he may have no choice but to grant him an audience.

And where Julian might not be so articulate and polished, he's genuine and straightforward. Considering how powerful and wealthy Khan is, Julian standing up to him may demonstrate more than any words, just what this showdown is all about."

The Field Commander doesn't respond at first, but I get the impression that he follows my reasoning. He looks over his shoulder out the rear window at the wooded scene, brilliant with fall colors. Then he looks back at me with a look of resignation and sighs.

"You know, Ira, this isn't going anything like I thought it would."

"I know what you mean, but maybe that's a good thing."

"How do you figure?"

"Because than it's probably not going anything like they thought it would either. And the government is in a tough position. They're being pushed by Khan to end this confrontation, and yet they still don't know exactly what they're up against or how far we're prepared to go. That's a reason they might welcome Julian's proposal, any opening for some sort of resolution."

"All right then. Let's get on with it. I'll get Jerry Dale to work out the logistics. I can guarantee he won't like the idea, but he'll go along. He's not one to negotiate with the enemy, but he follows orders, and he knows better than to try to change Julian's mind when it's fixed. I can tell you one thing, without Julian as a counterbalance, Jerry Dale will be more likely to push his agenda going forward."

"Tommy, if this turns out badly, I can't say I'd blame him."

51

Don Oldsmar bears an anxious expression upon his arrival at the command center. Jerry Dale retrieved him from the Reams farm, and from Oldsmar's sullen demeanor as he exits the vehicle, my guess is that he was coached along the way as to how he should behave during the coming operation. Jerry Dale escorts him across the clearing toward Julian's truck and instructs another soldier to guard him.

Early this morning, Jerry Dale tried to talk Julian out of his plan to deliver Oldsmar to Lawrence Khan. Their conversation sounded somewhat heated and grew loud at one point with Jerry Dale raising his voice in anger. I couldn't help but note the exchange even though they were across the clearing and I was on the porch.

Julian cut him off, though. His voice was low but firm, and there was no doubt the senior Runnion had the final word. A hushed conversation ensued, and then in a complete turnaround, Jerry Dale approached the cabin to recommend that he go fetch Oldsmar.

I'm about to enter the cabin to announce Oldsmar's arival when Tommy steps out the door.

"How's Julian?"

"He's awake, but still on the couch. He seems worse, Ira. He was lying so still at one point, I went over close to make sure he was breathing."

"Did you talk to him any more about his plan to go down

there."

"A little, before he dozed off, but he was vague about it. Julian's never been at a loss for words when something is on his mind, so when the time comes, I expect he'll tell Khan what he thinks of him in no uncertain terms."

"Well the time is almost upon us. High noon is when they're expecting him, and the whole world is watching. It's an audience who has taken Julian's side for the most part. I don't think Lawrence Khan saw that coming."

"Do you think that matters to him?"

"Probably not as much as it should, but he'll find out. At some point numbers begin to trump money and power."

"Speaking of numbers, two more militias have arrived, one from Vermont and another from Texas, and you know, Ira, the message I'm getting from these people is clear: they're ready for a fight."

"Hell yeah, we are. I'm going to challenge Larry Khan down there to a good old fashioned bare-knuckle brawl."

Tommy and I turn to see Julian, leaning in the doorway, gazing at us with a comical, half-crazed expression."

"Julian, are you alright?"

"As right as I'm going to be Field Commander, sir. I'm reporting for duty, ready to keep my date with high society."

Julian gazes above us and shouts. "Hey Jerry Dale. Let's get this show on the road."

Jerry Dale stops conversing with the soldier who guards Oldsmar, and meets his cousins gaze. Even at this distance, I can see that his expression is grim. He salutes in a nonchalant manner, turns, and walks toward Julian's truck. He directs Oldsmar into the passenger seat, and as the soldier gets behind the wheel, I notice that Jerry Dale handcuffs Oldsmar to the door. The Ford grinds its way in a semicircle across the clearing and stops a yard from the porch.

The soldier exits the truck and nods as he walks past me on the stairs, then stops and salutes the Field Commander.

"You ready, Oldsmar? You ready to get back to your sugar

daddy?"

Don Oldsmar doesn't turn his head in response to Julian's question; he remains silent, eyes downcast.

The soldier helps Julian down the stairs, and I join them as they reach the truck. He peers at me through glazed eyes, sunken and dark, underlined by pronounced lines. Yet, he appears calm and confident.

"Well Ira, this is most likely it, you and me. The battle's over for yours truly. I don't reckon I'll be coming back. You'll have to get somebody else to get you wood now.

We got along pretty good, you and me. Who'd a thought it, an old hippie and an old redneck."

"Julian, I never once thought of you as a redneck."

"I know that, Ira. What would give you cause to? I was referring to myself when I said an old hippie."

I didn't expect Julian's sense humor to surface at a moment like this, but realize the tease when I see a smile playing on his lips. I take his hand as he extends it toward me. A once strong and sinewy grip now seems to barely hang on.

"Good bye, Ira, and good luck."

"Good bye to you, my friend. I don't want any more wood unless you bring it."

"Well, I can't make any promises there, but I do hope that we meet again someday, when this is all over."

Julian places his hand on Pete's shoulder, and the two of them work their way down the stairs. Another soldier opens the truck door, and Julian backs himself into the drivers seat. He positions himself behind the wheel, starts the engine and turns toward the porch, waving to us in one motion, almost a half salute. The truck is put in gear and lurches forward as the clutch is released.

I watch the vehicle disappear around the bend with a sinking feeling, not sure if we should be allowing Julian do this. His rationale doesn't really make sense to me and I can't help but wonder if his physical condition is affecting his reasoning. Julian will be treated as a criminal, a terrorist, and he may not get anywhere near Lawrence

Khan. Considering the advanced stage of his illness, I'm certain that none of us will ever see him again.

When I glance toward Tommy, his expression seems to mirror my thoughts. He leans on the porch railing, staring in the direction of the truck's departure. When he turns and enters the cabin, I opt to remain outside and let go of Julian in my own way before I resume my post at the computer. I'll find out soon enough the details of what takes place down below.

I walk away from the cabin, wrestling with my thoughts, trying to hold back a rising tide of guilt. Turning left, I traverse the path that Julian showed me months ago, a trail that leads to a rock outcropping and a magnificent view of Walnut Creek Valley. I know that the Community Center is visible from the outcrop, and while part of me doesn't want to see it, I'm drawn to the spot anyway.

As I make the final turn on the trail, I'm surprised to see a soldier lying at the edge of the cliff, peering through binoculars, and even more so, when he looks back in my direction, and I recognize that it's Jerry Dale. He turns back to the binoculars and doesn't look at me as he speaks.

"You come for the show, eh?"

"Uh, no. I don't know why I came here, actually."

Jerry Dale stops and stares above the binoculars for a moment, as if he's trying to understand what I mean, but lowers his head and resumes watching without comment. I wonder what his purpose for being here is, whether it's sentimental or tactical. Somehow, I sense the latter.

"There he is, right on time."

I take a step closer to the edge and peer down upon the small white building that is the Walnut Creek Community Center, looking somehow out of place among a cluster of large, dark vehicles. If Jerry Dale hadn't announced it, I would never have guessed that it was Julian's truck pulling into the drive. It looks so small and hopelessly outnumbered. Julian is met by a contingent of soldiers who walk up the drive and at the same time a vehicle pulls in close behind him.

This is what I feared, that he would be surrounded and arrested upon his arrival and never be given an audience with Khan as promised. *We should never have gone along with this plan.* The soldiers are near the truck now. It wouldn't surprise me if they fabricate some reason to abort the audience with Khan. In fact, I wouldn't be surprised if Khan didn't even bother to show up.

"Jerry Dale, can you tell if Lawrence Khan is down there? Do you see him."

"Yeah, he's there. See that black Humvee to the left and back a little? He's leaning up against it with his arms crossed like he's waiting for a bus. There's a couple goons nearby with guns."

"Well, at least he's there. I guess he had to make a showing after all the publicity. I wonder if Julian will even get to see him."

"Oh, I expect he will."

Just as Jerry Dale says this, there's the sound of an explosion, to the right of our observation. He stops and glances in that direction as a smoke plume rises above the treetops, and then returns his gaze to the Community Center.

"What was that?"

"Josiah Johnson blew up the other bridge, the one by your place."

"What? Why?"

"Because Julian ask him to."

I look toward the Community Center to see Julian's truck lurch forward, forcing soldiers to dive out of the way. Then it veers sharply to the left, plunging into an uncut depression. The vehicle bounces wildly, racing past the soldiers, and seems to go airborne as it returns to the drive, thirty yards beyond the armed contingent.

They run after the truck, leveling their weapons, and the sound of gunfire, a crescendo of cracking and popping noises reaches us on the summit. Julian doesn't slow down in spite of the offensive, instead, his truck appears to accelerate. It begins to swerve as it nears Khan, suggesting that some of the bullets have taken affect.

Bodyguards push Khan out of the way and open fire. Then, in

an instant, all is consumed in a violent explosion. The entire scene disappears in a shroud of smoke and flame.

"What the hell happened? Did they hit his gas tank? Did they shoot a rocket at him? Jerry Dale, what happened?"

He doesn't answer. The smoke partly clears and Julian's truck has vanished. The Humvee is on it's side, engulfed in flames. I think I see a figure lying on the ground, but soldiers swarm the scene, blocking my view. Jerry Dale stands and turns toward me.

"We need to go, Mr. Stone. We got to tell the Field Commander what's happened."

"Right, well, first tell me. What the hell happened?"

"You're the one who put the idea in his head, like your buddy in Afghanistan."

"No, my God no, I told Julian about Mahmud because he wanted to know about him. I never suggested . . ."

"We got to go, Mr. Stone. Everything's changed now."

"But Julian told me that the battle was over."

"It is. The Battle of Walnut Hollow is over. Now the war begins."

Finis

www.ingramcontent.com/pod-product-compliance
Lightning Source LLC
Chambersburg PA
CBHW062020170626
46813CB00001B/236